To Charlie -

Will war ever end?
Let's hope

SO BEWARE

Best wishes -

A Novel by James Hockenberry

James Hockenberry

Published by HN Books, LLC, James Hockenberry and Colleen Nugent
HN Books, LLC, P.O. Box 4214, New Windsor, New York 12553, USA

Endpapers, maps, interior and cover illustrations by HN Books, LLC
 Library of Congress Cataloging-in-Publication Data
Hockenberry, James L.
So Beware/James Hockenberry
422 p., | c22.86 cm.
ISBN: 978-0-9915612-2-3 (paperback)
ISBN: 978-0-9915612-3-0 (e-book)
Library of Congress Control Number: 2017910499

1. Action & Adventure, 2. Suspense Thriller, 3. Thriller, 4. Fiction, 5. Literature & Fiction, 6. Spy Stories & Tales of Intrigue, 7. Contemporary Literature & Fiction, 8. Mystery, Thriller, Suspense, 9. Historical Thriller, 10. Teen & Young Adult, 11. World War One, 12. War, 13. Military History

Printed in the United States of America
Book Design by HN Books, LLC

First Private Edition 2017

For

John Fedden

and his daughters:

Mary, Frances, Ruth

REVIEWS OF *OVER HERE*

The first book in Hockenberry's "World War One Intrigue Series"

Synopsis: A thriller set in America beginning in 1915, *Over Here* by James Hockenberry depicts German clandestine activities culminating in America's entry into World War One. The plot is fast-paced and duplicitous. *Over Here* is an international intrigue, a tale of espionage that unfolds as German agents attack America to stop the flow of goods and supplies to the Allies in a desperate German attempt to win the war.

Critique: An inherently fascinating and deftly crafted action/adventure tale of unexpected plot twists and turns, *Over Here* clearly established author James Hockenberry as an extraordinarily gifted writer who will leave his fully entertained readers looking eagerly toward his next literary venture. *Over Here* is enthusiastically recommended and certain to be an enduringly popular addition to personal reading lists and community library collections.

— James A. Cox, Editor-in-Chief, *Midwest Book Review*

+++

In his first novel, *Over Here*, Hockenberry does a terrific job of bringing New York City to life in this fast-moving spy thriller set during WWI. The book's hero, NYC Bomb Squad Detective Sergeant Gil Martin, and its primary villain, Boer war veteran Danie Caarsens, are well-rounded characters whose family circumstances turn out to be equally tragic. A great deal of hard work has gone into researching the details that make *Over Here* both fascinating and historically accurate. For example, I learned that the first international terrorist act in NYC history took place during WWI. *Over Here* would make a wonderful movie.

— Mort Zachter, author of *Dough* and *Gil Hodges - A Hall of Fame Life*

+++

Rarely do I rate a novel so highly deserving of 5 Stars, but Hockenberry earned every one of them. So moved was I by the way Hockenberry weaved a brilliant story, yet taught me so much history of WWI I knew nothing about, I went out and researched where we were as a nation to commemorate the heroes of that forgotten war... . Brilliantly written!

- Sandra Brannan, author of the Liv Begen Mystery Series

REVIEWS OF *OVER HERE*

The first book in Hockenberry's "World War One Intrigue Series"

+++

James Hockenberry's *Over Here* explores little-known but significant events in the history of the United States — acts of German sabotage during World War I on American soil. Meticulously researched; the story is told with drama and flair, and fictional characters and events are seamlessly integrated with the true-to-life story.

— Daco, author of *The Libra Affair*, *Electromancer,* et.al.

+++

The section illustrations are beautiful... . Good use of dialogue and descriptive narrative... . I loved the pace and complexity of the story. There were no loose ends. I really liked that Mr. Hockenberry tells quite the tale with precision and deceptive simplicity. I was gripped and wracked and tense as I forded the chapters, absorbing the words that took me to the conclusion that Martin understands his own tortured soul. For WWI aficionados, this is a must read. For mystery and suspense devotees, this is something unique and interesting.

— 2015 Independent Book Publishers Association,
Ben Franklin Awards

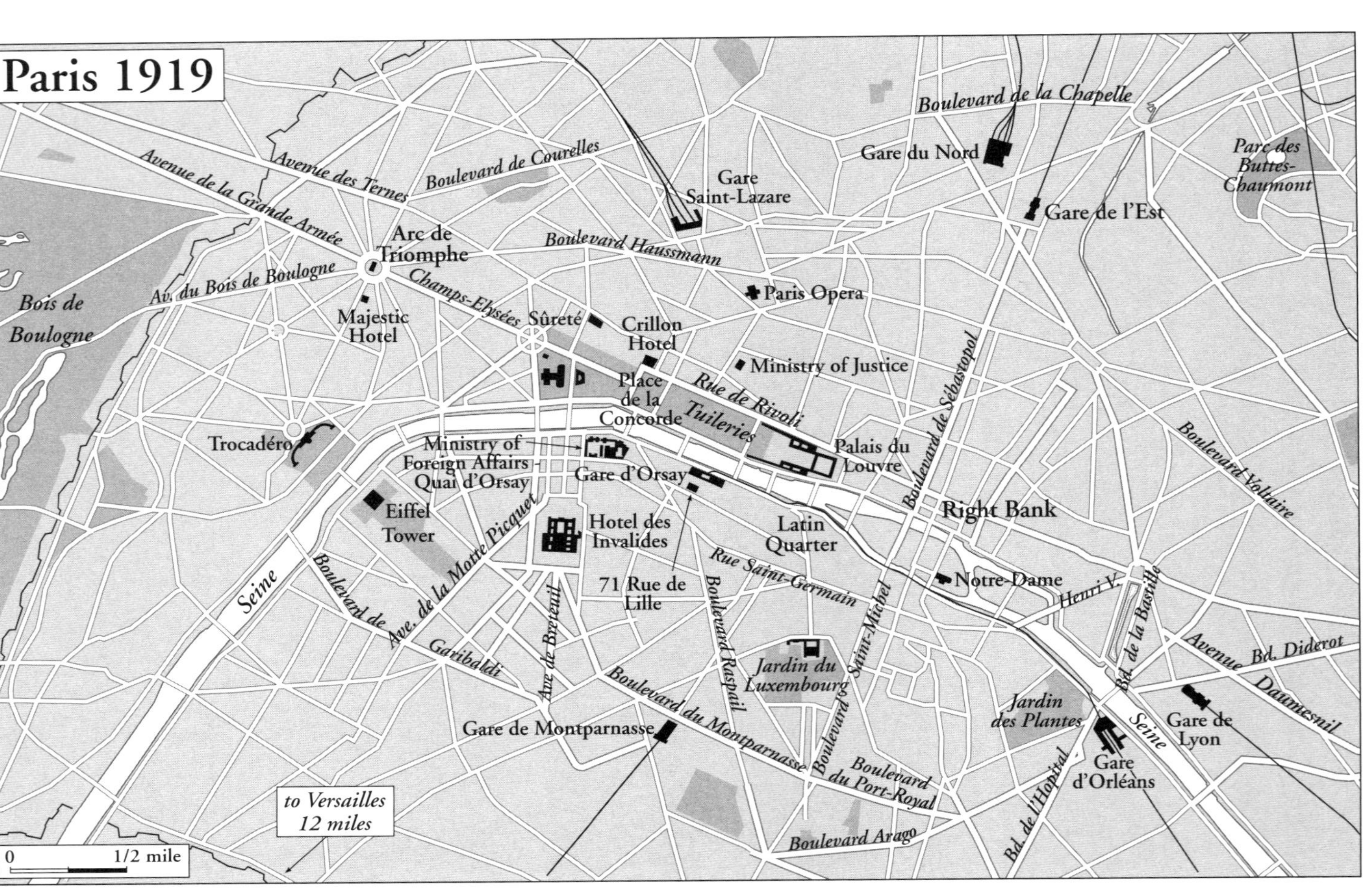

Paris 1919
Boulevard de la Chapelle
Gare du Nord
Parc des Buttes-Chaumont
Gare Saint-Lazare
Gare de l'Est
Avenue de la Grande Armée
Avenue des Ternes
Boulevard de Courelles
Arc de Triomphe
Boulevard Haussmann
Av. du Bois de Boulogne
Champs-Elysées
Paris Opera
Bois de Boulogne
Majestic Hotel
Sûreté
Crillon Hotel
Ministry of Justice
Place de la Concorde
Rue de Rivoli
Tuileries
Trocadéro
Ministry of Foreign Affairs - Quai d'Orsay
Gare d'Orsay
Palais du Louvre
Boulevard de Sébastopol
Boulevard Voltaire
Eiffel Tower
Right Bank
Hotel des Invalides
Latin Quarter
Seine
Boulevard de Garibaldi
Ave. de la Motte Picquet
Ave de Breteuil
71 Rue de Lille
Rue Saint-Germain
Boulevard Raspail
Boulevard Saint-Michel
Notre-Dame
Henri V.
Bd. de la Bastille
Avenue Daumesnil
Bd. Diderot
Jardin du Luxembourg
Jardin des Plantes
Gare de Montparnasse
Boulevard du Montparnasse
Boulevard du Port-Royal
Gare d'Orléans
Gare de Lyon
Bd. de l'Hopital
to Versailles 12 miles
Boulevard Arago
0 1/2 mile

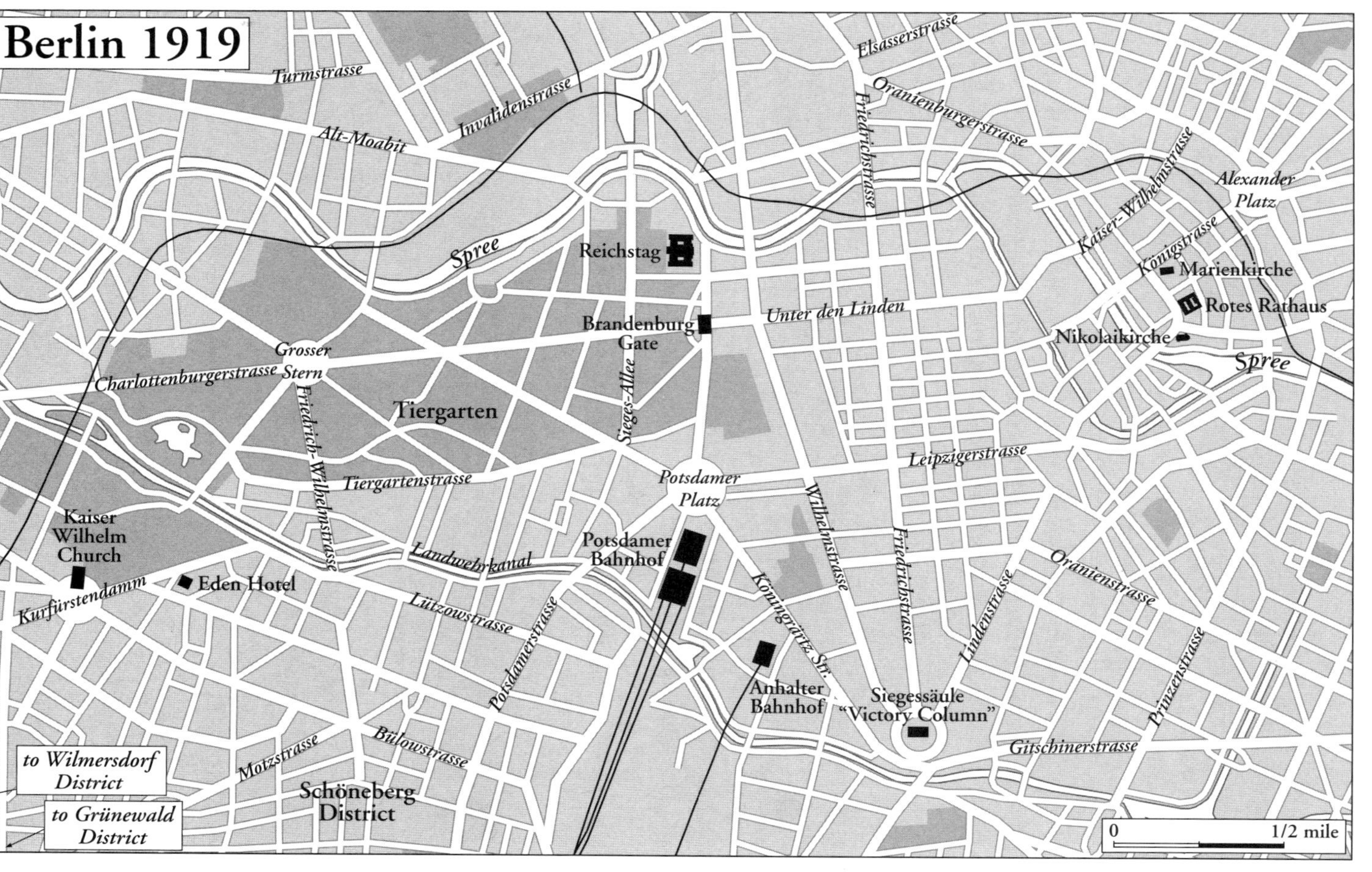
Berlin 1919
Turmstrasse
Invalidenstrasse
Alt-Moabit
Elsasserstrasse
Oranienburgerstrasse
Friedrichstrasse
Alexander Platz
Kaiser-Wilhelmstrasse
Königstrasse
Marienkirche
Rotes Rathaus
Nikolaikirche
Spree
Reichstag
Brandenburg Gate
Unter den Linden
Grosser Stern
Charlottenburgerstrasse
Tiergarten
Sieges-Allee
Friedrich-Wilhelmstrasse
Tiergartenstrasse
Leipzigerstrasse
Potsdamer Platz
Wilhelmstrasse
Friedrichstrasse
Kaiser Wilhelm Church
Landwehrkanal
Potsdamer Bahnhof
Eden Hotel
Kurfürstendamm
Lützowstrasse
Königrätz Str.
Oranienstrasse
Lindenstrasse
Potsdamerstrasse
Anhalter Bahnhof
Siegessäule "Victory Column"
Prinzenstrasse
Gitschinerstrasse
Bülowstrasse
Motzstrasse
Schöneberg District
to Wilmersdorf District
to Grünewald District
0
1/2 mile

Cast of Characters

I. On November 11, 1918

   a. Main Characters

      - Captain Gil Martin (later Major), former member of NYPD's Bomb Squad, transferred to military intelligence at start of the war, head of security for the U.S. delegation in Paris, widowed (wife, Corinne)
      - Lieutenant Paul Keller (later captain), uses aliases "Karl Brandt" and "Andreas Sund." Martin's best friend and right-hand man in the Bomb Squad and during the war. Becomes undercover agent in Germany after the armistice
      - Shannon Keller (Paul's wife), worked with the Bomb Squad before the war, becomes translator for the U.S. delegation in Paris. Good friend to Martin

   b. Others

      - AEF General Donald "Iron Head" Prescott
      - Prussian Major von Ohlmann

II. In USA / Washington

      - Herbert Hoover (historical figure), head of America's Food Relief Organization for Europe. Also, appears in Paris for this story
      - Allen Dulles (historical figure), early organizer of America's spy efforts in Europe. Keller fictionally joins his organization
      - Thomas Tunney (historical figure), was head of NYPD's Bomb Squad before the war, moved to military intelligence in 1917. Shannon's beloved uncle
      - Gary Cleveland, works for Dulles in the Food Relief Organization

III. In Paris

   a. U.S. Delegation

      - President Woodrow Wilson (historical figure)
      - Colonel Edward House (historical figure), President Wilson's chief personal advisor, lead negotiator in Paris, and Martin's direct superior in Paris

Cast of Characters

- John "Black Jack" Pershing (historical figure), AEF Commanding General
- Robert Lansing (historical figure), U.S. secretary of state
- William Bullitt (historical figure), junior delegate who will lead mission to Russia.
- Charles Culpepper, U.S. delegate and math expert
- Harrison Davenport, U.S. delegate
- James Brown Scott (historical figure), lawyer in U.S. delegation
- Ulysses Wentworth, delegate sent home in disgrace
- Sergeant Andrew Cooper, top sergeant of Marine guards and Martin's key non-executive officer

b. French Characters
  - Prime Minister Georges Clémenceau (historical figure), French head of state
  - President Raymond Poincaré (historical figure)
  - Commandant Emile Truchon, head of Paris branch of the Sûreté, the French National Police
  - Captain Alain Durand, French Military Intelligence
  - Sergeant Fornay, one of Durand's men

c. British Characters
  - Prime Minister Lloyd George (historical figure), U.K. head of state
  - John Maynard Keynes (historical figure)
  - Colonel T.E. Lawrence (historical figure)
  - Harold Blum, U.K. delegate and math expert

d. Other Characters
  - Ana Primakova, mysterious Russian journalist
  - "Mal," primary assassin for French Communists
  - Alexei Bukin, former Tsarist aristocrat, now living in Paris
  - Queen Marie of Romania (historical figure), descendant of Queen Victoria
  - Nguyen Ai Quoc (historical figure), Annamite patriot

Cast of Characters

- Louise Cromwell Brooks (historical figure), rich American widow whose townhouse in Paris is a popular meeting place for U.S. delegates and other important people
- Elsa Maxwell (historical figure), Mrs. Brooks's protégé

IV. In Germany

a. Retreating German Army

- Major Erich Landsmann (later Freikorps colonel)
- Lieutenant Max Reick (later Freikorps captain)
- Sergeant "Jawbreaker" Jens
- Wolf, teenage soldier, a hunter and killer

b. In Berlin / Weimar

- President Friedrich Ebert (historical figure), German head of state
- Defense Minister Gustav Noske (historical figure)
- Karl Liebknecht (historical figure), leader of the Communist Spartacist uprising
- Rosa Luxemburg (historical figure), Liebknecht's wife and leading German Communist
- Hermann Goering (historical figure), former Lieutenant Colonel in German Army, flying ace and German hero
- Major Jacobs, Freikorps Internal Security
- Lieutenant Kolbar, Freikorps Internal Security

c. Freikorps Soldiers

- Sergeant Dengel
- Heizer, jittery flamethrower man
- Miltz, local Berliner
- Sergeant Steffen
- Ritter, marksman

d. Others

- Frank Larsen, Dulles's man in Berlin. Keller's contact there
- Andreas Sund, German naval *Volksmarine* fighting for the Communists

Cast of Characters

- Gottmann, innocent ex-soldier caught in the fighting
- Gehrke, former German soldier Keller meets along the road

V. In Russia

- Captain Pavel Vasin, of the Russian Secret Service, the Cheka
- Nicolai, anti-Bolshevik who spreads warning about the Communists
- Boris, one of Vasin's agents

VI. In Denmark

- Major Frederick Rask
- Lieutenant Harald Fisker
- Asger, Danish soldier
- Finn, Danish soldier

VII. In Versailles and Environs

- Count von Brockdorff-Rantzau (historical figure), Germany's chief foreign minister to the peace talks
- Dr. Johannes Bell (historical figure), signs the Versailles Treaty for Germany
- Hermann Mueller (historical figure), signs the Versailles Treaty for Germany
- Major Victor Fauchaux, Durand's replacement in French Military Intelligence
- Colonel Favre, French commander leading attack to retake the U.S. Air Acceptance Base
- Captain Leblanc, French officer in charge of the U.S. Air Acceptance Base
- Captain Reinhardt Voss, second-in-command of Goering's air assault team
- Sergeant Albrecht, German in charge of blocking traffic into Versailles
- Rudi, one of Albrecht's soldiers

Acknowledgements

The creation of *So Beware* was a collective effort. I owe a debt and words of thanks to so many. Without their help, support, and inspiration, I could not have completed this book.

As she did for me in *Over Here*, my brilliant editor Gayle Wurst, of the Princeton International Agency for the Arts, has raised my level of writing, challenged me when necessary, and guided me through the various levels of completion. Her advice was outstanding and artfully presented, always for the betterment of the book. She helped with my research and taught me to question every word. Her contacts and advice have been invaluable. She sees things through my perspective but provides a critical and objective lens. This is a better book because of her.

Colleen Nugent, my longtime friend and stalwart partner in my book company, worked with me during every stage in the process. Her dedication and confidence in this book's success have fortified and guided me. She is a silent strength behind this work.

I give special thanks to Philip Schwartzberg at Meridian Mapping, my mapmaker; Howard Brower, my artist; and Hope Yelich and Diana Groden, my outstanding copy editors and proofreaders.

I also want to thank Anne Waldron Neumann and her writing group – David, Cecil, Mort, and Sue. They helped to launch the book. The group sharpened the plot, improved my prose, and identified problems I missed. I finished each session with greater insight, confidence, and improved ability. They steered me away from my worst tendencies and made me a better writer.

My beta readers added the "special sauce" to this book. Thanks to Hung Do, Glenn Eichen, Mary Jenkins, Greg Schaub, Charlie and Lynn Watkins, and Mort Zachter. They saved me too many times to count.

I would also like to thank my friend Christine Held, who helped transform me into an author, not merely a writer. She has taught me so much about the world of books.

This book visits many foreign locations and has recruited people from different nationalities. Many friends have helped me understand foreign cultures, language, and behaviors. Thanks to Armand Deuvaert for all things French and German; Pia Bogh for all things Danish; and Elena Grishkevich for all things Russian and chess.

Finally, I am most grateful to my friends and family, who always supported and encouraged me. You have made me a better person.

Historical Background

The spark that ignited World War One occurred in Sarajevo, Bosnia, on June 28, 1914, when a Serbian nationalist shot and killed Archduke Franz Ferdinand of Austria. Threats followed and hostile nations began to mobilize, triggering war between the Allies (France, Great Britain, Russia, Serbia, and Japan) and the Central Powers (Germany, Austria-Hungary, and later the Ottoman Empire) in August 1914. Italy, the United States, and many others joined the Allied powers afterward. The Great War, as it was known at the time, lasted for four years of unparalleled "industrial" butchery. The use of modern weapons, including machine guns, advanced artillery, poison gas, and tanks, accelerated the killing. During the war, military and civilian deaths totaled almost 20 million. The number of wounded exceeded that. It was the third most costly war of all time.

The United States declared war against Germany on April 6, 1917. The year before, President Wilson had campaigned on the slogan, "He kept us out of the war." However, America's economic necessity to protect its vast investment in the Allies, combined with Germany's resumption of undeclared U-boat warfare and its ill-conceived plot to form an alliance with Mexico that was exposed by the British, gave Wilson no choice — war. America's vast resources and manpower were fully unleashed on Germany.

In the spring of 1917, America's standing and reserve army of 200,000 men was minuscule in comparison to the European combatants. It took more than a year to build the American Expeditionary Forces (AEF) into a powerful fighting force that achieved significant battlefield success during the last 100 days of the war. Its breakthrough of the German Hindenburg line defenses during the Meuse-Argonne offensive was a spectacular, yet bloody achievement that contributed to Germany's plea to stop the fighting. When the armistice was signed on November 11, 1918, two million American troops in Europe held 21% of the Allied line.

According to the terms of the armistice, Germany had to: (a) withdraw from occupied Belgium and France by December 31, (b) move its forces beyond the Rhine River, and (c) surrender the bulk of its heavy weapons, airplanes, and the modern elements of its fleet.

The final peace was not concluded until June 28 the following year when the Allies and Germany signed the Versailles Treaty. The story behind the aftermath of the armistice and the talks leading up to the signing of the peace treaty provide the underpinning of this book.

QUOTES

"We are dealing with men, not angels."
– Colonel Edward House (chief advisor to President Wilson)

~

"No! No! No! We must go right to the heart of Germany. The Armistice should be signed there. The Germans will not admit they are beaten. You do not finish a war like this … .
It is a fatal error and France will pay for it!"
– French General Charles Mangin

~

"The statesmen have … made a peace that renders another war inevitable."
– Jason Brown Scott (U.S. legal expert at the peace talks)

~

"We all desire to see a League of Nations established in some form or another, but it must be remembered that nations, like animals, have different weapons.
One animal has teeth, another tusks, another claws, and so it is with nations."
– Sidney Sonnino (Foreign Minister of Italy)

~

"According to the most conservative estimates, during the last day of the war, principally in the six hours after the armistice was signed, all sides on the western front suffered 10,944 casualties, of which 2,738 were deaths, more than the average daily casualties throughout the war. Putting these losses into perspective, in the June 6, 1944, D-Day invasion of Normandy, nearly twenty-six years later, the total losses were reported at 10,000 for all sides. Thus the Armistice Day casualties were nearly 10 percent higher than those of D-Day."

– *11th Month, 11th Day, 11th Hour, Armistice Day, 1918 —World War I and Its Violent Climax* by Joseph E. Persico, Arrow Books, 2005

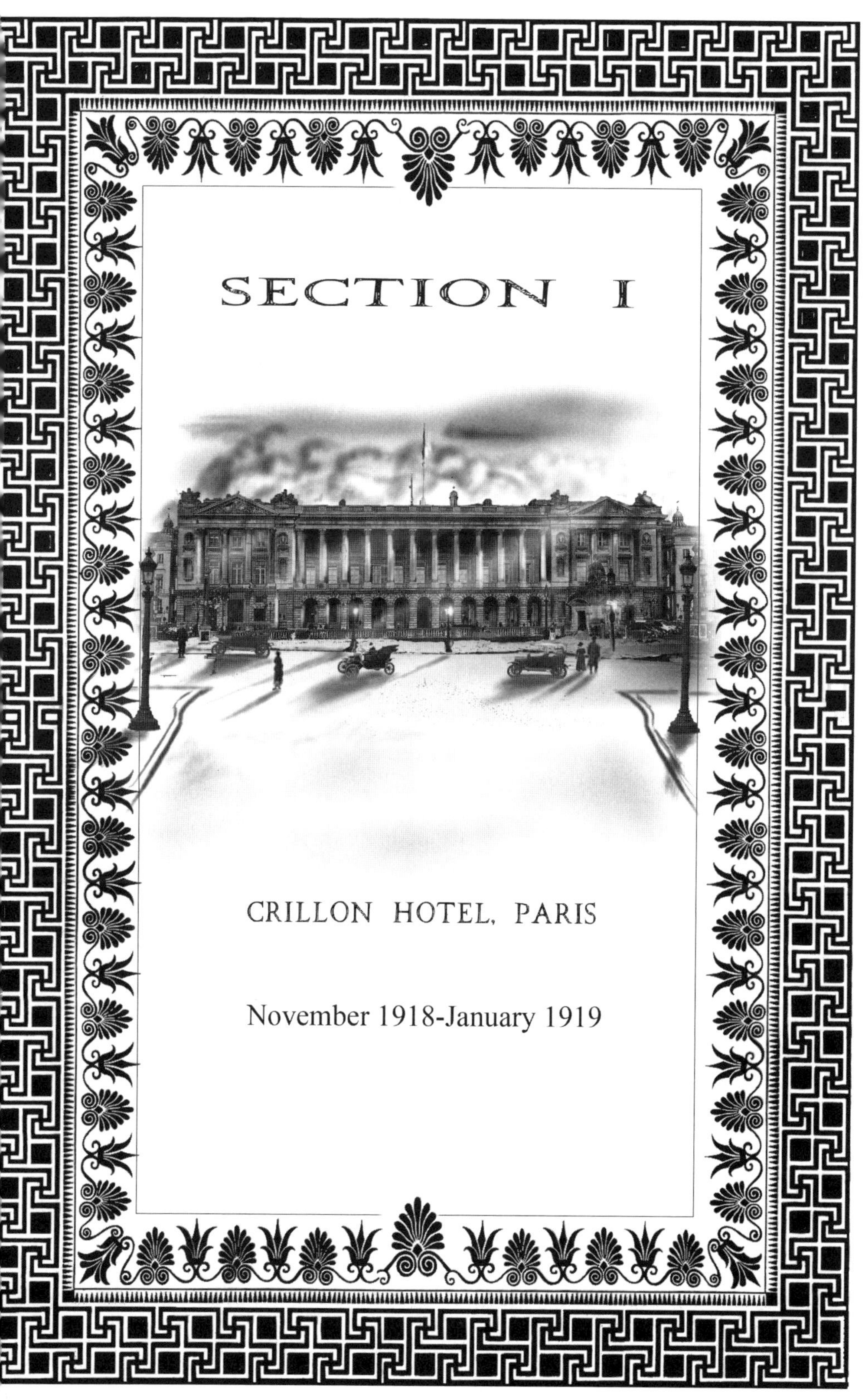

SECTION I

CRILLON HOTEL, PARIS

November 1918-January 1919

Chapter 1
The Last Day

The Western Front, Meuse-Argonne Sector, France: Nov. 11, 1918

05:00: "Gil, wake up! Now!" Captain Gilbert Martin of Army Military Intelligence recognized the voice — Lieutenant Paul Keller, his longtime friend and assistant. Martin, alert and focused despite his all-night trek from Allied headquarters, lifted himself from his cot in the basement of an abandoned church. After eight months near the front, he was accustomed to crises, but he had not expected problems today.

"Paul, what's wrong?" Martin grabbed his boots from under the bed. He trusted Keller with his life. "What in God's name is it? The war's almost over." The armistice between Germany and the Allies was to take effect on the 11th hour of the 11th day of the 11th month. Six hours away.

"Not yet. The general's sent the reserves up." In General Donald Prescott's part of the line, American troops had assembled in their forward positions. They were about to fight for ground the armistice would grant them for free a few hours later, a senseless waste of blood. "All hell's about to break loose. We're preparing to — "

The deafening barrage of American artillery commenced. The explosions rattled Martin's eardrums. "What did you say?" Martin hollered.

"Prescott has ordered an attack," Keller yelled back.

"He's not that stupid."

"I was on forward watch. I saw the build-up."

The artillery fire intensified. Martin cupped his hands around his mouth and yelled. "I have to stop him." They rushed to their motorcycle outside the church. Keller, the fastest driver in the division, grabbed the handlebars and started it up. Martin hopped on the back, and Keller skidded away, kicking dirt behind him. They were at Prescott's division headquarters in five minutes. General Pershing, the Commanding General of the American Expeditionary Forces (AEF), had assigned Martin and Keller to Prescott. Pershing said he trusted their judgment. Prescott called them Pershing's spies.

Martin and Keller smoothed their uniforms. Prescott was adamant about neatness. Martin marched into the general's tent with as much authority as he could muster. Keller followed. Prescott's aides stood aside and let the intelligence officers through. Everyone liked and respected Martin, and they had witnessed Keller's fearless aggression when provoked. The general, concentrating on his maps, did not look up.

Martin walked right up to the general and saluted. "Excuse me, General. May I have a word?"

Prescott glared at him. "How dare you barge in like this. Leave."

Martin maintained his best parade-ground posture. "Permission to speak freely, General." The request sounded like a demand.

"Denied." Prescott looked back at his maps. He smelled like cigar smoke and expensive Parisian soap.

Keller stepped back and stood at attention with clenched teeth. Martin advanced one step and pointed to Prescott's maps. "Listen, General."

Prescott's chief of staff backed away as if he expected an eruption.

The general's bristly white hair stood at attention. His barrel chest puffed out. "Get out of my way."

"General Prescott, this is slaughter," Martin said grimly.

"Go to Hell. I don't care who you report to. I'm going to give those Fritzes a final kick in the balls."

Martin understood why Prescott's staff called him *Iron Head*. "For Christ's sake. Hasn't there been enough killing? For what? A field we can walk across like it's Central Park in a few hours." Martin knew all too personally the value of human life. "Show some mercy."

"You're wrong, Captain. We've got these bastards on the ropes. I want to kill as many as I can. I'd march to Berlin if I could."

"But we've won," Keller said.

"Another word out of you, Lieutenant, and I'll have you court-martialed."

Prescott's icy stare failed to intimidate Martin. "I'm calling AEF headquarters." He turned and walked away.

"Stop," Prescott yelled. "That's an order. Sergeant, remove these officers. Keep them under guard until we finish the attack." The sergeant and a burly corporal pulled their Colt .45 semi-automatic pistols and pointed them at Martin and Keller.

On their way out of the tent, Prescott's chief of staff approached them. "Come with me." As he escorted them away, he whispered to Martin, "Sorry."

"Glory will be mine at last!" Prescott shouted behind them.

Once outside, Keller paced. Martin lit up a Camel and smoked it in seconds. His next one went just as fast. The chief of staff returned to the tent. The sergeant looked on apologetically. Minutes later, the barrage stopped and Martin heard distant whistles and yells from the front lines. The inevitable machine gun and rifle fire began to chatter.

"Shit." Keller kicked the ground.

"I failed." Martin shook with rage.

The wounded began to flow back from the front lines. Sick of the butchery, Martin prayed for these men with deep sorrow. The last American soldiers were dying in the war.

~

11:01: Shouts of joy erupted from both lines. Martin and Keller followed General Prescott and his senior officers and staff into no-man's land. Half-way across, Prescott stepped into a mud hole. He ordered a staff officer to wipe off his boots while everyone waited.

This walk was unlike any other Martin had made across a battlefield. Except for the cries of the wounded, it was so quiet he could hear his timepiece tick. No machine guns, no shells bursting, no confused orders. But some things had not changed. A nine-inch rat ran across his feet with something in its mouth. Another chewed on the face of a soldier blown apart at the waist. Martin was not sure if the man was American or German. The smell of cordite, decaying flesh, and onions filled his nose. He wondered if this field would ever yield crops again.

Martin reached for another Camel. Smoking was his one solace. Since he had landed in France, he had smoked two packs a day. When the war had started, the army transferred Martin and Keller's entire police unit, New York City's elite Bomb Squad, into military intelligence. That was almost a year ago, an eternity. His lungs were still recovering from exposure to poison gas two summers ago, and his doctors had told him to stop smoking. Die now or die later — what difference would it make? Nothing at home to go back to. He had expected to be buried in France.

Martin surveyed the field. He estimated the attack had cost more than forty American casualties. Stretcher bearers continued to carry the wounded back to the field station. A soldier with a Red Cross band around his arm picked up human remains too small to be identifiable and dumped them into a sack. Martin had seen death up close as a New York policeman, but the killing in this war was beyond his comprehension. Industrial murder. He longed to go away. Someplace quiet. Someplace where he could forget.

They followed General Prescott to the German position. The Germans in their tattered gray uniforms stood weaponless. "Bavarians," Keller said when he saw their uniform markings. Although defeated, they looked tough and proud. A one-armed German major stepped forward and saluted crisply. He offered Prescott his Luger. The general grabbed it and pushed him aside. "Where is your commanding officer?"

Keller translated. The German major replied. Keller turned to Prescott. "They're all dead, General. Major von Ohlmann was ordered here last week to take command of this sector."

Prescott grumbled and shouted orders. Keller and von Ohlmann talked for a few minutes. Martin understood enough German to know that Keller had softened Prescott's orders. Keller turned to Prescott. "These men are hungry, General. Can we bring some food over to their lines?"

"Don't give these bastards a damned thing," Prescott said.

"General, I apologize for saying this, but Major von Ohlmann is from a long line of Prussian officers," Keller said. "He's an honorable man and deserves respect."

"He's lucky I don't shoot him." Prescott looked around and seemed bored. "I'm done here. You so-called intelligence officers can do what you want. You will anyway, Lieutenant." Prescott instructed his master sergeant to supervise the collection of German weapons. He told a corporal to remain with Martin and Keller and left with his staff.

After he was gone, von Ohlmann approached Keller. "Am I to understand you are intelligence officers?"

"Yes. We are part of General Pershing's staff, not his." Keller nodded his head toward Prescott.

"*Gut*. Then, may I speak to you and your captain in private?" the major asked, looking suspiciously at the American corporal standing nearby.

"Of course. Where?"

Von Ohlmann pointed to his command bunker behind a series of communications trenches. The three men walked there in silence followed by the corporal. Three times von Ohlmann looked behind him. Martin followed his eyes to a German sergeant with a red arm band and a curious stare who never took his eyes off them.

"Corporal Wasek, please stand guard outside," Martin ordered. He, Keller, and the German major descended several steps into a 10 x 12 foot bunker. Three layers of stout timbers formed the roof, which was reinforced with layers of sandbags. Keller had to bend down to enter. It smelled of sweat, human waste, and turnips. Two sagging cots, a small table, and a chair were the only furniture. Rats moved unmolested. A dim light completed the bleakness. Von Ohlmann looked nervous but said in good English. "We can speak freely now." His voice was dry. "You noticed that my men are Bavarian, did you not?" Von Ohlmann swallowed hard and stopped. He looked at the entrance to the bunker.

"Is something wrong?" Keller asked.

"Go on," Martin said. "We're alone."

Obviously distraught, von Ohlmann looked toward the entrance again.

"We're safe," Martin said. "That corporal is a good soldier. I know him."

Von Ohlmann breathed deeply and said in a low voice, "I love Germany, but these Bavarians, they are not German. They are traitors." He squeezed his fist so hard his knuckles whitened. "You must tell General Pershing this. It is critical."

"What?" Martin and Keller both said.

"The junior officers. They are planning a coup. They want to break Bavaria away from Germany and make it Communist. That would be a catastrophe. You must stop them!"

Martin heard a faint gasp outside, the sound of a man falling, and footsteps. A shot went off. Von Ohlmann grabbed his chest and slumped to the ground. Martin and Keller reached for their .45s and dived for cover. In the confined bunker, Martin looked up and saw the German sergeant with the red arm band in the entrance. He fired two more bullets from his Luger, but they missed. Martin's return shot bored into his heart.

Keller examined the assassin, while Martin tended to von Ohlmann. His dying words were, "The German Revolution has begun."

Chapter 2
New York Celebrates

Bronxville, New York: Monday, November 11, 1919

Shannon Keller waited on the Bronxville platform for the train to go to New York City. She wondered if she was a wife or a widow. She had not heard from her reckless husband Paul in more than three weeks. The fighting had been hard on the Western Front since then. Despite his few letters denying his front-line action, she knew he was in the thick of it. He craved adventure and had been recommended for a Distinguished Service Medal. They do not give those to rear echelon officers.

A nurse approached Shannon. "Excuse me, Mrs. Keller, but I want to thank you for your talk at the library the other day."

"You're welcome," Shannon said, still lost in thought.

"You're an inspiration. My twelve-year-old daughter talks about you all the time. Your suffragette support, your work in the police department."

"My family, God bless them, encouraged me. I hope I don't disappoint them." Shannon enjoyed working in New York City's Detective Bureau, but she had lost her ambition to become the next Lieutenant Isabella Goodwin, the highest-ranking woman police officer in the United States. Her beloved uncle, Captain Thomas Tunney, who had been head of the NYPD's Bomb Squad before the U.S. entered the war, said he understood. But Shannon knew better.

"Not possible. You've made a believer out of my daughter. You seem able to do anything."

"Hardly. I'm still trying to hit one of my husband's fastballs."

"How is he? You mentioned he's fighting in France."

"I wish I knew. I truly wish I knew." With Paul still in the midst of so much dying on the Western Front, Shannon had sought solace in church and camaraderie with other "war matrons." To her surprise, marriage and worries about her husband had made her more aware of her own mortality. *Would they ever have children?*

As a detective before the war, Keller had stood firm when other men had faltered. He thought clearly when many panicked, qualities that made him a great cop and a superb officer. Now on General Pershing's staff, Keller had the respect of the enlisted men. They admired his "get-it-done" attitude, but superior officers frequently reprimanded him. He did not pay attention if he thought he was right. His cavalier attitude about outdated conventions was something she loved about him. Something they shared.

A paperboy ran up to the platform and shouted the news. "Armistice signed! The war is over!" Everyone on the platform cheered. Strangers hugged. Shannon lifted her face to the sky, closed her eyes, and said, "Thank you."

The joy continued during the twenty-five-minute train ride into Manhattan. Grateful people walked up and down the car shaking hands. The woman next to Shannon wept tears of joy. *The war was won.* Amidst the commotion, Shannon recalled her days with Paul. Her initial work in the Bomb Squad. Their investigations of German saboteurs. Their failures. The risks that almost killed her. The ultimate success that had brought them together. His departure for France.

She exited the train at Grand Central Station and, instead of going straight to the subway, headed toward the spontaneous celebrations outside. Children who had skipped school ran around. Everywhere people waved flags. Shannon forgot her husband momentarily and joined the jubilee. She clapped her hands until they hurt. Sirens blasted ear-screeching victory wails. People were making a happy clamor, using whatever they could — whistles, car horns, and pots for drums. Paper, even dollar bills, floated from the windows above and covered the ground like snow.

Men in uniform received handshakes, pats on the back, and kisses. Their pockets filled mysteriously with cash. Despite the wartime prohibition still in effect, bottles of liquor appeared and were passed to anyone who wanted a swig. Shannon ducked popping champagne corks twice and was doused with bubbly spray.

She took a subway downtown and headed to Police Headquarters at 240 Centre Street. Officially, she did clerical work for a detective unit that investigated bank fraud and smuggling, but everyone knew she actively worked on investigations. She had just finished her last assignment, one vital to the war effort. It was a corruption / murder case involving a Tammany Hall treasurer, Murdock Kittridge, who had used Tammany money for his own political ends. Shannon had been fighting the Tammany bosses for more than a year. They considered her an enemy and had threatened her more than once.

On Centre Street, an effigy of the Kaiser hung from a building. She walked by a man pulling a child's wagon where a manikin sat, dressed in a German uniform and a *pickelhaube* helmet. His companion beat it with a nightstick. One passerby spat at it. Another punched it. Some sailors performed an Indian war dance around a circle of fire to great applause. A band turned onto the main street playing "There'll be a hot time in the old town tonight." A fire truck sped toward Canal Street to put out one of the many victory fires that had gotten out of control.

In the squad room, the detectives were hugging each other and singing "Over There" and "The Battle Hymn of the Republic." Before she could sit down, the detective-in-charge dismissed his team for the day. "Go celebrate, but don't come here tomorrow with a hangover."

He smiled. “That includes me.”

Shannon and the other detectives walked across the street to “The Headquarters,” a restaurant on Centre Street popular with the police headquarters crowd. Although she was a woman, the men included her in their group, a privilege offered to the few people they liked and trusted. She had spent many hours after work at the oak bar making friends, discussing cases, and complaining about the bureaucracy that interfered with their arrests. To commemorate the armistice, the bar broke open a keg in violation of the war-time ban. Who was going to arrest them? Shannon ordered her second beer.

What did the armistice mean? Shannon hoped for a better world. President Woodrow Wilson had pledged to fight “the war to end all wars.” After victory, he proposed a League of Nations, where the civilized world would unite to settle differences. Shannon prayed for both and wanted to help make them a reality. She had no idea how.

Chapter 3
New Orders

New York Harbor: December 1918

Martin crumpled the orders he had just received and threw them into the East River by the Brooklyn Navy yard. *Not possible.* Then he laughed joylessly. It was the only emotion he had left. Sick of the carnage at the front, he could not believe the army was sending him back to Europe. All he wanted to do was sleep. Sleep away the fatigue. The horrors. The grief.

He had returned to New York City on a troop carrier ten days earlier. His orders had come through so quickly he expected to be decommissioned. His sharp intuition rarely got something so wrong. He had to read his orders twice to make sure: "You are assigned to Colonel Edward House until further notice. Report to him on the liner *USS Huron* at 17:00 hours tomorrow. Departure at 21:00. House will give you further instructions." Something about the *Huron*'s name triggered Martin's memory, but filled with concerns about his future, he could not remember what it was.

Martin had met House, President Wilson's chief personal advisor, once before in late 1916 when House had come to New York to discuss German sabotage activity. Martin could not remember much about the man, but he had read that House, not Secretary of State Robert Lansing, had been acting as Wilson's lead diplomat with the Allies during the war. Peace negotiations were soon to start in Paris, and Martin guessed House would have a key role there. Likely, that was where they were headed. Despite his misgivings about returning to Europe, Martin was intrigued to know what his role would be. He accepted the orders without comment; he was still a soldier.

The next afternoon, Martin took a taxi to 50th Street and headed to Pier 90. With his duffle bag over his shoulder, he hunched to counter the cold wind and pulled his military trench coat across his ribs. Stopping at the gangplank beside the *USS Huron*, he looked intently at the ship and froze. This was the liner that would take him back to Europe? It couldn't be, but there it was. The irony struck him hard. The prospect was as absurd as the Great War just ended.

He knew this liner by its previous German name, *Friedrich der Grosse*. It was one of eighty Central Powers ships the British Navy had chased into neutral New York Harbor at the start of the war. When the United States declared war against Germany, she had impounded these ships and renamed them.

Martin had arrested three German sailors disembarking from this very ship three years ago. In his investigation against German saboteurs, he had discovered that the *Friedrich der Grosse* had been a German bomb-making factory and had shut it down. His investigation had required much time on the ship, and he despised the thought that he would now have to cross the ocean on it.

Martin tripped as he walked up the gangplank. Only a desperate grab onto the railing saved him from falling into the water. Did the ship blame him for its fate? Stranger things had happened in the war. Martin reported to the ship's captain and was told his cabin number. He needed no help to find it. He stowed his gear and walked to House's suite, the most luxurious on the *Huron*. House sat behind a large mahogany desk writing a letter.

Martin saluted and studied House's narrow face. He had forgotten how physically unassuming the Texan was, but he knew that House was a man with considerable power. House stood up and extended a cool but surprisingly strong hand. "Thank you for coming, Captain, or I should say, Major." House reached into his pocket and handed Martin his oak leaf clusters. "This is a bit unusual, but congratulations, Martin. I need a major working for me." House pointed to the leather chair next to his desk.

"Thank you, Colonel. It will be an honor." Martin sat and rolled the bronze insignias in his hand. The oak leaves gave Martin a jolt of energy and a sense of recognition he had not felt in a long time. He had thought his military career was over, but he welcomed the promotion and the challenge to work with possibly the second most powerful man in America. He was not sure what he would do when he left the army, but those thoughts could wait.

"When I learned about this trip, I asked General Pershing for his thoughts. He recommended you. 'Sharp, fearless, has the conviction of his beliefs. Respected by the men,' Pershing said. Looking at your record, I see you have what I need. Language skills too. We're headed to Paris, the peace talks."

"I guessed that, Colonel."

"Analytical too." House's thick white mustache twitched. "I'll need a head of security, a military liaison, and a French translator. I don't trust the French. I want my own man. Keep your ears open."

Martin began to wonder what he himself would confront in Europe. Anarchists had already tried to disrupt New York. But who was House? A bureaucrat playing a game with the lives of millions? A powerful man who would succeed because of his abilities or fail for the lack of them? At least he was not some high-ranking fool with connections, like General Prescott. "I'll do what's necessary."

"Good. I'm interested in your ideas about the peace talks."

Martin spoke with his usual care, not sure how much he could trust House. "I think President Wilson's Fourteen Points are the hope for the world. We need a League of Nations. How to do it? That's the challenge."

"Honorable thoughts but academic." House hesitated for a minute. "I'm a practical man, Major. My job is to turn those ideas into terms the Allies can accept. You see, I will be the chief architect of the peace."

Not foolish but certainly arrogant, Martin thought.

House looked at him sternly. "You do realize the world is still at war?"

Martin was stunned. "But ..."

"The armistice?" House scoffed. "It has stopped the fighting but not the conflict. Bolshevism and revolutionary fervor are on the rise. Hatreds continue. Ethnic conflicts are everywhere. Rising nationalism too. The winners want vengeance, compensation, and new empires. Germany wants its glory back. And all America wants is world peace. Not much to ask, right? Just the impossible."

"What is?"

"If we can't agree on acceptable terms, we'll be at war again. Maybe sooner, maybe later. Fighting is already going on inside Russia. Germany is a powder keg inches away from a match. Eastern Europe wants self-determination. Ireland will revolt again. Civil war could erupt in the Balkans tomorrow. The Ottoman Empire is shattered beyond repair."

Martin felt the *Huron* slip away from the dock. Cheers rose from the top decks.

"Everything's to be negotiated: borders for new countries, reparations, the fate of the Central Power colonies. The list goes on."

"What's the biggest threat?" Martin asked.

"Your report about the assassination of that German major on the last day of the war was the first time I realized how dangerous the worldwide Communist movement is."

"You know about that?"

“I know everything the president knows.”

“They’re murderers, the Communists.” Martin would never have believed that a German soldier would assassinate his commanding officer if he had not seen it himself. The fabric of German order was unraveling.

“On the other hand, reactionary German imperialists are looking to restore Germany’s glory,” House said. “They might be worse than the Communists.”

“Never.”

“We’ll see.” House shrugged. “My biggest worry is the Allies. They’re out for vengeance.”

“To the victor belong the spoils?”

“God help us when our Allies realize that our president’s promise to make this ‘a war to end all wars’ was not just a propaganda slogan.” House paused to light a cigarette. “Those hyenas will want to expand their empires by feasting on the carcasses of the Central Powers. Imperial grandeur restored.”

Martin had an irrational thought. Were any German bombs still on board the former *Friedrich der Grosse*? But House’s words were explosive enough. The ship’s great whistle reverberated in Martin’s ears. Tugboats pushed the *Huron* into the Hudson River. “What about my partner, Lieutenant Keller? I’d like him to join us.”

“Impossible. Anything else?”

“No, sir.”

“Good.” House stood up. “The next few months will be unlike anything you’ve ever experienced before.”

Chapter 4
But, I Was a Cop

New York: December 1918

While the *USS Huron* was steaming its way through the choppy North Atlantic, Lieutenant Paul Keller boarded a train at New York's Pennsylvania Station bound for Washington, D.C. The athletic Keller walked with the confidence of a man who had faced death and survived. He wore his uniform with the pride and carelessness of youth, reflecting his concern for results, not rules. Fearless, he loved the thrill of trench raids and front-line attacks. He was considered one of the best snipers in the American Expeditionary Forces. He once had five kills in one night. Despite the admiring looks he received from young widows, he was devoted to his wife.

Perceptible only to him, he favored his right leg as he climbed the steps to the railroad carriage. The injury was a legacy of a wound he had suffered in 1916 at the hands of a German saboteur. At times, the leg would cramp during exertion and stress. His hand-written orders, neatly folded in his uniform blouse, were as puzzling as they were unexpected. "Report to Herbert Hoover, the head of America's food relief program for Europe, two blocks from the Treasury building; advise of your decision within twenty-four hours." *What does my army career have to do with a program to feed starving Europeans? What's so important that I have to decide immediately?* He tried to rest on the train but could not.

The building was nondescript, obviously not the official headquarters for the relief program. Keller was escorted to a small isolated room in the back-end of the basement. Civilian clothes did not hide his escort's lumberjack build and drill instructor ways. "Mr.

Cleveland will be here shortly." The escort closed the door with a bang and turned the lock. *Is this an interview or an interrogation?* The mystery grew.

Five minutes later, a man looking like a school principal appeared, carrying a thick notebook. "Gary Cleveland," he introduced himself. He asked Keller a series of detailed and personal questions: What were his parents' middle names? What was the color of the house he grew up in? The name of his dog? (Didn't have one. It was a cat.) The name of the desk sergeant in his first precinct. The description of every man in the Bomb Squad he had worked with. Details concerning his Distinguished Service Medal award. After Keller had answered, Cleveland stood up and said, "Thank you for your patience, Lieutenant Keller. I will take you to Mr. Hoover."

Cleveland and Keller took the elevator to the top floor. "Turn right," Cleveland instructed as the door opened. "Third door on the left. Knock four times. Good luck."

A boyish looking man with a thick mustache and high forehead opened the door and extended his hand. "Allen Dulles, Lieutenant Keller. Sorry about the questions. Please come in. Mr. Hoover and I are anxious to talk to you."

This was not what Keller had expected. Why the secrecy? The papers had reported that Herbert Hoover was Wilson's hand-picked man to head the $100 million American food relief effort for Europe. Hoover had a reputation for organization and efficiency, not duplicity. Keller had much to learn about the ways of Washington.

The damp, windowless room was two coat racks larger than a closet. Two folding chairs were squeezed in front of a card table. Hoover sat behind it looking stern. His square head barely moved. "Sit," he said. "This is important." Hoover rolled a pen between his fingers as he spoke. "Do you know, Lieutenant, that America is facing the greatest threat it has ever faced?"

"But the war is over," Keller said.

"The armistice? That's merely a pause in the fighting," Hoover said. "The whole world is breaking apart, not just Germany. Malignant groups want to start a world revolution and destroy our way of life. Others want to restore imperial control and colonial order. America is in the middle trying to reshape a violent world."

Hoover's words had a special meaning for Keller. His German-American roots went back several generations, and Keller had struggled between his outrage against German aggression and his love for the Fatherland. The armistice had stopped the first. Keller wanted to help rebuild the second. "What can I do to help?"

"A revolution in Germany is imminent," Dulles said. "We don't know which side will prevail — the Communists or the imperialists. A Bolshevik-style revolution in Germany would be a catastrophe."

"In other words, we need a different type of army for a different type of conflict," Hoover said. "Mr. Dulles is going to get it started."

Keller raised an eyebrow.

"I see you are skeptical, Lieutenant," Hoover said, "but I assure you that, despite his youth, Mr. Dulles is quite capable. He has been in the diplomatic service for years and has the confidence of the State Department. His uncle is Secretary of State Lansing. Allen, why don't you tell him your plan?"

"I am organizing a group of men to infiltrate Germany. We want to learn what is happening there from the inside." Dulles stopped to light a cigarette. Its pungent fumes filled the small room. "Some might call it spying. You have experience in this matter, I believe."

Keller tried to understand the implications. "But, I was a cop, not a spy."

"Exactly." Hoover flicked his hand as if he were shooing away the comment. "You *caught* spies. If you can shadow somebody, you can shake somebody shadowing you. I'm told you're smart, resourceful, and experienced. Your military record is impeccable. Your language skills and knowledge of German undercover activity in America make you the man for this mission."

"What mission, sir?"

"The German Army is disintegrating, but it is re-forming into a paramilitary organization called the Freikorps," Dulles said. "It is right-wing and imperialist. We believe some of its leaders are fanatics. Many of its soldiers are the cream of the German Army. We need to know what they are up to."

"That's where you come in," Hoover said. "We want you to leave the army and become one of Mr. Dulles's associates. You will join one of the German units withdrawing from France. We have chosen one whose leader will likely become a Freikorps commander. We'll give you money and papers."

"Do you remember one of the agents you arrested in 1916? Karl Brandt, case D-249?" Dulles asked. "It took some convincing, but he's cooperating with us."

Keller was stunned. Normally quick to accept the toughest assignments, he gulped and tried to understand what they were asking. "Yes, I spent a long time talking with him after he was convicted."

"He has no family," Hoover said. "No one cares what has happened to him. No one in Germany can vouch for him. We have arranged to make it appear that the real Mr. Brandt had never been arrested and remained hidden after we broke the spy ring in New York. At the same time, *you*," he pointed at Keller, "will take his identity. You will resign from the army and be hired by my Relief Agency. It will provide an excellent cover for Mr. Dulles's work. Officially, you will work for me."

Dulles leaned forward and smiled. “Unofficially, you will work for me as the ‘new Karl Brandt.’ Paul Keller will disappear ‘on assignment.’”

“General Pershing is very jealous about men who work for him. He won’t like you taking me.”

“Don’t worry. Let us handle him,” Hoover said.

This was beyond anything Keller had ever contemplated and more dangerous than the trenches. Yet, he was intrigued. “What happens if this German unit I join doesn’t become Freikorps?” he asked in a careful tone.

“Find another one,” Dulles said. “You will have no obligation to stay with this unit once it is disbanded in Germany. You’ll be another unemployed German looking to start a new life after the disastrous war.”

“What about the Communists?” Keller asked.

“Your assignment is the Freikorps. We believe they will clash with the Communists. Hopefully defeat them. We can deal with the Freikorps once the Communists are out of the way.”

Keller’s head was spinning. He was honored to be chosen for the assignment, but his biggest concern was how he was going to tell Shannon.

“This mission is vital,” Hoover said. “Your country needs you.”

His tone made Keller pause. *What aren’t they telling me*?

Chapter 5
Heimkehr: the Long Walk Home

The French - German Border: December 1918

Keller joined the withdrawing German Army in Eastern France. No one dared call it a retreat. He marched with men from an elite Prussian unit, one of the last to leave occupied France. With the November 11 armistice, the German Army was required to surrender its heavy weapons and leave all occupied territory by year end. No retribution was sought for the rank-and-file German soldiers. Like the soldiers he was marching with, Keller wore ragged clothes: a French Army greatcoat with blood stains and bullet holes, a German field cap, a thread-worn civilian shirt, trousers patched at the knee and seat, and old boots with thin soles. Nothing American, not his underclothes, not his socks. His once boyish face was hardened and lined, the effects of too many weeks in the front lines.

Keller felt strange walking with the German troops whom he had tried to kill six weeks ago and uncomfortable with the new name on his forged papers. The troops had been marching for days, twelve hours straight with a short break every hour and a twelve-hour rest as other units leapfrogged them. Horses died on the side of the road. Men pulled the wagons or left them behind. When the soldiers started to drag, the band played patriotic songs to re-instill esprit de corps and quicken the pace. The relentless sound of boots hitting the road mile after mile made Keller think of galley slaves rowing to the beat of a remorseless drum.

Keller spoke little, absorbed like the other men by the prospect of an uncertain and dangerous future. His future was perilous in different ways, but he pretended to share their burden of defeat. To them, he was just another straggler desperate to go home.

Despite the lack of decent food and sleep, the men marched in good order. They carried their flags reverently. The unit remained proud of their battlefield successes and maintained their morale and discipline. Some men coughed, but few complained. Keller wondered if the influenza epidemic that had struck the American Army so viciously had also struck the Germans as hard. Like others, he covered his mouth with a handkerchief to protect himself from dust. At least that's what he said.

A biting cold rain turned the road into a quagmire and slowed their pace to a grueling crawl. Keller pulled the collar of his greatcoat over his ears and slogged forward. He reached back and felt his valise stuffed with Dulles's money. His insurance or his downfall? Keller was not sure which.

Some of the men collapsed into the mud. They were helped up by the stronger men. One man leaned on Keller for more than two hours and begged to be left on the side of the road. "Get up," Keller said. "Don't you want to see your family again? They need you." His words revived the soldier, who stood and rejoined the others heading east.

As he staggered along, Keller reviewed his mission and remembered Shannon's warnings. "You're not a natural spy. You're too impetuous. That's fine for a cop, but a spy must disappear into his role. If you want to stay alive, don't give yourself away." Shannon smiled and softened her tone. "And lose those baseball gestures of yours. You use them without thinking. I know you love baseball, but they could get you killed." The rain now striking his face stung as strongly as her tears when they parted.

The rain continued for another six hours but stopped by the time they reached a train station. The tracks looked as decrepit as the older men. "This is it," the officer-in-charge yelled. "A train will take us the rest of the way to Germany." The men uttered a few exhausted cheers. "That is," the officer added, "if it can make it across those tracks before they're *kaputt*."

"Used up. Like us. We could have won," the lieutenant next to Keller said. Keller guessed they were about the same age, but the officer's unshaven face and battle-hardened body made him look older. He favored his right leg when he walked. His eyes were narrow squints, as though he was having trouble seeing clearly. He scratched his underarms — lice — and smelled worse than a Brooklyn slaughterhouse. His field gray uniform blouse was tattered and stained with dried blood, but he brushed away the filth as if he was preparing for inspection. His Luger holster was clean, and his pockets bulged with ammunition. He stared into the distance and said, "Fifty men, that's all that's left."

"Excuse me?"

The officer looked up at Keller with the face of a man who needed to talk and said with an East Prussian accent, "You're new to this column. We left Potsdam in 1916 as a regiment. We were down to a company this spring." He waved his hand with obvious resignation. "Look at us now." He slumped down, took off his boots, and rubbed his feet. Two toes on his left foot had been amputated. Keller tried not to notice. "Frostbite. Surgeon chopped 'em off without morphine. Someone owes me two toes, and I'm going to collect."

This war has left a lot of outstanding debts, Keller thought.

"My boots won't last another day. Socks long gone." He jammed his feet back into his boots and gritted his teeth to fight the pain. "I'm Reick. Lieutenant Max Reick." He extended his hand.

Keller shook it. "Karl Brandt." Not wanting to say too much, he deflected the conversation. "What will you do now, *Herr Leutnant*?"

"You've got to speak up." Reick pointed to his ear and scrunched his face.

Keller repeated himself. The lieutenant had endured too many artillery barrages.

Reick looked into the distance with the gaze of a lost sailor on a moonless night. "I've got nothing. My country has turned Socialist. My gallant friends are dead. I don't have a *pfennig* to my name. When are they going to pay us?"

"But you're alive."

"Alive? Hah. Call this living? I should be dead by now. All I know is fighting. Good at it too," Reick said with the same nonchalance and arrogance that New York City toughs said after they were convicted of murder. A skinny teenaged soldier with wavy blond hair and bloodshot eyes walked by. He touched his finger to his temple, and Reick nodded back. "That boy's the best fighter in the company. He's a true storm trooper. Has an instinct for killing. One time, he bayoneted three Welshmen just like that." Reick snapped his fingers. "Saved my life that day. We call him Wolf. He's a hunter. Loves to kill with a trench sword. Has more kills with that than most soldiers have with a rifle."

The boy's uniform engulfed his body. Keller tried to guess his age. "Isn't he too young to fight?" Keller asked.

"We called 'em up younger than that," Reick said. "He's like me — he comes from a good family and hates Bolsheviks." Reick pulled out a cigarette and offered one to Keller.

"Don't smoke." Keller knew he could betray himself by smoking like an American. He would have to learn the German way.

"We'll need that boy for the fight later."

Keller did not understand. Before he could speak, a volley of curses began down the tracks. He and Reick ran to see what was happening. By the time they arrived, the fighting had stopped, and a man lay bleeding across the tracks.

"Leave him," someone said. "It's Nathan. He tried to desert. We caught him hiding in that shed."

Wolf spit at the prostrate man and kicked him in the side. "*Verdammt Jude.*"

Keller imagined the man's pain, remembering when dock workers had broken his ribs back in New York. He started to help, but Reick held him back. "Don't. He got what he deserved. Fucking Communist. He's the reason we lost this war."

Keller walked away, fighting his basic nature. He could not risk his mission. He looked back to see Nathan vomit blood and convulse. Wolf pulled out his "Red" Mauser C96 and shot it into the air. The men cheered. Keller turned to Reick. "Germany was doomed when America entered the war. Too many men, too many resources."

"*Dolchstoss.* We never lost. Our lines never broke. No Allied soldier ever set foot on German land."

Dolchstoss, Keller thought. *Stabbed in the back? By whom*? At the end of the war, he had seen the German's poor equipment and inspected their overrun positions. He had interviewed many captured soldiers who complained of little food and poor morale. Allied intelligence reports had implied that one more push across the whole front would break the German lines for good.

"Traitors. Jews and Socialists lost the war, *not* the German Army," Reick said. "They infected Germany from the inside and forced the Kaiser to abdicate. The Socialist government signed the armistice."

The vengeance and aggression in Reick's voice stunned Keller into momentary silence. Somehow he would have to gain access to the ultra-nationalist movement and learn the extent of Communist activity. Reick's words convinced Keller that Dulles had chosen the right unit for him to infiltrate. The Allies had respected it for its tenacity and bravery. Its commander, now dead, was a Prussian aristocrat from a family known to hate Communists. The few prisoners from this unit were blindly loyal to their new commander and fiercely patriotic. They were the kind of men who would die to restore Germany's glory.

"Yes, we will stomp out these Bolsheviks!" Keller cried. "Germany will be great again."

A train whistle blew. "Come, Herr Brandt," Reick said, putting his hand on Keller's shoulder. Just before they jumped into a carriage, Reick paused, looked Keller in the face, and asked, "Have you heard of the Freikorps?"

Keller suppressed a wry smile.

Chapter 6
Wilson Arrives

Paris: December 1918

While Keller was marching with the withdrawing German Army, Martin sat in his room in the Crillon Hotel and spit-shined his boots. President Wilson's liner, the *George Washington*, had landed in Brest, and he was arriving today in Paris on the private train of the president of France. The world would be watching. Martin could feel the excitement in the city build to levels not seen since Armistice Day. He was honored that Colonel House had asked him to meet the president at Porte Dauphine Station.

Martin's admiration for Wilson matched that of a grateful French people, who called him "Wilson *le juste*." To Martin, Wilson and his fourteen-point peace proposal, which included his idea for a League of Nations, represented a radical change for an exhausted world. Despite the war, and to his own surprise, Martin had not lost hope.

With Wilson in Paris, Martin could now start the work he had come to do. Arriving a week earlier, Martin had had few important duties. House told him to see the sights. Martin became distraught by the piles of rubble from buildings shelled by German artillery, proof of how close the Huns had come. Even the Tuileries was scarred by a large crater from a direct hit. He sought spiritual guidance at Notre Dame but turned away when he saw that its stained glass had been removed to protect the windows from German bombardment. Everywhere he went, people wore black armbands. He wanted no more reminders of the war.

He walked over the Pont de Sully to the Left Bank and

wandered the streets of the Latin Quarter but became saddened when he remembered his wife's wish, never fulfilled, to see them together.

During the week, House had buried himself in his papers and rarely left the hotel. Visitors were frequent but never stayed long. On the fourth day, House told Martin at their 07:00 breakfast meeting that the conference facilities on the Quai d'Orsay were ready for inspection. When Martin presented his credentials to the French military police, they insisted everything was secure and needed no help guarding the facilities. Martin persisted. He examined every corner of the building with a detective's eye for detail and a military officer's understanding of tactics.

During his review, Martin met with Captain Alain Durand, French military intelligence, who was in charge of day-to-day security. They exchanged combat stories and police tips. "We must coordinate efforts," Martin said. "It's like the army — be sure everyone involved in security knows what's happening in other areas and departments. If we don't, we'll miss something, and something terrible could happen."

"Worry not," Durand said. "Everything will be fine. We will keep in touch."

~

For the first time in years, Martin had free time. Used to action, he became restless. Not needed by House or his French counterparts, he sat in cafés on the Left Bank and smoked one strong French Gauloises after another. He watched the boats on the Seine and dreamed of a better world. He visited Montmartre, but the risqué shows and lively atmosphere made him gloomy. He returned to his hotel room and read Victor Hugo, a welcome diversion that brought him closer to his French roots. But the sleepless nights he had experienced after his wife died in childbirth almost three years ago had returned.

~

On the day Wilson arrived, Martin left the hotel in full military regalia and joined House in a large staff car. House, dressed in a brown suit and narrow-brimmed felt hat, looked Martin up and down. "Impressive. Did you bring a weapon?" House asked.

Martin patted the chest of his uniform jacket.

"Good." House summarized the schedule for the rest of the day. "I don't expect any trouble, but be ready just in case. Stay in the background, smile at the cameras, and look for anyone suspicious. If you see someone wearing a red Communist armband, ready your .45." After a few minutes of silence, House added, "Try to get near President Poincaré, duplicitous bastard. I want to know what he says."

"Sir?"

"You're my eyes and ears. These French don't share our peace plans. I need to know what they think."

So that's why I'm here? To eavesdrop? Martin's apprehensions about his assignment swelled.

Presidents Wilson and Raymond Poincaré sat in an open carriage that led a procession of dignitaries. Martin and House rode in their staff car three cars behind them. "*Vive l'Amérique!*" people shouted and waved flags. A large French military guard marched on either side of them. In the background, cannons boomed. Martin tried to suppress his reflex to duck at each blast.

"Nervous?" House asked.

"Never got used to a barrage." Martin folded his hands and forced himself to relax.

The procession drove through the Bois de Boulogne, down the Champs-Élysées, and through the streets of Paris. The crowds cheered wildly along the entire route. At one point, they became so thick the French guard had to push them aside. The procession stopped at the Place de la Concorde.

Wilson jumped from the carriage and looked approvingly at the crowd. Joining his entourage, Martin heard Hoover say to House, "What a greeting! Terrific. No politician on Earth has combined the president's power and moral authority with messages of peace since the Good Lord preached the Sermon on the Mount."

Right, Martin thought, watching the hopeful and enthusiastic throngs. *Look what happened to Jesus.*

Chapter 7
Church Mice Have More

Kehl, Germany: December 1918

The men kept to themselves as the train wobbled toward Germany. Keller sat with Reick and Wolf in the first car, where they could hear the locomotive groan and grind. “Won’t last to Berlin,” Reick said. “Lubricants are scarce. This train must have been moving troops non-stop for the last month. Surprised we made it this far.” When he crossed over the Rhine on the ironwork bridge meant for trams, the engineer tooted the whistle several times to signal they had reached Kehl. Some men breathed a sigh of relief, others cheered, and a few sang *Die Wacht am Rhein*. Reick, who was scratching a letter, looked up and smiled while Wolf shuffled a deck of cards. Keller fought back his fear. He was surrounded by violent men who would butcher him if they knew what he was.

Moving at one-quarter its normal speed, the train swayed into the Kehl Bahnhof. The men were ordered to disembark while crewmen repaired the engine. Keller jumped off and landed on German soil for the first time in his life. Would his German-born grandmother recognize it? Despite his German roots, Keller felt disoriented by the surroundings. He was of German descent and as anti-Communist as the men in his unit, but he was an American spy.

“Your accent,” Reick said. “Where’s it from? Can’t place it.”

“All around,” Keller replied. True enough. Having grown up with two generations of German-Americans and living around Germans emigrating from every region of the Fatherland for his whole life, Keller spoke with a fluent but hard-to-place accent. It was further refined by all his years living in German-influenced New York City.

During the war, he interviewed soldiers from countless units and was able to discern and mimic accents pretty well. For this mission, he spoke with a modified north-central accent similar to that of the real Brandt. "My family moved a lot. Tough childhood. Great grandmother."

"Had a good one too." Reick said. Steam hissed from the locomotive. "We'll be here awhile. I haven't been in the Fatherland for eighteen months. Want to walk around?"

The rest of the men had all left the train, and some were saying emotional goodbyes. To his surprise, Keller saw a man pull off all his military insignia and badges and throw them to the ground. "War's over for me. I'm no longer a soldier," he said as he walked away with slumped shoulders. A sergeant pulled out a bottle of schnapps. "I was saving this 'til we took Paris. Guess this is as good a time as any to drink it." He lifted it to his mouth, drank about a quarter of the bottle, and handed it to another man. Wolf reached for it next and took two manly gulps and passed it along. The kid was too young to drink in New York, Keller thought, but old enough to be a decorated war veteran.

When the schnapps was gone, Reick, Wolf, and Keller headed to the riverfront where a French naval vessel was docking. Wolf's face constricted into bitter hatred. He reached for his Mauser. "God damned French. What they doing here?" He raised the automatic and aimed it at a French sailor.

Reick put his hand on Wolf's gun arm and forced it down. "Easy, boy. The armistice, remember? Hate to say it, but we let them come here. You've done enough killing for now. Stand down."

Wolf holstered his weapon, but said, "I've lost three brothers. The Russians killed my parents when they invaded East Prussia." With gritted fury, Wolf pointed toward the old town. "See how they ruined my country."

Keller wasn't sure who "they" were.

The three of them headed back into town along Kanzmatt Strasse. Along the way, they saw several women all in black who had the same thousand-yard stare as men who had been in the front lines too long. Three minutes later, they saw an old man in a soiled worker's cap and badly patched pants digging up the street. He looked too emaciated to do such work, but Keller did not see anyone else to do it. Reick asked the old man what he was doing. "Trying to repair these pipes." The man leaned over and gasped for breath. He pushed the shovel into the dirt, but stopped when it hit a rock with a sharp rasp. "Useless." He threw down the shovel in disgust. "The army stole our pipes to make bullets. Even my door knobs are gone. Now, no running water, no meat, no coal. It will be a cold winter. Church mice have more than we do."

"Sorry, old man," Reick said. "We had no idea. The censors made sure we never heard bad news."

"You lost. Waste of time, the war. Now we're done for. No army. No government. The French want to destroy us. The British want to starve us. And the Communists want to control us."

"We'll stop the Communists," Keller said boldly, trying to gain favor with his friends.

"Hah. Germany is ripe for revolution." The old man wiped his brow with a filthy cloth. "Now you soldiers will suffer like we did."

"I pray my family in Dresden is better off," Reick said. He looked at Keller. "You got a family, Herr Brandt?"

"All dead," Keller lied. The simpler the lies, the easier it is to remember them, Dulles had said.

His companions gestured knowingly. "Let's go," Reick said. "Try to find some food."

Wolf, burning with repressed teenage rage, yelled at the old man. "We never lost. We were stabbed in the back."

That phrase again! Reick grabbed the boy's arm and escorted him away. The old man resumed digging and mumbled to himself, "*Ja,* ripe for revolution."

Walking on, they met an amputee wearing an infantryman's field cap. He stopped, leaned on crutches to straighten up, and crisply saluted Lieutenant Reick. "Good luck, soldier." Reick saluted back. "More like you, and we would have won." The amputee nodded in agreement, a tear in his eye.

Around the corner and two deserted blocks later, the three men found a restaurant and entered. It was empty. "Can we order some food?" Reick asked the proprietor.

"Food? I got some turnips. You soldiers got the bulk of our food."

"Bread?" Keller asked.

The proprietor started to laugh. "If you like sawdust. Real bread was gone last year."

Reick and Wolf looked at each other in disbelief. "Impossible," Wolf said. "We've been on half rations since August."

"More than we've had. People are starving here, and the blockade continues." The proprietor pounded a table.

"I had no idea it was this bad." Keller was shocked to see a living ghost town more wretched than the slums of New York. He began to pity the land of his ancestors, and pity was the worst emotion. Uncomfortable feelings.

"Neither did we," Reick said. "We heard rumors, but the news was always upbeat. Nothing here for us. Let's go back to the train."

"Wait," Keller said. "I want to visit the church." He checked his watch. "We have time." Christmas, he realized, was yesterday, his first without Shannon in three years. Going there would bring him closer to her. He realized his mistake immediately. Returning soldiers did not visit old churches.

"You what?" Reick said.

"Why?" Wolf snarled. "You some kind of religious nut?"

Before Keller could defend himself, Reick calmed Wolf down. "Won't hurt nobody to look, son."

"Do what you want." Wolf sulked.

Keller feared what would happen if Reick was not around to steady the boy.

Coming upon the tall Lutheran church, Keller thought its reddish walls, high spire, and sleek but modest lines beautiful. Unnerved by what he had seen of the town, he wanted to go inside and pray for the first time since he could remember. Something had bothered him the whole day and at last he realized what it was — no church bells. A man in a black robe exited the church. Keller asked him about the bells.

The vicar looked at Keller curiously. "Gone. Melted down for shell casings." He closed the door to the church, locked it, and walked on. *"Guten Tag."*

"Typical. They turn their back on you when you need them," Reick said.

"Worthless pieces of shit," Wolf said. "I've seen too many of them Bible lovers bless someone and send him to his death."

"Hell with that." Keller shrugged. "Didn't want to go anyway. Let's go back." He doubted that his companions had a God. Did he?

As Keller and the others waited to board the train, the station master ran over to *Leutnant* Reick full of news. The revolution had begun. Sailors had mutinied and were marching on Berlin. They called themselves the *Volksmarine*, the people's naval division. Joining them were the Spartacists, the most radical political group in Germany. Soldiers assigned to defend Berlin had left their posts.

Hostages had been taken. Ransoms demanded. The Reich Chancellery was under attack.

"We have to move fast," Reich said. "These *Volksmarines* only know one thing — guns." He looked at Keller and said, "Well, Herr Brandt, will you join us?"

Chapter 8
The Freikorps

Berlin: December 1918

The train stopped on the wooded outskirts of Berlin just before midnight. Of Reick's remaining men, more than two-thirds had agreed to join the Freikorps to defend Germany against revolutionary and outside forces. Keller felt alone, more than he ever had. He was surrounded by tough, skilled, and aggressive fighters willing to die to restore Germany's honor. Volatile and angry, they had nothing to lose in trying.

Waiting for them was Major Erich Landsmann, commander of the Freikorps's newly formed Landsmann Battalion. When the last man stood at attention, Landsmann spoke. "At ease. Thank you for volunteering. You are patriots and trusted men. Our leadership has failed. The government should not have agreed to the armistice. The German Army has disintegrated, but the Freikorps will replace it!" The men applauded and whistled. "The Communists want to take over our country, but we'll stop them." More cheers. "And unlike the regular army, we'll pay you steady. And well." A loud ovation.

"I ask you to raise your right hand and swear you will serve the provisional government loyally." After every man, including Keller, recited the pledge, Landsmann saluted and pointed to a hunting lodge by the side of the woods where they would be equipped. Before he could say "Dismissed," a rifle flash came from deep inside the forest. Landsmann's aide fell with a bullet through his heart.

Keller ducked while the other men drew what weapons they had. They spread out and advanced. Wolf was the first to reach the trees. Reick waved directions to his soldiers. Knowing he had to earn the other men's respect, Keller ran to the dead aide and zigzagged forward, his Walther handgun readied.

Another shot cracked from the trees, whistling inches past Keller's head. He dropped to the ground and saw half of Reick's men form a defensive line along the edge of the woods. The shooting intensified. The storm troopers, heavily armed elite troops specializing in attack and infiltration, concentrated their fire on the flashes, and the sniping stopped. The rest of the men split into two groups and flanked the shooter from opposite directions. The storm troopers, unhindered by the night and the cover of the forest, moved with precision and confidence. Wolf maneuvered ahead of the rest. His short blond hair bristled. His agile movement and fierce concentration reminded Keller of a hungry lion hunting for prey.

Keller picked himself up and hurried to join Reick's men. Another flash came from a new location; the sniper was on the move. A private spun quarter-circle with a bullet in his shoulder. He never uttered a sound. A soldier in the defensive line pulled out a grenade, but Reick signaled to put it away. He told the men to advance behind him. Except for the sound of boots crushing twigs and leaves, the area turned silent. Suddenly, Wolf called out, "Got him." The soldiers lowered their weapons but maintained their vigilance as they scanned for more threats.

A few minutes later, Wolf and another man dragged a dead body behind them by his legs. Reick followed carrying a rifle by its sling. "He was alone."

Landsmann dashed forward. "Form a perimeter. Just in case." The men were in position before he finished his sentence.

"My first Communist. Got him from behind." Wolf wiped his trench sword across his trouser leg and scratched a notch on the handle to match the twelve already there. Keller understood how Wolf had gotten his name. The men slapped him on the back and laughed. The dead man wore a red armband and the blue sailor uniform of a *Volksmarine*. His throat was sliced from ear to ear.

"Good work, men," Landsmann said. "That boy gets an extra ration of schnapps."

The men talked about the attack and said it was good to fight again. Keller was given a soldier's tools: a Kar98A carbine, the rifle of choice for storm troopers, a cartridge pouch with 120 rounds, a uniform blouse, some potato-masher grenades, and a helmet with a skull and crossbones painted on the front. He had never seen one like it before. On his way out of the supply lodge, Keller overheard a conversation between Landsmann and Reick in the command tent adjacent to the lodge. "You're my second-in-command now, Captain Reick. No one I trust more."

"*Danke, Herr* Major."

"*Bitte*. One thing. What about that new man, Brandt?"

Keller stopped, bent down, and pretended to patch a minor wound on his leg. He would be in trouble if he were caught, but he needed to know what Reick said.

"The men like him. Don't know much about his background. He says he worked in the foreign service, stationed in America and Mexico. Says he has military training. Came back late in the war. He believes in the imperial government and hates the Bolsheviks. Says he's an excellent shot."

"We'll see." Landsmann paused and lowered his voice but not enough. "Just so you know, that *scheisskopf* Liebknecht just declared the *Spartacists* are now the German Communist Party. They'll call for strikes. More *Volksmarine* are arriving every day in Berlin. The government expects more trouble. They want us in Berlin to suppress any revolution."

“We’ll need more than carbines and hand grenades.”

“We have machine guns and flamethrowers in the city. Mortars too. We’ll get them tomorrow. I have orders to show no mercy.” Landsmann’s mouth curved into a smile.

“No restriction on force?” Reick questioned.

“Kill them all. This isn’t Russia. Those Bolsheviks will be no match for us. Form your units. Have them ready in three days.

As Keller walked away, an older soldier with tobacco-stained teeth approached and jammed his finger into Keller’s chest, almost knocking him over. Keller pretended nothing had happened. “You say you are one of us, but we don’t know you,” the old soldier rasped. “I’ve lasted four years on the front trusting my comrades. They call me Jawbreaker — remember that. And next time, you need to fight better.”

“I’m a sniper, not a storm trooper.” Keller walked away feigning indifference but wondered if Jawbreaker had seen him eavesdropping on the officers. A street fight with the Communists was coming. There was a good chance that either the Communists or the Freikorps would kill him within a week.

Chapter 9
What Are We Doing Here?

Paris: January 1919

Martin's problems started when President Wilson arrived in Paris. No other American president had ever been to Europe during his presidency, and Martin swore that Wilson would not meet the same fate that befell President McKinley and Archduke Ferdinand. Not on his watch.

The U.S. contingent for the peace talks grew daily. Martin had to supervise the safety of scores of diplomats, researchers, military men, and various experts now staying at the Crillon Hotel along with a detachment of Marines. They were in Paris to analyze the peace proposals and parcel out the spoils. The Americans favored national determination; the European Allies wanted to expand their empires. Irreconcilable differences.

Sensing danger and needing to discuss his growing problems for the safety of the American delegation and that of the president, Martin headed to House's suite for a meeting. He overheard House talking loudly with Herbert Hoover. Martin stood to the side of the door in the hallway and waited.

"Are we being played, Mr. House?" Hoover asked.

"I never wanted these talks in Paris," House said.

"A neutral site would be better, of course. Lausanne, perhaps?"

"Too late. We must make do here. France wants to make Germany pay," House said.

"Excuse me, Mr. Hoover," Martin heard House say. A moment later, his face peered through the doorway. "Major, come in. Mr. Hoover and I are almost done."

Caught off guard, Martin said, “I’m sorry, sir. I didn’t mean to listen — ”

“Nonsense. You’re right on time.” House sat down and draped a blanket over his legs. “This hotel is terribly drafty.” He folded his arms over his chest and shivered. “Come, sit. You need to hear this.” House turned back to Hoover. “They’re stalling, the French and the British.” He explained that both President Georges Clémenceau and Prime Minister Lloyd George had delayed the talks because they had scheduled new elections they expected to win by large margins. The renewed domestic support would increase their leverage during the negotiations.

“Then what are we doing here, Mr. House?” Hoover said. “Why don’t we just go back home and let them know when *we’re* ready. Make *them* wait. We hold the purse strings.”

House looked at Martin. “You look concerned, Major. What is it?”

“Security, sir. Or lack of it,” Martin said. “These diplomats and professors have no concept of danger. Too many people are coming and going. It’s hard to keep track of them all.”

“Aren’t Marines at the entrances and lobby enough?” House asked.

“Hard to say. I see too many people I don’t recognize moving about. I suspect the hotel is keeping something from us. I’ve asked, but they’re not telling me. We’re their guests; I don’t want to create a scene.”

“Do what you have to do,” House said.

~

A day later, after interviewing many of the Americans, Martin found the source of the unexplained guests. While talking with a maid in an obscure back corner on the second floor, he saw one of the American researchers stagger onto the main corridor right after lunch. An attractive woman with too much makeup, strong perfume, and an easy walk accompanied him. Martin approached and demanded how they got here.

"None of your business," the professor said, struggling to stand upright. Martin recognized him from the dossiers and photographs of the U.S. delegation — Ulysses Wentworth, a Yale professor and expert on the Middle East, the classics, and fine wines.

"It is, and I can make this embarrassing for you. You're married, aren't you?" Wentworth fixed his eyes on his shoes. Martin looked at the woman and said, in French, "*Madame*, I'm sure you visit this hotel frequently and don't want trouble." The woman tried to walk away, but Martin pulled her back.

She raised her hand to slap him in the face, but stopped at the last second as if she understood the gravity of the situation. She gritted her teeth instead.

He whispered, "I don't care about your affairs. I just need to know where you came — "

"Maxim's," she said.

"The restaurant?" Martin asked. "How?"

"Shut up," the professor said. "You'll spoil all the fun."

Martin silenced him with a stare. He reached for the woman's arm and squeezed. "How?"

She pointed with a jerk of her chin. "Through that door. There's a passageway."

Martin let her go. "Get out of here and don't come back." She hurried away, and he turned back to Wentworth. "Don't mention this, professor. We'll deal with you later."

~

The next day around lunch, Martin, dressed as a bellhop, waited near the door to the passage. Eighteen minutes later, a panicked woman from the U.S. delegation ran through the door. "He has a gun."

"Who?"

"I don't know. Some man!" she cried.

"Go. Tell the Marines downstairs." Martin drew his .45 and ordered everyone in the area to their rooms.

As he had done countless times as a police officer, Martin approached the unknown passageway carefully. He knelt low and slowly turned the door handle with his left hand as he raised his .45 and pointed it up to chest height with his right. He felt a charge of adrenaline.

Using the wall for cover, he pushed the door open. The stairway was dark; someone had turned off the lights. He listened for a sound — breathing, a gun, footsteps. Nothing. He called. No response. He moved into the doorway, but a sudden reflex pulled him back just as a shot rang out. Large caliber. The bullet grazed his scalp. He fired two shots into the stairway. Heavy footsteps bound down the stairs. They stopped. Wait. Take cover. Two bullets hit the wall protecting him. Chunks of plaster peppered his face, and white dust stung his eyes.

Martin leaned over and peered into the darkness with watery eyes. He fired at a silhouette and heard a cry. Something dropped. He moved into the stairway. Another shot drove him back. He fired two more rounds and charged. He stopped when the stairway bent at ninety degrees. No return fire. A trap? Martin pointed his .45 and peered around the corner. He saw a satchel eight steps down. He started to retrieve it when the intruder let off two more bullets at him. Footsteps raced toward him. The intruder wanted the satchel back.

The hallway light flickered on, and two Marines entered the staircase above Martin. They hurried by him, raised their Springfield rifles, and fired. The intruder retreated. Footsteps descended. A door slammed below. Martin and the Marines maneuvered down. When Martin opened the door to the restaurant, there was no sign of the assailant. The attacker had vanished into the crowd. The few patrons gave conflicting stories about the fleeing man, but they agreed on one thing: he was holding his shoulder. Some saw blood.

Frustrated, Martin returned to House's office with the satchel. "My God," House said. "Are you all right?"

Martin nodded and rubbed his eyes.

"Who was it?"

"Don't know. We'll have to improve security."

"We must go on as if nothing has happened," House said. "We can't let them think we're intimidated. Our plans for peace are now more important than ever. We are obviously upsetting someone powerful. What was he after?"

Martin shook his head. "Let's see what's in here." He opened the satchel, a French military issue used to carry hand grenades, and found a newspaper picture of Colonel House and a hand-drawn map of the Crillon Hotel. House's room number was marked on it.

Chapter 10
The Spartacist Uprising

Berlin: January 1919

Germany was disintegrating, but events were so chaotic that Keller could not tell how fast. Would the Communists, now rising up to control the capital, take over as they had in Russia? Not if he could help it. Keller's German patriotism now matched that of his fellow soldiers in the Landsmann Battalion heading into Berlin. They were spoiling for a fight.

The battalion moved into the city from the south, along Belle Alliance Strasse and up Friedrich Strasse to the center of town. Although they had not yet encountered resistance, the men heard rumbling in the distance. Dead men with red armbands littered the streets. As they marched, women in black and men with missing limbs and disfigured faces cheered them on. A few pensioners begged for bread.

The name of Karl Liebknecht, the Spartacist and Communist leader who had called for the overthrow of the government, was on everyone's lips. Talk of last week's 700,000-man Communist demonstration passed through the ranks as the soldiers learned more from the few brave pro-government sympathizers lining the roads. The latest news was that Liebknecht had urged his KPD Communist party to take up arms in the struggle. Its fighters now ruled key areas of the city.

At Unter den Linden, Captain Reick ordered Sergeant Steffen to command a platoon and remove the Communists from the Berlin Tägliche *Zeitung* newspaper offices on Linien Strasse. Steffen's platoon broke away from the main unit and continued east. *Soldat* Brandt carried a sniper's rifle over his shoulder in Steffen's second squad. *Stay alive,* Keller reminded himself. *Stay alive, but gain the Freikorps's trust.*

Next to Keller was Corporal Jawbreaker Jans who held a MG 8/15 7.92 water-cooled portable machine gun. To his left, a man lugged a sack filled with 100-round steel ammunition drums. Behind them was Heizer, a quiet man who carried a flamethrower. The petrol tank looked small on his large back. He had survived longer than flamethrower men should. The last two men pulled a small wagon with a trench mortar and shells.

The men followed Miltz, who had grown up in the neighborhood, through side streets and shortcuts. Steffen walked a step behind him and whispered what Keller guessed were instructions. The streets were empty except for some scavengers going through the possessions of dead Communists, and a few scared dogs. The men, alert and cautious, spread out in groups of three or four. They moved methodically and studied every open window, rooftop, and ambush point. Rifle and heavy weapons fire barked farther east, and the soldiers became more determined as they approached. As the sniper, Keller concentrated on the roofs. First up a block, then down, then back up again. He fought to control his nerves. If someone in his platoon were shot, they would blame him.

After twenty-five minutes, they reached the end of a narrow unguarded alley that fed into Keibel Strasse. Steffen gestured for the men to stop. Only locals, like Miltz, would know its location. Keller could hear men humming the *Internationale*, the Communists' revolutionary song, and building a barricade around the corner. The platoon was close to its quarry and well positioned for an attack. His platoon ducked down along the alley, staying low. The men readied their carbines. Keller reacted slowly, provoking disapproving looks from the other men. The mortar team began to assemble their weapon.

Steffen signaled Keller and Wolf to join them. Keller peeked around the corner to Keibel Strasse and saw the barricade about forty yards south on the other side of the street. A pile of overturned wagons, furniture, and mattresses defended by seventy armed men with red armbands and banners blocked Linien Strasse. A Maxim MG08 machine gun was positioned in its center. Miltz said the newspaper office was thirty yards behind it. “What do you think, Brandt?” Steffen asked.

Keller, understanding his life depended on his assessment, turned back to the safety of the alley way. “They’ve set their position all wrong. They expect a head-on attack down Linien Strasse. We can hit them from the side along this street. The machine gun can’t get us there. Two men with grenades can take them out.”

“They’re not soldiers,” Steffen said. “They’re fools.”

“Fun.” Wolf smiled gleefully across his lopsided face. He massaged the handle of the trench sword attached to his belt.

Keller took a deep breath, prayed. “Let me lead the attack.”

Jawbreaker circled back along the alley to Linien Strasse, faced the barricade head-on, and opened up with his MG 8/15. A squad climbed to a rooftop overlooking the barricade and emptied clip after clip from their carbines. The eight inexperienced sentries standing in front of the barricade died without firing a bullet.

Protected by the overpowering suppressing fire, Keller dashed onto Keibel Strasse, hurled a smoke grenade toward the barricade, and ran to cover on the opposite side of the street, limping to safety as his bad leg cramped. Behind him were Wolf, Miltz, and Heizer. The quiet flamethrower man said something Keller could not hear amidst the deafening gunfire.

Ignoring the drifting smoke, the men inched toward the barricade, protected by the building which blocked the angle of opposing fire. Wolf exchanged hand signals with Sergeant Steffen at the front of the alley. He cupped his hands and yelled in Keller's ear. "Fifteen seconds. Go for the machine gun."

Keller counted down the time. He removed two potato masher grenades hooked to his belt. Just then, a mortar round exploded in front of the barricade, blowing a gap right through it. Yells of confusion and desperation filled the air. When Jawbreaker emptied another drum at the Communists, Keller turned to the three men behind him and said, "*Mach schnell!*"

Hugging the building, Keller reached the edge of the wreckage and flung his two grenades over the top toward the machine gun. Two from Wolf followed. Miltz fired twice, toppling two men from the barricades. The grenades detonated within seconds of each other and obliterated the rest of the barricade. Keller felt the vibrations and heard the screams of dying men through his ringing ears. Keller and Wolf stepped aside while Heizer dashed forward and doused the area with bursts of liquid fire that cooked whoever was left. The smell of burning flesh and disemboweled bodies was overpowering. Things quieted. Heizer walked across the carnage with the distant expression of a man who had done this once too often.

Keller raised a Luger and jumped over the debris, which was covered by syrupy red slime. Wolf raced by him. Keller found two Communists, both lying prone with severed limbs. Wolf shot them both. "Just making sure," he said as he ran into the newspaper building. Miltz followed. A few minutes later, Miltz exited. "They're all dead," he declared.

Sergeant Steffen approached with Jawbreaker, whose MG 8/15 barrel was still steaming. "Casualties?"

"Watch out," Keller shouted and tried to push Steffen to safety. A rifle shot sung out above them. Keller pointed his Luger toward a window and emptied his clip. A man fell two stories and landed with a bone-crunching thud.

"Bravo," Steffen said just before he spit out red foam and collapsed, gasping for air. Jawbreaker ripped open Steffen's shirt, but he was already dead. Three men charged into the building and the rest pointed their carbines at the newspaper office.

"*Christus*," Wolf moaned. Looking like a little boy, he rubbed his nose with his sleeve and slumped down on the street. "I missed one."

A basement door opened behind them, and everyone in the platoon pointed their weapons at the noise. A frail man with a worker's cap climbed the stairs to the street and waved a white handkerchief. "Don't sho—" A volley of bullets silenced him.

Jawbreaker assumed command. "Man the perimeter. There may be more around." He walked over to Keller and patted him on the back. "Good work. I know only three other men who could have made that shot," he said and saluted.

Keller saluted back in the manner of a German soldier. He was not sure if he had become a Freikorps soldier, a spy, or somehow both. Worse, he did not know if he had a choice.

Chapter 11
Liebknecht

Berlin: January 15, 1919

Keller, manning the checkpoint across Linien Strasse with Wolf and Heizer, strained to see in the moonless night. Concerned about anarchist reprisals after the Communist defeat in the last two days, he aimed his carbine at the voice coming at him from the dark. It was past 20:00, the time when innocent people should be home. "Halt," Keller warned, but the intruder continued forward. Wolf reached for his Mauser pistol and moved to circle behind the voice.

"It's me."

Recognizing Miltz, Keller lowered his guard warily, but Heizer, whose eyes could not seem to focus, jerked his carbine up in shaky movements.

Miltz stopped at the wooden horse and barbed wire barrier in front of Keller and said, "I've found him." He slumped down and put his hands on his knees to catch his breath.

"Who?" Heizer asked, steadying his weapon.

"Liebknecht. I've found him, I tell you," Miltz said excitedly.

Keller's eyes widened. Liebknecht was the German Communist Dulles and Hoover had most feared when they assigned Keller the mission. Now, the Freikorps was going to do his work, but at what cost?

Wolf joined in. "You sure?"

"*Ja*. And that red bitch of his."

"His wife — Red Rosa?" Keller asked, trying to confirm the electrifying news. Even though the Freikorps had suppressed much of the revolt, Karl Liebknecht and his wife Rosa Luxemburg, the leaders of the Spartacist uprising, were still at large. A city-wide manhunt continued.

"Where's Captain Reick?" Miltz asked anxiously. "We need to move fast."

Wolf pointed his head to the new company headquarters in the Tägliche *Zeitung* newspaper offices. "Go."

Fourteen minutes later, Keller and the other men scrambled to collect the tools they needed for close-quarter combat. On his way out, Keller grabbed a sledge-hammer. The men jumped into a black Mercedes coupe and headed to the quiet middle-class Wilmersdorf section in the western part of the city.

Miltz drove. Captain Reick sat next to him studying a map. Keller was squeezed in the back seat between Jawbreaker and Heizer. Keller swallowed back the bile rising from his gut. A truck with twenty-five heavily armed soldiers was right behind. Wolf followed a block away on a motorcycle to make sure no one followed them. They sped down Konig, south on Friedrich Strasse, and west on Leipziger; the street lights flickered on and off, another sign of physical decay.

"That coward, Liebknecht," Jawbreaker said, fondling the brass knuckles that earned him his nickname. "Hiding in the bourgeois part of town. Some Communist." As they drove west, the scars of war began to fade. No walls marred by bullets. No abandoned burned-out wrecks. The houses were well-kept. Some with gardens growing badly needed vegetables. Jittery, Heizer worked the bolt of his carbine back and forth — click, click; click click — again and again. Click, click; click, click. Keller had seen men acting erratically like this before. In the American Army, they called it shell shock. Exchanging looks, Jawbreaker leaned toward Keller and said, "Watch him."

Click, click; click, click.

"There in ten more minutes, Captain." Miltz made a hard right turn onto Grunewald, spilling the three men in the back seat into each other.

"Slow down, *Soldat*," Reich said. "It's past curfew. Our friend isn't going anywhere."

"What the crap you doing?" Heizer asked angrily.

Jawbreaker, reaching over Keller, rested his hand on Heizer's arm and said, "Calm down, soldier. This mission is important. No mistakes. That's an order." The flamethrower man, who had defied Satan's arithmetic for so long, relaxed.

Once in Wilmersdorf, Miltz downshifted. They cruised up Sigmaringen Strasse and rolled to a stop at Wegener. "Mannheimer Strasse's the next block, Captain. Number 33 is a few minutes' walk."

Reick called all his men together and gave them final orders. He awarded Jawbreaker's squad the honor of taking the prisoners. "Remember, I want them breathing." The storm troopers advanced down the street with the same discipline and silence they had employed during a night-time trench raid. For Keller, this was like a police action, but he feared the combat mentality and aggressive nature of the group could force him to accept murder. These men would kill anyone who stood in their way.

When Jawbreaker's squad moved down Mannheimer, lights on the buildings on either side became dark. Curtains closed — soldiers patrolling at night meant danger. Wolf led the way, followed by Miltz, acting as a guide. Jawbreaker and Keller walked several paces behind. Heizer was last. Truncheons and clubs hooked to their belts instead of potato-masher grenades bounced against their legs. Each man carried a carbine, an automatic pistol, and a weapon of choice — Jawbreaker's brass knuckles, Wolf's trench sword, hatchets for Miltz and Heizer, and a sledge hammer for Keller.

Reick joined Jawbreaker's squad at the front door of 33

Mannheimer. The rest of the men had surrounded the house so completely it might as well have been a coffin. "Second floor, third door to the right of the stairs, 2C, that's where Liebknecht's staying," Miltz said.

Reick turned to Jawbreaker. "Proceed, Sergeant."

Jawbreaker gave the signal, and the men ran into the house and up the stairs. Reick was right behind them. When they reached the second floor, Wolf stopped and peered along the poorly lit hallway. As they waited, Heizer began to work his bolt as he had in the car — click, click; click, click; click, click. "Stop that." Jawbreaker pushed Heizer against the wall and waved a finger in his face. "I won't warn you again. If you compromise this raid, I'll kill you." He looked at Keller. "You're responsible for him, Brandt. No excuses."

Heizer's wild eyes turned fierce.

"Stay out of this one, soldier," Keller said, trying to be soothing.

Heizer snarled back.

Wolf moved toward 2C, and the rest of the men moved forward, except for Heizer, who remained on the steps. At the door, Wolf signaled for Keller. The voices inside seemed unaware of the danger. "Go," Jawbreaker ordered. Keller raised his sledge hammer and bashed in the door.

Wolf was into the apartment before the door buckled to the floor. A woman yelled and a thin middle-aged man fumbled with a revolver in the hallway. Before he could fire a shot, Wolf swung his trench sword at the man's wrist. Liebknecht's arm was saved by an identity bracelet. Jawbreaker moved forward and smashed Liebknecht's face with his brass knuckles. The teeth-breaking sound sickened Keller. "Fucking Communist. Bolsheviks killed my wife." Jawbreaker swung again, this time crushing Liebknecht's nose and shattering his pince-nez glasses. Blood spurted out of his face. He collapsed.

The captain entered the room. “What the Christ happened?”

Jawbreaker moved away and said, “He’s still breathing, Captain.”

“Patch him up, Brandt, and get him out of here,” Reick said.

Keller began to attend to Liebknecht when Heizer ran into the apartment, yelling, “Where’s that bitch?” Saliva foaming around his mouth like a rabid dog, Heizer stepped over Liebknecht and Keller. Keller tried to tackle him, but Heizer broke away and bounded into the living room.

Red Rosa charged at Heizer from the next room with her nails raised. Heizer grunted and jabbed the butt of his carbine into her face. The force of the blow stunned her, but she stayed upright, angering Heizer even more. After too many years of trench warfare, he exploded and hit her twice more with the carbine. He pulled out his Luger and pistol-whipped her until she fell.

“Don’t kill her!” Reick yelled, but Heizer administered blow after blow.

A shot rang out, and Heizer fell, dead on his side with a bullet through his ear. Jawbreaker holstered his Walther semi-automatic. “Couldn’t let him ruin our mission.” He turned to Keller and said, “I should shoot you too. *You* should have stopped him. Not me.”

“Clean up this mess,” Reick said. “Get them over to the colonel at the Eden Hotel. We’ll interrogate them there.” He pointed to Heizer’s corpse. “Take him.”

Keller, stunned and revolted, failed to move.

Jawbreaker stared at him. “You’re weak. You don’t have the stomach for battle. I’m watching you, Brandt.”

Chapter 12
The Ball

Paris: January 1919

Martin woke up repeating three words to himself: anarchists, assassins, spies. Four years and a great war later, he was confronting the same enemies he had defeated as a New York City detective. But this time, he was in Paris. Enemies were everywhere. Even America's friends could not be trusted. President Wilson was challenging their colonial ambitions and demanding payment on their debt.

Who was that on the staircase? A Russian who wanted to start a worldwide revolution? A German monarchist? A paid killer? An agent from a foreign government? Five days had passed, and the mystery continued. The chance of finding the man on the staircase worsened. The local police considered him merely a robber. Commandant Truchon of the Sûreté, France's National Police, had more pressing concerns: "I can't help you now. I'm sure you understand."

Only Captain Alain Durand, Martin's counterpart in French military intelligence, understood the threat. A common thief would not be carrying a picture of Wilson's top advisor and the location of his suite. Durand did what he could to further the investigation and updated Martin every day on his lack of progress.

To prevent further incursions, Martin forced the manager to board up the secret passageway to the restaurant despite his loud protests. To make sure it stayed that way, Martin posted a Marine twenty-four hours a day. He also commandeered a platoon of Marines from American Expeditionary Forces (AEF) headquarters and doubled the guard at the Hotel Crillon's entranceways. He assigned a man to stand by House's suite at all times. He doubled President Wilson's guard at the elegant Hotel Murat, the former palace of the Prince of Murat, which was provided by the French government.

At their daily morning briefing, House announced that Ulysses Wentworth, the professor who had brought the prostitute into the hotel, had been sent back to America. "When the president learned about the incident," House said, "he insisted we make an example of him. Mr. Wentworth will be on the next liner home. Steerage class." He added that his replacement, a most impressive individual, would be arriving soon.

With new dignitaries and interested parties converging on Paris each day, Martin tried to anticipate all possible threats, but there were too many to deal with. Tonight, he had a new problem. President Wilson was languishing in boredom and irritation while the other Allied leaders prepared their arguments and improved their political positions for the coming talks. *Monsieur le Président* Poincaré had thus organized a gala ball to entertain President Wilson at Le Grand Hotel facing the Paris Opera House. Every dignitary already in Paris was invited.

House considered it a great opportunity to assess the opposition. When Martin balked, saying it was too dangerous for so many world leaders to be in one room at one time, House said, "Before a battle, doesn't a good general scout the terrain and probe his opponent's lines for weakness? Diplomacy is a different game, but the tactics are the same. Our delegation will go to the ball in force."

"Of course." Martin did not mention that his last experience with such an affair in New York had almost ended in the death of a major industrialist. A timely confession from an informer had prevented the tragedy, but Martin knew he could not count on such luck a second time.

~

Colonel House announced that he could not attend. Coughing phlegm and running a fever of 102 degrees, House had finally succumbed to the Parisian weather. Fears about the influenza epidemic, which was causing the deaths of millions, made the doctors order rest. House protested, insisting he could go, but Herbert Hoover, who seemed to have a greater role in U.S. policy than his position might imply, said he could stand in for the colonel. House reluctantly agreed. Much to Martin's dismay, competition within the U.S. delegation was intensifying.

Martin arrived at Le Grand Hotel two hours before the start of the ball. Captain Durand greeted him at the entrance. "Everything is secure, Major. My president is pleased. This will be the first event in Le Grand Hotel since the war started. Thank God it is no longer a military hospital. This is a hotel for kings. Come, let me show you the facility."

At the main entrance, two guards dressed in Napoleonic-era cavalry uniforms jumped to attention, looking huge in their shiny silver breast-plates and *Cuirassier* curved helmets. Their sabers rattled against their legs when Martin and Durand walked by.

When Martin reached the circular grand ballroom where the gala would be held, he was impressed by its elegance and beauty. Louis XIV would have approved. Paintings from Ruisdael to Delacroix rivaled anything Martin had seen in a museum. The dance floor gleamed. The walls smelled of fresh paint. But, despite these cosmetic improvements, the ballroom showed its age. The mirrors, taller than three men, had cloudy spots across their surfaces and gray reflections. Nicks and small splinters marred the wood panels. He chastised himself. He had more important things to observe.

Martin asked about the ten-piece orchestra setting up in the far corner of the ballroom. Durand assured him every one of the musicians had been in the French Army and could be trusted. Just to be sure, Martin walked over, politely introduced himself, and spoke with each of them. They seemed friendly and honored to be there. The second violinist was quiet and tugged at his collar as if it did not fit well. Martin would ask Durand about him.

Martin looked up. The magnificent chandelier that dominated the high, arching, circular ceiling was so large he was not sure how it stayed up. If someone wanted to kill a number of people in the crowded ballroom, causing it to fall would be an excellent way to do it. He asked Durand about its supports and whether any explosive devices could be placed near them.

"Excellent point, Major. I will post extra men to guard it."

One less problem. Martin wished he had Keller with him. There was too much to do and too few people to trust.

~

Guests started to arrive an hour later. Lines of taxis, military vehicles, and cars full of diplomats and high-ranking officials lined up in front of the Opera House, all waiting to drop off their passengers. Herbert Hoover's car bearing President Wilson was second in line. While Martin waited nervously to escort the president into the hotel, he studied the roofs, open windows, and streets. He and Durand, who stood next to him, exchanged observations.

Excited civilians crowded the area. Amidst the throng of reporters by the hotel, one woman stood out. In the competitive arena of newspapermen, a woman journalist was rare, and this one was striking. Taller than most of the men, she wore a Siberian fur coat and walked with grace and confidence. Her light brown hair shimmered in the street lights and flowed in the breeze.

"Who's that?" Martin asked Durand, pointing in her direction.

Durand chuckled. "Everyone wants to meet her. That's Anastasia, 'Ana', Primakova, a Russian correspondent. She's been here since the Tsar was murdered. She claims she's a Tsarist, but we're not sure. We're watching her just in case she's a subversive. She's tougher than an army field nurse and smarter than Marie Curie. Some say she's a Russian noblewoman. Others say she was Trotsky's mistress. You're intrigued like the rest of us, *n'est-ce pas*?"

"No," Martin said, trying to deny the truth to himself.

"She's beautiful. Speaks excellent French and English and writes a good story. She's a puzzle, that's for certain. Come, your president has arrived."

Wilson's car pulled up to the entrance, and Martin stepped to open the door. Two Marines in their finest dress blues exited and stood guard as President Wilson and Herbert Hoover emerged. The crowd cheered, and Wilson waved back. Hoover pulled Martin close to him and asked, "Everything secure?"

"Yes, sir, but please go into the hotel quickly."

Hoover rested his hand on the president's wrist and whispered something. They moved briskly to the entrance escorted by the two Marines under Martin's watchful eyes.

Martin followed them into the crowded grand ballroom. The men wore dress uniforms or elegant white tie and tails; the women wore long, flowing gowns. He heard French, English, Italian, Japanese or Chinese, he could not tell, and better Polish than he had ever heard on the New York docks. The only language he did not hear was German. Waiters carried large oval trays of champagne flutes. Others offered *foie gras* and *terrine de canard*. The band played Chopin. The atmosphere was loud and festive.

"Excuse me, Major." Martin turned. Gunnery Sergeant Andrew Cooper, a three-time Purple Cross recipient and a member of the Marine guard, saluted. He had worked with Martin at the end of the war. Martin liked his efficiency, calm, and sound judgment. "You asked me to let you know if I saw anything unusual."

"What is it, Sergeant?"

"I saw a priest mingling among the guests. Harmless enough, but when I approached, he smiled, pardoned himself, and walked away. Like he was trying to avoid me, so I watched him. When he spotted you, he moved away quickly."

"Any unusual features?"

"He wore an eye patch."

"Means nothing to me. Go on, Sergeant."

"I tried to follow him through the crowd, but I lost him. He's disappeared."

"Good work. If you see him again, detain him and get me. Excuse me, I must find Mr. Hoover. Carry on, Sergeant."

Martin found Hoover after several minutes talking to a small man in grand white robes. Hoover waved, said something to the man, and walked over to Martin. One of the waiters, a short curly-haired man, clumsily ran into him. "*Excusez-moi, monsieur.*" Hoover chastised him and complained to Martin.

"Who was that man in the robes?" Martin asked Hoover after he calmed down. "He looks Western."

"Don't you know? That's Colonel T. E. Lawrence. A few of my British friends mockingly call him Lawrence of Arabia. Difficult man. More concerned about the Bedouins than us."

"What's he doing here?" Martin asked.

"He thinks he's some kind of Arab prince," Hoover said. "Represents the region, so he claims. They want independence. The British don't trust him. They want to expand their empire into the region. Petroleum is what they're after, I think."

"Where's the president?" Martin asked.

"Last I looked, he was talking with Président Poincaré. They're surrounded by guards — theirs and ours. They're safe."

"Pardon me, sir, I need to talk to my French counterpart," Martin said. He found Durand, who assured him nothing was amiss. He did not recall a priest on the invitation list. "What harm could a one-eyed priest do? Just in case, I'll have my men detain and question him. Come, let's check outside." Together they questioned the exterior guards and circled the area. "Too quiet." Martin's police senses suspected something.

"We have done all we can, Major. Let us return inside. My men are everywhere."

"The violinist and the curly-haired waiter are two of them," Martin said.

"*Très bien*. Come. Let's make sure that chandelier won't drop." After inspecting the well-guarded chandelier supports, they moved to the kitchen, where the head chef chased them out with a cleaver, exclaiming his cooks were preparing the food. Martin would go back when he had the chance. No one would accuse him of ruining dinner. As they returned to the main ballroom, Martin mused that Le Grand Hotel, like all old buildings, was largely wood. Nothing he could do about it, but it bothered him. Needing to report back to Hoover, he pushed his concerns away.

He found Hoover talking to a balding, unassuming English-looking gentleman with a high forehead and full eyebrows. Hoover waved him over. "Major Martin, let me introduce you to John Maynard Keynes. He's the financial representative for the British Treasury. He may be the shrewdest man in Britain and the most sensible man in Europe."

They shook hands. "Your Mr. Hoover is generous with his comments," Keynes said.

"Your reputation precedes you, sir." Martin thought Keynes

looked like a college professor. All he needed was a pipe.

"Listen to him, Major," Hoover said. "Continue, Mr. Keynes."

"The British people are demanding Germany pay the full cost of the war," Keynes said. "I insist they should pay what they can afford. We cannot crush their economy or bankrupt them without grave consequences." The deep intensity of his eyes hinted at a brilliant mind. "I fear less reasonable heads will prevail," he continued. "I heard one member of Parliament say, 'We'll squeeze them like a lemon until you can hear their pips squeak.' We will have a bigger problem later on."

"I'll relay your thoughts to President Wilson," Hoover said. "We agree and maybe we can help each other. We'll have much work to do at the talks."

Out of the corner of his eye, Martin noticed a husky man walk across the ball room. He appeared to come from the kitchen and was heading to the main entrance. He walked suspiciously, as if he had a stiff arm and shoulder. Sensing trouble, Martin followed him. His size and shoulders seemed familiar, but he looked different. Gray hair. Trim mustache, glasses. Able to look through disguises, Martin was sure it was the man who had shot at him at the Crillon stairway. He tried to maneuver closer, but too many guests stood in his way.

"Stop," Martin said in a low voice, trying not to cause concern. But his words were lost in a crash. Smoke poured from the kitchen.

"Fire!"

Chapter 13
Tiergarten

Berlin: January 15, 1919

The raid on apartment 2C had taken minutes. Reick's storm troopers traipsed through pools of blood covering the front hallway floor. They smoked cigarettes and made jokes. "Too easy," Wolf said.

Animals, Keller thought.

Captain Reick looked at Karl Liebknecht and Rosa Luxemburg, both sprawled on the floor like slabs of meat. "Can we get them to Colonel Landsmann alive?" he asked Keller.

"Don't know." Keller said, noticing the other men's disapproving looks while he checked Liebknecht's pulse. "He's still breathing. I need to — "

"Make it fast and make it hurt." Jawbreaker flicked his cigarette to the rug and rubbed it out. "Not sure about that one." He gestured toward Red Rosa.

"She's a whore," Wolf said, shuffling his deck of cards.

"Heizer's dead. Lost control. Had to put him down," Jawbreaker said to Reick.

"You did what you had to, Sergeant." Reick shrugged and asked Jawbreaker for a cigarette. "Good soldier. Bound to happen. Too many fights. Brave man."

Keller applied a tourniquet to Liebknecht's arm and bandaged the wound. He cleaned his damaged face as best he could and moved near an open window away from the other men. The outside chill revived him. A drink would have been better. He had violated the storm troopers' unspoken code. Mercy meant weakness. The looks of the other men indicated they would not trust him in a fight.

Jawbreaker oozed contempt and looked like a boxer just before the bell to start round one. *Just one punch.* He glared at Brandt. *That's all I need.*

"Let's get out of here," Reick said after he returned from Liebknecht's desk with his hands full of papers.

"Get up, coward." Jawbreaker kicked Liebknecht in the ribs. The Spartacist leader leaned forward, spit out bloody teeth, and fell back. Jawbreaker kicked harder. "Come on, traitor. Your revolution is over."

"My arm." Liebknecht struggled to get the words out. The area around his eyes had swollen. Blood leaked from the remains of his nose. "Water."

"Get up, or I'll kill you right here." Jawbreaker reached for his brass knuckles. Liebknecht managed to stand but withered seconds later. "Help him," Jawbreaker said to Miltz. "You, Brandt, take Heizer," he told Keller. "And don't drop him."

"But —" Keller stopped in mid-sentence. He knelt down, took hold of Heizer's thigh, and praying for strength, stood up and draped the two-hundred-pound body over his shoulder in a fireman's carry. He nearly buckled under the weight, but he regained his balance and headed to the door.

Liebknecht, almost delirious, put his good arm around Miltz's shoulder and hobbled away. Jawbreaker and Wolf carried Red Rosa by her shoulders and feet. On their way out, they knocked her head against the door frame with a loud thump.

What was left of Heizer's head bounced against Keller's back. He stumbled on the stairs but managed to stay upright. He continued on, fearing Jawbreaker might shoot him if he fell. The old wound in his leg began to ache. He stopped to regain his strength, hoping the others would not notice. When he reached the truck, he leaned down and placed Heizer's body on the ground. He covered him with a blanket one of the soldiers gave him. Two other men helped Keller put the corpse in the back of the truck with the reverence due a fallen friend who had fought one too many fights.

Jawbreaker and Wolf rolled Red Rosa into the truck. She landed face-down. Jawbreaker jumped into the truck and pushed her over with his feet. She uttered a weak groan and barely moved. Miltz handed Liebknecht to Jawbreaker, who lifted him like he was made of straw and forced him to sit on his haunches.

During the ride to battalion headquarters at the Eden Hotel on Budapester Strasse across from the zoo, Rosa Luxemburg's pulpy face turned pale. She started to twitch uncontrollably. Liebknecht kept calling, "Rosa, Rosa." Jawbreaker silenced him with another kick to his lower intestines, which emptied, releasing a foul stench. Despite the blistering cold, Wolf opened the canvas flap at the back of the truck.

By the time they stopped at the well-guarded servants' entrance to the hotel, Red Rosa was dead, and Liebknecht was unconscious. Jawbreaker and Keller carried him to the basement, cleaned him up, and gave him some morphine. Colonel Landsmann would interrogate him soon.

"What do we do with the whore, Captain?" Miltz asked. "Can hardly tell who she is."

"Drop her in the Landwehr canal. Under the Lichtensteinbrueke. She won't turn up for months. Or longer."

Keller did what he could for Liebknecht while Jawbreaker taunted him. Reick and Colonel Landsmann entered the dank basement. "Guard the door, Brandt. Don't let anyone pass," Reick said, slamming the door before Keller could finish his salute.

For the next fifteen minutes, Keller heard demands, slaps, and curses from the officers. If Liebknecht said anything coherent, Keller could not tell. What were his own chances of surviving the night? 50-50, if all went well.

He heard Landsmann say, "We're done. He's tough, I'll give him that." One last punch and Liebknecht went quiet. Was he dead? The door opened and Landsmann walked past with an angry face.

Reick ordered Keller inside. The smell of vomit filled the room. "Take him to my car. We're going for a ride," Reick said.

"*Jawohl.*" Jawbreaker saluted and smiled malevolently.

Keller gulped.

Reick looked peeved, worsening Keller's odds. "What's wrong with you? Got something better to do?"

Keller and Jawbreaker carried Liebknecht to the captain's car at the back of the hotel. The motionless Communist leader felt like a sack of potatoes, and his face looked like unused grindings from a sausage machine. Reick opened the back door of his car. They tossed Liebknecht inside on his stomach. Reick drove, and Jawbreaker sat beside him, forcing Keller to sit next to Liebknecht's curled up legs.

They drove into the Tiergarten woods near the Rickard Wagner statue and stopped in a dark, secluded clearing beyond the Queen Luise monument. A thin layer of ice shrouded the ground. "Here," Reick said. Keller slipped when he got out and looked around for help he knew was not there. Jawbreaker went over to Liebknecht, still lying flat in the car, and yanked his body upright, causing howls of pain. Reick seemed to enjoy his agony. Jawbreaker pressed smelling salts into the cavity that was once Liebknecht's nose and jolted him awake. "We're going for a walk," Jawbreaker said.

"Can't," Liebknecht said. "Kill me now."

"I can make your death last a long time." Jawbreaker pulled out a lighter, flicked it on, and started to heat his knife. "Better do what we say."

Somehow, Liebknecht lurched out of the auto and started to walk. When Liebknecht had gone six paces, Reick glowered at Keller. He took a Mauser from his holster and handed it to him. He pointed to Liebknecht. "You do it, Brandt."

Chapter 14
Freikorps Justice

Berlin: January 1919

Ten minutes after they dumped Liebknecht's body in front of the morgue by the entrance to the Tiergarten zoo, Reick, Jawbreaker, and Keller returned to the nearby Eden Hotel. With martial law in place, Landsmann had secured first-class accommodations for his headquarters staff. Reick and Jawbreaker were ready to be heroes. Miltz and Wolf were drinking beer and celebrating with the rest of the battalion. They had thrown Red Rosa into the canal. Captain Reick confirmed that Brandt had done what he needed to do, and the men once again welcomed him into their ranks. Keller pretended to enjoy the praise and chugged a Paulaner, appearing to partake in the camaraderie. Nevertheless, he stayed aloof, which was his nature.

Early the next morning, a battalion sergeant walked from the Eden Hotel and "accidently found" an "unidentified" body where Reick had told him it would be. Reick wanted to pretend he had nothing to do with the dumping of Liebknecht's body. The sergeant picked it up and carried it into the morgue as ordered. The mortician recognized the badly mauled corpse as Liebknecht's and reported he had been shot.

The news of Liebknecht's death spread quickly across Berlin. Rumors about his last minutes varied. He had been shot in the back of the head execution-style. No, he was killed trying to escape. You're wrong. He was lined up against a tree and shot by a firing squad. He had committed suicide. Not possible. Where was Rosa Luxemburg? Although certain the Freikorps had arrested her at the same time as her husband, the newspapers could only speculate. There was no trace of her body.

The celebration at the Eden lasted until early morning. Having gone to bed at 04:00, Keller woke up tormented. Last night would haunt him the rest of his life. Under Reich's orders, he stayed in the hotel for his own protection until the speculation over Liebknecht's death quieted down. Revenge-minded Communist sympathizers remained in the city. Keller felt as if a piranha was trying to eat its way out of his stomach. The harder he tried to erase last night's memories, the more vivid they became. As far as he was concerned, he was a murderer. On one of his last cases in the Bomb Squad, a German sympathizer got mixed up with German spies and became complicit in murder. After that, the Germans had manipulated him and ruined his life. He had claimed he had no choice, but he was guilty anyway. So was Keller, in his own mind.

Unlike Keller, Colonel Landsmann spoke proudly of last night's events. The next afternoon, he invited pro-government sympathizers and friendly newspaper people to the hotel for a talk in the ballroom. Jawbreaker, Miltz, Wolf, and Keller stayed in the back. Reick stood next to Keller. From the podium, Landsmann confirmed that men from his battalion had captured the two Spartacist leaders and taken them for questioning. Rosa Luxemburg had been allowed to leave, but Karl Liebknecht was arrested. On the way to the Moabit prison, the car broke down. Liebknecht tried to run but was shot after several warnings.

"Questions?"

What about the condition of the body? "Liebknecht was uncooperative and abusive to his questioners. Force was needed to restrain him. Some of his injuries may have occurred before my men arrested him."

Listening from the back of the room, Keller was used to police and military officials lying to the public, but he had never heard anything so implausible.

Why dump the body at the morgue? "The men were wrong to do this. They realized their mistake and reported the incident. As soon as I learned about it, I sent out a patrol to retrieve the body." Landsmann had neglected to say the men who brought the body to the morgue claimed the man was unidentified.

Who were the men involved? "I am going through my own investigation. Until it is complete, I cannot disclose names. I will say this: Those men are heroes. Luxemburg and Liebknecht were Communist traitors looking to destroy Germany!"

Did any useful information emerge from Liebknecht's interrogation? "His revolution failed. Everything else is confidential."

Rote Fahne, the extreme left's paper, is demanding a civil court trial. How do you respond? "I have nothing to say. I don't care what they want."

What is your reaction to Prime Minister Ebert's request for an independent investigation? "This is a Freikorps matter, and we will conduct a military tribunal. We respect the law and want justice for all concerned, but it will be our justice. Good day, gentlemen."

Keller returned to his hotel room. He shuddered at the possibilities. The news of an independent investigation, or worse a Freikorps one, hit him in the gut like a punch from Jack Johnson. He could already picture himself in front of a firing squad. If an independent investigation did not discover his identity as an American spy, a Freikorps one would, and they would likely dispatch him as they had Liebknecht. Keller could already feel the cold slab in the morgue. No one would care, and Shannon would never know what had become of him.

~

Confined to his room, Keller had nothing to do but think before the military tribunal. The Freikorps had not treated him like a prisoner — "detained comfort" Reick had called it. It was a spacious, quiet room with decent food, but the guard at the door prevented him from any outside contact. Not even a newspaper. During the sleepless nights, he formed a plan, risky but bold. Thankfully, Miltz had brought him all his things, including the leather valise he had brought from Washington. It was his only hope. Could he pull it off? Bad actor or not, he had to try.

~

A few days before the tribunal was to begin, Colonel Landsmann and Captain Reick came to Keller's room. They controlled Berlin and told him the Freikorps would never allow the government to usurp their investigation. The outcome was already determined.

Was this good news or bad?

"The trial is for show," Landsmann said. "Miltz, innocent. Lack of evidence. Luxemburg's body is missing. Wolf was pardoned because he's too young. Your name was never mentioned in the Liebknecht incident. We told them Heizer was on Liebknecht's assassination detail, not you. Sergeant Jawbreaker Jans and I, sentenced to two years, but we'll be out in two weeks."

Keller was relieved to be excluded from the proceedings, but worried that Jawbreaker would be close by to threaten him. "Thank you, Colonel, but may I ask you something?" This was the moment — time to make his pitch. All or nothing. He'd not get another chance, but failure meant certain death. "Do you trust me?"

"You're not a storm trooper. We hardly know you, but you're smart and follow orders."

"I'm more than that. I can help more than you realize."

Landsmann looked at him skeptically. "How?"

Keller opened the hidden compartment of his valise and showed him Dulles's money.

Chapter 15
Panic

Paris: January 1919

Martin choked on the thickening smoke, his visibility reduced to a few yards. Screaming people stampeded toward the main entrance. The heat in the ballroom began to build. Lights flickered, and flames attacked the swinging doors between the ballroom and the kitchen. *Where was President Wilson? And Durand?*

Martin's lungs, weakened from past exposure to chlorine gas, began to constrict. Here and there in the crowd, people were collapsing and falling to the floor. Others passed out. A stout man shouldered by, almost knocking Martin down. Desperate, heart-rending cries from workers trapped in the kitchen cut through the surrounding screams and groans. They were condemned to die in the fire. Martin called out for help, but his voice vanished amid the uproar. His eyes stung so badly he could barely see. He knelt down and gagged on the smoke. He felt something by his foot — a bottle lay in a puddle of spilt champagne. He pulled out his handkerchief, mopped it in the puddle, and placed the wet cloth over his mouth. His breathing eased.

Crackling sounds alarmed him. The fire had intensified and would soon be feeding on the wooden beams, ballroom floor, and elaborate draperies. As Martin rose unsteadily to his feet, a shrill military whistle pierced the commotion. *"This way, hurry! Over here!"* came Durand's authoritative voice. *About time he showed up.* The ballroom could erupt into flames at any moment, but Durand remained in control. He supervised his men, who guided those who could walk to the exits, helped the feeble, and carried the injured to safety.

The first group of firemen dashed into the ballroom. Some smashed windows with axes, allowing the smoke to escape. Others, led by Durand's blond-haired waiter, dashed by Martin with a long hose. More followed carrying tablecloths, buckets, anything to fight the blaze. The second violinist and several fellow band members frantically began to take down priceless paintings and move them to safety. Through the thinning smoke, Martin noticed several guests, including Keynes and the pretty woman journalist, working with the firefighters.

Almost afraid to look, he glanced upward. Miraculously, the chandelier remained fixed, the ceiling so far intact. The exits now were clearing and from what he could tell, the evacuation was almost complete.

Martin, still lightheaded, struggled to get to his feet, but toppled again in a fit of violent coughing. Durand darted by him. "Alain," he called weakly.

Durand hastened over. *"My God!"* he cried. "Are you injured?"

Martin shook his head. "President Wilson?"

"Safe. He is on his way back to his hotel. My president too," Durand replied, helping Martin to his feet.

A new crew joined the firemen and directed another hose at the dying blaze. Fire turned into hissing steam. The temperature in the ballroom began to drop.

"We've contained the fire!" Durand cried with relief.

"Mr. Hoover?" Martin asked.

"Outside, helping to organize the medical team with Colonel Lawrence," Durand said. "We're setting up a triage and first aid station at the Opera House."

A noise roared from above. The chandelier broke away. "Get away!" Martin shouted as he ducked and covered his head.

The chandelier broke into thousands of glass projectiles. One man underneath died instantly, and two others suffered deep lacerations. Luckily, most of the other guests had already reached safety. Martin's back and arms had protected him from major injury. Durand was unhurt.

Martin ignored the cuts on his arms and looked at the destruction. "How many more are hurt?"

"Hard to say. No way to know about the kitchen staff. We're still trying to get to them."

"Too late," Martin replied. "The arsonist —," he began to cough.

"This is a conspiracy," Durand declared. "One man alone? Impossible. Powerful men with resources did this."

"And good intelligence. This was well-planned. What will happen next?" Martin fought to regain his breath. "The man who shot at me in the hallway — I saw him just before the fire started."

Durand did not seem to hear him. "What?" After Martin repeated himself, Durand said, "We'll find him. First, you need to see a doctor."

"No," said Martin. "We need to find him now." He started to run when he saw a woman holding onto her leg fall and could not get up.

"I can't move. Help me."

Martin picked her up and carried her to the street where he handed her to a medical team in front of a Ford ambulance. They loaded her in and dashed away. Another ambulance took its place. *How many times have I seen such scenes? How many more will die?*

Martin painfully moved up the street to the Opera House, fighting his way through hundreds of hotel guests who had already escaped. His constricted lungs begged for air. Still coughing, Martin entered the foyer of the Opera House. A doctor directed stretcher bearers. Three nurses administered morphine and a second doctor sutured a wound. Martin asked about the injured.

"Three gravely, with burns. We need a priest."

"There was one across the street performing last rites," a nurse said. "Never saw him before. He had an eye patch."

"And the rest of the injured?" Martin asked.

"Most suffer from smoke inhalation." The doctor gestured to a line of fourteen stretchers placed along the wall.

"May I see them?" Martin asked, hoping to find the arsonist. The doctor nodded.

"Water," a raspy female voice called as he walked by. Martin looked down and saw a tangle of light-brown hair. He recognized Ana Primakova and saw she was concealing a gun. Another mystery for another day. She tried to sit up, and fought for air. Her arms were blistered by burns, her cheeks covered with soot, her eyes watery and red. He had seen similar symptoms after a gas attack. "You'll be fine, Madam," Martin said. "I'll get you a drink." He gently eased her down, went over to a small table, and filled a glass with cool water from a pitcher. Returning, he gently raised Ana up, supported her back with his broad hand, and put the glass to her lips. "*Merci,*" she said simply, drinking between coughs. And then, as her breathing eased, "I am so stupid."

"Madam?"

"I rushed in. People needed help. Anyway, I wanted a good story. The smoke became too much and I collapsed. I don't know what happened next. Lucky to be alive I guess."

"The firemen performed well."

"Who are you, *Monsieur?* You are very kind," she said weakly.

Martin had not heard that from a young woman in a long time. He was not sure what to say, except, "Major Martin, with the U.S. delegation."

"*Un Ami*? *Bon*. I am Madam Prima — " She lapsed into a shock-induced sleep.

I know. Martin sat by her stretcher and looked at her for a long time. High cheek bones accentuated an angular face more Nordic than Slavic. Her strong jaw seemed too heavy for her otherwise delicate face. *Who are you, really*? he wondered. *And why are you in Paris?*

Chapter 16
Questions

Berlin: January 1919

Reick looked at Keller's stacks of Swiss Francs and gaped. Landsmann raised his eyebrow and said, "Who the hell are you?"

Keller recited the response he had practiced endlessly with Dulles before he left America. "I robbed a bank in Mexico City. With the help of a friendly banker who took his cut, I transferred the money to Geneva."

"What are you doing here?" Landsmann asked.

Reick reached for the money and began to count.

"I worked for Felix Beck's East Coast organization in America."

"Beck?" Landsmann looked surprised. He and Reick exchanged confused glances.

"Section III-B's man in New York," Keller said, referring to Germany's military intelligence unit during the war.

Landsmann nodded. "Beck died, didn't he?"

Yes, and I was there when he was killed. "That was the end of his organization." Keller glanced out the window where ice was forming outside. The trees in the Tiergarten bowed in the distance.

"Why?"

"Beck controlled everything. After he died, his saboteur tried to blow up Wall Street but failed. The New York police hunted down his agents. I was in danger. I ran."

Landsmann stared back. "How did you get here?"

"I hid at a friend's house in St. Louis. When America declared war, the police started to round up German sympathizers. My friend was one of them. I was afraid he'd give me up, so I went to Mexico.

Other German agents did too." In case the Germans checked his story, Dulles had established the necessary documentation and had destroyed any record of the real Brandt's arrest and incarceration.

"Then?"

"I returned to Europe last August. It was clear we were going to lose." Keller began to sweat. Did they believe him? He breathed in and continued. "The Mexican government didn't want us any more, so I robbed a bank." He smiled. Dulles had even faked the bank robbery.

"Is there more than this?" Reick looked up, his hands full of bills.

Keller ignored the question. Contacting Dulles's man in Berlin for money was a complicated process used only for emergencies. "From Mexico, I bought passage to Spain and crossed into France by motorcycle. I caught up with your army outside Strasbourg."

Landsmann leaned back in his chair. "What did you do for Beck?"

"I handled his spy in the New York Police Department and helped his harbor master, Traub," Keller said. Having helped stop these people and wipe out Beck's organization, he knew the details. He supplemented his knowledge with information he had gathered from the real Karl Brandt, who had agreed to cooperate after he was arrested.

"Tell me more." Landsmann shifted his eyes toward the money.

"I only know my part in his organization," Keller said. "Beck kept his agents separate from each other. He disguised our names when he reported to Berlin. I can give you specifics about his saboteur. You may have read about his work?"

"Major attack in New York? A gold shipment was involved, I think. The attack failed. What happened to the saboteur?" Landsmann asked.

"Body never found, presumed dead."

There was a knock on the door. "Come back later," Landsmann shouted. He studied Brandt. "Go on."

I have his interest. "I'm a German patriot. I want to help."

"*Scheisse.* What are you doing here?" Landsmann leaned forward, chin on his folded hands.

"I'm useful." Keller reached for a glass of water and took a long sip.

"Your money's useful. Not sure about you," Landsmann said. "Why did you come to us?"

"Nowhere else to go. America will jail me. The Mexicans will kill me. The Allies know I worked for Section III-B. Germany was my only option."

"Why didn't you tell us sooner?" Reick asked.

"There was no time for explanations. I was just another German straggler running from the French. Things moved fast after that."

"Not fast enough to —"

"If I had come up to you in Kehl with a lot of money, you never would have believed me, *Kapitan.*" Keller prayed they bought his story.

"Why should we believe you now?" Landsmann stared back.

"What have you got to lose?" Keller paused. How much deeper into Hell could he go? "Besides, a lot of people want me dead for killing Liebknecht. Outside of the Freikorps, I'm already a corpse."

"Where did you get your military training?" Reick said. "You're good with a gun."

"Beck insisted on it. I've been shooting guns all my life. I spent much time with the saboteur, Caarsens."

The two officers looked at each other. "Haven't heard of him," Landsmann said. "Describe him."

He knows Caarsens. Landsmann is testing me. "A Boer.

Tortured by the British. Cigar burns on his arms. Worked for the Ottoman Sultan before the war. He was an explosives expert. I worked in his New Haven Projectile Company. Taught me tactics and bomb-making. He blew up Black Tom Island and almost destroyed lower Manhattan."

Landsmann seemed satisfied and stood up. "I have to go. Let me think about it. Come *Kapitan* Reick, we need to talk."

The door shut with a bang. He heard Landsmann and Reick arguing outside. Keller heard the words "Swiss Francs" several times.

How well have I sold my story?

~

Keller remained confined to his hotel room for two days. He received no word from Landsmann. With every day that went by, his chances of survival worsened. He felt like a man on death row. On the night before the Freikorps tribunal, the outside guard was doubled. He tried to sleep but could not.

The next morning, a cold wind rattled his window and invaded his room. Keller put on his heaviest wool sweater, but it did not help. Nothing left to do but wait. He went back to bed and closed his eyes.

Heavy steps down the hall woke him. A reprieve or an execution? The footsteps got closer. He heard Reick say something to the guards. A knock. Keller opened the door, expecting to be shot.

Reick was alone and unarmed. "Pick up your things, Brandt, you're moving. I don't like it, but you're free. The colonel wants you on his staff," Reick said. "He'll want more money — another ten thousand dollars in Swiss Francs. Everyone in Berlin needs that money. Friends as well as enemies. Understand?"

It had almost cost him his life, but Keller had reached the highest level of the most powerful anti-Communist force in Germany.

Chapter 17
Shadowed

Berlin: January 1919

Two days after joining Landsmann's staff, Keller walked toward his secret meeting with Dulles's man in the Potsdamer Bahnhof. Because the city was now under Freikorps control, he wore an ordinary suit to look less conspicuous. Alone for the first time since he had joined the withdrawing German Army six weeks ago, he was desperate for the additional $10,000 Landsmann had demanded from him.

After leaving the Eden Hotel, Keller walked along the Tiergarten Strasse for fifteen minutes when he sensed someone following him. What was it? A nervous glance? An awkward gesture? An ill-timed movement? His pulse quickened. Having chased German agents in New York City, Keller had become expert at surveillance and shadowing. Was he now the mark?

Keller doubled back on his route and headed north away from his meeting with Dulles's man. He shifted his bag from one hand to the other and stopped twice unexpectedly. Any unusual movements? He spotted someone slowing his pace to match his. He stopped in front of a parked car and used the reflection in its window as a mirror. There he was, Shadow #1, a middle-aged man with a trim mustache. He could have been a former soldier. Were there others?

Keller turned south and stopped at Lutzowplatz to wipe dung off his boot. There he was again, Shadow #1, across on Cornelius Strasse. His gray suit was too tight for his heavy-set body. He looked away as soon as Keller spotted him.

Keller walked back north, returning to Tiergarten Strasse and turned as if he was returning to the hotel. Shadow #1 followed. On the other side of the street, a younger man in a trench coat was walking toward him. He made a hand movement, what Keller guessed was a signal to Shadow #1, and turned around to tail Keller. Keller had found Shadow #2. Both shadows stopped when Keller stopped, then followed him south to Hoherzollen Strasse. #1 maintained a discreet distance. #2 stepped up his pace and moved closer.

In his Bomb Squad days, Keller had always needed at least three men to shadow a suspect properly. He wondered where the third shadow was. Keller almost missed him, but spotted him at the corner of Hildebrand Strasse smoking a cigarette. As Keller neared him, he noticed the man's scuffed shoes did not match his well-pressed business suit. The unmistakable outline of a gun bulged from his coat pocket. #3.

Three shadows meant someone was determined to know his business. Who was shadowing him and why? The Communists because he was now on Landsmann's staff? Someone looking for revenge for Liebknecht? Landsmann's men because they distrusted him? Keller's suspicion that the colonel had not completely believed his story grew stronger. Until he could identify his pursuers and determine what they wanted, he was in grave danger. Should he ask Dulles's man to get him out of Berlin immediately? He had broken every pledge he had made as a police officer to reach the top echelon of the Freikorps. Though frightened, his competitive nature and love of action welcomed the challenge. He would not give up now.

Keller bent down to tie his shoe and waited for #2 to come closer. As he neared, Keller stood up, reversed directions, and bumped into him as he walked by. He looked right at #2 with an "I know what you are" expression. Having been recognized, #2 skulked away.

Across the street and a block away, #1 stopped when his partner retreated. Keller was now the hunter. Using a trick he had learned from German agents in New York, Keller looked at #1 and called, "*Guten Morgen*. You look lost, friend. Can I help you?" #1 stood petrified. Keller waved good-bye, leaving the man confused and impotent.

#3 was nowhere to be seen, though he had to be lurking nearby. The game had now switched from deception to chase. Keller continued east at a fast clip and entered the Nollendorf Bahnhof, where he bought two tickets, each in a different direction. Although it was mid-day, the station was crowded, making it easy for Keller to hide among the other passengers. He headed to the men's toilet, where he changed into the hat and coat he was carrying in his bag, and went to the platform for the east-bound train.

Keller spotted #3 farther down the platform looking as bored as everyone else. This man was good. Keller had given himself away by scanning the posted schedule. Only an expert would have spotted him, knowing that regular riders would not need to look at departure times. Keller waited until the last second to board, but he jumped back immediately before the doors closed. #3, who had followed him onto the train, stared at him angrily through the train's window as it passed. His pock-marked face and slick black hair registered in Keller's mind.

Moving to the west-bound platform, Keller scanned its length for other possible threats. He repeated his previous steps as the train headed into the station and continued to observe all passengers as it came to a halt. Just as the train doors started to close, he jumped onto the train. Looking out the window, he verified no one else had boarded with him, but he did see a small man with a taut face and a black leather coat standing alone on the platform shouting for the train to stop. Shadow #4?

Keller disembarked at the Potsdamer station, where he mingled in the waiting area to make sure no one else was tailing him. He bought a different hat and walked around the station once more as a triple check.

As he passed by the café inside the station, he recognized Frank Larsen, Dulles's man, sitting in the window drinking a coffee. He was pleased to see him at the exact place and time. One of the newest members to join the Bomb Squad, Larsen had started at the height of German sabotage in New York. Like Keller, he was fluent in German and had moved into military intelligence when the United States declared war on Germany. They had worked together during the war. Keller rubbed his eye as he walked by and Larsen countered with a cough, signals they had used in their police days. It was safe to meet.

Thank God. Dulles had known communication would be difficult in Berlin, so he had devised a simple code using the days of the month. At scheduled times, Keller could meet Larsen at one of four prearranged places one time per week: week one, place 1 at 12:00; week two, place 2 at 15:00; etc. Larsen would wait at each spot for one hour. Dulles guaranteed that Larsen would always be at the assigned place and time, even if Keller could not.

Larsen walked outside, bought a newspaper, and pretended to read it. Three minutes later, Keller returned, collided with Larsen. At the same time, he pressed a small piece of paper into Larsen's hand and walked away. Larsen pretended to scratch an itch and eyed the note. It only showed the number six. He ripped it up and continued to read his paper. When enough time had passed, he folded the newspaper and headed inside the station.

Keller waited for him on a bench by platform 6 as a train to Hamburg prepared to depart. The conductor was calling for final passengers when Larsen reached the bench and stood near Keller. He opened his paper and said, "Thank God, you're alive, Paul. You look terrible." The noise of the departing train was so loud no one could have heard their conversation.

"Nightmares. Worst month in my life." Keller leaned forward, placed his elbow on his knee, and covered his mouth with his hands. "I'm being followed." Keller quickly summarized the major events that had happened since he joined the Freikorps, except for the details of Liebknecht's death. No one would ever hear that story. "I need — "

The train whistle drowned out his words.

"What?" Larsen asked.

"I need $10,000 in Swiss Francs right away."

Larsen's eyes widened. "Impossible." He moved to the bench next to Keller. "I can't get that kind of money."

Keller stood up and looked away. "Meet me in two days with the money, or you'll find me floating in the canal."

Chapter 18
The Investigation

Paris: January 1919

The day after the fire, Martin checked every member of the U.S. delegation. Only two men had been hospitalized for smoke inhalation. He reviewed all security procedures and promoted Andrew Cooper to top sergeant of the Marine detail. Once the Crillon Hotel was secure, he and Colonel House visited France's national police, the Sûreté, at the Ministry of Justice on Place Beauvau for another confrontation with Commandant Emile Truchon.

"I'm taking charge of the investigation," Truchon said despite the obvious connections between the failed attempt on House and the fire. "We've concluded the fire was deliberately set. There was a loud noise just before the kitchen erupted into flames."

"I heard it," Martin said.

Truchon ignored him. A study by teams from Durand's Military Intelligence, local police, and the Sûreté had discovered the ovens were not well maintained. Apparently, a grease fire in the main oven had ignited bottles of cooking oil and alcohol. Management swore the bottles were kept safely away from the stoves when not in use.

Truchon paused to check his notes. "We found broken glass from several different bottles near the main stove. By itself, this is not conclusive but their intermixed pattern suggests more than one bottle was tossed onto the fire. There are no traces of explosives, but we think the arsonist used kerosene — we noticed its distinct odor — to feed the blaze. It's the only explanation for why the fire got out of control so quickly."

Don't like him, but competent assessment, Martin thought.

“What do we know about the kitchen staff?” House asked.

“Their bodies are charred beyond recognition. We are trying to identify them. One man is unaccounted for. The autopsies are going on now; it will take time before we can identify the missing man.”

“I think I saw the perpetrator,” Martin said. “I can — ”

“Le Grand Hotel is one of the finest hotels in all of France!” Truchon boomed. “It is our honor and duty to find the arsonist — not yours. We will not permit you to assuage your guilt and minimize your incompetence by — ”

Martin fought to control his temper. He was seconds away from lashing out and creating a diplomatic incident. The haunting possibility was that Truchon might not be totally wrong. Martin regretted that he had not had time to check the kitchen after the head chef forced him away, and he was too slow to catch the man in the Crillon passageway, even though he had wounded him. Martin would keep these concerns to himself.

House put a calming hand on Martin’s arm and looked coldly at Truchon. “We understand this is a French matter, Commandant. However, it is in everyone’s interest to cooperate. After all, our president was threatened too.”

“*Non,* you don’t understand.” Truchon’s face turned red. “France has suffered greatly the last four years. You Americans are naive. Your fourteen points. Bah. Prime Minister Clémenceau said it best: ‘The Good Lord needed only ten.’ We *must* punish Germany. They can never be allowed to threaten France again.”

Is this what all these accusations are really about? Martin wondered. *Driving us away from the peace talks or undermining our position? Truchon doesn’t know us as well as he thinks.*

“May I remind you, Commandant, America has contributed mightily to the Allied victory,” House said.

"And has earned much money in the process. Let me state this bluntly: The best thing you Americans can do is leave. Let *us* conclude the treaty. We understand Germany as you do not."

"That will not happen, Commandant." House fixed his eyes on Truchon.

"So you say. Regarding this investigation, it is mine. But if you insist, I will send someone over to speak to you, Major Martin. Good day." Truchon left without the customary courtesies and handshakes.

~

After a brief talk with House, Martin went to his room to make sense of his confrontation with Truchon. The commandant was arrogant, hiding behind the guise of honor. Martin could understand why he would want to handle the investigation. He would want the same responsibility. But without help? Something else was happening. Was Truchon trying to cover up his bureau's incompetence? Was he part of a French plan to disrupt America's role in the talks — perhaps to encourage the U.S. to leave the conference altogether? Was the Sûreté or Truchon himself involved in the fire? The more Martin considered it, the more possible their complicity became. But why? Martin was certain of one thing: Truchon knew more than he was saying, and by controlling the investigation, he would try to keep it that way.

Unless Martin could foil him. He decided to concentrate on solving the case alone, staying wary of French intrigues. He would learn the truth only if he discovered it himself, but Martin had few leads. He concluded, as Truchon had suggested, that the arsonist had help from someone inside the hotel. German agents had used this tactic in New York, both in the Hotel Biltmore incident that Martin had helped to thwart and the January 1917 Kingsland, New Jersey, explosion that he had investigated after it occurred.

Martin considered the possibility that anarchists were

responsible, but he rejected the idea. The fire was beyond their capabilities. Whoever did this was bold, smart, and determined.

He had to talk to Durand.

~

At Durand's office in the Ministry of Justice on Rue Saint-Dominique, Martin discussed the case with the captain but said nothing about his earlier confrontation with Truchon. Both Durand and Martin believed the best place to start was the man in the Crillon stairway, whom Martin had also seen at Le Grand Hotel. Someone else must have seen him before the fire started, if not after. Martin worked with an artist to sketch him. The drawing was a good likeness, and Martin handed it to Durand. "Add my physical description of the man and we've got an excellent chance to catch him."

"We will spread the picture and your description all over Paris. He will be the most-wanted man in France tonight," Durand said.

"Show it around the brothels and ask the streetwalkers," Martin said. "Who else would have told him about the secret passageway?"

"He must have connections with the Communists too," Durand said.

"Possible. Look what's happening in Germany." The newspapers had been full of the bloody accounts of the unsuccessful Communist coup d'etat in Berlin. "I pity anyone in the middle of that mess."

"We will follow up the Communist connection," Durand said. "Lenin and his worldwide revolution are a threat to France — to all the world's democracies."

Durand's confident and determined manner reassured Martin, but he had a lingering concern. Could he trust any French official?

Chapter 19
Surrounded

Berlin: January 1919

Three days after his meeting with Larsen, Keller left the Eden Hotel with an empty briefcase. It was Saturday, January 25. Keller headed to his meeting with Larsen at the popular Romanisches Café at 238 Kurfurstendam near the Kaiser-Wilhelm Church at 15:00. Keller had chosen the café because of its close proximity to the Eden, a risk he had to take. He could not be away from headquarters too long.

He left the hotel through the staff entrance and, instead of walking along Budapester Strasse as he had for the previous meeting, he headed south. At Hildebrand Strasse, he looped back north and entered the Tiergarten. Although its woods provided numerous places for an ambush, they gave Keller good opportunities to spot anyone who might be following him and, if the chance arose, to maneuver behind any pursuers and ensnare them. He had to find out who they were.

The January wind and raw air gnawed into him. His breath turned into fog as soon as it left his mouth. His teeth felt like they could crack. He pulled his coat collar around his neck and leaned forward to counter the numbing gusts. His leather gloves would limit his ability to use the Luger in his pocket, but better to have warm hands than useless frozen ones. His gloved hands could still handle the knife strapped to his ankle. It had saved him more than once.

Despite its discomfort, the icy weather was his ally. Few people would be walking outside without a good reason. Anyone following him would be more conspicuous and deprived of common observation techniques. No one could stand idle in this weather. Like Keller, any shadow would also be encumbered with clothing that would reduce his ability to handle a firearm, another advantage to an expert knife-fighter like Keller.

Keller reached Grosser Stern and did not see any tails. Time was short. He had to make the rendezvous. He found some taxis idling around the nearby Tiergarten Bahnhof.

He rejected the first one to offer a ride — the driver seemed too keen and was young enough to be a shadow. The second taxi driver was an old army veteran with only one eye. Turning his face to avoid recognition, Keller got in the cab. "*Kaiser Wilhelm Kirche, bitte.*" He removed his gloves, placed the briefcase at his feet, and reached into his coat pocket to ready the Luger. He spied out the back window several times.

"You looking for something?" the driver asked.

"No. Just don't take the direct route."

The driver shrugged. "Your money."

With each turn and deviation south and west, Keller continued to check the streets behind him. He grew confident that he had avoided any tails and enjoyed the brief minute of safety. At Augsburger Strasse just down the street from the Kaiser Wilhelm Church, Keller gave the driver a tip and watched him drive away. He breathed easier when he saw him pick up an old lady near the church, something a shadow would not do.

Keller circled the block, then headed to the Romanisches Café. He looked at every patron to see if someone from the Eden would recognize him. Confirming he was safe, Keller found Larsen at a table near the front. A briefcase identical to Keller's sat by Larsen's leg. Keller sat down and placed his case next to Larsen's.

"Not easy, but you got your money. Swiss Francs," Larsen said, looking down at his coffee.

"Good."

"Boss is mad as hell. He hopes this is it."

"Me too."

"What's next?"

"We're moving out," Keller said. "Now that Germany has elected a Parliament, Chancellor Ebert wants to move the government to Weimar. We can protect it better there. The Communists are still a threat."

"I can't help you there. Do you want out?"

"No," Keller said defiantly. "I must go, but you keep things going here. I'll need you later."

"Count on me," Larsen said.

Keller downed his schnapps in one gulp. "You're a good friend and a good agent." He took Larsen's briefcase and stood to leave. "This will keep me alive for a while."

"Hope it's worth it." Larsen dropped some coins on the table and put on his coat.

"Landsmann has something big planned. I'm sure of it. And I aim to find out what it is."

~

Keller now faced the most dangerous part of the day — getting back to the hotel. It was a short distance. He had to return to duty, as his shadows would likely know too.

He would sneak back the way he came — through the Tiergarten. The sun was going down and the darkness reduced visibility, but the weather had warmed and the wind had died down. He no longer needed gloves, but neither would an assailant. Relying on speed, not stealth, Keller walked fast and stayed on the main paths. He clutched Larsen's briefcase with his left hand and kept his Luger ready with his right.

His chest pounded. Acid rose from his stomach. Being alone and in constant danger was taking a toll. Waking up at all hours of the night had made things worse. Oh, to be a policeman again. To kiss Shannon once more.

Through the trees, lights from the Eden Hotel glowed in the distance. Almost there. He relaxed for a moment, and stretched to relieve the tension in his lower spine. He lowered the Luger for just an instant to rub his back and realized his mistake immediately.

Almost like a ghost, a pockmarked man with slicked black hair emerged from behind a tree fifteen yards in front of him. Shadow #3 from three days ago flashed a Mauser carbine at him. Keller ducked right.

Blocked. A burly man with a scarred face pointed a pump action shotgun at him. Shadow #2 looked like he wanted to even things out.

Behind and to the right of #2 stood the same heavy-set middle-aged man Keller had seen before, Shadow #1, his finger on the trigger of a Mauser semi-automatic. "I'd love to shoot you right here."

Keller looked for some advantage but stopped when he heard another voice.

"Don't move. Drop the gun." A voice from behind. It sounded like a hiss. Keller let the Luger fall to the ground. "Turn around." The small man with a taut face and a black leather coat he had dodged at the Potsdamer station held an M1917 Smith & Wesson revolver. Shadow #4. "We waited for you to come back," he said with the authority of a leader.

Keller froze.

"Who do you work for?" #4 demanded.

Keller fought to regain his composure. "Colonel Landsmann."

"Hah. We both know that's a lie. What is in there?" #4 pointed to the briefcase.

His attackers had chosen an isolated ambush point with dense tree cover and narrow paths. They blocked all avenues of escape.

Keller would have to fight his way out.

Chapter 20
Russians

Paris: January 1919

The day after meeting Truchon, Martin crossed the river on the Pont de la Concorde. He was dressed in worker's clothes. Alain Durand accompanied him. The peace talks were to start in two days. A cutting breeze swept along the Seine, forcing Martin to shield his face with the side of his hand. They headed to a quiet café in the Latin Quarter to meet Durand's friend, Alexei Bukin, a Russian émigré who had escaped the revolution. Bukin had retained his imperialist fervor throughout his exile and still had good contacts in Moscow and Petrograd.

On the way to the meeting, Martin confided to Durand that the incident at Le Grand Hotel confounded him. Durand smiled dryly and said, "We have a development. Your sketch has produced one result. A Bois de Boulogne prostitute remembered the man in the picture. She was scared when she saw his face and said he was a "monster." He threatened her with a knife and forced her to do unspeakable things. Called himself Mal."

"I've known those types in New York." Martin could barely contain his disgust.

"He's in his mid-thirties, strong as a mason. Average height. Dark hair, closely cut. Bad teeth. Had two knife wounds on his chest and a bullet hole in his upper thigh. Missing part of his right ear. Might have been a soldier."

"Could be our man. How long ago did she see him?"

"Last month. Hasn't seen him since. She'll contact us if she sees him again." Durand admitted he felt bad for the woman. The Germans overran her farm, and her husband was killed on the Marne. "Came to

Paris without a *centime*. I hate what this war has done to my country."

They walked through narrow back streets in silence. Durand looked around to make sure no one was listening and said, "My contact may be risking his life if he's seen with us."

"These Russians don't trust anyone, most of all their own," Martin replied.

"Just let me do the talking. We're here."

The two-story building, painted in faded German-uniform gray, jutted onto an intersection of three oddly angled streets. The sign over the door read *Café du Centre* and swung like a pendulum on its one hook, scratching its wooden support with each sway. Its high-pitched squeal reminded Martin of the voice of a harsh nun from his childhood. The café was popular with locals who appreciated low prices; criminals who valued its discreet proprietor, who kept away nosy *cognes* looking to make easy arrests; and ambitious journalists who had discovered it was an excellent source of information impossible to find in more reputable establishments. Just the type of place Martin had liked to meet informants when he was a cop.

The café smelled of stale liquor and dirty patrons, a few of whom sat at broken-down tables in front of bottles of wine in various stages of empty. There was a low hum of chatter. Bukin sat in the far corner talking to a man in a large hat that concealed his face. They were both drinking *pomme*, distilled apples. Bukin looked up and waved them over. Durand approached and reached out his hand. Bukin took it with a grunt.

"Thank you for seeing us, Alexei," Durand said.

"The owner is a friend," Bukin said. "Everyone keeps his mouth shut. Make it fast."

"May I introduce my friend, Gilbert Martin," Durand said.

"*Monsieur*." Bukin was a thin man whose face showed ridges

of age and torment. He was dressed in a suit that at one time may have been fashionable in St. Petersburg, but it hung loosely and was wrinkled out of shape. He introduced his colleague, "Madam Anastasia Primakova." She removed her hat and looked up.

Martin, speechless, tried to avoid her eyes. "Good to meet you," he said with as blank a tone as he could fake.

"And you." She said nothing more. She glanced at him, her eyes so sapphire Martin could almost feel them burn. Either she did not recognize him — she was groggy when he gave her water — or she was pretending not to know him. Martin tensed.

When everyone was seated, Bukin cleared his throat. "Enough pleasantries. What did you want to discuss, Alain?"

"The Bolsheviks. I'm worried," Durand said.

"If I tell you what I know, what do I get in return?" Bukin asked.

Martin watched the verbal volleys. He looked at Ana out of the corner of his eye. Her gaze was fixed on Bukin.

"I know who you were, and who you are now. I know your friends and your enemies too," Durand said. "My silence should be enough."

"We shall see."

"What are the Russians up to?" Durand said.

"Fighting each other. Their civil war is more vicious and bloody than the war against Germany. Who will win, you want to know?" Bukin let the words linger.

Martin understood the Bolsheviks' problem. Their Red Army troops were fighting former supporters of the Tsar, ex-military, landed aristocrats, and other nationalists in a loose alliance called the White Russians. The Western Allies were giving them support while maintaining a blockade against Bolshevik Russia.

"Exactly," Durand said.

"Depends on you," Bukin said. "American troops are already in Siberia. How many Allied troops are willing to die for the White Russians?" He glanced at Martin.

Does he know I'm American? Would Ana have told him? He could not read her expressionless face.

"Are you listening, *Monsieur* Martin?" Bukin said.

"I apologize." Martin quickly looked away from Ana.

"Can the Bolsheviks win, Alexei?" Durand asked.

"Yes. They are determined and ruthless. They're fighting for their noble Communist cause. Lenin and Trotsky are strong leaders. The White Russians are fragmented and soft. They're fighting to restore a failed and much despised system."

A waiter interrupted and asked what they wanted to drink. He had a limp, dirty hair, and the nervous twitch common to front-line soldiers. Martin ordered wine. Bukin another bottle of *pomme*. "So what you really want to know is if the Bolsheviks are planning something against France or the peace talks," Bukin said.

"Lenin has declared a worldwide Communist revolt," Durand said. "We have reason to believe they are — "

"You should be wary of the Communists, *mon ami*, but do they speak for the Russian people?" Bukin shrugged his shoulders and downed the remaining *pomme* in his glass. He refilled it to the top. "Don't forget that Lenin possesses all of the Tsar's secret papers. All those special deals France and Britain struck with the Tsar before he was deposed. Could prove very embarrassing to the Allies and provocative to the Russian people. Don't think for a second Lenin won't use them."

"But the peace talks. I believe the Communists started the fire at Le Grand Hotel." Durand summarized some of the findings from his investigation. "What do your sources say?"

"Anything is possible." Bukin leaned back and lit a cigarette. *Stalling for effect?* "The Russians have cause. The Allies are trying to topple the Bolsheviks. Why shouldn't they do the same to you?" Bukin smirked and took another drink.

Who is deceiving whom? Martin wondered.

Ana jumped in. "And why isn't Russia attending the conference? They're the only country that fought for the Allies that was *not* invited. It's an outrage."

Knowing the Allies prayed for Lenin's downfall, Martin did not answer. Durand coolly said, "You lost your war and your Tsar."

"I think we are done here. Good day, *Messieurs*. Come, Ana." Bukin downed his drink, put on a threadbare overcoat and left. Ana followed without saying another word.

Martin was left wondering which side had gained more from the meeting.

~

Ana was upset when she and Bukin returned to his attic apartment in the poor outskirts of Paris. An educated voice from the shadows asked, "What did you learn?" The man played with a standard French military Lebel 1892 revolver, swinging its chamber open and closed.

"God damn it, Truchon. I told you never to come here," Bukin said.

"I need to know, Bukin. What did Martin and Durand say?"

"And you brought *him*." Bukin pointed to a stout dark-haired man in his mid-thirties.

Ana gasped when she saw Mal but quickly steadied herself.

"He is necessary for my plans," Truchon said. "Does Durand suspect anything?"

"He thinks the Communists are involved in the fire. They have a lead on your friend." Bukin gestured toward Mal. "Some whore identified him from the drawing the American made."

"Should have killed him when I had a chance," Mal said through his yellowed teeth. He grimaced and reached for his wounded shoulder.

Truchon turned to Mal. "One mistake I can forgive. You were once a good operative, but you have now failed twice. I wanted that hotel burned down. That I cannot forgive." Truchon raised his Lebel and pulled the trigger before Mal had time to react.

Ana squeezed her eyes shut. All she heard was a click and Truchon's taunting laugh. "If you fail me again, the next time my gun will be loaded."

Ana opened her eyes. Mal's left hand was clenched into a rock-crushing fist. His head bowed in surrender. "I will do better next time, Commandant."

"Now for you." Truchon waved his pistol at Ana.

Ana had survived the threats of such men most of her life. She remained calm and tried to guess Truchon's next move, like the good chess player she was.

"Why did you run back into the fire?"

She had guessed right. Truchon was the greater threat. Knowing he hated weaklings, she turned aggressive. "Mal dropped his pistol when he ran out. I ran into the flames to recover it."

"He what?" Truchon shouted.

"I did not," Mal protested. "Someone took it."

"Shut up." Truchon demanded.

"He showed it to me earlier that evening. He bragged he had used it to shoot at Major Martin. The Sûreté could have traced it back to you, Commandant — military issue, all those engravings on the handle."

"She's lying!"

"Do you have the gun?" Truchon asked Mal.

"No, but I — "

"Let her finish, or I will kill you. Where is it now, Ana?"

"I threw it in the Seine," Ana said.

"I'll get you, *putain*," Mal said.

Truchon slapped Mal hard. "Touch her and you will die very slowly." He sat down and stared at the window with his piercing gray eyes. He swung the chamber of the Lebel open and closed. Open and closed. Finally, he said, "We need to stop these talks another way."

Chapter 21
Chances?

Berlin: January 1919

Keller assessed his chances. Every pathway was blocked. If he ran, he would be shot before two strides. He could fight and get to #4, the leader, with his knife. That would give him enough time to reach for his Luger lying on the ground, but he would be riddled with bullets before he could pull off a round. If he could just get them closer together, they might miss and shoot each other in the crossfire.

The leader must have been thinking the same thing. He kicked Keller's Luger farther away, moved a few steps back, and ordered his men to spread out.

Words were Keller's only weapon. "What do you want?" he demanded loudly, hoping someone else would hear him. His grip tightened around the briefcase, and his eyes jumped from #4 to #2. They stood in front of him. The other two men in back. Surrounded.

"Listen to me, *Schweinhund*," the leader demanded.

Keller turned back and faced him. Mustering as much calm as possible, he stared straight into his assailant's eyes. "I can help you."

"The briefcase will be enough. Toss it over, or I'll shoot you right now."

"If you take it, you'll have the entire Landsmann Battalion after you."

"Why should that bother me?" The leader laughed, spurring the others to snicker.

Who were these men? Were they Landsmann's agents after all? Maybe rogue operatives working both sides. Keller could not tell, but cash trumped everything these days. *Play indignant. Be bold.* "Do you know who I am?" Keller forced himself to continue his hard stare.

"I know more than you think."

Keller fought back the fear they knew he was a spy. "I wouldn't rob someone on Landsmann's staff."

"That's not my concern." The leader pulled back the hammer of his revolver. "The briefcase."

Keller placed the briefcase on the ground and edged toward the Luger. #2 kicked him to the dirt and pointed his shotgun at Keller's head.

Keller closed his eyes. *The Lord is my Shepherd ...* A deafening explosion thundered and a light flashed in his head. Keller's eyes flew open. *Grenade — thirty yards away.* Shrapnel and forest debris swept forward, killing #1 instantly. Keller, lying low, was safe. The other men seemed dazed but unharmed.

Keller's warrior instincts took over. But before he could unsheathe the knife from his ankle, a shot rang out. Assassin #3's head evaporated into a gray and crimson mist.

Assassin #2 dropped his shotgun and fled. He moved fast despite his burly physique and successfully dodged a hail of rifle shots.

Knife in hand, Keller ducked and rolled on the ground toward the leader. In one sweeping movement, he rose and slashed up at the man's face, cutting deep and low. #4 grabbed his throat and fell down.

Keller knelt over him. "Who are you?"

His face full of hate, the man gagged and tried to spit his last bloody breath at Keller.

"Don't die, damn you! Who do you work for?" Keller pounded the man's chest, but he was dead. He picked up the carbine and aimed it at the fleeing man. When the man moved into a small clearing, Keller fired. #2 shrieked and fell face forward. Keller turned when he heard something behind him.

"Good shot, Brandt." The voice emerged from the trees. Miltz appeared, working the bolt of a long-barreled Mauser rifle. "You were a trigger-finger faster than me."

"*Mein Gott*, Miltz, what took you so long?" Keller started to shake, a delayed response.

"When I told the colonel you hadn't come back, he ordered me to find you. He acted pretty anxious. 'I must have that briefcase,' he kept saying. He seemed worried that someone would try to steal it. Too many traitors, informants, and spies around."

Keller glanced at his briefcase. He was glad he had told Miltz about his route.

"Dusk makes it hard to see," Miltz said. "The Tiergarten is a big place. We discussed the paths you'd take on your return, but I still couldn't find you. Good thing you started talking so loud. Otherwise, I might have been too late. Come on. Let's clean up this mess." Miltz pulled some red arm bands from his uniform blouse and tossed them to Keller.

"What am I to do with these?"

"Tie them around their arms. People around here are used to seeing dead Communists. Nobody's going to say nothing."

"Do you recognize these men?"

Miltz rolled over the man killed by the grenade. "Not much left to look at. Can't say." He went over to the man he had shot. "Seen worse in the trenches, but don't recognize him."

"What about this one?" Keller pointed to the leader.

Miltz used his boot to move #4's head side to side. "You cut him good, Brandt. Head's hardly attached. Don't recognize him."

"Look closer."

Miltz bent down. "Holy mother of God. That's Major Dietrich. I know him from my army days as a courier. He's Section III-B."

"What was military intelligence doing following me?"

"I'd heard he had gone AWOL. Out for himself, I guess."

Obviously, he had connections to Landsmann's HQ if he knew about me, Keller thought.

"The colonel will be glad he's dead. He hates rogue officers. He must have suspected a traitor in his midst and sent me out to protect you, or," Miltz pointed to the briefcase, "that."

"Thanks. I owe you one, Miltz."

"We're moving out for Weimar tomorrow."

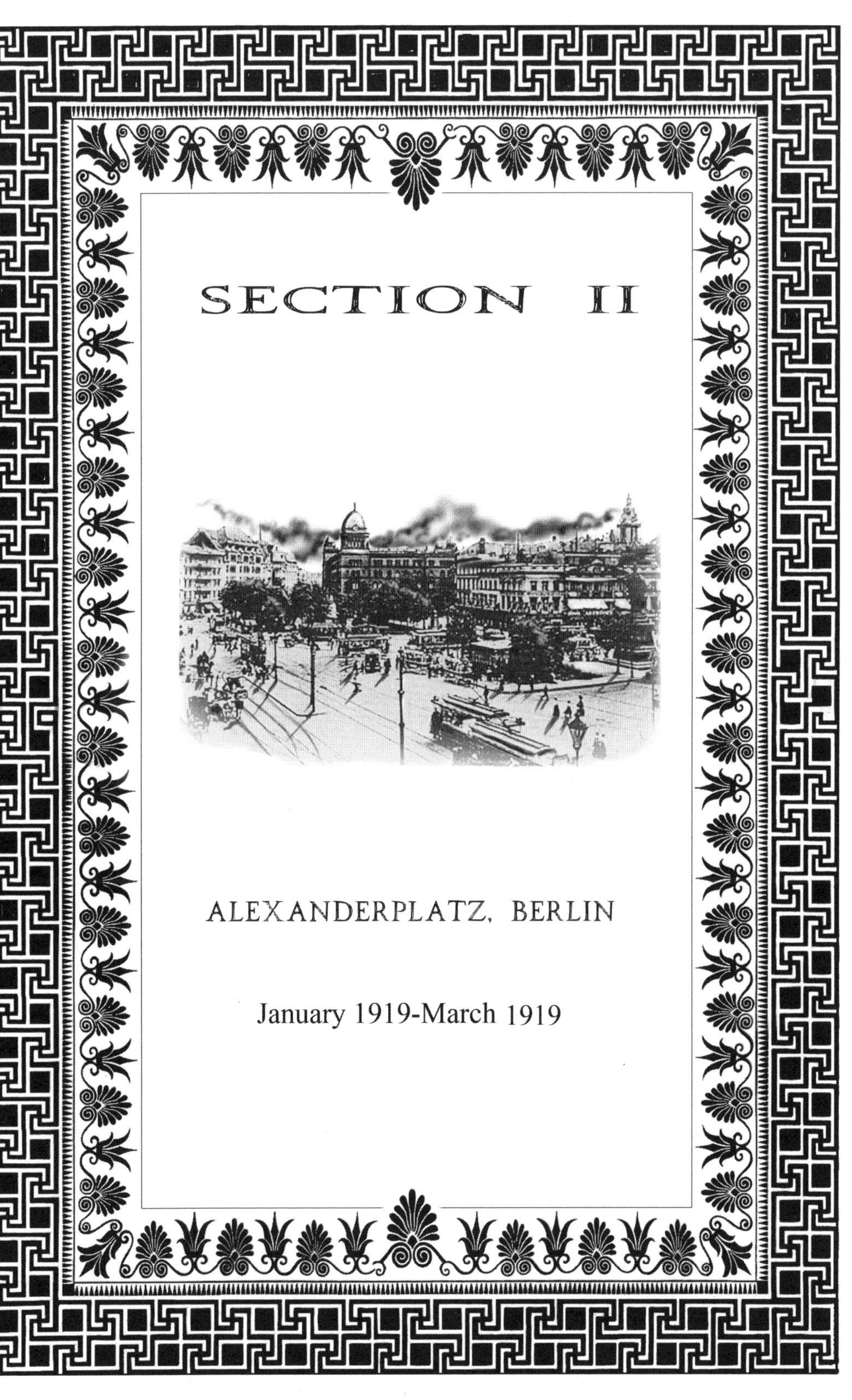

SECTION II

ALEXANDERPLATZ, BERLIN

January 1919-March 1919

Chapter 22
A Riot in a Parrot House

Paris: January 1919

"Now I know how God feels," Colonel House told Martin. They sat in House's suite at the Crillon after the first day of preliminary talks with two representatives from each of the five major Allied powers on the Supreme War Council. They called themselves the Council of Ten. "Everyone is pleading his case to me — Poles, Czechs, Baltics, Arabs. After President Wilson, I must be the most popular man in Paris. A distinction I'd rather not have. All these countries hope America will bring them salvation, or at least self-determination." House collapsed in his favorite chair and began to cough. "Damn this cold."

Martin covered House's legs with a blanket and asked Sergeant Cooper, guarding the door, to bring tea. "Isn't that what we were fighting for?" Martin asked.

"Not you too," House said. "I'm a practical man. I can't please everyone. Just as I got back here, an Indochinese man approached me outside the hotel and argued for his people. His English was pretty good. He was more persuasive than most. I actually listened to him for a few minutes."

"What was his name?"

"Nguyen Ai Quoc, I think. Said he will become his country's George Washington. Good luck to him. He gave me this report. It's in French. Here."

Martin translated the title. *Eight Claims of the Annamite People*. He scanned the document and put it on a side table. "Looks compelling."

"With all we have to deal with, we will not argue with the French about some faraway Asian colony of theirs."

"What happened at the meeting today, Colonel?"

"Chaos. One of the British delegates called it 'a riot in a parrot house.'"

House summed up the meeting at the French foreign ministry along the Quai d'Orsay as a mass confusion. The meeting took place in the "clock room," known for the small clock on the mantelpiece. There was no agenda and too much of everything. Too many nations. Too many people. Thirty-two separate delegations — everyone had his own experts. Too much information. And too many languages. "I felt like I was in the Tower of Babel," House said. "Poincaré, the host, rambled on for half an hour. The interpreters were a disaster. I want my own. Luckily, Ulysses Wentworth's replacement is due to arrive later today. That will help."

House told Martin the delegates had chosen Georges Clémenceau as the conference president, as if that were a surprise. The "old tiger" had once again announced the desire for heavy reparations against Germany. They had also agreed that English and French would be the joint official languages at the conference. "That's something, at least."

"Did the topic of Russia come up?" Martin asked. He had briefed House on his meeting in the Latin Quarter with the Russians.

House sighed. "The French are unanimous on the subject. Russia abandoned them in their time of need. As far as they're concerned, the Bolsheviks can go to hell."

"We will have to deal with them at some point," Martin said.

"Any progress finding the arsonist?"

"No, but I'm worried what Commandant Truchon will — "

"Without more information, I don't want to hear anything else about him. I have enough problems with the French as it is."

"French police are combing the streets and brothels for another lead. We still haven't identified the missing man from the kitchen. I'm sure he helped the arsonist and maybe even started the fire. The coroner says we'll never be able to identify all the bodies."

"What about their families? Aren't they pleading for answers?" House asked.

"Not a word. Most of the dead were foreigners. They had no families in France. You're tired. I'll leave, Colonel, unless you need me further."

"No. Go."

"Let me take these 'Eight Claims' and summarize them for you. Our delegation is thin on Indochina experts." As Martin picked up Ai Quoc's document from the side table, a piece of paper dropped out. He picked it up and started to read, but stopped with a jerk of the head. "What the — "

"Something wrong?"

"Your Annamite friend has sent us a message. 'I used to work in Le Grand Hotel. I know all the kitchen staff and can tell you where the man you are looking for is hiding.'"

Martin felt a jolt of excitement. *Can this be true*? He stared at the neatly lettered message and tried to sort out his questions and doubts. *Who is Nguyen Ai Quoc? Can we trust him? Why is he telling us this?* Had his luck, the envy of everyone on the Bomb Squad, returned? Captain Tunney, his NYPD commander, had always distrusted such miraculous breakthroughs, but cases had been solved with less than this note. Instinct and experience told Martin this was a legitimate lead. The arsonist case had reached that point when an investigation turns into a chase. It was the part of police work that thrilled Martin most.

The Marine at the door knocked to announce the arrival of a

new delegate to see Colonel House.

"Excellent."

When Shannon Keller walked in with her natural poise, Martin could not believe it. "What are you doing here?" was all he managed to say.

~

Shannon smiled. "I wanted to join the fun. It was getting lonely in New York." The chance to participate in the peace talks had intrigued her, and she wanted to be part of the adventure that would shape the world for the next hundred years. True to character, she jumped at the chance when she learned that the U.S. delegation needed Middle East experts and translators. Fluent in French and German, and having studied the classics and Byzantium at Vassar, she was well qualified for a position. Being a woman had never held Shannon back. She applied for a job, but initially was not selected.

"Keep trying," her Uncle Tunney said. "I'll see what I can do." He approached Treasury Secretary McAdoo, President Wilson's son-in-law, who knew her capabilities and volunteered to help. After all, she had helped Martin and the Bomb Squad wipe out a German spy ring in New York. He offered to intercede in her favor if a suitable assignment should turn up.

After the U.S. delegation sailed to France, Shannon continued to press for an assignment at the talks, hoping something would develop. When Ulysses Wentworth was sent home in disgrace, she was selected immediately.

Shannon took off her coat, but Martin noticed that her long gloves covered the lower portion of her arms, undoubtedly to conceal the burn marks she had suffered at the hands of the German spy master who had kidnapped her in New York. "I'm ready to get started, Colonel House," she said. "I understand there have been threats against you and the president. Should we start there?"

Martin suppressed a smile. Shannon was cut from the same cloth as her tough, no-nonsense uncle. When he had first met her, her directness and confidence had disconcerted him until he discovered she was also smart, brave, and caring. It had now been almost two months since he had seen her. She had a deeper maturity than Martin remembered.

"Slow down, young lady," House said. From his look, Martin could tell the colonel was impressed. "I already know from your record that you're discreet and comfortable around powerful people."

Martin knew that, through her uncle, Shannon had met governors, senators, business leaders, and other influential men. She generally got what she wanted. *And you can handle a gun better than most cops.*

"Thank you. My uncle taught me well." Shannon gave a well-timed smile. "I can serve as a researcher, an interpreter, or a police investigator. I spent a summer in Paris before the war and know it quite well. What do you need, Colonel?"

"Right now, I require a translator I can trust," House said. "I need you with me at the conference meetings."

"I could use her help with my investigation," Martin said. "She's the best analyst I know."

"I am aware of her capabilities, Major. But I don't want her in harm's way. Just to be clear, you work for me, Mrs. Keller," House said. "We leave the hotel tomorrow morning at 7:30 sharp. My car will be outside."

~

Two hours later, Shannon met Martin in a secluded section of the hotel lounge. At the table nearest them, a man was playing chess with one of the Marines. "Who's that?" Shannon asked.

Martin chuckled. "Harrison Davenport, one of our legal advisors. He's at that table every night asking anyone to play him. I gather he's pretty good. Bit touchy, I understand."

"I should play him sometime. See if he can beat me. What about Colonel House? Is he always so difficult?"

"He's been sick and under pressure. I don't think his life was ever in danger before, and he doesn't get along with the French." Martin finished his wine and said, "I'm glad you're here, Shannon. You and Paul are my only true friends."

"Thank you for your letters during the war, Gil. Paul's not much of a writer. I worry about him. I wish I knew where he was."

"I can't help you. He was called to Washington the same time I left New York. His mission is secret, that much I know."

Shannon had not heard from Paul in more than six weeks, and Martin's words confirmed her worst fears. He was deep under cover in Germany. Not wanting to burden him, she masked her concerns. "How can I help you, Gil?"

"I need to follow up this message. Here. What do you think?"

Chapter 23
The Annamites

Paris: January 1919

The next day, Martin showed Captain Durand the note from the Annamite man. “Nguyen Ai Quoc? We know him. He’s a dangerous subversive,” Durand said. “We’d arrest him if we could. He writes articles in the liberal press challenging France’s authority and rule over Indochina.”

Martin fidgeted in his chair. *A trap*? Maybe this note was not the lead he thought it was. He and Shannon had discussed the note at length, and she believed it was legitimate. Based on the document Ai Quoc had given House, he was intelligent, determined, and sincere. Shannon thought he was using his knowledge of the unidentified man in the kitchen to gain access to key members of the American delegation, something that an unknown Asian could not do otherwise.

Martin trusted her insight, yet — “Who is this man?”

“Right now, he works as a busboy in the Ritz Hotel,” Durand replied. “He’s well-traveled. Even worked for a while in London and New York. He’s a patriot and motivated. He wants independence for his people. That makes him dangerous to France.” Durand reached for a cigarette and offered one to Martin.

Martin lit up. The smoke flowed into his lungs and calmed him down. “So there’s a chance he would have known the kitchen staff at Le Grand Hotel?”

“We don’t normally keep track of such men, but yes.”

“Does Commandant Truchon know this man?”

“Undoubtedly.”

Martin frowned. “Is Ai Quoc a Communist?” He inhaled another satisfying drag on his cigarette.

"A devout socialist, *oui.* A Communist? Hard to say. Do you know where to meet him?"

Martin nodded.

"You're on your own," Durand warned. "The Sûreté and Truchon have jurisdiction over subversives like him. I can't help you in this matter. Bureaucratic restrictions. My apologies."

~

That night, Martin met Shannon over dinner after she returned from the Peace Conference. He needed her insights on his investigation.

"When will you meet him?" Shannon asked.

"He works at night. His note said to meet him at midday."

"I assume Captain Durand will provide help."

"No. He can't, and I don't trust Truchon. I'm going alone."

Shannon tried to conceal her gasp with a cough.

Martin sensed her alarm but did not acknowledge it. "None of our Marines speaks French well enough. It's less dangerous on my own."

"Can't I — "

"No. You'll be at the conference. Anyway, Ai Quoc wants to speak to a high-ranking American. I'll be fine."

The waiter brought over a basket of fresh bread and a bottle of vintage claret. He poured a finger for Martin to sample. "Excellent," he smiled.

"So what happened today?" Martin asked.

"President Wilson got what he wanted — the Committee approved the formation of a commission to set up a League of Nations."

"Hallelujah. A toast." Martin refilled their glasses.

"Gil, it was so exciting. The League will change the world. Someone should make a movie about it. Experts everywhere. Detailed maps. Powerful men debating. It'd be so inspirational — diplomacy at its best. It would make lots of money!"

Martin laughed. He had rarely seen Shannon so thrilled. *How ironic,* he thought. *We've exchanged roles. Before the war when it came to hopes for the future, I was the idealist and Shannon the practical one.* "So it's as good as done."

Shannon's enthusiasm faded from her voice. "It's not as simple as that." Colonel House believes the League is a noble concept, she explained, but making it work would be the challenge. Much needs to be decided. President Wilson is to chair the commission, but Colonel House will lead the discussion, running the meetings in his office. "I'll be here for the next month," she said. "A comprehensive draft for the League is due on February 14."

"Not much time."

"I'll find time to help with your investigation. Be careful tomorrow."

~

The Red Dragon Café was in a rundown section of Paris north of the Gare du Nord. Martin felt as if he had walked into another world. The signs were in Chinese. The air was laden with the smell of raw fish, oriental spices, and hashish. The place hummed with human activity. Small men in bright robes and jackets smoked from a water-pipe or played mahjong. They chatted in cadences strange to Martin's ear. They all turned when he entered. Their faces were weathered and their arms tattooed. Speaking French, he asked the tiny gray-haired woman at the register if *Monsieur* Ai Quoc was present.

"Who you?" she asked after a few uncomfortable seconds, spitting through the gap of a missing front tooth. Two men standing by the swinging door to the kitchen approached. Martin tapped his chest where his .45 rested in a shoulder holster. He did not want a fight, but would if necessary.

One man carried a heavy machete in his right hand. Two fingers on his left hand were missing. The other man was a good four inches taller, with a long scar across his left cheek. He curled his hand ominously around the handle of a pistol stuck in the sash around his waist. Two other men stood between Martin and the entrance. The other patrons moved aside.

Outnumbered and outflanked, Martin raised his hands and said in French, "A friend. I want to talk to Monsieur Ai Quoc about this." He nodded toward his coat pocket and slowly reached in. The taller man pulled his gun. "*Du calme*," Martin said and showed him Ai Quoc's *Claims for the Annamite People*. The two toughs backed away, and Martin's pulse returned to normal.

"Come," the old woman said.

Martin followed her up a narrow staircase to a dingy room about the size of three closets. An Asian man sat at a desk with a wooden top and crates for legs. He stood up and bowed his head. "Allow me to present myself. I am Nguyen Ai Quoc." He extended his hand. "Thank you for coming, Major Martin. You have received my note?"

Martin nodded.

"Excellent. Please sit." Ai Quoc turned to the old woman and said something to her in Chinese. She bowed and left the room.

After the exchange of a few pleasantries, Martin asked Ai Quoc what he was trying to accomplish by approaching House.

"You have time to relax for a minute, yes? You are my honored guest."

The old woman returned with a steaming pot of tea, and Martin detected a hint of lemon mixed with other enticing aromas. Both men tasted it appreciatively, and after a moment, Ai Quoc spoke. These were historic times, he said. He admired America and President Wilson's

Fourteen Points, but he had a problem. "I am from a small country in the grip of a powerful one. We wish to be heard like the rest."

"What do you want for Indochina?" Martin asked.

Ai Quoc's posture became more erect. His face beamed. His voice projected energy. "*Monsieur*, all I want for my people is what your colonists wanted from the British."

Martin was impressed. Ai Quoc had learned his history well. Based on the American Constitution's Bill of Rights, his *Eight Claims for the Annamite People* were simple, logical, and profound — political autonomy; freedom of assembly, religion, press, and movement; the rule of law, not decree; and representation in the French Parliament. "Thoughtful and just," Martin said. "You present your case well."

"But, ...? You are not sure. Let me explain what it's like to be colonized." Ai Quoc described beatings, legal farces, and rapes. "My thirteen-year-old niece was sodomized with a bayonet by a French soldier."

"I will make sure your case is heard."

"I can ask for no more." Ai Quoc reached for a pen, scribbled something down, and reached to hand the paper to Martin, then pulled back as if reconsidering. "My people suffer under the yoke of the French. We will break it with or without your help. It is only a question of time, sixty years even." He stood up and extended his hand. "Take this." He bowed.

Martin clasped the paper, but out of respect did not open it. "*Merci*."

"That is the address where you can find the kitchen worker you are looking for. I give it to you as an act of friendship. I do not know this man. I am not involved with his affairs or his politics. He is Chinese, not Annamite. He is a beast. Wounded and trapped — you know the dangers such men pose."

Chapter 24
Weimar

Outside Weimar, Germany: February 1919

Keller was relieved to be out of Berlin. It had been a month since the Spartacist revolution, and he was now seven miles outside of Weimar, where he patrolled the defensive perimeter of the Landsmann Battalion's camp. Selected as the seat of Germany's new government, Weimar was a medieval town of 50,000 people located in central Germany, one hundred fifty miles southwest of Berlin. It was deeply linked to Germany's cultural past by Wagner's operas and Goethe's philosophy. More importantly, it was not part of Prussia, whose leadership had brought Germany into the Great War debacle.

It was 04:06. The trees seemed to cower against the night's bleakness. Snow dusted the ground, providing an uneasy shroud of stillness. Keller welcomed the monotony of his guard duty. At least he could be alone with his thoughts. His cheeks were red from the biting wind, and his feet ached from the cold rising through his old boots and worn-out stockings. The discomfort reminded him he was still alive, having survived the madness of last month's Spartacist revolution in Berlin. The image of Landsmann's bloodied driver hanging from a tree near the Eden Hotel lingered in Keller's mind. A wooden sign saying "traitor" fell from his neck. Landsmann had identified Dietrich's spy and had dispatched him ruthlessly. *What would he do to me?* Keller cringed at the thought.

Keller continued to anguish over his role in Karl Liebknecht's assassination. An isolated spy doing his enemy's bidding, he was plagued by remorse. *Since I can't sleep,* he reasoned, *why not volunteer for midnight patrols? On guard duty, at least, I don't have to pretend to be Karl Brandt.* Everyone knew Brandt to be a loner, so no one thought much of it. No man in the battalion, including Keller in the guise of Brandt, was above any job, even those assigned to Colonel Landsmann's staff, as Keller had been. Most of the men thought his promotion to sergeant was a reward for pulling the trigger on Liebknecht, but their concerns and jealousies remained unspoken. Good German soldiers did not challenge authority.

The battalion had been pulled out at night under secrecy. Keller hoped Larsen was smart enough to figure out how to communicate with him in Weimar. Until then, he had to act like a regular soldier and keep his ears perked to learn as much as possible about Freikorps activities. Above all else, he had to keep sane and stay alive. He was not sure which would be the bigger challenge.

With each step over the snow-crusted leaves, Keller wondered what he was doing in these woods. He had been in Germany more than seven weeks, but it felt much longer. Last month, Friedrich Ebert, who had been appointed the German Chancellor when the Allies forced Kaiser Wilhelm to abdicate at the end of the war, called for elections across the country. The Allies wanted to create a German republic, and Ebert wanted to secure his position through a democratic process and to establish a new German constitution.

Despite the Spartacist threats, thirty million citizens had voted, including newly enfranchised women. The turnout had been remarkable — more than 80 percent of the potential electorate. Ebert's Social Democratic Party (SPD), the moderate social democrats, won a convincing victory with 40 percent. Still worried about Communist activity, Ebert had moved the government and the constitutional convention to Weimar, where the Freikorps could better guarantee security. No one wanted a repeat of a Russian-style revolution in Berlin.

Keller relieved the stress and boredom by thinking of better times back in America. It was late spring 1917. He and Shannon had just become engaged. They are speeding along the Boston Post Road north of New York City on his Harley-Davison model J motorcycle. The rough grips feel good in his hands. His goggles fit securely around his eyes. The wind in his face is as refreshing as lake water. Without a care in the world, he shifts the bike into top gear. It lunges into full acceleration. He leans into a corner. The machine and he merge into a combined entity. Shannon, her scarf waving in the wind, sits in the sidecar beside him. She laughs and shouts, "Faster!"

Something rustled in the underbrush, startling Keller out of his thoughts. He aimed his carbine at the sound. He hoped it was not human but was prepared to kill if necessary. He was surrounded by a jungle of human predators where life was no longer precious and every atrocity applauded. Finger on the trigger, he slowly knelt down in an icy puddle and waited.

Two gleaming eyes poked over a fallen tree and stared at him. A rabid growl grew into a fully grown Rottweiler. Foam dripped from its clenched teeth. Angry vapor spouted from its large black nostrils, as its well-muscled neck prepared to attack. Just as it sprang, Keller squeezed off a round that struck the beast in the face. The dog whimpered and dropped five feet in front of him. Blood, brains, and foam expanded on the ground. Keller stood over it and fired another round into its head, ending its dying wails. "The scavengers will pick your bones clean, just like they will mine," he said, and resumed his patrol.

"Got a problem, Brandt?" A soldier called out.

"No. Just a dog," Keller answered. Or was it an omen?

He finished his shift as the sun began to rise and headed for the mess hall. A full belly was one of the benefits of fighting in the Freikorps, whose solders were always sufficiently fed, while the rest of Germany, still plagued by the Allied blockade, starved. He filled his plate and sat alone at a table at the far corner of the room. The scrambled eggs were dry. The bratwurst tasted like — Keller did not want to think about it. At least he was full. He finished his breakfast with bread that was equal parts sawdust and grain, and washed it down with something brown called coffee that was satisfyingly hot.

The next room erupted into jeers and whistles. He wiped his mouth, returned his plates to the counter, and went to investigate. "What's going on?"

"Moscow Magda," Jawbreaker said, putting on his coat to start patrol. "She's at it again, subversive whore. We just got her latest pamphlets from Russia." They contained the ususal Bolshevik platitudes in German, calling for the formation of a new Communist international organization.

"They want to start a worldwide revolution," said a lance corporal from Frankfurt.

"Their ideas spread like the plague," contributed a Prussian private.

"I thought they'd had enough when we crushed the Spartacists in Berlin last month," Jawbreaker growled.

"She proclaims Karl Liebknecht and Rosa Luxemburg heroes," the lance corporal added.

Jawbreaker snickered. "Not if they'd seen how they died."

Keller's stomach turned — *that's not the way it was* — but he laughed anyway in an automatic, life-saving response.

"I hope the Communists keep at it. I love killing them," Jawbreaker grinned. "From what I hear, we might have to go into Munich next."

"I don't trust those cursed Bavarians," the Prussian said.

"They're lousy soldiers. I hated when we had to fight beside them," the lance corporal agreed.

Keller had fought against Bavarian units and considered them excellent fighters. Looking at the ground, all he said was, "Second-rate troops."

"Them or us," the Prussian said. "I don't even consider Bavarians German."

"I'm ready to fight anywhere, any place. Germany must regain its glory!" exclaimed the Prussian. He looked at Keller, who remained silent. "What about you, Brandt?"

"Whatever it takes. I hate those bastards." Keller played along. "I'm going to rest." The strain was getting to him. One thing was certain. He was trapped and had little chance of help. *Lord, give me one more chance to see Shannon.*

Chapter 25
The Raid

Paris: February 1919

The morning after Martin spoke with Ai Quoc, he reported to Durand's headquarters with the location of the missing kitchen worker. "To hell with the Sûreté. I'll make this arrest," Durand said. Within half an hour, he had organized a raid. Three military cars carrying a posse of thirteen heavily armed men were heading to a poor section of northeast Paris. Martin would have preferred a more cautious approach, but he had no jurisdiction here. The one thing he and Durand agreed on. Speed counted.

The military cars stopped at an arched entranceway. Was Ai Quoc's information good? From the car, Martin peered into the courtyard from the car and checked the address Ai Quoc had given him. "Place Henri Lefebvre. This is it." Armed with a Winchester Model-12 pump-action shotgun, his favorite weapon for such raids, a .45, two hand grenades, and a U.S. M1917 "Knuckle Duster" trench knife borrowed from one of the Marines, Martin walked with Durand to the entranceway. "Let's take a look. Your men ready?" Martin asked.

"*Oui.*" Durand ordered three men to guard the back of the buildings and two men to stay outside and protect against a rear attack. At the entranceway, Martin and Durand eased through a five-yard-long stone corridor, wide enough for a horse and wagon, and peered into the courtyard.

"I don't like it," Martin said, surveying the square of dilapidated four-story buildings that enclosed the unpaved courtyard. The curtains to every window were closed. The height of the buildings and angle of the sun rendered the courtyard cold and dark, and the ground, gray with soot and ash from crumbling chimneys, was dotted with puddles of brown. The smell of overcooked food assaulted his nose. Rats the size of army boots rummaged through overturned garbage cans. A baby carriage with no wheels lay on its side. Threadbare sheets and women's undergarments wilted on sagging laundry lines. An eerie quiet reigned over the area.

This was a tactical nightmare. From the roof and third- and fourth-story windows, an adversary could catch them in a downward, four-sided crossfire. There would be no cover unless they could fight their way into the buildings, and no chance to use grenades against defenders far above them. He and Durand exchanged knowing looks.

Martin squinted into the gloom. "We could be slaughtered."

Durant pointed out Building #1 to their left. "I know this neighborhood. Many subversives live in this *arrondissement*." The door was about thirty yards diagonally across the courtyard from the entrance. "Our man is there, #1B. We'll have to move fast."

Durand split his remaining eight men into three groups: the first group of three men would charge Building #1. Two men at the entrance would provide cover fire with an FM Chauchat light machine gun. Sergeant Forney, Durand's second-in-command, and the remaining two men would maintain a defensive position at the entranceway. When the first team reached Building #1, Forney and his men would follow across. Together they would storm the flat where the Chinese kitchen worker was allegedly hiding. Durand told Martin to stay behind.

The soldiers shed their canteens, bulky jackets, and personal belongings. Durand peered into the courtyard, studied the roof and every window for movement, and signaled the first team to advance. Martin pointed his shotgun at the roof. Exposed, they sprinted across the courtyard to Building #1. To Martin's great relief, there was no firing.

Sweating and ducking low, Martin zigzagged across the courtyard to the other men. Durand pointed up — #1B was on the right side of a landing twenty steps up a narrow flight of stairs. Positioned on the first step of the foyer, Martin was the last of ten men lined up along a staircase only wide enough for one man to pass. An assailant on the staircase above could kill them all with a hand grenade or two bursts of an automatic weapon.

Martin felt anxious and helpless in the role of observer, but this was a French operation. Durand drew his Lebel pistol and ordered the first three men to advance. They readied their carbines and crept up a step at a time. The floorboards creaked under their weight, and Martin heard something dart at their feet. The lead man pointed his rifle at the sound but relaxed when a fat gray cat scampered down the stairs. The soldier wiped his brow and chuckled.

"Continue," Durand said.

The lead man reached the first floor landing in front of #1B without incident. The next two men moved next to him. One man pointed his rifle at the door as the other two shoved up hard against it. The door gave way with a tremendous blast that rocked the building.

The staircase shook so hard Martin feared it would collapse. Temporarily blinded, he felt his face. Blood ran down from numerous small cuts, but all was intact. His lungs contracted as smoke filled the staircase. Through ringing ears, he heard Durand groan and fall. Martin rubbed his stinging eyes, and his vision, though blurred, returned. The three soldiers in front of him seemed paralyzed by shock but unharmed. Martin moved to Durand, who was sprawled on the stairs, still groaning. His pulse? Strong. His breathing? Steady. Wounds? Nothing visible, maybe a concussion.

The soldiers positioned outside ran in. "Get back!" Martin shouted. "Secure the perimeter. No one leaves. Call for back-up."

The youngest of the soldiers to survive the blast panicked. "Where did they go? They're gone. Where are they?"

Martin had to slap him back to reality. "You and your men take your captain to the street. Help is on its way."

The highest ranking soldier still alive, a sergeant, with a large Gallic nose, protested. "Who are you to order us around?"

"A bomb expert," Martin said. "Get your men out of here! There may be more traps." At the top of the stairs, a spatter of red mist on the wall and mutilated body parts were the only evidence that the first three soldiers had ever existed. Aside from the distinct possibility that there might be more bombs, Martin worried that the explosion might trigger more blasts or ignite a fire along the old wooden staircase.

The next few minutes could determine whether he survived. Heart racing, Martin closed his eyes. *Collect your thoughts. Control your breathing*. He became a Bomb Squad sergeant once again.

He sniffed — dynamite, just as he suspected. He walked to what was left of the entrance to #1B, studying every inch of ground and fragment. The bomb maker was an expert. Durand's first team never had a chance, but the rest of the men had been low enough on the stairs to avoid the force of the blast. Durand was lucky to be alive.

Martin put down his shotgun, pulled out the trench knife, and began to poke at the debris. Crouching low and taking a step at a time, he entered #1B looking for hidden wires and booby traps under the rugs, in crevices, and behind furniture and doors. Thirty-five minutes later, he had cleared the hallway, front closet, and living room.

He opened the door to the bedroom. Hanging from a rope, next to an overturned stool, was the body of the Chinaman.

Chapter 26
The Apartment

Paris: February 1919

Martin studied the hanging body. Judging from its condition, the man had been dead for more than a week. The only injury on the body was a deep gouge on the back of the head — someone strong had bashed him with the butt of a gun or a truncheon. The Chinaman was likely unconscious when they necktied him. Two killers at least. Who? He examined the noose — nothing special about the rope, but the knot was looped expertly. He scratched some notes on a pad and cut the body down. He rested it gently on the floor and crossed himself.

Martin guessed the Chinaman knew his killers and had let them in. He looked around and noticed a crusted brown patch on the rug. He leaned over and examined it. Dried blood with black hairs, the same color as the dead man's. The murder had happened here.

Martin went to the window and spread the curtains, but instantly realized his mistake and drew them shut again. *Careless, Gil.* He ignored a photograph of Lenin on the wall, but a chessboard in mid-game intrigued him. Chinese kitchen workers playing chess?

Littered on a rickety bureau were Communist pamphlets and manifestos in Russian, German, and French. Most interesting to Martin were numerous newspaper clippings of articles by Ana Primakova. He quickly ran his eyes over a few in French. They were well-written despite her revolutionary observations. There were also some handwritten notes in Chinese. Martin folded them neatly and put them in his side pocket for one of the American experts to translate.

By the bed, a nightstand drew his interest. There was something curious about it. He opened the drawer and poked along the edges with his trench knife. Nothing. One of the German spies he had investigated owned a similar nightstand with a secret drawer that opened by a clever device. Martin pulled out the drawer, turned it over, and probed again. He spotted a tiny button camouflaged to look like a knot in the wood. He pushed it. A flap sprang open and a page fell out. It contained a rectangular grid with letters and numbers, a code. He tossed the drawer on the bed. *Who was this dead man? No ordinary kitchen coolie, that's for sure. What was his connection to Ai Quoc? Was he just an Asian co-worker or something more?* Ai Quoc was involved politically, but Martin did not believe he was involved in the fire or this killing. After all, Ai Quoc had given him this address. A trap? Maybe. Martin had thought Ai Quoc was more patriot than Communist, but — Sergeant Forney appeared at the bedroom door. "Find something?"

Martin turned to face Forney. "Just some articles. Typical Bolshevik rubbish."

"I brought you your shotgun. Captain Durand is conscious and will be on his feet in a few days," Forney said.

"Good news. The other men?"

"The two still alive are searching the rest of the flat."

"Check for fingerprints, hidden compartments, weapons. Be careful. Post a guard at the door."

"Right." Forney walked into the living room. "I'll let you — " Before he could say another word, a fusillade of gunfire opened up from the front door. Forney took three bullets in the chest and spun half-way around, spitting up blood. Martin ducked as two Slavic-looking men charged into the apartment, guns firing.

A wounded French soldier cried for help and died. More gunshots. The other soldier fell. Quiet. Martin was alone. Hearing his attackers creeping up to the bedroom door, Martin reached for his shotgun and kneeled behind the bed. They would either charge or toss in a grenade. He considered using one of his grenades, but he figured the old apartment, already damaged by the first blast, might give way, killing him too.

Martin checked the tubular magazine of his shot gun. Fully loaded. Six shots. Good. Attack. He stood and pumped off six powerful rounds as fast as he could, guessing the positions of his attackers. The bullets tore through the paper-thin wall, eliciting screams. With no time to reload his shotgun, Martin drew his .45 and moved forward. The sight of the carnage he had inflicted met him at the bedroom door. The shotgun had shattered both men's bodies so badly he could not tell which crimson-soaked parts belonged to which man.

Martin stepped over the gore and searched the front of the apartment, looking for other attackers. He moved into the hallway. The door to #1A was open across the way. His attackers must have come from there, but he did not want to chance going in alone. Something stirred in the stairway above him, and he pointed the .45 toward the sound. An old woman looked down at him with a frightened face. He ordered her to get inside.

He had to finish the fight. Despite his concern for the structural integrity of the building, a grenade was his best option to clear the apartment without risking his own life. Martin moved to #1A and called a warning through the open door. No response. He called again and waited. Ten seconds. "Last chance!" He pulled the safety pin of the MK I fragmentation grenade, pushed off the cap, and moved the switch on the lever away to start the fuse. Six seconds. He rolled it into the apartment and prayed the floor would not give way. It should not. The blast would go sideways, not up and down. He ducked for cover on the stairwell and felt the force of the explosion through the wall.

The grenade fragments would have maimed anyone in the room, but there were no cries, just the hissing of a busted pipe. He recovered the shotgun, loaded it, and moved into #1A. The room was full of smoke. The furniture was broken and shredded, but the shrapnel-scarred walls remained intact. No bodies. Despite the cold, the back of his uniform was soaked. He realized how thirsty he was. He found a canteen on the body of one of Forney's men and emptied it in three gulps. All he could do now was wait for reinforcements.

To his shock and bewilderment, Ana Primakova was the first person to arrive. "What are you doing here?"

"Major Martin? You shouldn't be — " Ana seemed as surprised as he was. But her demeanor changed quickly, and she began to act as though he were a complete stranger. "There was an explosion. I'm a reporter. I was nearby. Here I am."

Liar. You must have been nearby, expecting something to occur.

She took out a pencil and notebook. "Can you tell me what happened?"

"Madam Primakova ..."

"Call me Ana." She smiled.

She was changing again. "You need to wait for the French authorities. This is a crime scene, Ana. I'm a guest here and can't help you."

"Do you mind if I look around? I won't touch anything."

Something inside him wanted to oblige, but he remained resolute. "Go."

A squad of French soldiers arrived, led by one of Durand's officers. Martin recognized him and turned to explain what had happened. Ana hurried behind his back and glanced into the bedroom. Her eyes lingered on the bed.

"Damn. Madam Primakova," Martin declared.

"I'm leaving. I will see you again, Major Martin."

~

Two hours after she had left Place Henri Lefebvre, Ana Primakova sat on her favorite bench by an apple orchard in the Luxemburg Gardens. She stared blankly at the frozen ground. She needed time to think before she reported to Bukin. How had her once good life turned to this? Things had begun to change in January 1905 when the Tsar's Imperial Guard fired on striking workers at the Bloody Sunday massacre in Saint Petersburg. Ordinary citizens were caught in the volleys. An estimated one thousand people, including her mother, were killed. Ana was at her mother's side when the bullets whizzed over her head and struck her mother in the chest. Covered with her mother's blood, Ana wondered if the shooting and shrieking would ever stop. They never had.

She hated the Tsar from that day forward even though her husband was a nobleman. Commissioned at the start of the war, he was mortally wounded leading an attack in the Brusilov offensive in September 1916. Ana fled to France to stay with his uncle. When he joined the French Army, she returned to Petrograd, where her husband's gambling debts caught up with her. She was living on rats when the Bolsheviks took over.

A woman walked by pushing a baby carriage. Ana was reminded of her own daughter, Sonya, and wondered if she ever would see her again. Conscious of the cold seeping through her coat, she headed to the Metro. She opened the door to Bukin's office to discover Commandant Truchon sitting in Bukin's chair. He was tapping his fingers on the desk. "What did you learn?"

Bukin remained in the shadows drinking whiskey.

Ana patted her arms against her chest. The radiator was broken and the room was cold. She described what she had seen.

"How did military intelligence know the Chinaman was there?" Truchon demanded.

Ana did not know. “Someone must have talked.”

“Who?” Truchon’s tapping increased. “Good thing Mal took care of that slant-eye when he did.”

Bukin poured himself another whiskey. “I never trusted that Chinaman in the first place. I told you not to use him to help start the fire.” He glared at Truchon.

“Shut up. He served his purpose,” Truchon said. “Why was the American with them?”

“I don’t know, but he seemed in charge after Captain Durand was wounded.”

“He’s becoming troublesome,” Truchon said.

“What about the coded message?” Bukin asked. “We never should have left it there!”

“The American didn’t say anything,” Ana said.” But, I got a look at the bedroom and saw a drawer tossed open on the bed.”

Truchon waved his arm dismissively. “Even if Major Martin has the note, he’ll never break the code in time.”

Chapter 27
The Bloodhound

Weimar: February 1919

Keller's duties in Weimar had become routine. Instead of fighting street-to-street in Berlin, the Landsmann Battalion protected the city, and its men listened to elected delegates construct Germany's future government. Although guard duty was hardly the work of an elite unit, Keller was pleased to stand down. For two weeks, the politicians debated, cajoled, and argued their case as the members of the Peace Conference in Paris must have been doing. He had little knowledge of what was happening in Paris. German leadership was concerned they had not been invited, an ominous development that shattered long-standing diplomatic protocol. The snub suggested the Allies would impose terms so harsh the German population would rally against them. What then? Might he have to remain a spy? His stomach cramped at the prospect.

Weimar's citizens let the politicians work unhindered — no strikes, no uprisings, no Communist threats. The streets remained quiet as though people recognized that drafting a new constitution, agreeing on new leadership, and building a new country demanded the delegates' full attention. Ebert had chosen the location well. The intimidating presence of the Freikorps, which patrolled the town and controlled Weimar's railway station, post office, and National Theater, contributed to the order. The government made it known that the Landsmann Battalion, with its reputation for military efficiency and ruthless brutality, would provide shock troops if necessary. The only incident was a feeble march of workers whom the battalion turned away with quick-triggered efficiency. After that incident, no one questioned who ruled Weimar's streets.

On February 13, the newly elected head of the cabinet, Philippe Scheidemann, of the majority moderate Socialist party, stood in front of the assembly to announce the new Germany's foreign goals at the assembly of delegates. Keller, Captain Reick, and Jawbreaker were present to protect Friedrich Ebert, who remained head of state as President. Keller wondered if he was seeing history in the making. Had four years of tragic war forced Germany to reform? Was the country that had marched across France twice since 1870 finally ready to reject its imperialist and military traditions and join the Western democracies to form a new world order? If so, he could go home. Naïveté or wishful thinking?

Scheidemann loudly rattled off his positions. In foreign affairs, he would work to establish a final and fair peace settlement with the Allies, restore Germany's colonies, end the Allied blockade, make a full exchange of prisoners of war, and participate in Wilson's League of Nations based on equal rights for all nations. Domestically, he proposed to improve education, create a People's Army, form a democratic national government, and restore a decent normal life.

Like everyone else, Keller applauded. It was a good start. On the way out, Keller overheard Jawbreaker ask Captain Reick about the People's Army. "What the hell is that?"

"Don't fret, my Prussian friend," Reick said. "General Noske is still in charge of defense. We control things despite what these politicians think."

Careful to make sure no one saw him, Keller silently cursed. The new Germany had not changed.

~

That night, Keller escorted Colonel Landsmann and Captain Reick to a meeting with Defense Minister Gustav Noske. Keller had never met the man and wanted to measure him against General Pershing and his generals. If a new war were to break out again, Noske would be the man to overcome. He was popular among the officer corps and known for his decisive actions and stalwart leadership. He had gained national attention when he almost single-handedly ended the Communist-inspired Sailor's Revolt in Kiel at the end of December. Ebert had then put Noske in charge of Germany's military affairs, leading to the defeat of the Spartacists last month. *The Red Flag*, a German Communist newspaper, called Noske the "bloodhound" because of his relentless determination and indomitable will. Without him, Reick had said, the Freikorps would not exist; Germany's military would be toothless; and the Communists would likely be running the country.

Flanked by two motorcycle riders, Noske's staff car pulled up in front of the post office that served as the Freikorps central command. Colonel Landsmann stood at attention on the curb. Reick and Keller, weapons ready, waited in front. One of the motorcyclists hurried to open the car door for the defense minister and a German Army major, his aide. Noske was dressed in rumpled civilian clothes and an unbuttoned wool coat that reached below his knees. A German officer with a steel jaw and strong military bearing exited the car behind him, wearing the fur-collared leather coat of an airman. The famed Blue Max, the mark of a superlative combat flier, hung from his neck. In the U.S. Army, such officers were called "hard men."

"Who's that?" Keller asked.

"You don't know? That's former *Oberstleutnant* Hermann Goering, one of our greatest pilots. Twenty-two kills. He supports the army and is advising us on air tactics."

Noske walked up to Landsmann and whispered something. Landsmann broke out into a smile and escorted the defense chief into the building. Goering, Reick, and Keller followed them. Although he was almost as tall as Keller, Noske was an unimposing man with a thick middle, little hair, and round glasses. He looked older than his fifty-one years and lacked a leader's swagger. He reminded Keller of a research scientist.

This was the highest level Freikorps meeting Keller had ever attended, a possible intelligence coup if he could ever get the information back to Dulles. In the conference room, he overheard Noske tell Landsmann, "These Socialist fools think that just because I'm a Social Democrat, I'm one of them." He said he was waiting for the Freikorps financier and asked to speak with Landsmann and Goering in private. Landsmann seemed to know the financier. "Our friend will be most welcome," he said. "We owe him a great deal." The spy inside him told Keller the identity of this man would be priceless information.

Ordered to the front foyer to protect against intrusion, Keller stood guard with a watchful eye, hoping to catch a glimpse of the financier. If he had arrived, it was not through the front door. Keller began to fret. The intrigue and stress of being an undercover agent and a Freikorps assassin had ravaged his stomach. Cramps and nausea were constant. Worse, he could not see a doctor without revealing its cause.

Keller wanted to go home and be a detective again. Tired, he nearly made a deadly mistake. His mind relaxed, and he started to imitate throwing a baseball, but Shannon's warning months ago alerted him, and he stopped himself before anyone noticed that most American gesture. He began to contemplate escape from the Freikorps. But without help, his chance of escaping the Freikorps was slim.

An hour passed. The financier was late. Keller, continuing to guard the front door, sensed tension. One of Noske's motorcycle riders appeared every few minutes, looked outside, and grumbled when the street remained empty. He returned to the meeting without saying a word. Five minutes later, Noske's aide stormed out of the building, almost forcing the door off its hinges. He ordered Reick to follow him. Keller watched the army major and Reick argue by the staff car but could not hear what they were saying. The major threw up his hands in obvious disgust and sped away.

Reick clenched his fist but released it when he noticed Keller observing him. "What are you looking at, Brandt? This is none of your concern."

Startled, Keller jumped to attention. "*Jawohl, Kapitän Reick,*" and saluted crisply.

"Don't ever spy on me again."

Chapter 28
The Code

Paris: February 1919
Martin was troubled. He sat at his desk and emptied the remains of a large pot of strong coffee into his cup. It was going to be a long night. Two days had passed since he had discovered the coded message, but neither Durand's cipher experts nor anyone in the American delegation could crack it. By mutual agreement, Durand and he had withheld the message from Truchon and the Sûreté. They did not trust him. Martin had shared the message with Shannon, who had a mind for these things. But she continued to be as mystified as everyone else.

After another long day, Shannon met Martin in House's office at 21:00. The conference had become a routine series of endless discussions, presentations, and pleas. Self-interest, not compromise, dominated. Shannon could not distinguish one day's activities from another. The end result of each day was another long list of unresolved topics to discuss tomorrow. Finances caused constant commotion. The Allies, particularly Britain, wanted relief from the debt they had accumulated with America, but Wilson insisted on payment in full. Everyone wanted Germany to pay enormous reparations, which saner experts, including Keynes, argued would destroy its economy. "Open up our markets so Germany can earn the money it needs to pay us back." Few listened to him.

The Japanese were frustrated with the lack of interest in their demands. They continued to argue with Britain about the future of the naval bases Germany had established in China, which China wanted back. The Italians kept insisting they must annex the Adriatic port of Fiume. The "Big Three" — France, Great Britain, and the United States

— remained unsympathetic. Italy accused them of reneging on their promises at the start of the war. The Polish question caused endless contentious debate. The fates of Czechoslovakia and the Balkan region remained unresolved. Palestine's future produced bitter arguments. Britain and France clashed over competing mandates concerning the rest of the Ottoman Empire.

Martin looked up when Shannon entered. "I hope your day was better than mine."

She sat down and sighed. Her face was etched in shadows Martin had never seen before. "Any more coffee?" she asked.

Martin ordered coffee from the guard at the door and slumped back in his chair. "Shannon, are you sure Ai Quoc didn't set us up?"

Shannon rubbed her eyes. "I've gone over it from every perspective, and no, he didn't set you up. Yes, it was a trap, but I don't think he knew about it. The proof?" Shannon pointed to the coded message on the table. "Men died to keep that out of your hands."

"Durand agrees. Ai Quoc was looking to curry favor with us. The Chinese kitchen worker helped the arsonist and was killed to shut him up." Martin filled Shannon's cup from the newly arrived pot and topped off his own. "So," he said, "what about the code?"

"I've studied it for two nights. I think about it all day. But nothing." Shannon stared down at the message in frustration.

W	S	M	C	H	4	9	2	A	K	B	X	N	C	M
2	1	1	6	V	8	4	B	L	F	2	J	H	H	5
1	0	6	3	H	F	T	V	H	I	G	Q	V	U	T
2	2	2	8	X	Z	5	W	V	B	B	Z	i	W	Z
1	1	9	5	C	8	S	F	P	S	8	F	P	F	L
2	2	4	4	B	Q	X	J	K	G	O	K	T	G	Q
2	2	5	7	F	E	8	B	0	P	0	A	Q	E	9

If I could just make out the beginning," she said. "W S M C H 4 9 2 A K B X N C M. Letters? Initials? A date? These first numbers mean something. They must. I've gone over this so many times, I'm confusing myself."

"This message was sent to the men in that apartment. They were foot soldiers. The message is telling them to do something. But what? When? Where? Whoever sent it took great measures to protect it. Was the kitchen worker killed to prevent him from talking? He recruited the men in the apartment across the way to watch for intruders. They defended that apartment — more likely the message — with their lives when we showed up."

Martin did not say it, but he increasingly believed that Madam Primakova was involved in the conspiracy. Her arrival at the scene so soon after the fight was no coincidence. That, he would deal with himself.

"What language is the encryption?" Shannon asked.

"Assume it's in French," Martin said. "It's the only common language among those involved."

"The code is a mix of alpha-numerics. No obvious pattern. A horizontal sequence? Maybe a vertical one. It's clever; I'll admit that." She studied the code with the intensity of a surgeon about to perform a delicate operation. "There must be a master key that transcribes these lines. But what could it be and where is it?"

~

The next night in House's office, Shannon admitted she remained baffled. Durand's code-breakers were equally stymied. Martin sensed that something terrible was going to happen, and soon. "Shannon, think," he said. "What are we missing?"

"Tell me everything you saw in that apartment. Go over every detail."

Martin closed his eyes and relived every moment. He opened his eyes to see Shannon shaking her head. "You've left something out, Gil. Concentrate. What seemed out of place? Odd?"

Martin's eyes widened. "The chess set! There was a chess set. I never figured out why it was there. It didn't fit with uneducated Chinese workers."

"My God! That's got to be it!" Shannon said. "This code must be linked to chess!"

Martin called Sergeant Cooper at the door. "Sergeant. Go to Harrison Davenport's room. Bring him here immediately."

Eighteen minutes later, Davenport arrived with red eyes and tousled hair. "This better be important," he grumbled, but soon calmed down after Martin explained the magnitude of the situation.

Martin handed him the code. "Does it mean anything to you? It's a cipher, but we think it's related to chess."

Davenport scrutinized the code with his lawyer's sense of detail. "It might mean nothing, but "WS" might mean "Wilhelm Steinitz."

"Who's he?" Martin and Shannon asked simultaneously.

"Maybe the greatest chess player of all time. He was world champion about twenty years ago. He played Mikhail Chigorin — MC? — for the title. The fourth game was famous. There, #4." Davenport pointed to the number on the first line.

"When?" Martin asked.

"1892. There's your '92'. Your code looks like it relates to that game."

Martin and Shannon looked at each other as if they had found the clue to the Holy Grail itself. "Where did it take place?"

"Havana."

"The H," Shannon declared, amazed. "The first line definitely could relate to that game."

"Possible," Davenport said. "Maybe the position of the pieces on the board. Every square on a chess board has a column and row reference. "I'm no expert. If you really want to know more, go to John Maynard Keynes. He loves chess. He can help you, but I think you will need whatever key the code-makers used to make the encryption."

"The key must be on the chessboard. I've seen it!" Martin sprang to the door and ordered Cooper to get their car and drive him to Place Henri Lefebvre. "Bring your best men," he said, checking to see if his .45 was fully loaded. On the way, he silently prayed no one had yet recognized the importance of the chessboard.

~

Three hours later, Martin returned to House's office carrying a folded chessboard under his arm. Shannon, who had been working at the code since he left, looked up in anticipation. Davenport seemed perplexed.

"Gold!" Martin shouted. "It was hidden in plain sight, right on the table where I'd seen it. I wrote down the position of each of the pieces and examined the board. Look! I found this under it." He opened the board and spread it on House's table. "It must be the key!"

The alphabet and numbers were scratched on each of the sixty-four squares in random sequence:

K/V	P/E	A/T	3/X	0/Q	E/B	9/R	G/J	8
Q/D	T/P	1/C	Y/K	C/U	6/i	U/o	M/H	7
4/G	N/A	7/M	W/U	H/W	Z/S	2/F	R/Z	6
F/2	X/N	D/K	8/H	S/3	B/U	i/Y	V/L	5
L/W	D/2	0/M	J/S	5/Y	L/F	Y/7	F/T	4
H/P	C/E	X/V	K/Q	0/A	E/1	B/N	V/4	3
A/6	P/C	T/Z	W/G	R/8	G/o	1/X	J/L	2
Q/J	M/o	2/D	U/5	N/i	Z/R	i/B	S/9	1
A	B	C	D	E	F	G	H	

Shannon added the standard referencing to the board, writing A through H horizontally on the bottom to indicate the eight columns. Starting with white on the bottom, she numbered upward from 1 through 8 along the right-hand side to indicate the rows across. Every square thus had a unique reference based on column and row. For example, the designation for each corner is: A1 (Q/J), H1 (S/9), A 8 (K/V) and H8 (G/J).

"Now we have something to work with," she declared.

Davenport shook his head in bewilderment. "How will you ever crack it?"

Chapter 29
The Chessboard

Paris: February 1919

The American delegates chosen to break the code gathered in Colonel House's office, waiting to learn more about their new assignment. House announced that Shannon Keller would lead the decoding team. Some of the men expressed their displeasure. "No woman is going to tell me what to do," said Charles Culpepper, the Brown University mathematics expert.

Martin pulled Culpepper aside and told him that Mrs. Keller had more brains and guts than he had in his fat belly. If he didn't like it, he could talk to President Wilson. "If you want to leave, go," Martin said. "But if you do, you are no longer required in Paris."

"If that woman doesn't measure up, I'll let you know," Culpepper said.

"Don't bother unless you tell me how you can do better," Martin retorted.

Disgruntled chatter turned into a hushed silence a few minutes later when John Maynard Keynes, on loan from the British delegation, entered. Martin introduced him to respectful nods.

Colonel House had used all his diplomatic persuasion to bring Keynes to the decoding effort. British Prime Minister Lloyd George was skeptical and distrustful when House first approached him about borrowing Keynes. Lloyd George changed his mind when House explained the gravity of the situation, the shortage of time, and the complexity of the problem. In addition to Keynes, Lloyd George volunteered two more men from his delegation and asked House for everything the Americans had on the codes. Within two hours after

Martin had delivered copies of the code, the chessboard key, and all other relevant details on the case, they were off to British Military Intelligence in London. Now, three teams were working on breaking the code: Shannon's American team, Durand's French military cipher experts, and British intelligence.

The question House and Lloyd George had to decide was what to do with Truchon and the Sûreté. The French would be furious if they learned that Britain and America had withheld information that could have prevented a disaster on French soil. The Peace Conference would collapse. But if they gave the information to Truchon, and he was involved, the specific plot might be thwarted, but the general threat would remain. House and Lloyd George agreed to say nothing for the time being. Decode the message first.

Many people were now working on the code. House commandeered the billiard room in the basement of the Crillon. The hotel manager protested until two Marines escorted him away at bayonet point. American soldiers replaced the billiard tables with desks, and eight men in green eye shades or thick glasses sat where privileged men in tuxedoes had rubbed chalk on their cue sticks less than twelve hours before. One of the Englishmen remarked that it was an odd place to work. Without windows, the low-ceilinged room was dark except for the dull overhead lights and the gray metal lamps placed on the desks. They reminded Martin of the lamps used to interrogate prisoners. The biggest advantage to the room was that it was secure.

House ordered the room cordoned off, and passes were given to Shannon, the Americans recruited to help, Keynes, and the two other Brits. Sergeant Cooper led the security detail. No one without a pass could enter unless approved by House or Martin in writing.

Shannon, Keynes, and Culpepper debated the possible logic behind the code. The other men worked through possible permutations and combinations. It was tedious work. Nothing made sense. Late that afternoon, Keynes asked Shannon, "Could all this be a diversion? A tactic to waste resources?"

"We have no choice but to continue."

While Shannon led the American decoding effort, Martin spent much time with Durand. They concentrated on improving security, finding Mal, and preparing for any sabotage attempts they could imagine.

Everyone involved was pledged to silence. Food was brought into the billiard room, and anyone needing to use a water closet or to visit his room was escorted there by a Marine. By late that night, scraps of paper and piles of pencil shavings covered the floor. The only results were more theories about the cipher and predicable failure.

Just before midnight, Martin met Shannon in the billiard room and reported that Durand's team had encountered the same frustrations and lack of progress. Keynes talked with the London code breakers, whose initial reaction was that the chess angle may not be correct. The first line in the code might be there to mislead and confound. They would look at it further. Martin, with his detective's sense of a case, was sure that chess would guide them to the solution. Shannon agreed, but thought there were further layers of intricacies they had not identified. Keynes said, "This will take time."

Time, Martin suspected, they did not have.

~

Two days later, the number of desks in the billiard room had increased by three, but the code continued to perplex them. The night before, Shannon had thought she had a breakthrough but was stymied soon after. In the meantime, the peace talks continued in the same unproductive and contentious way.

That morning, Shannon walked into the billiard room after her breakfast of tea and rolls. The room smelled of old food and anxious people. Ventilation in the room was poor and temperature control erratic. It was either too cold or too hot. With so many bodies in the room, the air was stale. A blanket of cigarette smoke hung overhead and seemed to deaden the exhausted men. Shannon sensed defeat when Culpepper started to argue with his British counterpart, Harold Blum. Men pulled them apart before they could start swinging. She told Culpepper to take a rest; he was too tired to help. She calmed Blum down with praise and encouragement and asked him to have a good English breakfast upstairs.

In deep concentration, Keynes had either not noticed the scuffle or had chosen to ignore it. He sat in his chair in the back of the billiard room scribbling mathematical formulas as Shannon approached. He looked up and rubbed his eyes. "Could we talk in private, Mrs. Keller?" he asked.

Alone in House's office, Keynes said, "First, I'd like to ask a question, then I'd like to make a comment."

"Certainly." Shannon sat down on a leather couch. She shifted uncomfortably. Keynes remained standing.

"The question." Keynes reached into his rumpled tweed coat for his pipe. "Is there a chance that by killing the men at that apartment your man Martin has foiled the plot we are trying to uncover?"

Shannon and Martin had discussed this possibility. "A chance? Yes, a small one," she said. "But we can't take that chance. We must assume another attack is coming. We believe the decoded message will reveal the plot."

"That is what I thought you would say." Keynes tapped the bowl of his pipe into his hand and then blew air through the stem to clear it. "Second, my comment. Whoever designed this cipher is very clever. We will either need one thousand monkeys or a new approach."

"One thousand monkeys?"

"Yes. A metaphor for using a random approach. One thousand monkeys with typewriters typing completely at random for one thousand years, twenty-four hours a day, could transcribe all the possible permutations of the symbols. One of them, by pure probability, would provide our solution. If you are right that the message is in French, of course. Another language will take another thousand monkeys."

Shannon was taken aback. "But we don't have a thousand years."

"Or monkeys," Keynes said deliberately. "Therefore, we need to rethink our approach." He dug into his pocket for a tobacco pouch.

"What do you propose?"

Keynes moved to House's chair, sat down stiffly, and started to fill his pipe pinch by agonizing pinch. Shannon waited for his response. "First, I believe British intelligence is right. Not every letter in the code means something. I believe your Thomas Jefferson devised a seemingly unbreakable code using this technique. The chessboard itself contains many such false references. This could be why each line to the code uses only 15 letters or numbers. If I am right, breaking this cipher will be that much harder. False references increase the number of permutations and disrupt discernible patterns."

"Assuming you are right, what do we do?"

"Instead of taking the message and working backwards to a solution, I suggest we look at this from the perspective of the person developing the code," he said. "Based on the first line of the code, we believe the cipher relates to chess, specifically to the 1892 match between Steinitz and Chigorin. Game #4 to be exact. If this assumption is wrong, we will do well to use the monkeys."

"No, I'll bet my life on it," Shannon countered. She sounded more confident than she was.

"Mrs. Keller, you have proven to be an excellent abstract thinker. Assume we are designing this code, how would we go about it? We will ask each other questions. Start with what we know, and we will go from there. Me first. Using this chess match, what complexities would you build into the cipher?"

Shannon was thrilled and intimidated at the same time. One of the most brilliant men at the conference was testing her intellect. "Let your mind wander." Keynes struck a match and lit the pipe. He seemed to enjoy the taste. "Together, we can decode this."

Chapter 30
The King

Paris: February 1919

Determination, the magnitude of the stakes, and sheer stubbornness kept Shannon and Keynes working. They sat in a private room, now their office, on the second floor of the Crillon Hotel. *Evaluate the evidence,* Shannon's police training told her. She placed the chess board and the coded message side by side on the big table near their desks. Above them, she placed a list of all the moves from the 1892 Game 4 championship and another chess board ready to recreate the game. She stared at them both intently, hoping to find a hidden link to the cipher.

The office was located in the back of the hotel, overlooking the maintenance garage. Below, she heard mechanics working on an automobile. Despite their noisy efforts, the men were unable to repair a vehicle that continued to stall.

"Ignore them. Look at the key, Mrs. Keller. Forget everything we have discussed about the code so far. Let us figure this out together. What do you see?"

"The chessboard key, obviously. A sixty-four square grid, each square with two characters on it. But what does it mean?" Shannon asked.

"This is a chess game, correct? Expand your thoughts." Keynes filled his pipe.

"Two opponents — white and black. Each moves in turn. Could our code work the same way?"

"Each of the sixty-four squares has a distinct reference, right?"

Shannon nodded, not knowing where Keynes's thoughts were heading.

"Let's assume our cipher-maker is using the standard numbering for a chess board. Letters A through H for the column, and 1 through 8 for the rows." Keynes rolled his pipe around in his hands, obviously thinking. "Now, he has to design a code that his user can both understand and manipulate to find the proper square on the chess board key. Once the user knows which square and symbol — right or left — he can decode the real message." Keynes stopped, put his elbows on his desk, and leaned forward, resting his head on his folded hands.

"I'm not following, Mr. Keynes."

"Patience. I'm trying to examine the problem differently. We're designing this code right now, not trying to break it." Together they looked at the board, went over the number and letter combinations, and tried to identify duplications or patterns for a quarter of an hour. The economics and numbers genius saw it first. "For the code to work, we require a grid that contains the 26 letters of the alphabet and the digits zero through nine — that's 36 spaces. Therefore, of the 64 boxes on the board for any individual cipher, 36 spaces relate to the code whereas the other 28 boxes mean nothing and serve to confuse us. Our code-maker has designed the key to work from two perspectives — black or white. That's why there are two characters on every box of the chessboard key."

Shannon studied the contents of every box. "Are you saying the chess board key is really two keys? But how would someone know which one to use?"

"The chess game. We're back to that 1892 match." Keynes jumped up so fast his pipe flew out of his hands. "By the moves!"

"That's the connection to the game we've been struggling to find." Shannon became as excited as Keynes. "The moves dictate the position of the key for the conversion from the real message to the code."

"We've just linked the key, the board, and the game. The code-maker needs to indicate which move, black or white, so the person reading the message can establish a starting point for the conversion key. This gets us back to the code itself," Keynes said. "The first four letters of each line. They're numbers. What do they mean?"

"Two numbers to indicate the move, another to indicate black or white, and a fourth for a false reference or something else," she said.

"Odd and even — black and white. But which is which? Which of these four positions represents the mysterious fourth reference?"

They looked at the first characters of each line in the message:

2116

1063

2228

1195

2244

2257

"For days, our mathematicians in London were certain there was some numerical pattern to this sequence, but they were wrong," Keynes said. "It's not an algorithm. It's a logic pattern."

Shannon looked blankly at Keynes.

His hands still folded, Keynes tapped his two index fingers together rapidly. "This is it. So the first line in the message tells the reader how to use the code. The remaining lines contain the real message. Here's my guess. The first digit — 1 or 2 — indicates whether the code is using the white or black perspective. If it's white, look at the left side of each box. Black uses the right side. The next two numbers indicate the move of the game. The pattern changes with every line, which simultaneously changes the reference point on the key. Devious."

Shannon tried to comprehend everything Keynes had said. "Let's see if I understand." Shannon swallowed hard, hoping she had gotten it right. "There are 3 alphanumeric sequences used to make the cipher — the actual message, the code key, and a middle conversion key used to translate the actual message to the coded one, right?"

"Precisely."

"We have the chess board key and the coded message. We need the conversion key. You believe it is based on the position of certain pieces in the actual game?"

"Yes, but that takes us only to the first three numbers of the code. That fourth number in the sequence mystifies me."

"But we still don't know the starting point on the chess board key. Could the fourth number give us a clue?" Shannon asked. Outside, she heard an automobile engine rev up and then backfire.

"Why not the square where the piece lands after the move?" Keynes asked.

"But which piece?" Shannon wasn't sure she knew what she was asking.

"Let's go back to my idea of thinking like the code-maker," Keynes said. "I'm guessing he's a chess lover."

"So what?" Shannon said.

"What's the most important piece on the board?"

"The king!" they exclaimed in unison.

"It's the only piece that's always on the board during any game ever played. The code-maker did not devise this code for one message, did he?" Shannon said.

"No," Keynes said.

"This is a code that is meant to be used often. Why can't the king be the starting point for the code?"

"That's the significance of the fourth number in the code. It's the number of places away from the position of the king. That's the starting point!" Let's share this with our code-breakers downstairs."

Keynes ran out so fast he forgot his pipe.

~

The British mathematician Harold Blum decoded the first line as the sun began to rise. "Everyone, come here. I've got something," he shouted. "*Plan tigre es* ..."

Shannon ran over to his desk. "You've cracked it?"

"The first words." Everyone in the room stood up and cheered. "We need to set up the chess board based on the information on the next line," Blum said. "Where is the position of the king?"

Keynes moved the pieces quickly. He had recreated the game so often it was almost mechanical. Blum determined the starting point and set up a new conversion key. "Let me work with this. Give me some time," Blum said. After twenty minutes that seemed like forever, he scratched out the new solution key. "Got it." Everyone crowded around his desk.

Blum followed the same procedure for the second line as he had for the first. When he had finished, he read the second line. "t prêt 18 fev... I need to work on the rest."

"They're giving us a date. Hurry, finish!" Shannon said.

Blum methodically transcribed every letter and line but it took time. A few minutes after 8 a.m., he gave the finished decryption to Shannon.

"*Plan Tigre est prêt 18 février. Commencez à préparer. Details plus tard. Ours.*" She gasped. "It's an operation to kill the Tiger — that's Clémenceau. Start to prepare. February 18. That was yesterday! Details later. Bear — must be his code name. My God, that means they could attack him at any time!"

Chapter 31
Clémenceau

Paris: February 19, 1919

"Clémenceau is in danger! We must warn him!" Shannon dropped the decoded message. "It's 8:28. We might be too late," Shannon said, fearing they had failed to decode the message in time. "Colonel House called a meeting here at the Crillon. If we're lucky, Clémenceau hasn't left yet." Keynes was all business. "I'll tell Mr. House to call Clémenceau's home immediately and contact my Prime Minister. He could be in danger too."

Within minutes the hotel lobby resembled a staging point for a major attack. Everyone had a grim face. Marines scrambled. Sandbags piled up on the front walk. Telephone lines heated up. Heavy weapons were sent to key defensive points around the hotel. Martin's security planning and drills had proved their worth.

House left an urgent telephone message for Prime Minister Clémenceau, who had just left his house. French security forces hastened to intercept him. House put down the phone and ordered all non-military personnel to the basement. Luckily, President Wilson was back in America.

~

Martin was in his car heading to Durand's office when he heard the news. Stuck in traffic, he stopped a newspaper boy running by and asked what had happened.

"Don't you know? Clémenceau's been shot!" the boy exclaimed as he scurried on. "What? How? Anyone else?" Martin asked, but no one heard him above the commotion. People on the street were turning unruly and shouting threats. Martin headed back to the hotel. His first duty was to protect his delegation. When he arrived, security was tight.

A platoon of Marines with fixed bayonets and belts full of grenades patrolled the perimeter. Two snipers looked down from the roof, and three men set up a machine gun at the entrance.

Sergeant Cooper approached Martin and saluted. "Glad you're safe, sir. Colonel House has asked to see you as soon as you arrive. Come with me."

Martin ran up the stairs two at a time, not waiting for the elevator. Shannon was already there, sitting in front of House's desk. Her pallid skin signaled she had not slept in days. Martin had known her long enough to read the horror and defeat in her usually composed face. "Clémenceau — is he still alive?" he asked, fearing the worst.

"The wound was not fatal." House had been on the phone ever since Shannon had warned him of the plot. The Prime Minister had been shot at 8:40, just as he was leaving his house. Someone dressed in work clothes had approached Clémenceau's car and started shooting with a pistol. His driver sped away, but the assassin continued firing. One of the bullets struck the Prime Minister in the back, between his ribs and lung. "He's a lucky man. One inch either way and he'd be dead or paralyzed."

"Twenty minutes more and we could have saved him," Shannon mumbled to herself.

"The gunman's name is Emile Cottin," House informed them. "He shouted, 'I am a Frenchman and an anarchist.' The crowd almost lynched him." House clenched his fist. "The guillotine is too good for him."

"Will I be able to talk to Cottin?" Martin asked.

"Probably not. The French must handle this from here on, Major. Let them interrogate their own rat," House said.

"But he didn't act alone. The decoded message proves that," Martin said.

"Not necessarily. This may have been a different plot." House opened his desk drawer looking for something.

Does House know something I don't? Martin wondered. "Cottin's a Communist stooge. Someone forced him to shoot Clémenceau."

"Here they are." House pulled out a stack of letters marked 'confidential' in his own precise handwriting. "Anarchist threats. We get them every day. So do the British and French. I show you these because we can't jump to conclusions. I never took them seriously before. The French are capable of learning whether Cottin acted alone. They'll use methods on him I'd rather not know about. You and Mrs. Keller have done remarkable work, but your job is to protect the American delegation."

"The conspiracy and protecting our people are related to the same threat, Colonel House," Shannon said.

"We should — " Martin read House's eyes and stopped.

House slammed his desk drawer shut. "We can't get involved in unpleasant French affairs. This assassination attempt complicates my work enormously. Clémenceau may be alive, but he is far from healthy. The bullet is near his lung and can't be removed. I don't know when he'll regain full strength. If he ever does. He's at home resting and insists he'll be at the conference tomorrow. I doubt it." House sighed. "I fear the conference will last far longer than I had hoped."

"I understand, Colonel." Martin tensed; he had almost overstepped his rank and knew when to back off. "The code? What will the French tell the press?"

"We'll let the French handle them. The Big Three leaders all agree that we must keep what we know about your code to ourselves." House looked at Shannon, who nodded in agreement. "France has had enough setbacks — the Dreyfus affair, Germans at the gates of Paris, mutiny in their army. We don't want another one now that the country is regaining her honor."

"But who's behind the code?" Martin asked.

House told him he was closing the decoding operation and returning Mr. Keynes to the British delegation. He ordered Martin to give Captain Durand the solution and help him in any way possible without getting directly involved again. "The French insist that we call this assassination attempt the act of a crazy man. If the public finds out there was a conspiracy to kill the greatest man in France, the repercussions could be catastrophic. You and I know the Communists are a threat, but do you agree to say nothing about this affair?"

"I understand," Shannon said. "The U.S. government and New York City officials tried to downplay the truth about the poison gas attack on lower Manhattan in 1916 as well. We had to manage the press to calm passions and maintain order. We have to do the same thing now."

"Of course," Martin said, knowing he could say nothing else. *But the conspirators are out there, and they're still deadly.*

Chapter 32
Martial Law

Berlin: March 1919

Dressed in battle gear and equipped with extra cartridges and grenades, Keller and the Landsmann Battalion boarded a train in Weimar for Berlin. Once again he was heading into a fight. The quiet in Berlin had not lasted. Word had quickly spread around the men that the radical German Communist party — the KDP — and the Independent Democratic Socialist Party — the USPD — had declared a general strike in Berlin. They wanted to take over the city. "Never," declared Colonel Landsmann. President Ebert immediately imposed martial law and ordered the Freikorps to enforce it.

Acting as bodyguard for Landsmann, Keller accompanied the colonel to the Freikorps headquarters on the outskirts of Berlin, and was present when Noske briefed his commanders. Noske had ordered 30,000 Freikorps soldiers to prepare to attack the city. The Landsmann Battalion would spearhead the assault against the Communists' strongpoint on Alexanderplatz in the eastern sector, where the Communists had taken over police headquarters and fortified the area. This battle would be harder than the one in January. Radical units from the sailors' revolt in December had joined the insurgents. They were formidable opponents, well-trained and experienced.

Later that night, Landsmann told Captain Reick that his company had the honor of leading the battalion. "How will we take Alexanderplatz, Colonel?"

"From all directions. Your men will make a direct assault up Koenig Strasse. Other units will flank them from the northwest."

"Any restrictions on use of force?" Reick asked.

"No. Kill them all if you have to, but try not to flatten the city." A messenger interrupted to hand Landsmann a note. He read it and turned to Reick. "Get your platoon leaders and meet me outside my tent in an hour. I'll give you some additional firepower."

When Jawbreaker saw Landsmann's additional firepower, his faced beamed as if he were beholding Helen of Troy. Captain Reick called it a "self-propelled artillery vehicle" — a 7.7 cm light field gun mounted on the back of a Daimler truck with armored side plating. Its intimidating muzzle pointed forward. "It's as mobile as a truck and faster than a tank," Reick said. "The cannon is powerful. Its range is limited, but that won't matter in a street fight. We have plenty of high explosive shells." The 15.1-pound shell contained 294 lead balls and a half-pound of TNT and could obliterate anything they would face.

"I'll call her Gertrude," Jawbreaker said, rubbing his hands together.

Reick laughed. "She's ugly, but you want to get your hands on her anyway, don't you Sergeant? She'll knock you silly when she's angry."

"Better that way." Jawbreaker jumped on the truck to admire the gun close up.

"Mount machine guns on it," Keller suggested. "Double its effectiveness and help protect it." Gertrude's lack of protection from above, a real problem in street fighting, worried him. Mines could also destroy her from below. Still, Gertrude gave them firepower they had never had before and were likely to need.

"Excellent suggestion. Gertrude'll be unstoppable then," Reick said. "Paint a skull on her radiator. Let 'em know what's coming."

"Those Bolshevik bastards will break and run when they see her," Jawbreaker said.

"Don't be so sure," replied Keller.

~

Dawn found two point men leading Reick's one hundred and fifty men up either side of Unter den Linden. Two squads followed ten yards behind, each armed with a Maxim MG08/15 hand-carried light machine gun. Miltz drove Gertrude behind the lead squads with Jawbreaker in the passenger seat manning the front-mounted heavy Maxim machine gun. The two best marksmen in the battalion, Keller and the new man, Ritter, stood on the truck at either side of the cannon, scanning the windows and roofs. Reick, his staff, and the rest of the men crouched low behind Gertrude as the company moved forward, searching for mines, snipers, and ambushes.

The battalion stopped at the end of Unter den Linden at Platz Zeughaus to redeploy. Reick, Sergeant Dengel, and Keller continued up Kaiser Wilhelm Strasse, turned right on Spandau and stopped at the red city hall on Koenig Strasse. They assessed the approach to Alexanderplatz about five minutes away. Keller could see the Bolshevik red flag wave defiantly over the square. Ahead of them, Koenig Strasse was empty — too empty. "A trap," Keller said.

"I don't like it either, but orders are orders. Move out," Reick said, pointing his arm forward.

Keller returned to Gertrude. He sensed in the other men the same gut-tightening acceptance of potential death that he felt. Crackling gunfire and numerous explosions erupted to the east, broadcasting the start of the battle. The company turned northeast up Koenig Strasse. A heavy volley of gunfire opened up two blocks later, and the point man to Keller's left went down. Enemy fire rained down from everywhere, concentrating on Gertrude. Miltz slumped over the steering wheel even as Jawbreaker countered with burst after burst of machine-gun fire.

Keller knelt close to Gertrude's steel side-plates and looked for targets, but the enemy was well concealed. The best he could do was to fire at the muzzle flashes. Ritter took a bullet in the shoulder and was out of the fight. With no driver, the truck stalled, helpless in the middle of the road. The ambush was well planned and executed. The main fire came from a butcher shop, half a block up the street.

Reick's men moved into a defensive position inside the adjacent buildings, but Gertrude was isolated, immobile against the murderous gunfire overhead. The gunner managed to load the cannon, but was hit numerous times before he could shoot. Bullets flew close to Keller's head, striking the truck repeatedly. Two Freikorps men moved to Gertrude but were cut down in seconds. Jawbreaker's machine gun stopped. Heavy enemy fire prevented him from poking his head up to replace the overheated barrel. Counter-fire by the rest of Reick's men turned the fight into a stalemate.

Knowing Gertrude was doomed unless he acted, Keller jumped off the truck and was nicked several times in the process. He crawled on his belly under the truck and inched his way back to the rear, then got up and crouched against it for protection. He motioned to Reick in a nearby building. Reick ordered his men to lay down a torrent of suppressing fire against the butcher shop as Keller climbed back onto the truck, aimed the cannon, and pulled the lanyard. The butcher shop exploded into smoke, dust, and shrieks. The gunfire from it ceased.

Reick's men charged forward in the smoke and confusion, throwing grenades and firing wildly. Jawbreaker, his machine gun repaired, raked the enemy buildings with murderous fire, shouting curses as he shot. Men tossed potato-mashers into every building they passed. A soldier with a flame thrower finished them off. Keller retrieved his rifle and picked off three men on the rooftops. When Reick's men reached the smoldering butcher shop, the street went eerily silent.

Reick sprinted up to Keller. "Good work, Sergeant. How is Gertrude, Jawbreaker?"

Jawbreaker checked the engine. "Good thing we put extra armor around her," he reported. "I can get her going in fifteen minutes."

"Captain!" called Sergeant Dengel from the wreckage of the butcher shop.

"You, Brandt, come with me," Reick said to Keller. "Jawbreaker, get that truck ready to go. The rest of you, finish cleaning out those buildings. We'll reform in front of the butcher shop."

Keller followed the captain into the shop. The smell of sausage, cordite, and human remains permeated the smoky, dust-filled room. Pieces of bodies lay scattered and broken, like half-eaten bones around a campfire.

"This one's alive." Behind the counter, Dengel pointed to a man in a sailor uniform wearing a red arm band. The man held his head in obvious pain. "Traitor. I bet you know something." Dengel kicked the man in the gut with his heavy boot.

"How bad is he hurt?" Reick asked.

"Not bad," Dengel said. "No wounds. I think he got hit in the head. A concussion maybe." Dengel pulled the man to his feet.

Despite his wobbly stance, the sailor spit in Dengel's face. "I won't talk."

Dengel drove the butt of his rifle into the man's groin. He doubled over, shrieking. "Take him to the back room," Reick ordered. Dengel wrenched the sailor's arm behind him until it cracked. He pushed the sailor forward with his bayonet; the man cried out with every jolting step. Keller followed, knowing the next few minutes would be sickening.

"There, by the butcher's table." Reick walked up to the sailor and glared at him. "I need to know the number and location of your men. What heavy weapons do they have? Their plans? This could go easy or hard for you."

The sailor tried to stand upright. "Go to hell."

"Stick his hand in that meat grinder. I'm going to enjoy turning the crank," Reick said. Dengel and another soldier forced the sailor's hand into the thing. Despite his exertions, he could not free himself. He looked desperately at the grinder. Reick took the handle and said, "Last chance."

"You're all monsters. Die!"

Reick turned the crank a touch and the metal grinders bit into the sailor's hand with crushing power. The man howled unearthly obscenities. Another partial turn. Blood spit from the grinder in pulses. "Talk," Reick demanded. Starting to slip into unconsciousness, the sailor shook his head. "Douse him." Reick ordered, handing over his canteen. He turned the crank again.

The sailor's cries of agony bore into Keller like a drill as the meat grinder pulverized his bones and devoured his fingers. "Wait!" Keller said, "Let me handle him, Captain."

Chapter 33
Alexanderplatz

Berlin: March 1919

"I've descended into hell," Keller thought numbly, staring at the meat grinder that had gobbled up the sailor's hand.

Captain Reick, beads of sweat dripping from his brow, stopped turning the crank. "If he hasn't talked by now, he won't." With that, he pushed hard on the crank. "Will you?" The sailor's screams chilled the room.

The man squeezed his eyes shut and collapsed onto his knees, yelping a mix of incoherent laments and curses. The only words that made sense were, "Kill me."

"He's yours, Brandt." Reick said. "He's about dead. Do what you want with him. I'm going out to ready the assault." Dengel and the others followed him out of the back room.

When they were alone, Keller reversed the crank and extracted what was left of the sailor's hand. He'd seen newly amputated stumps that looked better. He agreed with Reick on one thing. The sailor was a dead man. Even if he survived the day, gangrene would finish him off. The man was about Keller's age, and his pain affected Keller acutely. He knelt down and held his flask of schnapps to the sailor's lips. "You know you won't last long, don't you?" Keller asked.

The sailor drained the flask and looked at Keller. "*Ja.*"

"Do you have kids?"

With his good hand, the sailor raised two fingers. Mercy demanded immediate death. "Tell me what we need to know, and I promise I'll get money to your family."

The sailor moved his lips as if to say, "*Danke.*"

"Where are your papers?"

The sailor pointed his chin to his uniform blouse. Keller unbuttoned the shirt and glanced through the papers. "Andreas Sund of Bremen. I'll find your family. I'm deeply sorry all this has happened. I'll let your wife know you died bravely."

"I love her." Andreas struggled to say the words.

"I'll tell her." Keller, self-hate and bile rising up from his stomach, pulled out his Mauser semi-automatic and said, "Tell me something useful, Andreas. I'll make it fast."

In a barely audible voice, the sailor revealed what he could as he fought death. Keller believed him. When the man could no longer speak, Keller saluted and pointed his gun at the sailor's heart. The sailor did his best to salute back. Keller pulled the trigger and blood spattered onto his face. *Will I ever be human again*? He massaged the sailor's eyes closed, crossed his dead arms over his chest, and said a short prayer. He folded Andreas's papers into his own blouse and went to tell Reick what he had learned. The information would save lives, at least those of the Freikorps men. *It's something.*

Keller found Reick in the middle of Koenig Strasse talking to Dengel and Jawbreaker next to an idling Gertrude. "You can't make a direct assault on police headquarters," Keller said.

"What do you know, Brandt?" Reick asked.

Keller conveyed Andreas's information. The Communists had posted more than a hundred men at police headquarters. Some had moved forward to the butcher shop. Impossible to say how many were at the headquarters now. They had four heavy machine guns, at least one on the roof. No flamethrowers but plenty of grenades.

"Mortars?"

"Not sure," Keller said. "But they have enough firepower to slaughter us without more support. They have a Mauser 1918-Tank Gewehr."

Jawbreaker seemed stunned. "An anti-tank rifle? How did they get that?"

"It could take Gertrude out at a range of six hundred yards," Keller said. "They've planted mines in the street. We'll never get through, Captain. You need to rethink your attack."

"I'll send word to the colonel."

Keller finished briefing the captain and Dengel called him over. "I don't like you, Brandt, but I admit you're useful in a fight."

For thirty minutes, Reick's men waited nervously for the order to advance. By now, every soldier knew what Keller had told the captain and was wondering what the colonel would do. "He'll think of something," said a private with a long scar across his face. As he and the rest of Reick's seasoned veterans prepared for the bloody frontal assault to come, revenge was foremost on their minds. They had already lost six men and eighteen were wounded, including Keller, who had been stitched up and declared fit for duty.

The runner returned from battalion headquarters with Colonel Landsmann's reply. Reick nodded stoically after he had read it, and ordered Jawbreaker to move Gertrude into long-range firing position. "We're going to blast them from a distance," the captain said.

At that moment, engines roared above them. Four Fokker D VII biplanes suddenly appeared, flying low in the direction of Alexanderplatz. The lead pilot waggled his wings and waved. Keller thought he recognized Goering. Seconds after the Fokkers sped past, the rat-a-tat-tat of their machine guns opened up on the square. The Communists countered, but the aeroplanes flew through the curtain of bullets and— circled overhead for a second pass. As they flew away, a giant Gotha bomber soared into the melee and dropped its bombs. Keller could feel the ripples of their impact.

Reick checked his watch and then ordered Jawbreaker, now

acting as Gertrude's gunner, to shell Alexanderplatz. Jawbreaker and his loader set to work quickly just as a second Freikorps unit moving in toward Alexanderplatz from the northwest began to rain mortar rounds down on the Communists. The bombs, artillery shells, and mortar rounds were as intense as a coordinated pre-attack barrage during the war. Keller guessed the ferocity killed no more than half the Communists. Men had survived worse in the trenches. However, the bombardment had given them a temporary advantage. Reick blew his whistle, and to Keller's surprise a trolley with armor plating and heavy machine guns on either side rolled up Koenig Strasse. The driver wore a Freikorps uniform. "Last-minute idea from the colonel," Reick said. It'll lead the charge. I need two volunteers to man the machine guns." Dengel jumped onto the trolley, immediately followed by a new man Keller did not know.

"It won't go a hundred yards," Keller commented to Reick.

"I know. A sacrifice for the greater good. It'll draw fire and reveal their positions. Get to your position, Brandt."

Ducking through side streets and back alleys, Keller snuck onto the roof of the tallest building on Dirksen Strasse. His concealed position gave him an excellent view of Alexanderplatz. He was now the most forward man in the company.

Attentive to possible mines, the company moved forward with the trolley in front. With classic storm-trooper attack tactics, the soldiers moved behind it — grenade men first, rifle and machine guns next, a flamethrower man behind them. Gertrude stayed back as Jawbreaker continued to shell the square.

The Communists opened up from Alexanderplatz with formidable firepower. More had survived than Keller had expected. At first, the trolley advanced powerfully, spitting out devastating machine gun fire. The men ran to catch up. Jawbreaker proved to be an accurate artillery gunner. His shot blew open a gap in a barricade placed across the road and scattered the surviving defendants.

Disaster struck as high-caliber rounds from the insurgents' anti-tank rifle pounded the trolley. Moments later, it hit a land mine. Its front end lifted five feet off the ground before it landed on its side. Cheers rose from Alexanderplatz. Miraculously, Dengel crawled from the wreckage, dazed but unhurt.

Undeterred, the lead men threw smoke grenades for cover, and the light machine gunners ran through their ammo drums and scrambled to reload. Two soldiers dragged a scratched and angry Dengel to safety.

Gertrude's devastating cannon fire and mortar rounds from the Freikorps unit pressing in from the northwest gradually silenced the Communists. Position after position fell like tall grass before a scythe.

Through his sniper's scope, Keller spotted an enemy machine gun atop police headquarters. Taking careful aim at the man feeding the gun, he squeezed the trigger of his Mauser carbine. The man's chest exploded in red mist. Keller worked his bolt and waited. The gunner stuck his head up to see where the bullet had come from. Keller nailed him in the helmet. The firing ceased.

Keller's next priority was the anti-tank gun, the most powerful weapon the Communists had. He needed it to fire again so he could locate it, but the Communists were smart and conserved its use. Keller studied the rooftops through his scope. The rifle would most likely be emplaced on top of police headquarters, the strongest enemy position. Keller concentrated on that spot. It had to be there.

Keller heard the low rumbling of a tank coming down Alexander Strasse. The other Freikorps unit had arrived, unaware of the anti-tank rifle. The tank operators were dead men unless — there, a movement. Keller spotted a man with the anti-tank-Gewehr over his shoulder running to the other side of the building. A tough shot, but the soldier was moving just slowly enough, weighted down by the weapon. A good target. Keller shot. The man spun around and tumbled. Two others tried to reach the fallen weapon, but he kept them at bay with well-placed shots. Reick's advance would prevent the enemy from attacking his building. Keller kept low, safe and vigilant.

Reick's men moved forward methodically, silencing any resistance they encountered. The lead squad, now commanded by Sergeant Dengel, had reached Alexanderplatz when the other Freikorps unit battled its way in, led by a Leichter Kampfwagen II light tank. The two units converged at the copper statue of Berlina in the middle of the square. Dengel and the other squad leaders huddled together planning the final assault. The tank moved into position and poured machine-gun bullets into police headquarters. The Communists had nothing to counter it.

Firing from police headquarters ceased. Shouts followed, and a man dressed in the blue uniform of a sailor from the rebellious *Volksmarine* Division walked out of the building carrying a white flag. Another twenty men with arms raised joined him. Dengel quickly rounded them up and forced them at gunpoint to line up against the wall.

Before Dengel could organize his firing squad, Colonel Landsmann rode into the square atop Gertrude. "Halt!" he shouted. "Those men are my prisoners. Put your rifles down."

Dengel maintained his stance.

Landsmann pointed his Luger at him. "Do not disobey my order, Sergeant."

Jawbreaker jumped off Gertrude and headed toward Dengel, who lowered his rifle and walked away. Reick went over to the flagpole in the square and lowered the red flag, then tossed it on the ground and spit on it. Another soldier hoisted their own Freikorps flag, a skeleton head on a black field.

From his sniper's position, Keller was relieved. He had survived the fight. But what about the next?

Chapter 34
New Assignment

Paris: March 1919

Two weeks had passed since the attempted assassination of Clémenceau, but Martin and Durand had made no further progress unraveling the conspiracy that Martin was sure existed. Much to Colonel House's consternation, and despite Durand's best efforts, Truchon and the Sûreté usurped the entire investigation. Martin considered much of the information he had received to be unreliable gossip and exaggeration. All he had learned was that, despite persuasive French measures, the accused assassin, Emile Cottin, continued to insist he had acted alone.

House's diplomatic efforts to obtain access to Cottin had failed. An experienced investigator, Martin was furious because, after interrogating scores of German prisoners during the war and criminals before that, he was sure he could get at the truth, even if Cottin said nothing. "What men don't say can be more revealing than what they say," he told Shannon that night when they met at the Crillon. "And more honest." He ordered another glass of brandy, which the hotel seemed to have in large supply. He had come to enjoy its taste and calming effect at the end of his day.

The next morning he met House before the colonel departed for another long and unproductive day at the Peace Conference. House admitted that, although Clémenceau had returned to lead the talks, he lacked his usual quick mind and forceful vigor. Martin again raised the issue of Cottin despite House's obvious discomfort. "The matter is delicate, and America's involvement — " House stopped and pointed at Martin, "*yours* in particular, is unwanted and unworkable. Commandant Truchon has expressly stated you are unwelcome in his office and on this case. His government is backing him up." While the French appreciated Martin's work obtaining the code, Truchon nevertheless insisted it did not matter since it had failed to stop the assassination attempt.

Martin pleaded yet again for access to Cottin, but House supported the French position. The assassin was a Frenchman. The target was the French Prime Minister. And the crime occurred on French soil. The French must handle it themselves. He finished by saying, "You're on your own. Don't ask me again," he warned.

After the meeting, Martin ordered additional Marines to protect the U.S. delegation and increased security around the hotel. Off-duty, he inspected the street where Clémenceau was shot, interviewed potential witnesses, and paid and tricked informants inside the Sûreté with Durand's help. But he learned nothing more. In the newspapers, Truchon insisted that Cottin had acted alone. The case was solved to his satisfaction, a conclusion the French press accepted without challenge. No one in France wanted another disgrace. Clémenceau seemed to be recovering, and the matter was best forgotten.

Security tightened around the Quai d'Orsay, and the Peace Conference continued on its sputtering, contentious way. President Wilson had delegated Colonel House the authority to act on his behalf and returned to the United States. Several members of the British delegation privately told Martin they applauded House's work because the rigid and idealistic Wilson was becoming a detriment to the talks.

Two days later, when Martin reported to House before the morning's conference sessions, he was surprised to see a young man speaking to the colonel. He recognized William Bullitt, a junior U.S. delegate, whose high forehead, balding head, and pinched face reminded Martin of an oversized peanut. Bullitt talked more than he listened and managed multiple view-points as long as they were all his.

He came from old money and liked to show it, despite the aristocratic preference for modesty. He wore a well-cut suit, like that of a Morgan Bank partner. Early baldness made him look older than his twenty-eight years.

Martin's security duties had made him privy to the details of everyone in the U.S. delegation. Bullitt, one of the youngest men, prepared their daily intelligence reports. Born into Philadelphia society, he had graduated from Yale and married into an equally prominent family. He had started his career as a correspondent for a Philadelphia newspaper. Before the peace talks, he had worked as an aide to Secretary of State Robert Lansing, who was said to favor the young man. How else did a low-level staff member get invited to Paris?

Some in the U.S. delegation considered Bullitt brilliant, but he was brash and conceited. He represented everything Martin despised — unearned privilege, flashy displays of wealth, and an oversized ego. Martin admitted to himself that he might dislike Bullitt because he himself had felt socially inferior as a child. He still had lingering memories of growing up poor with ailing parents. But no. After surviving the war and seeing the worst that humans can do, Martin no longer felt envy. He cared only about who a man was, what he believed in, and how strongly he would fight for his beliefs. He decided he did not like Bullitt because, neither honorable nor brave, he was condescending. What was he doing in House's office? Martin felt an itch under his neck but refused to scratch it.

The colonel introduced Bullitt and called him "my protégé." Martin looked straight at the young man and saw that he was avoiding his gaze. Bullitt had something to hide. "Gentlemen, sit," House said. "Something urgent has come up." Martin tried to read the colonel's expression, but the wily Texan's face was indecipherable. "I have asked you here today because I am giving you a new assignment."

Was he about to be punished for continuing to investigate Clémenceau's shooting? Out of the corner of his eye, Martin saw Bullitt begin to smile. Peanut-head already knew what the meeting was about. Very bad start. Martin was going to be a fifth wheel in this mission, whatever it was. "I'm here to serve, Colonel," Martin said without conviction. He would guard his options, learn what he needed to, and react accordingly.

"What is it?" Bullitt said excitedly.

"We need a new approach to Russia," House said. Since the Peace Conference had started, the topic of Russia had provoked contentious debates and emotional fears among the participants. No one could decide what to do about the Bolsheviks, but ignoring them was no longer viable. Thousands of Allied troops were stationed on Soviet soil, poised to help the White Russians in their bloody civil war against the Bolsheviks. The British blockade continued to starve Russia as it had starved Germany during the war, and the Allied public was strongly anti-Communist.

"We need a dialogue with Mr. Lenin," House said. "Neither the French, nor the British, nor the Americans want to commit thousands, perhaps hundreds of thousands, more soldiers to Russia."

Martin fidgeted in his chair. Tough call. He knew the Doughboys and agreed they would not want another war, but Communism was a threat to the Allies that needed to be stopped.

"I believe the Bolsheviks have solidified their position as Russia's rulers," Bullitt said. "Their form of government can be a model for poor counties trying to modernize. The Red Army will win the civil war unless we make a commitment similar to what we made fighting Germany." Bullitt had just confirmed that he admired Lenin.

"What about Lenin's call for worldwide revolution?" Martin tried to soften his tone to mask his anger.

House ignored him and addressed Bullitt. “I’m ordering you to Russia. Major Martin will accompany you. Officially, Mr. Bullitt, your mission is strictly fact-finding. Unofficially, you are to start preliminary negotiations with the Bolsheviks. Talk to Lenin and his advisors. See what they want. Tell them what President Wilson wants.” House outlined the terms America would accept: cessation of hostilities on all fronts; the end of the blockade and full resumption of trade between Russia and the rest of the world; and withdrawal of all Allied troops from Russian soil following complete demobilization and disarmament of Russian armies. Full diplomatic relations would follow.

“What about forgiveness of their debts?” Bullitt asked.

House’s disapproving look needed no interpretation.

“But — ” Martin hesitated. Was he being sidelined for the rest of the peace talks and sent away from Paris? This was not the time to press his thoughts on the Communists and clarify his role, he realized.

House turned to Martin. “Stay here, Major. I need to brief you further. Mr. Bullitt, you leave in two days. Thank you.”

Bullitt dismissed, a cold silence settled in between Martin and House. Martin broke the tension. “Why him?”

House’s eyes widened into an owlish grin. “I’m amazed by your question, Major. You’ve worked with me long enough to know the answer.” He paused, but Martin remained silent. “Bullitt is a junior delegate. Any risk of failure stays with him. Of course, if by some miracle he achieves something, well ... if anything goes wrong, we blame him and say he overstepped his authority and acted on his own.”

“Why me?” Martin asked.

House leaned forward. “So nothing will go wrong.”

Chapter 35
The Tailor Shop

Berlin: March 1919

For three successive days after the battle, Keller and Reick's company guarded the strategic central location at Alexanderplatz against another attack. It took another week for the Freikorps to finish off the Communists. Enemy dead were estimated at 1,200 with more than 10,000 wounded. Their own casualties were light. With this second uprising, the Communists had pushed Defense Minster Noske too far. He issued an order: "Any person who bears arms against government troops will be shot on sight." There would not be another Berlin uprising.

When the fighting was completed, the Freikorps blockaded the streets in the eastern section and isolated rebellious neighborhoods with barbed wire. Well-armed troops manned checkpoints. Notices were posted: "Halt! Anyone who goes past this point risks death." Jawbreaker volunteered for duty at the Koenig Strasse checkpoint. "I'll be happy to enforce Noske's order," he said. Of that, Keller had no doubt.

Landsmann ordered a block-by-block sweep of the secured area as part of a massive Freikorps effort to remove the Communist threat in Berlin once and for all. At daybreak the next day, Keller left with Sergeant Dengel's ten-man squad to search houses that had been sympathetic to the insurgents. Keller protested to Reick that, because of his rank, he should lead his own team, but Reick said he was short of men. *Short of trust, maybe?* Ritter, now released from the hospital, was also on the squad.

The men entered a rundown boarding house owned by an ex-soldier missing an arm. He offered Dengel tea, but the sergeant pushed him aside and ordered a search of the house. Ritter discovered a Luger semi-automatic and fifty rounds of ammunition in the basement. When he showed the pistol to Dengel, the sergeant grabbed the one-armed proprietor by the collar, dragged him into the street, and pointed a rifle at his head.

The ex-soldier swore he was not a Communist. He was poor, and this was the only part of the city where he could afford to live. He needed the Luger to protect his two young daughters. Under the Communists, the area had turned lawless. “Please,” he begged. “My wife is dead. My daughters need me.”

“Where are they?” Dengel asked with predatory interest.

The man’s pleadings grew louder and more impassioned, reaching Keller’s ears. He sped outside and fired his carbine in the air. “Stop!” All eyes turned to him. “If you pull that trigger, Dengel, I’m going to shoot you where you stand. That man was a German soldier. He has done no wrong.”

“He’s a Communist. He deserves to die,” Dengel countered.

“He’s no threat to us. Let him protect his family. We’ve done enough killing.”

“What’s he to you? You want his daughters for yourself?”

“Back down.” Keller aimed his carbine at Dengel.

Dengel pushed the ex-soldier away and stepped back. “I’ll give you this man, Brandt, but only because of what you did at the butcher shop. I’m taking his Luger. Never cross me again.” Dengel ordered his squad to move on, leaving the ex-soldier prostrate on the ground.

Keller lagged behind, trying not to look at him for fear his concern would betray his thoughts. Walking slowly as he passed, he surreptitiously dropped his pistol near the ex-soldier. *At least I saved him. One life protected against three months of killing*. The scales of humanity still balanced heavily against him.

An hour later, after searching two more houses without incident, Dengel's squad approached a tailor shop with an apartment above it, set back from the street. The pavement was crumbling, the hedges were twisted, and refuse sullied the yard. Upstairs, the shutters were broken and the big front glass window was held precariously together with tape. Inside, all looked dark and empty.

"Don't like the look of this place," Ritter said. He worked the bolt of his carbine and readied a round.

"Careful," Dengel replied. "Informants report it's a staging point for Communist fighters."

A shot from inside the building missed Dengel by inches. "It came from there." Dengel pointed to the second-story window just above and to the right of the front door. Every man in the squad fired into the window. Ritter sprinted toward the building and tossed a grenade through the window next to the door. Two more men followed, throwing grenades into different parts of the building.

Silence followed the explosions. A voice called out, "We surrender."

"Throw out your weapons. Come out slow with your hands up!" Dengel ordered.

The front door tilted open and fell off its hinges. Three rifles followed — one with a broken stock, an old hunting rifle, and a military issue Mauser. Three men in ordinary civilian clothes walked out. Unshaven and grubby, all wore red arm bands, red scarves, and oversized worker caps. Their army belts contained empty ammo cases and naked hooks that normally held grenades. A frail man with a limp led the way. "Don't shoot. We didn't fire on you. That was that bastard Lau. He's crazy. He's dead upstairs. I'm Gottmann."

Keller and four others searched the building. They found three dead men in the tailor shop blown to pieces by the grenades. Another lay dead near the upstairs right window, just as the frail men had said. The building was secure.

When Keller walked outside, he saw that Dengel had lined the three Communists against the wall of the tailor shop. One was on his knees, pleading. The second was frozen in panic. Gottmann was talking to Dengel. "I'm a veteran like you. I fought at the Marne, Verdun, Ypres. I was gassed and wounded four times. I don't deserve to die like this."

"You're a turncoat," Dengel said. "You know Noske's orders. I condemn you to die."

"I'm a patriot. I want a better Germany, like you. There must be a better way," Gottmann said.

Dengel commanded every man in his squad to line up and shoot on order. Keller reluctantly joined the squad.

"We didn't shoot at you. Lau did. Have mercy."

After saving the ex-soldier an hour ago, Keller could do nothing for these men without endangering himself.

"Ready!"

The kneeling man clasped his hands together and looked to the sky. The second man appeared to soil himself. Gottmann ripped open his shirt and said in a dignified voice, "Shoot here and don't miss."

Keller fought the urge to get sick.

"Aim!"

Keller's trigger finger began to shake.

"Fire!"

Keller controlled himself and aimed carefully. His shot clipped Gottmann's ear. He would not be an assassin. The three men fell. Dengel removed his Luger and fired a bullet into each man's head. "Leave them. Move on."

Walking away with the rest of the squad, Keller swore with

each step that he would find Larsen his contact. He had to get out of Germany while he still retained a shred of humanity. He'd leave a message for Larsen at the drop-off point the first chance he had. With all the fighting, he was not sure Larsen was even in Berlin. Or alive.

~

Three days later, Keller went with Reick for a meeting of the Landsmann Battalion officers. Landsmann praised them. The city-wide search had uncovered hundreds of machine guns, thousands of rifles and side-arms, and stockpiles of ammunition. "Berlin is ours," he declared. "What now?" Reick asked Landsmann after the briefing.

"The Communists are still a threat to the country," Landsmann said. "Bavaria is in danger, but my bigger worry is the peace talks. My man in Paris tells me they are going against us."

"What will we do?"

"He has a plan."

POTSDAMERPLATZ, BERLIN

March 1919-May 1919

Chapter 36
We Have Seen the Future

On the Tracks to Moscow, Russia: March 1919

Martin stretched out on his sleeper bed but could not rest. He was cold and tired. He had secretly left France two weeks ago with Bullitt. Outside of House's inner circle, only Durand knew about it. Martin had confided in him because of the ongoing investigations. Martin had dressed as a civilian, although he kept a full dress uniform in his suitcase for his meeting with Lenin. Bullitt dressed in a suit.

They had traveled from Paris to the coast and on to Stockholm in a British warship. As ordered, Bullitt and Martin had spoken little with the British seamen, who kept their distance and asked no questions. Even the ship's captain knew nothing of their mission. From Stockholm, they had journeyed overland to Finland. At Helsinki, they boarded the overnight train to Moscow. They were just two more diplomats scrambling around, trying to patch up a broken world.

Martin turned over on the hard bed, more a wooden platform with blankets. Every position was uncomfortable. The frosted cabin windows leaked freezing air mixed with locomotive fumes that turned his eyes red. The thin pillow with its lumps of greasy sawdust made him itch. Awake and nearing Moscow, he had misgivings about the erratic Bullitt.

The voyage had given Martin another chance to assess him, and he grudgingly admitted that Bullitt was bright and energetic. He could be charming if he wanted to be, but he was naïve, overconfident, and rash. Martin wanted to prevent the ambitious Bullitt from blundering and accepting a deal that suited him better than his country. Martin had the impression Bullitt spoke in monologues, as if Martin were not even there. Worse, he had shown little interest in Martin's opinions.

Martin opened a tin of peaches and savored their sweetness. Despite the seemingly well-stocked larder on the train — was that a ruse to impress them? – he was glad House had insisted they bring their own provisions. At least they would not starve like the war-torn Russian people. The train bounced and rocked side to side. The clamor of the rusty wheels grinding into the tracks gave him a headache.

Martin had an even larger concern than Bullitt: Russia itself. He did not speak the language, and Russia was fighting a disastrous civil war. With all the hatred and competing factions, the risk of something deadly happening was high. Rogue units, of which there were plenty in this civil war, would care little about diplomatic conventions if they thought they could profit by capturing or murdering the Americans. Martin carried only a .45 pistol. He doubted Bullitt would be much help in a fight.

Despite his fears, counter-revolutionary units had seemed to have understood House's secret warnings that nothing should threaten his envoys if they, the anti-Bolshevik White Russians, wanted American help. If gunfire erupted, their diplomatic protections would mean little, and armed men would likely steal the $50,000 secretly secured in Martin's suitcase. But, it was all he had.

Martin finished his peaches and reclined on the bed. He decided to confront Bullitt over dinner that night and would persuade him to accept his advice.

~

Martin woke up two hours later and made his way to the dining car. He found Bullitt chomping on a large, rare steak. *Hope it's horse.* He knew illiterate soldiers with better manners. Martin sat down, and Bullitt just grunted, spearing his potato with a fork. "Sorry, hungry."

"Mr. Bullitt, before we get to Moscow, I think we have some issues to agree upon."

"I'm fully capable of negotiating with the Russians myself." Bullitt dabbed his napkin on his lips. "You're a military man, not a diplomat. I don't know why you're here."

So you'll be able to keep your head on your shoulders. Martin reached into his pocket for a Gauloises. He needed to calm down and fight his growing irritation. He inhaled deeply and said, "Colonel House expressly asked me to raise my concerns."

Bullitt's attitude changed. "Of course. Please proceed, Major."

Over his bread and soup, Martin began to probe Bullitt. "I understand you don't speak Russian. How will you communicate?"

"Minister Zinoviev, Lenin's delegate, will provide translations," Bullitt said, looking out the window. Heavy falling snow reflected the moon's brightness and blanketed the scarred earth.

At least that confirmed what House had told him. "How will you know if the translations are accurate?" Martin asked. The train screamed to a stop. People were thrown forward, and plates crashed to the floor. Martin became wary. He regretted leaving his .45 in the cabin. He stood up to get a better look, but a conductor appeared and informed them a snow drift had formed on the tracks. No need for concern. Martin grabbed a knife from the table, went outside, and checked the train up and down the tracks. Men were working to clear the impasse, but Martin returned to the dining car unconvinced this was a weather-related obstacle. He would stay vigilant. The delay could take hours.

"The October Revolution is one of the most dramatic events of this century," Bullitt declared after Martin sat down. "We have seen the future, and the Bolsheviks represent the hope for the downtrodden."

The two men sat in silence. A few minutes later, the train lurched forward, then stopped again. The dining car began to turn cold, and the lights began to flicker. Martin closed his eyes.

"Tired?" Bullitt asked.

"Worried."

"The Bolsheviks need a deal. I'll get us a good one."

"How will you trust Lenin? You've read the stories about the Bolsheviks. The starvations. The executions. Even the Tsar."

"The Tsar deserved to die. The Bolsheviks are honorable men."

The train began to chug forward with intermittent spurts. Those still in the dining car applauded. "Mr. Bullitt, you grew up privileged. You know little of the real world. Lenin wants a deal. He wants to push us aside and consolidate his position in Russia so he can launch the next phase of his worldwide Communist plan."

"You don't know that."

"We need to be aware of the realities and negotiate accordingly."

"I know what I need to do. We must contain the revolution. Not stamp it out."

"You're being played for a fool. Good night, Mr. Bullitt." Martin stood up and left.

It was close to 23:00. Martin entered the carriage that contained his cabin just as a woman in a black woolen coat scurried toward the next carriage. From the back, he could not guess her age, but from her lithe movements he guessed she was no older than thirty. The proportion of her shoulders in comparison to her head, a feature unique to every individual, looked strangely familiar to Martin, a trained observer. But she disappeared into the next carriage before he could recognize her.

An envelope protruded from under his cabin door. He picked it up and bolted his door. "Major Martin" was scratched on the front of the envelope. Inside was a note written in French with a delicate, almost spidery hand. "Be careful. Men have just boarded the train. Danger imminent."

Chapter 37
A Noise

On the Tracks to Moscow: March 1919

"Imminent." The word struck Martin like a high-caliber bullet. He read the note twice, and retrieved his .45 from his valise. He slammed a magazine into the grip, knelt behind the door, and listened. The noise from the grinding wheels and piercing train whistle made it difficult to hear. The train continued to sputter and stop.

Then he heard it. A slight noise. A shuffling foot? He listened again, ear to the door. A slight squeak as if someone's shoes needed a new heel. Whispers. Two men. The hammer of a gun pulled back. Crouching low, Martin moved as far away as possible and aimed the .45 at the door. The cabin was narrow, wide enough for the bed, hardly enough room for one man to fight for his life. Vulnerable, he could only wait.

The door to his cabin splintered open. The lead attacker burst into the room with a Russian Nagant revolver. Stumbling after him, the second man, built like a longshoreman, gripped a Luger in his right hand and a twenty-five-inch Lebel bayonet in his left. Off-balance from his effort against the door, the first man made a sudden sideways turn. Martin pulled the trigger but missed as the train lurched forward and stopped again. His second shot hit his attacker in the left shoulder below the collarbone. Blood spurted, but the man seemed to absorb the blow. He raised his revolver and grunted something. *Was that French?* Before his assailant could squeeze off a shot, Martin steadied himself and fired. The bullet hit him in the jaw. The assailant froze. His eyes glassed over. He fell to his knees and collapsed onto Martin, causing his next shot to miss the second attacker.

Pinned by the downed assassin and trapped in the narrow space, Martin pulled the dead body over himself for cover. The unsteady train was Martin's ally. The second man's bullet lodged in the dead man's back. Martin's .45 caliber slug hit the attacker's hand, knocking away the gun. Two bullets left. The man righted himself and gaped at his bloody hand, breathing hard as watery mucus gurgled out of his nose.

The tiny cabin made Martin feel like he was fighting in a coffin. The attacker pointed the long bayonet and charged. Martin ducked to the side at the last moment. The bayonet lodged in the wall below the window, leaving the attacker vulnerable. Martin shot him close up. The powder singed the man's clothes and the bullet lodged in his gut. He doubled over, but amazingly did not fall. His flailing arm hit the ceiling of the cabin. He backed away, reached into his coat with his good hand, and pulled out a six-inch blackjack with metal studs. His vicious backhanded swing landed a blow on the right side of Martin's head between the hairline and his eye. The pain was immediate and crippling.

On reflex, Martin shot again. His last bullet. The man grunted in pain and dropped. Dizzy, his vision blurred, blood seeping to the floor, Martin struggled to reload his .45 just as a third attacker entered. His gun empty, the Russian revolver out of reach, Martin flopped down, feigning death. The bluff worked. The third man ignored him and lifted the gut-shot man to his feet with a grunt. The two attackers picked up their dead comrade and fled.

Martin tried to stand, but fell. He pushed a new magazine into the .45 and crawled by act of will to the doorway, stopping to fight back nausea and vertigo. He peeked into the corridor, pointing his gun at the fleeing men. The wounded one was coughing and struggling to keep pace. "Stop!" Martin ordered with the little energy he had.

The third man stopped, turned, and fired two wild shots. Martin ducked back into his cabin. He fainted to the sound of shouts.

~

Martin felt someone dabbing his throbbing head. He blinked. His left eye opened, and he realized he was lying on a bed. His right eye stung from his bloody wound.

"Are you all right?" Bullitt asked, sounding genuinely worried.

Next to Bullitt stood a man in a Russian captain's uniform who seemed to be in charge.

"Where are they?" Martin asked.

"Who?" The Russian captain said in passable French.

"Three men. Military types. Well-built, around thirty years old. Peasant clothes. Well-armed." *French speaking?* Martin paused at the thought.

"Robbers?"

"Assassins. They must have jumped on the train when it stopped to clear the snow." Daylight was shining in from the window. "What time is it?" Martin asked, alarmed. "It's morning? The investigation? We must hurry."

The Russian captain said they had followed the trail of blood to the adjacent carriage, where the assailants must have jumped off. He and his men had interrogated potential witnesses, but no one saw anything useful. The train had already made its morning stop, and many passengers had disembarked. New passengers had boarded. "What about the woman who ..." Martin stopped.

"What woman?"

Martin touched his head, pretending to look confused. "Who? Sorry. Mistaken."

"I regret, but we will never solve this case," the Russian said. "Too many other concerns now you're safe."

"We have to think about our mission," Bullitt said.

"We will get your friend to a hospital when we reach Moscow in a few hours," the Russian captain added. "Rest until then, Major Martin."

Martin closed his eyes and wondered. Many questions in his mind followed him into unconsciousness.

Chapter 38
Moscow

Moscow: March 1919

Martin felt a debilitating pain in his head. He touched his face and felt a bandage partially covering his right eye. He strained to open his left. Blurs. Had he survived the Western Front just to be cracked in the skull by a ... what? Assassin? Imperialist? Communist? A Frenchman? He felt anxious, vulnerable, alone. He struggled to lift himself up but fell back down on the bed. A bed? Blessed Mary.

Where am I? A fearful antiseptic smell, a soldier's nightmare, stung his nose and mixed with the sour odor of stale vomit on his roughly starched sheets. He felt the metal rails on his bed and heard muffled chatter — Russian? — and frantic activity outside his room. He rubbed his good eye, willing himself to see, and his vision began to clear.

A woman dressed like a nun entered and said something he did not understand. She had the cold, detached face of someone who had seen too many men in his condition. He spoke to her in English and French, but she shrugged her shoulders, gestured for him to open his mouth, and shoved a thermometer in it. She tapped her feet, appearing to count off the seconds. A minute later she checked the reading, smiled reassuringly — could mean anything, nurses never conveyed the truth — and wrote something on a chart by the foot of his bed. She left without further comment.

What day was it? What was happening with Bullitt? Martin's suitcase was on the floor by the chair near his bed. A change of clothes hung over it. He prayed House's money was still there, safely hidden. He swung his feet to the floor and tried to stand, but he lost his balance and crumpled back onto the bed and renewed blackness.

A deep voice startled him awake. Martin tried to concentrate. The door to his room was closed, and the curtain was drawn. A man began to speak French with a strong Russian accent. Martin collected his thoughts and assessed him. He wore an encouraging smile, a grayish-white doctor's coat, and a cap like Lenin's. His reddish beard was well-trimmed in pre-revolutionary Tsarist style. Martin could not guess the man's age, but his sagging gut and slight stoop hinted at affluence now gone. Something was not right.

"Where am I?" Martin asked.

"Moscow. This hospital now serves the proletariat elite. One autocracy replaces another. No change. Except for the dead."

"How did I get here?"

"You've suffered a concussion. You're lucky that's all. There was some worry it was worse. The men who attacked you were not Russian. Their remains will never be found. Attacking American diplomats invited here by the Bolsheviks was foolhardy." The man peeked through the curtain and surveyed the street. He was more relaxed when he turned back to Martin. "Call me Nicolai."

Martin was confused and unsteady. "Who are you?"

"We have a mutual friend and share common interests. What I am telling you is important. In Russia, we hide secrets from friends and reveal all to strangers. Curious world." Nicolai checked his watch. "Time is short. Listen. Ask your questions when I'm done."

Martin nodded, but wondered how much to trust.

At a noise in the hallway, Nicolai reached toward the shoulder-holster bulge in his coat. He waited nervously, but withdrew his hand when the steps moved away. "I am not Bolshevik. The danger you face and the threats to the American delegation in Paris do not come from Moscow. Look to French radicals."

"Who?"

"The world has fractured into competing forces. Good? Bad? Who can tell? What difference does it make? Danger is everywhere, so beware."

"What are you trying to say?"

"The Western Allies have made a mistake by thinking of Communism as one world force. Lenin might believe that will happen in the future, but not now. Today, Lenin is too preoccupied with problems in Russia to cause trouble in Europe. His government is barely hanging on. His Red Army is battling the White Russians on six fronts. Your Allied powers have sided against him and have troops in Siberia, Murmansk, and elsewhere. An army of former Czech prisoners is rampaging across the country, and Moscow has no means to stop them. A British blockade has cut off foreign trade. Russia is facing economic collapse. Its energy and transportation sectors are crashing. Moscow has no chance to repay its war debts even if Lenin were so inclined. Dead bodies litter the streets because there is no means to collect and bury them. More than sixty percent of the population is starving. In short, Major Martin, Comrade Lenin's position is desperate. He will do anything — lie, cheat, plead — to improve it."

How does he know my rank? "Who has attacked us in Paris? And the Communist insurrections in Germany? They originated here, did they not?"

"A dish can have many varieties. Recipes change as they cross borders. Political thought too." Nicolai paused to recheck the window. He turned back; a muscle twitched over his eye. "The Communist menu has mass appeal. Many believe it will spread."

"You mean the Bolsheviks haven't yet started to expand their reach in the west?"

"Propaganda, yes. Ideas, literature, talk, yes. Money,

sometimes. Fighting, no. That is local. Germany is ruined. It is ripe for Communist takeover. Anarchy and revolution are main ingredients in such a rancid stew."

"What about France?"

Nicolai checked his watch and stood up. "I must leave."

"And the woman on the train?"

Nicolai waved away the comment. "Last thought. The Bolsheviks need a treaty with the Allies. Concede, gain time, grow stronger, refute prior commitments, attack. That is how Lenin operates. He did this with Germany in 1918."

"The Brest-Litovsk treaty was a disaster for Russia," Martin said.

"Lenin needed to end the war. He didn't care how or what he had to sign. Stopping the war let him consolidate his revolution. He had no intention of honoring the terms when they no longer suited him. The man who helped negotiate Brest-Litovsk is talking to your Mister Bullitt right now."

"Georgy Chicherin?"

"A capable man. Lenin needs that treaty."

"How long have the negotiations been going on?"

"A day and a half, right after they brought you here."

Suddenly, Martin heard several cars drive up fast to the hospital. Brakes squealed. Doors slammed. Men shouted orders. Nicolai jumped to the window, peeked out the curtains, and started to tremble. "I've stayed too long. Good luck." He pulled out his revolver and dashed out.

Martin struggled to the window. As far as he could see, the hospital was surrounded with military and other vehicles. Police and men in leather coats were patrolling the area, guns drawn. A few minutes later, Nicolai, now wearing a heavy sweater instead of a doctor's coat, tried to sneak out but never had a chance.

Martin turned away. The volley of gunshots rang in his ears. Screams, then silence. He checked his suitcase. The money was still there.

~

After a period of fitful rest, Martin slid out of bed. Wincing, he began to put on his clothes. It took several painful minutes. He had just buttoned his shirt when the Russian captain from the train breathlessly entered his room. He seemed startled to see Martin dressed. "Leaving?"

"What just happened? I was asleep and heard gunshots."

"A counter-revolutionary was shot. We've been looking for him for a long time."

Did they find him through me? Who are my enemies? My friends? Martin sat back on his bed and pretended to fight a headache. On guard, he studied the captain for clues.

"Pain? I expect so. Two inches either way and that baton would have cracked open your skull. I was coming to check on your condition when my men spotted him. Lucky break."

Does he know Nicolai spoke to me? Martin squeezed his eyes shut to exaggerate his pain. It was not much of an act.

The captain took off his coat and sat on the chair by the bed. He gave the suitcase a knowing look. He crossed his legs leisurely, but his eyes were steady, never blinking, always questioning. Martin had used the same look on suspected saboteurs in his Bomb Squad days. The captain took out a pack of cigarettes and offered one to Martin. "Russian. Strong, but good. I know you smoke."

How does he know that? Martin took a cigarette knowing it would be better not to accept anything from the captain. "Never had a bad cigarette."

The captain took a long pull on his cigarette and exhaled a cloud of smoke right at Martin. "I have more questions about the incident on the train. Let me introduce myself. Comrade Pavel Vasin of the Cheka."

Martin gulped. He had read intelligence reports about the Cheka before he left Paris. *Extraordinary Commission. State security, Lenin's henchmen. Avoid at all costs.* Martin detailed all he could remember about the train incident, excluding the note. Vasin asked about his recent visitor. If the Cheka was interested in Nicolai, Nicolai's warnings took on greater meaning and truth. Martin admitted that a man had come by his room, but said he had not recognized him. His vision was still poor. He was mostly asleep and did not understand why the man had come to his room. He had no idea how long the man had stayed.

Vasin seemed to accept the story. He stood to leave. "The doctor has said you can go. Your safety is my concern. My men will escort you to the hotel where Mr. Bullitt is staying. He should be there shortly." Vasin seemed amused about something. "The hotel used to be the palace of a count. Now it's the People's Residence. I understand Mr. Bullitt is making progress with the talks."

Now under Cheka protection, Martin was not yet a prisoner, but no longer free. No more unexpected counter-revolutionary visitors. Only his diplomatic status and America's growing importance in international affairs could protect him.

~

Martin found Bullitt at the People's Residence spooning caviar onto toasted bread and looking pleased with himself. It was late afternoon and already dark. He looked up and said through a mouthful of crumbs, "How are you? We were worried."

Martin shrugged. "Better."

"My meetings are going splendidly. I met Comrade Lenin today." He washed his caviar down with champagne. "Impressive man. He seems amenable to our terms. He's letting Georgy Chicherin complete the deal."

Comrade Lenin? Nicolai had been right. "What terms are you offering?" Martin asked.

"I have written instructions from Colonel House." Bullitt patted his coat.

"Can you trust the Russians?" Martin remembered Nicolai had warned him that Lenin would sign anything to reach an agreement. He also knew the Allies had no stomach for a fight. United States military advisors had estimated 500,000 Allied troops would be needed to defeat the Bolshevik Red Army. The American people would not tolerate so large a commitment.

"I can make a deal with them."

"Don't overstate your authority."

"Once I have a deal, everyone will agree to it. President Wilson. Lloyd George. I spoke with him before I left."

"Don't be so sure," Martin said. "The situation is changing quickly, and the Russians are treacherous partners."

Chapter 39
Terms

Paris: March 1919

Five days after Martin left the Russian hospital, Bullitt's talks ended. Pavel Vasin and eight well-armed toughs escorted the Americans to the Moscow train station. Much to Martin's displeasure, Vasin insisted his men carry their bags. He pitched his suitcase hard at Vasin, who smirked as he picked up the case. The case was fifty thousand dollars lighter; someone had stolen the hidden money. Most likely it had been taken from his room after Martin had recovered enough to attend the last days of the meetings. The Cheka was the obvious suspect, but Martin had been in Russia long enough to know it would not have mattered even if he had solid proof.

Martin was not surprised when Vasin and his men accompanied them onto the train and kept watch over them. One of them had a deep red scar that cut across his cheek. Martin would never forget it. Martin called him Boris. He had the cold steely eyes of a killer and served as an armed guard, posted by his berth at night. He was rough and uncooperative whenever Martin wanted to leave his cabin. Were he and Bullitt prominent Russian guests the Cheka needed to protect, or dangerous subversives to be isolated from the masses? Martin concluded they were both and was relieved when Vasin bid them a terse goodbye at Helsinki. Martin arranged for two U.S. Marines to escort them to Paris.

During the long trip, Bullitt could not hide his excitement. "We have a deal. Excellent terms," he repeated frequently and loudly, ignoring Martin's warning to be more discreet. Despite Bullitt's confidence, Martin remained skeptical, the memory of his talk with

Nicolai still vividly fresh. He kept his distance from Bullitt when possible and ate with him out of courtesy, preferring to play cards and share war stories with the Marine veterans. The stitches in his skull were healing. His headaches were less frequent and intense. No further incidents occurred on the trip.

When they arrived in Paris, Martin went to Shannon to learn the latest developments. The peace talks had continued as laboriously as ever. Japan's demands on Germany's former territories in the Pacific, particularly in China, had become another difficulty. Although many issues remained unresolved, the discussions were beginning to address the most important issues of the entire conference — reparations and the question of Germany's responsibility for causing the war. Clémenceau was still running the talks but lacked his usual fire, undoubtedly due to his injuries from the assassination attempt.

Concerning Russia, the counter-revolutionary White Russian armies had won some important victories against the Bolshevik Red Army. Nicolai's warnings gained further credibility. No wonder Lenin wanted a treaty. Much to the shock of the Western powers, Hungary's new government had just fallen to local Communist leaders. Bolshevism was on the march across Europe. Lenin's predictions were coming true. To further enflame passions, Britain's recently appointed Secretary of War, Winston Churchill, arrived in Paris to garner support for the White Russians. People were listening. Worse, newspaper editorials and public opinion in Britain were taking a more strident stance against the Bolsheviks. Mr. Bullitt's proposed treaty seemed doomed.

Early the next day, Bullitt and Martin headed to House's office. Martin could not tell what House was thinking from his body language and demeanor. Bullitt had already telegraphed him some of the terms. "Sit down, gentlemen. I commend you on your work, Mr. Bullitt," House said. Almost as an afterthought, he added, "I understand you are better, Major."

Martin nodded.

House asked Bullitt to detail the terms Lenin had agreed to. Bullitt produced the treaty with all the official seals and Lenin's signature. Speaking quickly and with conviction, he rattled off the terms. All conflicting Russian parties would retain control of the territories they currently occupy pending a formal Peace Conference to be held soon. The Bolsheviks would thus cede control of the Baltic States and Finland, most of the Urals, Siberia, and Ukraine, and the vital Archangel and Murmansk harbors to White Russian and local nationalist forces. They would recognize Tsarist war debts, something they had never done before.

The Allies would promise to remove their entire forces from Russia and end the blockade. They would also stop all financial and military aid to the White Russians and would guarantee the White Russians would accept the conditions. Lenin gave the Allies one month to accept the deal. Bullitt ended by saying, "These are excellent terms. Better than we could have hoped for."

House rubbed his chin. "I will take this up with the president. Come back tomorrow. Thank you."

~

The next day, House informed Bullitt and Martin that the president did not reject the deal out of hand, but was irked that Lenin had given him a deadline. Given current public opinion in Britain, Lloyd George could not come to terms with the Communists. French approval was out of the question. America would not accept the treaty alone.

"Let's be clear about this." House outlined his concerns. Another Peace Conference would confuse and delay the current proceedings in Paris. Accepting this treaty would give Lenin and the Bolsheviks international recognition as the legitimate successors to the Tsar in areas they now controlled. The Allies would be compelled to guarantee the end of the Russian civil war and would be forced to abandon their White Russian friends.

House finished by stating that American public opinion would also be averse to a deal with Soviet Russia. The negative backlash could compel the Senate to reject the treaty. The president's dream of a League of Nations could be stillborn. "I am sorry, Mr. Bullitt, but the answer is no. The Allies will not sign this treaty."

Bullitt dropped his head and froze. His jaw clamped down so hard Martin feared he would break his teeth. When he had composed himself enough to speak, Bullitt threatened to resign and tell his friends in Congress the details about his trip. "You could have gotten a revolt. Now you will get a revolution. You have missed a great opportunity. This failure will haunt you for another hundred years." Bullitt stormed out.

Martin was not sure what to say next. Before he could raise the issue, House asked about the fifty thousand dollars. When Martin confessed it had been stolen, House let out an uncontrolled laugh, the likes of which Martin had never heard from the colonel. Stunned, Martin just looked on.

"I thought that might happen," House said. "A test — how treacherous were the Russians? Case proved, I guess. Did you look at the money carefully, Major?"

Martin's face wrinkled in confusion.

"Counterfeit. We didn't lose a thing."

Martin left House's office a few minutes later wondering what the month-long trip had meant. An unknown woman had saved him. A man had given up his life to tell him about Bolshevik intensions. His words burned in Martin's mind: "Your threat is in France, not Russia." He needed to rethink his investigations.

Chapter 40
A Sick Man

Paris: April 1919

Dressed like poor students, Martin and Shannon sat in the back of a small bistro in the Latin Quarter. Shannon had chosen this meeting place because it was popular with locals, not known in the British or American circles, and discreet. Its patrons were often lovers on an illicit rendezvous, never anarchists or American diplomats. Candles stuck in empty wine bottles provided most of the light. Cheap wine flowed freely, and conversations were in whispers.

It was their first meeting alone since he had met her after returning from Russia ten days ago. He had looked forward to talking with her and had hoped to relax tonight. She was the only person in Paris he could trust; the only one with whom he could be honest and unguarded. Her direct knowledge of the peace talks helped him understand the participants. Her insights guided his actions.

Now recovered from his injuries, Martin had had little free time. Even though no further threats had occurred since Clémenceau's shooting, much work had accumulated. Aside from his normal duties, four problems dominated his time: Bullitt and the mystery surrounding his Russian trip, the investigations related to the coded messages, the attack on Clémenceau, and Mal the assassin.

Much to his dismay, Martin had to chaperone Bullitt everywhere. Whenever he could, the young diplomat told everyone that the Allied rejection of the treaty he had negotiated with Lenin was a tragic mistake. Bullitt bragged he would make sure Congress learned that he considered the rejection a folly. Martin had had to pull him away from a nosy reporter more than once, and he would be deeply relieved when Bullitt went home. “Soon,” House promised.

On his own time, Martin continued to investigate the attack on Clémenceau and the fire at the hotel. Aided by Nicolai’s information, he had narrowed his search to the French Communists, but he still was struggling to understand the depth of their threat. He needed Durand’s help, but was not sure how to get it. The French investigation had shut down since Cottin’s confession, and Durand was out of the country. Martin had neither the authorization nor the manpower to pursue a search. He hoped a lead would materialize, but despaired that one would not.

Martin vowed to uncover the men behind the attempt to assassinate him. This was as personal as his pledge to light candles for his wife Corinne, their baby, and Nicolai at Notre Dame Cathedral.

Shannon nudged him gently. “Gil, you listening?” The candles on their bistro table had burned down to nubs, and the café was emptying. Shannon peered across the room to see if anyone was listening. Martin sensed her suspicions, reached for her hand, and gazed at her. The nearly empty bottle of wine on their wobbly round table contributed to their masquerade.

“The president has aged considerably since you’ve been gone, Gil,” Shannon said softly in French. “He’s under enormous pressure. I’m worried. He’s not himself.” Shannon had been able to observe the president closely for several weeks, having returned to translation duties after her decoding work.

Martin agreed. “Something’s not right.” He confided that Colonel House had also been acting strangely. Sick and under great strain, the colonel seemed preoccupied. House had hardly spoken to Martin since his return from Russia, a sure sign something was amiss.

“The president is a sick man,” Shannon said. “Just look at him. He’s exhausted. His eye twitches. He’s abrupt and nervous.”

"Yesterday, the colonel told me he had argued with the president. I was shocked he mentioned it. The colonel is normally discreet. His frustration must be high."

"What were they arguing about?"

"The need for the Senate to confirm the treaty. House insisted he must obtain its approval. The secretary of state confirmed it, but Wilson disagreed. He's acting alone. We might never get a treaty unless the president starts to listen. Without a treaty, the League of Nations is dead."

"The president never meets with Colonel House anymore," Shannon said, redirecting the conversation.

"I overheard the colonel tell Secretary Lansing that Wilson is trying to do too much. He must delegate," Martin replied. Shannon's words forced him to confront something that he had observed since he had been back but had chosen not to think about — House's relationship with the president. It had deteriorated considerably in the last month. And if House's role in the talks had changed, so had his. Martin was House's man.

Shannon confirmed his suspicions. "I was told that the president mentioned to Lansing that you had done a bad job in Russia. Your security has been ineffective. Lies, I know, but if the president believes them ..."

Martin left the bistro wondering if he had wasted his time in Europe. Snow began to fall. Drops of melted flakes ran down his face. Could April start any worse? Maybe he would be fired and sent back to America. Fine with him. He had supported Wilson's League of Nations, but having seen how the peace talks had developed, Martin realized the "war to end all wars" was just a dream. The killing would go on, and he was still a cop pledged to capture the bad guys. And there were plenty of them in Europe — his trip to Russia had confirmed that.

He must continue until they fired him.

~

The following day, the peace talks started as laboriously as usual, but Shannon detected a new tension between the Big Four — France, Britain, America, and Italy. Japan had left the talks. The agenda had moved to the Balkans, and Italy's President Vittorio Orlando demanded that Italy be allowed to annex the Adriatic port of Fiume as a reward for its war efforts. The portly white-haired Italian looked more like a kindly grandfather than a world leader. He insisted Fiume had been promised to him when Italy joined the Allies in 1915. Now, Britain and France were reneging on their commitment, and Orlando threatened to leave the talks.

Shannon sensed a heated debate would erupt into an argument. President Wilson started to cough, and turned quiet. He looked dizzy, asked for a doctor, and suddenly collapsed. The doctor declared the president had succumbed to Spanish flu and prescribed rest. Shannon followed him to the ambulance in case he needed a translator.

~

That night at dinner, Shannon told Martin the doctors were covering something up.

"Why do you say that?"

"The president has circulation problems. I'm worried he might have had a stroke. If word ever got out ..."

"I can't believe it."

"The symptoms are there. At the hospital, the doctors seemed deeply concerned. Flu? No. I'm enough of a detective to add up the clues. Stroke." Shannon paused to collect her thoughts. The gravity of the situation made her lightheaded. She emptied her wine glass. "I've corresponded with Uncle Thomas. He's heard rumors about the president's health too. Who will replace him at the conference? Can it even continue without him?"

They ate in silence for a few moments until Martin broke the tension. "Colonel House confided to me that he'll take his place, but said nothing about the president's health. I'm going to escort the colonel to the talks tomorrow."

"He'll have a lot on his shoulders."

~

The day after House took over for President Wilson, an editorial from the London *Times* caused a ruckus throughout the U.S. delegation. It accused the president of hindering the talks with his rigid and impractical views, and went so far as to say Wilson had bungled negotiations at the conference. At the same time, it complimented Colonel House and suggested the talks advanced briskly under his direction in Wilson's absence. Wilson's idealistic advocates argued openly in the Crillon lobby with practical men who preferred House's approach.

Furious, House called Martin into his office. "Did you read this?" He threw the newspaper down on his desk. "Damn it. I don't disagree with everything they say, but the president will never trust me again."

"Maybe this will help him see the need for flexibility. He'll delegate more and let you make the deals," Martin said, trying to calm House down. But in his gut, he suspected the editorial was right. Everything he had heard from his friends in the Allied delegations confirmed it.

"The president is a proud and stubborn man. He's not open to suggestions that aren't his."

"What can I do to help?"

"Find out who's behind these attacks on us. That will let me regain my leverage with the president and deflect talks about our delegation's problems. It's up to you, Major. He'll be back at the talks in a few days."

~

The next night, when Martin met Shannon at the Crillon restaurant, she raised another problem. "Colonel Lawrence is fuming. He claims the Allies are neglecting Arab concerns. Today I overheard him in the hallway swear he will do something the Parisians will never forget. He doesn't make idle threats."

"Even the British say they're not sure he is one of theirs any more," Martin replied. "He's their problem, I say."

~

At lunch the next day, Shannon left for a walk. It was clear and sunny with a light, refreshing spring breeze. Several people looked up and pointed to the sky. A motor hummed, and a biplane with British markings flew low. The pilot's white Middle-Eastern headdress flapped in the wind behind him. He tossed something out. Sheets of white paper followed. Heavens, could it be toilet paper? Some people were shocked, others amazed. Shannon laughed. True to his words, Lawrence of Arabia had mocked the Peace Conference.

~

Not far away, Wolf, now in Paris on an advance scouting mission for the Freikorps, spied the biplane and had different thoughts. *If someone can fly over Paris and drop toilet paper without being shot down, ...*

Chapter 41
An Evening at the British Delegation

Paris: April 1919

Five days after President Wilson's collapse, Martin met Shannon in the lobby of the Crillon to discuss the president's first day back at the talks. Martin was keen to learn what had happened. "The president is fuming," she began.

"Not here." They walked in silence to a quiet section in the reading room. "The London *Times* editorial has hit our delegation like a bomb," Shannon continued. The president was incensed they called him a bungler. I have never seen him so angry. He told Secretary Lansing that Colonel House is not in charge of U.S. policy. *I* am."

"Let's hope things calm down. Nerves are frayed. Everyone is worried about Wilson's health. The rift between the president and Colonel House will be hard to close," Martin said.

"I have to admit Colonel House has done an excellent job at the conference. He knows how to get things done," Shannon said.

"That won't matter to the president."

"But if they can't reconcile, what does that mean to the peace talks? The president needs the colonel to get any treaty through Congress. If they're estranged, I have no idea what Congress will do. What will happen if they reject it?"

"It will ruin the president. Maybe kill him. And condemn Europe to a new, even bloodier war."

"Things will work out," Shannon said. "They must. We've both had a hard day, and I need a drink." They went to the bar and ordered a bottle of their best Château Latour Bordeaux. "Did you get an invitation to the British delegates' reception tomorrow night at their hotel?" Shannon asked, after enjoying a glass.

Still worried about the friction between the president and Colonel House, Martin was only half listening. "Sorry. What?"

"To the British delegates' reception tomorrow night at their hotel. I'm sure you've been invited."

"I'll check." His tone conveyed disinterest.

"Everyone will be there. Come on, we'll go together. I could use a change."

"If you insist." He did not have the will to fight her.

"I need to buy a new dress. I hear Maison Martine around the corner has all the latest fashions."

Martin shrugged his shoulders.

"Wear your dress uniform."

~

Their military driver pulled in front of the Majestic Hotel on 19 Avenue Kléber, three blocks from the Arc de Triomphe. As Martin escorted Shannon through the grand hallway, with its high ceilings, polished wood with gold inlaid decorations, and Louis XIV furniture, he noticed everyone looking at them. Despite the popularity of Americans and the medals on his uniform, he knew Shannon was the attraction. Her husband would have been speechless seeing her. She wore a wide-brimmed hat tilted at an alluring angle and pumps that made her almost as tall as he was. Her oriental-patterned silk dress made a swishing sound as she walked. The waistline was set just above the hips, and the hemline fell just below the knees, a recent fashion trend that Martin was having trouble accepting. His wife would never have worn anything so revealing. Much had changed during the war.

After checking their hats and coats, they entered the main room's gilded elegance through an archway that reached to the ceiling. The room was framed by Greek columns and intricate Roman mosaics along the baseboard. The artwork alone was worth a king's ransom. To Martin it was just another room in a fancy Parisian hotel. He was tired of Paris's past opulence and uncertain future. He preferred New York City's adolescent vitality and consuming energy.

Shannon and Martin mingled for a few minutes and said a few words in passing to members of the U.S. delegation. In the center of the room, Martin noticed the broad shoulders and stiff, but dashing, posture of a white-haired American officer at the center of a group of military men with competing amounts of braid and ribbons. General Black Jack Pershing himself. An attractive young lady, obviously not his wife, clung to his side. She and Shannon dueled momentarily with their eyes. Martin, aware of Pershing's reputation as a philanderer, was nevertheless surprised he had so little care for proper decorum. Embarrassed, he turned to Shannon. "Let's get out of here. I don't want to be privy to a scandal."

Before he could pull Shannon away, the commander of the American Expeditionary Forces turned around, winked at Martin, and smiled at Shannon in a way that made Martin uncomfortable. Pershing whispered something to his escort, who stomped back several paces. The general called him over. "Major Martin. Join us. Please bring your friend."

Shannon leaned over and whispered, "I'd like to meet him. This will be fun."

Martin walked over and saluted. "Good to see you, General. You look well. May I introduce Mrs. Paul Keller? She's part of the U.S. delegation and the wife of Lieutenant Keller. You surely remember him."

The general frowned. Five yards away, Pershing's companion stared at Shannon like a boxer measuring a foe at the start of a prize fight. Shannon countered by tossing her thick red hair and rolling her head toward the general. Martin had never seen her react to another woman like this before and was intrigued by the contest.

"Of course," General Pershing said. "Brave man. And how are you, my boy?"

"Fine, General. Thank you."

"By the way, where is Colonel House?"

"Not feeling well, General. He had to decline the invitation."

Pershing's attention moved to Shannon then back to Martin. "Heard you might have had some issue with the president concerning the Bullitt mission. Crazy business, that. We can't trust the Communists."

"I agree," Martin said, wondering about the general's motives. *Is he implying that he'd trade a few good words on my behalf for a chance at an evening with Shannon?*

"I'll speak to the president again. I'll straighten out any concerns he might have about you. The role of the AEF isn't completed here. We need our best men." The general leered again at Shannon.

True to her nature, Shannon took the offensive. She turned in a way that emphasized the profile of her slim waist and well-filled dress. "I've heard so much about your conquering ways, General," she said. "All of Paris talks about them." She reached for some champagne from the tray of a passing waiter and took a long sip.

Martin almost gagged but trusted Shannon enough to let her continue.

"My dear, you are most kind." Pershing moved closer and put his arm around her shoulders.

Shannon pivoted and spun away from his grasp. "You flatter me, General, but I am more interested in your marksmanship. I bet I can outshoot you in a contest."

Martin tried to keep a poker face. It was no secret in Police Headquarters that, before the war, Shannon had practiced for hours and hours with every firearm in its arsenal. She vowed to be as good a shot as any man on the Bomb Squad. According to the men who had seen her shoot, she was. In Paris, she had often gone shooting to relax, and Martin had supplied the guns and bullets. Shannon was likely to win, and he guessed the general knew it too.

"I'll bet you an excellent dinner on the town if you win. Just you and me," she said in a velvet voice.

"Such bravado. I like that," Pershing chuckled. "On the outside chance I lose, what do you win?"

"Bragging rights." Shannon smiled. "I'll tell everyone I beat you. I know some French journalists who would love to judge the contest."

Pershing coughed and checked his watch. "I shall try to arrange it. In the meantime, I have a meeting with the Belgians. It was a pleasure to meet you, Mrs. Keller." He turned to Martin. "Lieutenant Keller has quite a firecracker on his hands," he said under his breath. "I'll speak to the president on your behalf, Major."

As the general glided away with his companion, Martin looked at Shannon and tried not to laugh. Piano music filled the room as a few people cheered. The room quieted as everyone turned toward the sound. "Lively song. What is it?" Martin asked Shannon.

"'*Esmeralda,'* by Cole Porter. Everyone in Paris knows it. You must."

"I haven't had time for recreation in years."

"Porter himself is playing," said Shannon as her feet started to tap to the rhythm. Porter continued, playing a generous set that elicited claps and whistles so loud Martin could not hear what Shannon was saying. Porter stood, bowed, and urged on by the crowd, returned to the piano to play another song.

Martin noticed John Maynard Keynes near the bar drinking something colorless. He liked Keynes, but had not seen him since they had cracked the code, and was anxious to talk to him. A British colonel and another person he knew from the Canadian delegation moved toward the mathematician.

At the sight of their approach, Keynes squeezed his face as if he had eaten a lemon. He hastened to greet Martin and Shannon. "Good to see you, Mrs. Keller, Major. I have not seen you in weeks." A French reporter Martin had repeatedly chased away from the Crillon came within eavesdropping distance.

"Mr. Keynes, a moment. Let's move somewhere quieter." He looked at Shannon and gestured toward the reporter.

Shannon moved to intercept the reporter. "*Monsieur* Lebeau, isn't it? What interesting things can you tell me?" she asked in a voice of authority.

When it was safe to speak, Martin said, "I'm glad to see you. I wanted to get your thoughts about the progress of the talks."

"Worried about them?"

"That article in the London *Times* has caused a real stir in our delegation."

"The real concern is graver."

"I thought you might say that."

"The talks have moved to the question of reparations from Germany. Once decided, the Allies will invite German delegates to receive the terms, but there is a problem." Keynes explained that the Allies were seeking to impose such harsh reparations they could strangle Germany. No one had any idea how to calculate the damages caused in the war, and most of the proposals were ludicrous and destructive. The defeated powers needed to rebuild their economies, and that required money. Unfortunately, the Allies had rejected his proposition that poorer countries issue bonds guaranteed by America and Britain. "We have to give Germany a means to recover. Only then can Germany pay us back. My colleagues want revenge, but do not realize Europe is dying. I fear for the future, Major Martin."

"What can we do?"

"Hope more pragmatic heads will prevail. Talk to your Mr. House. I think he understands."

They shook hands. Martin needed quiet. He walked up the street, sat on a bench, and gazed at the Arc de Triomphe. While deep in thought, he sensed someone approach from behind.

A soft voice said, "Don't look at me. Be careful. Danger is everywhere." A deep breath. "Nicolai was my friend. You and I share a common enemy. Meet me tomorrow." Martin felt a paper slip into his pocket. By the time he turned around, the person had disappeared.

Chapter 42
Irrefutable Evidence

Outside Paris: April 1919

The next night Martin met his informant at a rundown café outside the city. "This is the man you want. If you don't believe me, go to his apartment. The proof is there. *Bonne nuit.*" They shook hands, and the informant crept back into the shadows.

Watching the flight of his perplexing new ally, Martin knew he had to act fast. Powerful forces were certain to marshal against him. His enemy had rank. He was convinced the informant had revealed the truth: details about the fire at Le Grand Hotel; the note on the train; Nicolai; the Cheka. Everything now made sense, except for one thing. Why had the contact come forward now? Battling his concerns, Martin called Durand, now back from Algeria, and asked to meet immediately on the Pont de Neuilly on the northwest outskirts of town.

~

One hour later, they were both looking down at the rushing water of the Seine. Martin disclosed the name of their enemy.

"Impossible," Durand said. "He's a war hero, one of the most influential men in Paris. I know he's hindered our investigation, but he's not a traitor."

"We have to raid his apartment. Can you arrange it?"

"If you're wrong, we'll both be guillotined."

"If I'm right, we could save France."

"Give me a day. I still can't believe it's Truchon."

~

The next afternoon, Martin, Durand, and six soldiers armed with shotguns, sword bayonets, and high-caliber handguns entered

Truchon's fashionable three-story apartment building. The men smelled of sweat, anticipation, and wine — a classic raid, French-style. The lead soldier, a sergeant, carried a sledge hammer. It was after 15:00 and noisy children were coming home from school. *Give up peacefully, Colonel. Please. We don't want innocents to die in a crossfire.* The lead soldier put a finger to his lips. The kids backed away and faded into their flats.

Martin prayed he was right to trust his informant. It was a gamble, but he was used to those. The sergeant rapped on the door. No answer. He looked at Durand, who gestured yes, and took a vicious swing with the sledge hammer. It smashed into the lock and the door groaned open. The only response was the angry yowl of a cat that retreated back into the apartment.

Martin pushed through the soldiers. "Me first." If this were a trap, Martin was determined to at least be the first victim. As instructed, his six-solider assault squad held at the door, all heads turned for instruction. Martin entered with careful and methodical steps, and looked for explosives as Durand posted more men around the building. After securing the apartment, Martin called him for support.

Together, they carefully searched for secret compartments in the walls, opened every container and cabinet in the kitchen, and checked for loose tiles in the bathroom. Nothing.

"You sure it's here?" Durand asked.

"It must be," Martin said, more from hope than conviction. "We'll tear this place apart later if we have to."

"What now?"

"We wait."

The minutes froze into hours. Sitting in the living room, Durand ran the flat side of his bayonet against his thigh. Up and down. Over and over. His eyes stayed fixed on the broken front door. He looked ready to pounce. To ease his own tension, Martin reviewed all possible scenarios. What would the confident and wily commandant do when he arrived? Lie? Protest? Confess? Martin hoped he would fight. He rubbed the scar, still red, on his forehead and looked at his watch. Three minutes had passed since he had last looked.

The sound of the elevator stopping at the top floor jarred Martin into action. He jumped to his feet and concealed himself behind the sofa. Durand stood to the right of the front door. His men, hiding in the foyer behind a bend in the hallway, would move behind the commandant, catching him in a trap. The elevator door opened.

The sound of boots headed toward the apartment abruptly stopped. "What the hell?" Martin realized Truchon had seen the battered front door. Martin stood and pointed his .45 as Durand pulled Truchon inside by his coat. One of Durand's men followed, poking the barrel of his shotgun into the small of Truchon's back.

"We need to talk, *mon Commandant*." Durand forced him onto the ground face first and dug his knee into Truchon's shoulder blades, pinning his head sideways into the rug.

"I'll have you shot for this," Truchon said through forced breaths. "What have I done?"

"You tell me." Durand dug his knee deeper into Truchon.

"Captain, why don't you let Commandant Truchon sit so we can talk to him like gentlemen," Martin suggested.

Durand extended a hand, but punched Truchon in the gut when he was upright. The commandant doubled over, gasped, and fought for air.

Martin wanted to strike him too, but controlled his temper. Durand and one of his men tossed Truchon, still coughing, onto the sofa as if he were a carcass of beef ready for the butcher.

The commandant did not react. He brushed off his clothes and sat up. *He doesn't rattle,* thought Martin. He related what he knew and added conjecture, presenting them as facts.

"Where is it?" Durand slapped Truchon across the cheek. Martin could almost feel the sting.

Truchon defied the insult. "When we finish here, you two will be breaking rocks on Devil's Island for the rest of your lives. I have nothing else to say."

Stalemate.

In a corner of the room, the cat was sniffing and scratching the rug near the window. When Martin walked over, the floor boards softened, then squeaked. He stopped and looked down. Suspicious, he stepped on the same spot with a heavy foot. The squeak was louder. Martin glanced at Truchon, but the commandant remained stone-faced. "Alain," he called to Durand. "Help me move this rug."

Martin knelt down and felt around the area as if he were looking for a bomb. One board seemed a bit out of alignment, its edges narrower than the rest. He pressed down, and the board weakened almost imperceptibly. He dug his fingertips into the narrow gap at the top corner of the board, but he could not lift it.

Durand handed him a bayonet, handle first.

Martin pressed the tip down into the crack and pried up. The board began to lift. He heard a mouse run under the floor. The cat chased the sound. Out of the corner of his eye, he saw Truchon's hand grasp the arm of the sofa. Martin pulled out a silver box, about six by nine inches and four inches deep, and a stiff piece of cardboard folded in half. He silently thanked his informant.

The cardboard opened into a chessboard with the same letter and number pattern as the one Shannon had used to break the cipher. Here was the key he had used to code and send out his secret orders.

Truchon groaned like a wounded animal at the sight.

Martin held out the chessboard. “Why didn’t you destroy it?”

“Why? I designed it.”

“Fool.” Martin gave the chessboard to Durand and punched out the lock on the box with the bayonet. Inside were papers and stacks of unused American currency in twenty and fifty dollar bills. He seized one stack and shuffled through it as if it were a deck of cards. He examined one bill. Definitely counterfeit. He pulled from his pocket the list of serial numbers House had given him. A match. Truchon had been paid by the Cheka with counterfeit money they had stolen from him. The Communist connection.

“Large sum of money.”

Truchon spat at him.

“Do you know the name Pavel Vasin?” Martin countered. Truchon’s surprised look told it all. “Did you look at these bills closely, Commandant? Counterfeit. Stolen from me in Russ—”

Truchon’s hand moved quickly. He pulled out a Lebel from the drawer next to the sofa and pointed the gun at his head. “I am a French patriot, and a Communist,” he declared. “*Vive la révolution!*” He pulled the trigger.

Chapter 43
71 Rue de Lille

Paris: April 1919

"That should end it," Martin said to Shannon when he returned to the Crillon. "At least I hope so. We've cut off the head of the French Communist movement. The only remaining threat is that assassin, Mal. He's alone without resources. The French manhunt will get him soon enough." After Durand's men chopped through a secret hollow wall in Truchon's apartment Martin had discovered, they found hand-drawn maps of the Crillon and Majestic Hotels; a list of men, probably agents, informants, and contacts; addresses of known Bolshevik headquarters in Hungary and Bavaria; a coded letter from Vasin; and *Communist Internationale* periodicals. "No doubt about Truchon's loyalties."

"You've cut away the cancer," Shannon said. "Just in time. The talks have reached the final stage. Clémenceau announced they would invite the Germans to receive the terms in less than two weeks." She added that Wilson and Lloyd George had guaranteed France's security against future aggression. Orlando was about to return from Italy. The final borders of the broken-up empires of Russia, Austria-Hungary, and the Ottomans still needed to be fixed. Shannon finished her tea, and they sat in comfortable silence for a few moments. "What now?"

Martin let out a deep sigh. "Plan what we'll do once the Germans are here. From what Mr. Keynes said, they'll be shocked when they learn the terms. They're a far cry from those they thought they had accepted when they signed the armistice. I'll be glad when it's over, and we can go home."

"Then you'll be free tomorrow? It's Saturday."

"Dare I ask why?"

"A party at Louise Cromwell Brooks's townhouse. The first this spring. Everyone talks about her parties. We can't miss it."

Martin frowned. "Wasn't the British reception enough fun?"

~

Martin parked his sedan on the Rue de l'Université two blocks away from the townhouse Mrs. Brooks rented at 71 Rue de Lille in the exclusive 7th arrondissement across the street from the Gare d'Orsay. The townhouse was located a block away from the left bank of the Seine across from the Jardin des Tuileries. The streets were already full of parked vehicles, presumably from people attending the party. When Martin reached the narrow Rue de Lille and saw 71 squeezed between two other houses in typical Parisian fashion, he was surprised. *This is what everyone is talking about? I assume the interior is more elegant.*

As they approached 71, a few members of the U.S. delegation walked in, looking drunk. Accompanying them were two young women who could not have been their wives. The men in the U.S. delegation had not brought their spouses to France.

"A quarter of our people go there every night," Martin said. In his job, he had heard much about these gatherings. "She is the center of the Anglo-American social world in Paris. She's Philadelphia Main Line upper crust."

"Some consider her beautiful. Others say she's a seductress," Shannon said. The glamorous Mrs. Henrietta Louise Cromwell Brooks, now divorced, had come to Paris with an unattached companion, Elsa Maxwell. Apparently, they were in the husband-seeking business, and gossips hinted that Mrs. Brooks was closing in on the youngest general in the American Army. "Watch out, General MacArthur."

"He deserves her." When Martin was on Pershing's staff, he had often disagreed with the young general, whom he considered a glory seeker and blindly ambitious. Brave, though, and a good commander.

Before Martin could ring the bell, a doorman in a waistcoat opened the door, took their invitations, and invited them in.

A few steps behind the doorman, an attractive woman in her late twenties stood in the richly decorated foyer. She had pale skin, white teeth, and moneyed airs. Her high cheekbones and fine-boned features conveyed a calculating intelligence. She introduced herself, "Mrs. Brooks," and extended her hand. "Welcome. I am so glad you've finally come to one of my parties, Major Martin. How nice to see you, Mrs. Keller. You two are friends, I gather."

"Thank you, Mrs. Brooks," Martin said. "Mrs. Keller and I know each other from New York. I worked for her uncle. Her husband is out of the country. I'm her chaperone tonight."

"Enjoy yourselves." Mrs. Brooks winked and moved on to her next guests.

Martin frowned. Shannon, always observant, placed her hand on his arm. "Relax, Gil. We will not be part of her scandals. Everyone in the U.S. delegation understands that I am happily married, and you are the most honorable man among them. She pulled him closer and whispered, "How does she know our names? She's never seen me before."

Martin laughed. "She makes it her business to know everyone with influence. If she doesn't know someone, she asks. She's everywhere. I've often seen her in our hotel."

They moved into the sitting room where several people, including Captain Durand, had circled around an overweight woman playing jazz on a piano. "Her protégée, Elsa Maxwell," Martin pointed out. "She plays quite well."

When Martin noticed General MacArthur among the onlookers, he said, "Let's move on. Nothing good will happen if I have to speak to him." On their way to the living room, they walked by a staircase where two men stood embracing. Martin was used to Paris's liberated ways and the lack of restraint in the post-war world. He did not care what people did in private.

"The old ways are gone, Gil. People are trying to forget the war however they can."

They moved to the large living room decorated in a blend of contemporary and traditional. It was crowded with people babbling away in at least five different languages. The overpowering smell of perfume permeated the room. A man in the shadows drew Martin's attention. He looked vaguely familiar, so Martin went over to investigate. By the time he got there, the man was gone. When Martin asked about him, people nearby said they had seen him before, but no one knew him. The only consensus was that he wore an eye patch.

Martin's attention was next caught by a woman looking, dream-like, through a window toward the street. From the way she was dressed, she craved attention. Her dress plunged at the neckline. Strings of pearls, some falling to her waist, cascaded in bunches from her neck. Colorful ribbons and medals of all sorts were pinned across the front of her dress. Her most striking attire was a golden headdress that looked like something an Aztec chief might wear. She was approaching middle age with a figure to confirm it, but Martin imagined that, at some point in her life, she had had few rivals. Tonight, she seemed more a curious artifact than a spidery temptress.

"Queen Marie of Romania," Martin said, anticipating Shannon's question. "Her scandals are the talk of Paris."

"That's her? You wouldn't believe what I hear about her at the Quai d'Orsay."

"She even tried to flirt with President Wilson."

"That Presbyterian? I would have loved to see that." Shannon continued to stare.

"Didn't bother her. She just moved on to her next conquest," Martin said. "She wants a good deal for Romania. And, from what I've heard, she's going to get it. They will annex Transylvania from Hungary."

"Oh, no — she's walking toward us."

The queen prowled toward Martin, put her hand on his arm, and said in accented French, "Major Martin, the hero of New York."

Martin cringed. He never considered himself a hero and hated to be called one. Had he not known the queen's father was the Duke of Edinburgh, he would have guessed she was a gypsy or an actress.

"What a pleasure to meet you." She kissed him on both cheeks, surprising him.

Although her direct assault made him uncomfortable, Martin quickly regained his composure. "Your Majesty." He bowed. "Your reputation in Paris does you no justice."

Shannon looked on in apparent amusement.

"I do so want to meet your Colonel House, Major," the queen said.

She'll have as much success with him as she had with the president, Martin thought.

"I understand he's the smartest man at the talks."

Flattery — her weapon.

Shannon curled her arm around Martin and pulled him close. "I am so sorry, your Majesty, the major is spoken for tonight."

"I'll give the colonel your greetings." Martin bowed again.

"Pity. Paris offers so many diversions these days," the queen said just before she turned away, heading for a British general sipping whiskey.

Martin saw James Brown Scott, a lawyer in the U.S. delegation, and waved to him. He respected Brown's competence and steadfastness.

A butler announced that a buffet, prepared by Chef Pierre, the former sous-chef at the Ritz and Mrs. Brooks's well-publicized friend, was ready in the dining room. People clapped. Everyone enjoyed coming to Mrs. Brooks's parties because of the excellent food.

On their way to the buffet table, Martin and Shannon walked into a parlor that was blocked by several men and at least two women. They were looking at a painter who was sitting in front of his easel finishing his work. His model, an exquisite beauty, stood with one hand on her hip and the other holding a snake draped over her shoulder. Nude, she looked at the artist provocatively. His painting had captured her raw allure.

"Another diversion, I guess. I'm jealous, though," Shannon said, studying the model head to toe.

Martin was not sure what to say. He had never before confronted such overt sexuality. This was not pre-war America with its prudish restraint. It was something else. Something new. Something dangerous. He was more intrigued by the confident and casual way the model displayed her nakedness than by its physical power. He overheard someone say she was one of the dancers at Paul Poiret's Oasis theatre and would dance later. Poiret was an inventive fashion designer and a popular social figure in Paris.

Shannon and Martin headed to the dining room where Martin began to fill his plate with oranges from Spain, slices of freshly baked baguettes, and a fragrant cheese soufflé. He looked up and did a double-take. To his surprise, Ana Primakova had just entered the room. She was staring at Captain Durand in the next room. Martin had to look twice to be sure it was her.

She was dressed in a sailor suit, a recent fashion sensation, which made her look athletic and feminine at the same time. Her light-brown hair was pulled back under a sailor's cap that added further mystery. She held a glass of red wine in a way Martin found entrancing. Ana's face was performance ready — one-half real, one-half staged, impossible to read, totally convincing. *Who was she acting for*? In the devious and treacherous Russian world, acting was how she stayed alive.

Ana was accompanied by a bald man in an ill-fitting suit. He was several inches shorter than she was, but he looked strong, and his lithe movements suggested he was fast. A Cheka man? He had his arm around her waist. Martin fought back a tinge of jealousy.

Shannon noticed Martin's reaction. "Who's that?"

"Ana Primakova. She's a Russian journalist." His eyes stayed fixed on Ana, but she did not appear to notice him.

"She's striking. How do you know her?"

"I met her during the fire." Martin could not disclose the details and the emotions he felt. He was not sure he understood them all himself. He was confused but could not deny his attraction to her. He admired her, yes. The story she had told him at their last meeting was sad but gripping. He understood she was a pawn in a global game.

But his attraction to her was deeper than that. Her bravery and intelligence were beyond question, but there was something else. The grace and dignity of a well-bred woman? Maybe, though Martin had never put much value in those things before. He had come to realize she had saved his life by placing that note on the train in Russia. His kindness to her after the fire at Le Grand Hotel was paid back in full, plus some. Yes, a lifelong debt.

But now, as his mysterious informant, she had reversed their roles by revealing Truchon's treachery. She had put her life in his hands, a trust he had to honor. Their mutual life-and-death bond was strong, but it did not explain everything. What else was it? Martin could not say, but he was sure it existed, yet uncertain how to confront it.

His concentration was disrupted when someone started to play a tango on a Victrola. People put down their plates and headed to the living room to dance to the decadent new rhythm. He heard the heels of the women's shoes strike into the floor to the music's beat. Shannon said something, but Martin shook his head and pointed to his ear.

Shannon cuffed her hands around his ear and said, "I don't trust her."

"I do. Come. Let me introduce you." They walked over to Ana, and Martin spontaneously kissed her on both cheeks. "Madam Primakova, it's good to see you. May I present Madam Shannon Keller?"

"My pleasure," Shannon said, keeping her distance.

Ana's Russian guardian tried to step between them, but she whispered something to him, and he walked away, maintaining constant vigil. Ana held out her hand and said to Shannon in excellent English, "I've seen you at the peace talks, Mrs. Keller. It is good to have a woman in such a prominent role. Congratulations. I am a great admirer of your Uncle Tunney."

Shannon seemed taken aback that a Russian journalist would know about the former head of the New York City's most elite police unit.

"I read your New York newspapers whenever I get a chance. I followed the stories about the German spies you brought down."

Martin interjected. "I'm surprised to see you here, Ana." As soon as he said it, he realized he had slipped and used her first name. Shannon looked at him curiously and excused herself to powder her nose. Martin guided Ana to a quiet corner of the room where her guardian could see but not hear them. "I thought you'd disappeared," he said.

"I can't. I'm still a journalist and have a job to do," Ana said.

"My guardian insists. I learn a lot when I cover these gatherings. I've never seen you here before."

"Your information was correct. Truchon is dead."

Ana closed her eyes. "Thank God."

"Who's your companion?"

"He watches me. I can handle him."

"I must escort Mrs. Keller back to the hotel. After that ..." Martin was not sure what to say next.

"When? Where?"

"Someplace private. I ..." Martin hesitated and looked deeply into her eyes. *Do I want to cross this bridge?*

Ana returned the look. "My place. One hour. Here's my address."

Chapter 44
The Treaty

Paris: May 1919

The sun was coming up when Martin, smelling of Ana's perfume, left her apartment in a rundown street near the Gare de l'Est. He was delirious with ... what? He had not tangled with these emotions in years. He felt exhilarated, numb, and conflicted. He had seen wounded soldiers in the same state of mind just before they died. He fought back guilt and prayed to his dead wife for understanding. *I'm sorry, Corinne. I succumbed to human weakness. No one can replace you. Not ... Ana. Ana? My God, what am I saying?*

Martin's car was parked on a dingy side street off the Boulevard de Strasbourg. The pavement was slick from a midnight storm. Fog cloaked the area like a thin veil. The streets, soon to be full of early morning laborers, were empty except for mangy dogs scavenging for scraps. The smell of decay and animal waste reminded him of the New York dockyards.

In this part of town, prostitutes, thieves, drunks, and destitute former soldiers prowled the streets looking for coin, drink, or opportunities, but Martin's thoughts were not on his safety. He scratched his day-old whiskers and wondered how he would return to the Crillon without someone asking a question about where he had been. Deep in thought, he neglected the first rule of the streets — be aware of your surroundings.

Two men in French Army field jackets stained in the back and armpits stood across the street from his car. Bulges at their sides and across their chests suggested they were heavily armed. The first man was turned away from Martin, but he was bald. Short but sinewy, he was built for speed, a runner. The second man was bulkier and had pulled up his collar. A blue service kepi hid the top of his face. They tossed away their smokes and pointed in his direction as if to say, "That's him."

Were they shadows looking to follow him or a direct threat? Without looking back, Martin crossed the narrow side street and walked toward the main boulevard to see how they would react. If they followed, he would lose them and double back to his car from a different direction. He quickly glanced over his shoulder and saw the men move toward him with the speed of elite soldiers. The heavy-set man made some gestures to the runner who sprinted away.

They were maneuvering to trap him front-to-back. Martin cursed his carelessness and reached for his .45. *Christ, no.* He had left it in his car when he had gone to Mrs. Brooks's party. He tried to remain calm and assess the situation. As the bulkier man drew closer, Martin saw the vicious scar that cut across his cheek. It was Boris, one of the Cheka men who had escorted him back to Helsinki. Martin felt sick when Boris drew a revolver.

Martin fought to regain his composure. Had Ana set him up? At twenty-five yards, Boris fired. The bullet whizzed by Martin's ear. He ducked low and zigged, trying to make it to the wide, busy boulevard where he would have a chance. A second bullet hit the street near his shoe. A chunk of pavement bounced up and nicked his leg. He was losing his breath. Martin ducked behind a wagon and looked for a weapon. Nothing, not even a rock. Two more bullets struck the wooden panel beside him. A splinter tore into his arm. His coat absorbed most of the force. Martin pulled it out, took two deep breaths, and ran.

Steal a car and crank it started? No time. Any moment, he expected to see the runner. If he did, Martin would be dead seconds later. He willed himself to outrun his pursuers, but his lungs protested.

Think. There — a shop door. If he could get inside, maybe he would have a better chance than — locked. Martin kicked it with all the power he could muster, but it did not budge. A bullet crashed into the door above his head. Boris was closing in.

Martin reached the Boulevard de Strasbourg but was losing ground with each step. He had the faint hope that someone would help, a cop starting his rounds maybe, but cops were as scarce as a table full of food around here, and this was a neighborhood where people minded their own business. Martin turned into a narrow alleyway. If he could hide there or crawl into a window ... . After three paces, he realized his mistake. Just brick walls. No doors. No escape.

He looked back in desperation. Boris was fifteen yards to his left. A gunshot came from his right. The runner. Martin recognized him — Ana's bodyguard from last night. The bullet grazed his arm. His two assailants converged, forcing him to retreat deeper into the alley. They had stopped shooting. They did not want to kill him. They wanted to capture and question him. *What had Truchon said before he died?* By running into the alley, he had made it easy for them.

As he raised his arms in surrender, the burning impact of a bullet struck just below the ribs. He reached to his side and felt the sticky wetness. His shirt began to turn red. He collapsed to his knees, expecting the next shot to hit his head. He closed his eyes and heard two shots in quick succession. Surprised to be alive, he opened his eyes and saw the bodies of both attackers slumped to the ground. Half their faces were missing.

~

It was 7:15 a.m. when Shannon finished her breakfast of hard boiled eggs, baguettes with strawberry jam and butter, and café-au-lait. Where was Martin? He would normally have met her by now. She smiled to herself and pushed away her concerns.

In the main lobby, most of the U.S. delegation was chatting with nervous anticipation. Shannon heard someone say, "It's done." She let out a deep sigh, "Thank God." James Brown Scott emerged from the group carrying a thick book with a white cover. "Conditions of Peace" in French and English adorned its cover in gold lettering.

Shannon noticed an athletic man in a business suit looking on. He wore an eye patch and seemed focused on the white book. *I've seen him before.* He looked in her direction, turned away, and vanished. Excited about the news, Shannon did not give him another thought. "Is that the treaty, Mr. Scott?"

"We finished it last night. I'm taking it to Colonel House," Scott said. The treaty was about two hundred pages long comprising nearly four hundred and fifty articles. It was about seventy-five thousand words.

It reminded Shannon of her first Bible. "You don't look happy, Mr. Scott. What is it?"

"The statesmen have made a peace that makes another war inevitable. Excuse me. I must get this to Mr. House."

Scott's words distressed Shannon. She was contemplating the implications when Sergeant Cooper approached her. "Excuse me, Mrs. Keller, do you know where Major Martin is?" he asked. "I haven't seen him all morning."

"No, I ..." Shannon stopped. "He had to leave Mrs. Brooks's party in a hurry last night. He didn't say much. Something to do with the attempt on Clémenceau."

She did not know if he believed her or not, but Shannon had a larger concern. If Shannon's instincts were correct and Ana was a Russian spy, Martin had walked into a trap last night.

"Help!" a woman screamed from the entranceway. "It's an emergency!"

“What the hell?” Sergeant Cooper ran toward the voice, pushing the delegates aside.

The delegates looked at each other with bewilderment. “What’s happening?” “Who’s hurt?” “Not today!”

Out of instinct, Shannon knew it had to be Gil. She followed Sergeant Cooper to the front but stopped short when she saw Ana Primakova. Her hands and sweater were stained with blood. She pointed to the street. “It’s Major Martin. He ..., he ...”

“Get a doctor!” Cooper yelled. He put his hands on Ana’s shoulders and tried to calm her down. “What happened?”

“He’s shot. He’s in his vehicle. I didn’t know where else to go. He’s lost a lot of blood. I tried to stop it. Hurry.”

Chapter 45
A Confrontation

Paris: May 1919

A frantic Shannon heard the siren of the approaching ambulance and was greatly relieved when Sergeant Cooper took control. A corporal ran by carrying a first aid kit. James Brown Scott led everyone in prayer. "Does he need blood?" he asked Shannon.

"I'm sure the hospital needs every drop," she replied.

Words of shock and concern spread through the crowded lobby. One man pushed forward. "I'm a priest. Does he need one?"

"He's Catholic. Go," Shannon said. Realizing she could do nothing more, she strode over to Ana Primakova, who stood staring at her bloody hands. "You Russian whore," Shannon said. "You got him shot, didn't you?" Shannon raised her hand and slapped Ana. The delegates nearby gasped.

Ana rubbed her face. "I am not what you think I am."

"What's he to you?" Shannon asked. The sound of the ambulance leaving seemed to echo through the hallway.

"A friend." Ana's cheek was turning red.

"Liar." Shannon spit out the words.

"How dare you call me that! I brought him here, didn't I? You don't know anything about me."

"I know you work for Russia."

"I no longer have a country."

"What does that mean?"

Ana looked dizzy and bent her head down.

Before Shannon could react, Sergeant Cooper returned with a somber expression. The delegates in the lobby formed around Cooper, straining to hear what he would say. “The bullet missed the vital organs and passed through his body. He’s lost a lot of blood.”

“Is he going to ...” Ana started to faint.

Cooper caught her before she fell. “Who is this woman?”

“Ana Primakova. She’s a Russian reporter. She’s involved with Martin’s shooting. He was with her last night,” Shannon said.

“Whoever she is, she saved the major’s life,” Cooper said. “Another twenty minutes and he would have bled out.”

“It’s my fault he was shot,” Ana said.

“I don’t understand,” Cooper said.

“Don’t trust her,” Shannon said.

Cooper stared at Shannon. “I’ll determine that myself. I’ll talk to both of you later.” Shannon became taut, but she knew Cooper was right and calmed down. Cooper consulted with Scott and announced to the delegates in the lobby that Major Martin had been seriously wounded. He was being taken to the Hotel-Dieu de Paris hospital near Notre Dame.

“Today is an important day for the peace talks,” he concluded. “Our work is complete. The draft is done. I left a copy at the front desk when Major Martin ... . He is in good hands. Please return to your duties. I need to talk to Colonel House.” Scott returned to the front desk, but the draft was gone. He asked, but no one had seen it. Too busy to continue looking, he decided to renew his search later.

Alone in the lobby, Shannon asked Ana to follow her to the billiard room, knowing it would be empty this time of day. They walked there in silence. “How did the major get shot?” she asked behind closed doors. Her words vibrated across the tables.

“He was ambushed near his car.”

“Back up to last night. Start at Mrs. Brooks’s party. Why were you there?”

Ana explained that she was there on orders from her Russian superiors. Such social gatherings provided useful information. As a newspaper reporter, Ana was skilled at soliciting information from loose-lipped drunkards, indiscreet braggarts, and romantically inclined boors who wanted to impress a beautiful woman. Afterward, Ana was to convey the news to her Cheka guardians. They had pressed her before the party to find out what had happened when Commandant Truchon was arrested. She was to make inquiries with her contacts in the U.S. delegation, but she had grown tired of being a Bolshevik puppet. She was surprised when Martin appeared. This was her chance to speak to him without raising suspicions. “I needed to escape. I asked Gil for help.”

Gil? “Why?”

“My reasons.”

“Do you expect me to accept that?”

“I can’t go back to the Bolsheviks. I’ve killed their men. I told all this to the major. Maybe he — ”

“If he lives.”

“Oh, God,” Ana said. Neither woman spoke for a few moments.

A Marine corporal barged into the billiard room and asked if Mrs. Keller was all right. It was time to go to the talks. “I’ll be there in a moment, Corporal. Thank you.” Shannon turned back to Ana. “Tell me what you told the major.”

“Why should I?”

“You’re not leaving until you do. You owe it to Gil, in case ...”

“Please, no. How did my life fall apart like this?”

Shannon tried to piece together Ana’s jigsaw puzzle life. “Do you mean you work for the Cheka against your will?”

“Two Cheka men were watching me last night. Gil got in the middle and was shot. I had to kill them.”

"You killed two Cheka agents?" *Who is this woman*?

"To save Gil. Now they will assassinate me." Ana's hands began to shake.

Shannon's police training told her Ana was close to breaking. "How did you get involved with the Bolsheviks?"

"My former husband was an imperialist. The Bolsheviks hated him, but he had important anti-Bolshevik connections in the Duma. They and his Tsarist friends protected him. When he died in the war, Lenin's people forced me to work for them."

"Why did they send you to Paris? I'm sure they didn't trust you."

"For the talks. My language abilities. My husband's contacts. They needed me. But they took insurance."

"How?"

"Believe me when I say I tried to help the major. I hate the Bolsheviks."

The corporal returned. The delegation had to leave. Shannon told him to stay. "Watch Madam Primakova. Don't let her leave." Before she closed the door, Shannon turned to Ana. "We'll continue this later."

~

Five days later, Shannon walked through the Hotel-Dieu de Paris to visit Martin. Spring had arrived in Paris. The air was fresh; the flowers were in bloom; but the tremors of the cataclysm that had ended six months ago rippled through the city in the form of grieving widows, maimed soldiers, and displaced citizens. Shannon imagined what Martin had been thinking when their roles had been reversed. Back then, he was visiting her at New York's Mount Sinai Hospital, where she was recovering from her kidnapping ordeal. She rubbed her arm where she had been tortured. The outer burn marks had healed, but the inner ones still hurt despite her efforts to will them away. *Our trials bring us together, don't they, Gil*? She wondered where her husband was. *How soon will it be before I have to visit you in a hospital? Or a morgue*? *Or ever?*

Shannon walked through the maze of hallways and staircases to Martin's room. Outside his door, she talked to two nurses discussing his case. "How is he, Isobel?" Shannon asked in French.

"Grouchy."

"That means he's getting better," Shannon said.

"We'll miss him. He's got some wonderful stories, but he doesn't like it when we call him 'the hero of New York.'"

"He's quite modest," Shannon said. "Thank you so much for everything you've done." She was about to open the door when John Maynard Keynes exited Martin's room. "Mrs. Keller, it is a pleasure to see you." Keynes cleared his throat, as if to change his cheery mood, and quickly added, "Except for the circumstances, of course. Our Major Martin is resilient. A near miss, I gather. I am glad he is better. He is not a man suited to the confines of a hospital. Get him out. He is needed."

~

"Thank you for coming, Mr. Keynes," Martin called from his bed. He propped himself up on his pillows and tried to smile when Shannon entered. The throbbing in his side was sharp but manageable. He had refused morphine for the last few days. He had seen what it could do to men, even the strongest ones. Being confined and forced to endure the regimen of the hospital bothered him more than the pain.

"How are you, Gil?" Shannon asked.

"Fit for duty," he said through a grimace.

"How are you really? Emotionally?"

Martin slumped back onto the bed. He never could hide anything from Shannon. She was too good a detective. "Fine," he said without conviction.

"What's wrong?"

"I'm better. I should be getting out soon."

"That's not what's bothering you. What is it?"

Martin started to say the words but stopped.

"I'll tell you," Shannon said. "Ana Primakova."

"I want a cigarette."

"You're dodging my question, Gil. What's your relationship with her?"

"She saved my life," Martin said. He recounted the Russian trip and the message on the train. He skipped details of the night he had spent with her and moved to the morning he was shot. "I'm still not sure how the Bolsheviks are involved, but I'll tell you this. I was trapped in an alleyway with no weapon. A dead man for sure. Ana appeared out of nowhere and killed those two men. Those were difficult shots."

"A reporter doesn't know how to shoot like that."

"She's not a reporter. She's a spy."

"On what side?

"Not the Bolsheviks."

"She does their bidding. Why?"

"She had to. They kidnapped her daughter, Sonya, and held her hostage. They blackmailed Ana into working for them. They watched her all the time, but that didn't stop her from saving me — twice. She warned me of an attack on the train to Moscow, and again last night."

"What has changed?"

"Sonya died. Influenza."

"What now?"

"Ana can't return to Russia. She's alone and can help us. Where is she?"

"We have her under guard at the Crillon. We don't have the full story yet." Shannon moved closer to Martin. "She told me you know everything."

"I doubt that, but I know enough to say she's a victim."

"How do you feel about her?"

Martin's mouth became dry. He wanted to avoid the question, but he had to tell Shannon, the only person in Paris he could confide in. Martin confessed his attraction to Ana. Her appeal was powerful: her grace and beauty; her stoic courage and intelligence; his need for the intimacy so lacking since his wife had died; his fatigue after years of fighting. Living in this Parisian cesspool of distrust had made him weak. His life was complicated enough without ... "She's a remarkable woman."

"What does she say about the Communist threat and the attack on you?"

"The attack on me was really about her. To keep her in line. If she's right— "

"Gil, that's a risky speculation."

"I don't think so. We must protect her. She's on our side now." Martin was too tired to continue. "What's happening in the talks?"

"The Germans are arriving in a few days to receive the terms."

"All hell could break loose when they arrive," Martin said. "Help me get dressed, Shannon. I need to get back to work."

Chapter 46
Café Josty

Berlin: April/May 1919

Keller was alone for the first time since he had learned the Freikorps had a secret plan to attack Paris. He had changed trains three times before his stop. A trench coat covered his Freikorps uniform. With the Freikorps in total control of the city and the revolutionary movement in Berlin effectively silenced, he and the rest of the Landsmann Battalion soldiers had been given their first day off in weeks. Desperate to flee the Freikorps, he had taken the rare chance to break away and get an emergency note to Larsen.

Once at Alexanderplatz, he walked around the neighborhood for twenty minutes, doubling back twice before he headed to the Marienkirk on Kaiser Wilhelm Strasse a few blocks away. Before he went to the church, he ducked into a store and exited with glasses, a different gait, and a hat. Avoiding shadows was a game of deception, and Keller had become an expert player. His life depended on it.

Certain no one was shadowing him, Keller entered the church from a side entrance, went to the tenth pew from the altar, and sat in the farthest seat to the left. He breathed easier. He had reached the location to hide his message. In the humbling confines of the old church, Keller felt a need to unburden himself in prayer. Three minutes later, he took a piece of paper from his pocket. It appeared to be blank, but it contained a coded message written in lemon juice. In the note, Keller asked for an immediate meeting with Larsen at their usual place. The message ended, “Get me out of here.”

He removed the knife strapped to his ankle and carved a narrow niche into the seat where it joined the side-rest. He folded the paper into a one-inch square, tucked it into the niche, and covered the niche with a sliver of wood he jammed over it. It would not be noticed. Even if someone found it, the message would appear blank unless a candle were held behind the page. And then, someone would have to decode it.

Keller carved a small “k” into the base support for the pew, signaling Larsen there was a message. He had worked out this procedure with Dulles before leaving for Germany. Larsen was to visit this church regularly and go to this seat. Dulles’s instructions were firm: “Use this means of communication only in emergencies.” Keller had no doubt his current situation qualified.

Feeling safe in the church, Keller postponed returning to his unit. His mind drifted to better times: eating his mother’s strudel, swimming in his uncle’s lake in Wisconsin as a boy, hitting his first home run. He recalled every moment of New Year’s Eve 1915, starting when Shannon appeared at Police Headquarters for their evening together. She looked like a goddess and sparked considerable jealousy among the unmarried men. That was when he realized he was falling in love with her. The pleasant thoughts were overtaken by a harsher recollection, the day Dulles had approached him about becoming a spy.

He should have listened to Shannon when he returned home after his meeting with Dulles. What a dreadful fight they had had, the first since their marriage, when he told her about his mission. She had warned him, but he did not listen. “You’re a cop, Paul, not an actor. You’re meant to chase bad guys, not hide as one.”

“But the work is vital,” he had argued, as much to convince himself as Shannon. He swallowed hard. “I’ll be fine.”

“You’re being impulsive. It’s your nature. I won’t try to stop you. I can’t. Just promise you won’t do anything crazy.”

Keller looked deep into her eyes. “I promise,” he said, knowing such a promise would be impossible to keep. Of course the mission would be dangerous. That was what excited him.

So much has changed.

Approaching footsteps from the front of the church jolted Keller from his thoughts. Instinctively, he reached into his coat for the small Mauser pistol, but stopped when he saw a man in a cassock walking toward him with his head bent. Keller studied his every movement until the man nodded at him and walked on. Keller watched him for a few more paces and relaxed, convinced the man was a pastor.

Again, he pondered Shannon's warning. When she said this mission would either get him killed or destroy him, she had been right, but for the wrong reasons. He had survived so far, if surviving was the right word. Guile, calm under pressure, and courage in battle had kept him alive in the Freikorps. Also luck. It could not last much longer. He had become a thug, a fanatic Freikorps soldier, and an assassin. He could accept the first two, but killing unarmed people violated every personal creed he had. In this living purgatory, he was dying from the inside out, not from the outside in, as Shannon had feared. He would have preferred the fate she had predicted.

~

A week later, Keller faded into a crowd of workers at the Potsdam Bahnhof. He headed to the emergency meeting he had arranged by message with Larsen. Exiting the station, he ducked into a haberdashery and purchased a sweater, a common brown overcoat, and a popular businessman's hat, which he placed in a bag. After another block, he entered a hotel and exited wearing his new outer garments. He pretended to be an old man with a limp and a crooked back. He circled around Koniggratz Strasse and walked back through the Bahnhof onto Potsdamerplatz. Safe, he headed toward the popular Café Josty, the meeting place.

At late afternoon, the café was not crowded. Keller sat at a round wrought iron table in front of a big window overlooking the street. No Larsen. Danger mounted by the minute. Pretending to be one of the bohemian and artistic patrons, Keller sketched the busy square where five main streets intersected. Drawing provided an excellent excuse to observe without attracting attention to himself and to assess possible escapes. Trams and buses nearly collided at the busy intersection. Flocks of pedestrians moved around in a typical urban frenzy. The bustle made him long for New York.

Business was sparse. Keller heard the bartenders washing glasses and preparing for the evening crowd. A fashionable woman led an equally fashionable but younger man upstairs for an obvious liaison. They did not seem to care who noticed them. Getting your pleasure where you could was a lesson many had learned from the Great War. He would never have seen this kind of behavior in his uncle's hometown of Milwaukee before the war. He enjoyed the diversion.

The festive decor and cheerful bartenders jarred with his somber mood. He ordered another beer. For the third time in ten minutes, he checked his timepiece. Keller's spine stiffened. Where was Larsen? He looked out the window again and was relieved to see Larsen running across the street to the café. A man in a brown coat and a fedora seemed to be following Larsen's movements.

Keller continued to survey the street after Larsen entered Josty's. The man in the brown coat sat on a bench outside facing the café and opened a newspaper. Larsen walked past Keller's table and adjusted his glasses, the "all-clear" signal. Keller countered by reaching for his glass but not lifting it. *Be careful.* Larsen moved on and sat at the bar.

Five minutes later, they went to the toilet separately. "What's the matter?" Larsen asked.

Making sure they were alone, Keller said, “We don’t have much time. Were you followed?”

“Don’t think so.” Larsen’s tone was not convincing.

“Man in a brown coat and a fedora. He’s outside watching us. He might be following you.”

“Can’t see how. I used all the precautions.”

“We need to split up and make sure.”

“But your note. What’s so important?”

A drunk entered the men’s room and headed to the urinal. “Outside,” Keller said. They washed their hands and continued their discussion at a quiet corner of the bar. “I’m going to die one way or another if I stay here much longer.”

“You must stay,” Larsen said. “You’re our best source in the Freikorps. Something big is about to happen.”

“How do you know?”

“Our sources. Don’t ask. I implore you to stay.”

“I’ll need money and papers.”

“If you stay.”

Keller suppressed his anger and scanned the café to see if anyone was watching them. He felt dizzy. Under his breath, he said, “I may be signing my death warrant, but I’ll give you a week. No more. I might not even have a day. After that, I’m gone with or without your help.”

“That may not be enough time.”

“I’m taking a big risk giving you that. Now go. I’ll watch.” As Larsen turned away, Keller pulled him back by his sleeve. “Tell my wife I love her.” He returned to his table and observed the street. The man in the brown coat stood up when Larsen exited the café. He gestured to another man in a business suit who began to follow Larsen.

Keller had to steady himself. *My God. We’re in trouble.*

Chapter 47
Alone

Berlin: May 1919

Keller watched the two men follow Larsen across Potsdamerplatz toward the Bahnhof and grew worried about his own safety. He scanned every possible outside vantage point. No one seemed to be watching him. He studied everyone inside the café. Just drunks, broken-down veterans, and lovers. If someone was shadowing him, he was very good.

All Keller knew was that Larsen was being followed. He could no longer risk being seen with him. *If "they" were following Larsen, were they after him too? Who were they*? Ruthless men surely, most likely anti-American provocateurs or Noske's agents. If they had penetrated Larsen's organization, it was only a matter of time before they learned about his false identity. Every man, even one as tough as Larsen, succumbed to torture.

Survival instinct told Keller to run. Practicalities stopped him. He did not have money, clothes, or papers. He was still a soldier in the Freikorps, and Landsmann had ordered deserters shot. Fighting to stay calm, he grabbed the first trolley at Potsdamerplatz. At the third stop, he jumped off and hopped back on just as the doors closed, apologizing to the driver, who shrugged his shoulders and pressed the accelerator. Keller transferred to another trolley after two more stops.

Once on the second train, Keller understood two facts. He was in danger, and he was alone. He got off, doubled back, and went to the Marienkirk on the outside chance Larsen had left him a message. It was a risk — they might have spotted Larsen there — but one Keller had to take. He sat in his usual seat and looked into the hollowed-out niche. Empty. He prayed Larsen would escape, but doubted it.

~

By the time Larsen reached the Bahnhof, he realized Keller's warnings had been true. He was being followed. The man in the brown coat now wore a tan one. The businessman was nowhere to be seen. *How many more are out there?* Larsen looked over his shoulder and to either side. Any others were not to be seen. He looked again. The man in the tan coat was gone.

He turned back and to his surprise, the man in the tan coat was in front of him. Larsen stumbled to avoid colliding into him. The man stood his ground, his arms folded across his chest. "We've been following you for weeks, Mr. Larsen, if that is your real name," he said in excellent English.

Larsen tried to swallow, but his mouth was too dry. He responded in German, pretending not to understand. "*Wass*?"

"What were you doing at the U.S. Office for Food Relief this morning?" The man in the tan coat continued in English.

Larsen shook his head and feigned ignorance, fighting back panic.

"Who did you meet at the Café Josty a few minutes ago?" he said in German.

Larsen held his arms up in mock confusion. Out of nowhere, the businessman appeared and punched Larsen in the kidney. He crumpled to the ground. The man in the tan coat stood over him and demanded, "What is so important at the Marienkirk?"

The words jolted Larsen like a cattle prod. He struggled to his feet and recalled his training. *Remain ignorant and contrite. Concede nothing*. He responded in his best German, "Don't hurt me. I'm just a simple man. I go to the church to pray. During the war, — "

The man in the tan coat grabbed Larsen's wrist in a vice-like grip and twisted. "Please follow us."

Larsen stammered. "Wh-what's wrong? I haven't done anything. You must have mistaken me for someone — "

The businessman pulled out a Mauser and pointed it at Larsen's head. "You're under arrest."

Two goons moved to circle them. An onlooker approached and asked, "What's going on?"

One of the goons intercepted the intruder and growled. "State business. Go." He reached for a pistol and shot into the air. The few remaining onlookers scattered. The goon stayed behind to make sure no one interfered again while the businessman nudged Larsen forward with his gun barrel.

Larsen pretended to limp to slow down the pace. *Think*. Dulles's final warning flashed through his brain. *If you ever get captured, assess your chances. Avoid being tortured. You will talk. Do what you must.*

"Move. *Rasch*." The businessman kicked Larsen in the calf. Larsen stumbled. The others yanked Larsen to his feet.

"We don't like traitors or spies," the man in the tan coat said. "We're going to have a little chat."

Larsen reached for the button at the bottom of his coat and pulled it off. He snapped it, releasing the poison. Before the Germans could react, Larsen swallowed it, hoping to protect Keller. The last words he heard were, "*Scheisse*. Now we'll never find out what he ..."

~

Keller rested for half an hour in the church pew and collected his thoughts. A sinking feeling struck him when he realized he could not avoid whoever might be tailing him. As he had learned chasing German agents in New York, shadows did not have to follow a mark if they knew where he would be next, and when. If these men were as good as he thought, they would know this too. It was late afternoon; Keller would have to report back to headquarters at the Eden Hotel soon. They did not need to follow him. All they had to do was to wait. If they were going to arrest him, it would be there.

As he neared the hotel, Keller realized his only chance to survive was to stand tall, stick to his story, and deny any charges against him. "Lies," he would maintain. "My involvement in Liebknecht's murder has brought me many enemies. There's a conspiracy against me. I'm a loyal soldier — look at my military record." *Chances of surviving to morning? Less than half.*

Two cold-faced privates eyed him when he entered the hotel. Their sidearms were visible. The other men in the area turned away. Jawbreaker, looking more surly than usual, approached. "Sergeant Brandt, the colonel has ordered you to report to him immediately. I'll escort you."

"In a minute, I need to — "

"Now."

Chapter 48
Disbelief

Berlin: May 1919

Flanked by two burly privates, Keller followed Jawbreaker down the corridor to Landsmann's office. Even if he had wanted to, he could not have escaped. The moment of truth had arrived. Had he been recognized at the café? The next few minutes would determine his fate. The fact that he was still alive was a good sign. Would they shoot him on the spot once they knew his real identity? Probably. Was it all in vain? Most likely.

Keller's knees buckled when he saw the man in the brown coat in front of Colonel Landsmann's office. He seemed to be arguing with a shorter businessman in a blue suit. His deep baritone voice carried more than it should have. The man in the blue suit tapped his feet nervously and slouched forward as if he were carrying a heavy field pack.

Play for time, think. Keller turned away so the two men would not see him and reached into his uniform for a cigarette. He pretended to be annoyed. "*Scheisse.* None left. Jawbreaker, do you have a *Zigarette*?"

"Since when do you smoke?" Jawbreaker offered a packet. "Here."

"*Danke.*" Keller took one and held the cigarette German-style. Out of the corner of his eye, he studied the man in the brown coat, who appeared not to notice him. *Maybe he doesn't realize who I am,* Keller thought. *I look different in my uniform. Bluff it out.* He turned to Jawbreaker. "Light?"

Jawbreaker struck a match and held it below Keller's face,

forcing him to bend to light it. "You're a strange one, Brandt."

Keller sucked in a lungful of tobacco, shrugged his shoulders, and said, "The war." The universal excuse. Everyone knew it gave men wide latitude to behave oddly. Keller blocked the view of the men in suits by holding the cigarette in front of his face. He took a quick look at them. The vein in the neck of the man in the brown suit pulsated wildly as he berated the smaller man in the blue suit, who, from his rigid jaw and fixed stare, seemed to accept the rebuke unwillingly.

"You don't say much, do you Brandt?" Jawbreaker asked. "Mind in the clouds again?"

Keller grunted and continued to eavesdrop. "It's your fault he's dead, Kolbar," the man in the brown suit said.

Who are they talking about?

"Why? You were closer to him than I was when he reached for the poison, Herr Jacob."

"Our investigation is *kaputt*, Kolbar," Jacob said. "Noske will have my head."

"I disagree. He was meeting someone today at Josty's. I'm sure of it," Kolbar said. "One of my men is interviewing people there now. They'll get a description. I'll get to the truth without that dead spy."

Larsen. Keller's mouth turned to cotton.

The door to Landsmann's office swung open, and Captain Reick emerged and saluted. "The colonel will see you now, Major Jacob. Lieutenant Kolbar."

They're undercover Freikorps agents. I'm a dead man already.

For twenty-seven minutes, Keller kept to himself while Jawbreaker and the two privates stood guard. They smoked cigarettes and joked about women. Finally, Reick opened the door and invited Keller and Jawbreaker in to join the two Freikorps agents. "Leave your weapons outside," Reick said. Jawbreaker looked at him curiously and handed his pistol to one of the privates. Keller did not know what to think and complied. Reick ordered the two privates to stay by the door.

As he walked in, Keller prayed Jacob and Kolbar would not recognize him. *Best stay quiet. Remain inconspicuous.* A piercing bugle call of a man practicing outside interrupted the silence and rattled Keller even more.

Keller kept his head down and followed Jawbreaker into the office. He positioned himself so Jawbreaker stood between him and the two Freikorps agents. Captain Reick was sitting in front of the colonel's desk writing something.

When Keller looked up, he was surprised to see Defense Minister Noske and Hermann Goering whispering to each other in the corner of Landsmann's office. Noske, his arms crossed, seemed interested in what the flamboyant Goering was saying. Landsmann concentrated on Jacob, ignoring the soldiers when they entered. "Before I get to the next matter, is there anything else, Major Jacob?"

"No, Colonel."

Keller tried to breathe normally and act soldierly.

"Keep me posted on your investigation," Landsmann said. The two agents saluted and turned to leave. On his way out, Jacob walked by Keller as if he were not there. Kolbar glowered at him but said nothing.

Keller felt unnerved and perplexed. *Why didn't they arrest me*? There were two explanations. His cover was still safe, or they were waiting to find out more and were continuing to observe him. Keller was only half-listening when Landsmann asked, "You, Sergeant Brandt, you speak good English, *Ja*?" Noske and Goering stopped talking and looked up.

"Why do you ask?" Keller said. He chastised himself for his defensive tone but knew every question could be a trap.

"Answer the question, Sergeant."

Keller cleared his throat. "Yes. I've told you before. I worked in America before they declared war. I speak English well."

"Tell me again. Places you lived. Details."

They're trying to catch me in a lie. Keller provided extensive information based on interviews he had had with the real Karl Brandt.

"Fine." Landsmann muttered something else then added, "I need an English translation. It's important." He looked at Keller with probing eyes. "What I'm giving you is most secret."

"You can trust me." Keller stood more erect.

"You're a brave soldier. You've proved your loyalty. Here." Landsmann handed Brandt a thick book with a white cover and gold lettering.

Keller tried to hide his shock, but his eyes doubled in size. He held in his hands the Paris Peace Treaty. "How did you get this?" he asked without thinking.

"That is no concern of yours, Sergeant Brandt," Noske said sternly. "Read."

When Keller finished translating the opening pages, Noske told him to go to the section concerning Germany. When he finished, the room was as quiet as a graveyard at midnight. Noske kept a poker face. Landsmann shook his head. Goering clenched his fist. Reick crossed his arms. Jawbreaker ground his teeth.

Noske broke the silence. "In your opinion, Sergeant, is this document real or a fake?"

"How can I answer that?"

Landsmann cut in. "My best agent in Paris took this from under the noses of the U.S. delegation, Defense Minister. It is not a fake."

Keller continued to translate.

"Outrageous!" Noske exclaimed. "The Allies force us to admit full guilt for the war. Pay an impossible sum. Give up all our colonies. This is not what we had agreed to at the armistice."

"The military — we give up our navy, heavy weapons. They restrict us to an army of 100,000 men," Goering said. "They're castrating us."

"They don't even want us in their League of Nations. How will that help the world order?" Landsmann asked. "Occupation of the Rhine valley. France retains rights to coal from the Saar Coal District. Germany will freeze next winter."

"If I'm right, we must give up about thirteen percent of our territory and ten percent of our population," Reick said. "The people will riot."

Everyone spoke at once, each man expressing outrage. "Quiet, all of you," Noske ordered. The voices died down. "Obviously, Germany cannot accept this."

"If we don't," Reick said, "the Allies will invade. They will enslave us."

"No," Noske said. "We will stop the signing. How are your plans progressing, gentlemen?"

"The air attack on Alexanderplatz was a preview," Goering said.

"My agent is working out details, Minister. My men will be ready," Landsmann said. "What does our banker say?"

"Wait. See if our diplomats succeed where the army has failed." Noske sneered. "If they fail to change the terms, we will proceed."

SECTION IV

PRESIDENT WOODROW WILSON
AND COLONEL EDWARD HOUSE

May 1919

Chapter 49
An Old Friend

Berlin: May 1919

Awake in his bed, Keller now had two reasons to reach friendly territory. His own life was at risk, and he had vital information for Dulles: Freikorps agents planned to stop the signing of the Peace treaty. This was the reason he had become a spy, to do something significant. Now he had his chance. If he could disrupt the Freikorps plans, everything he had endured since he entered Germany would have been worth it.

But how to escape Berlin? Colonel Landsmann kept strict control of his battalion. Roll calls were twice a day, and every movement outside of the base was questioned. Free passes were rare, and Keller had used his quota. Until yesterday, he had managed to avoid suspicion during his absences, but it would be much harder now he believed he was being watched. Any unexpected move on his part could prompt intense questioning, likely torture, and possible execution.

He rolled over in bed and reviewed his options. He would flee as soon as possible, but how? *Strategy first. Work backwards to tactics, just as we did at AEF headquarters.* Once he had escaped Berlin, where would he go? East toward Russia and away from the Allies was out of the question. South to Switzerland was an option. Once he crossed the Swiss border, he would be safe and could easily travel to neighboring France. Getting through Germany, where Noske could deploy considerable resources to chase him, could be difficult. Even if his pursuers did not find him, he risked capture in insurrectionist Bavaria, where Communists and government troops alike would hate a Freikorps deserter. Too much uncertainty.

Go straight west, the most direct route to Allied territory. It might be the fastest, but it was also the most likely course. Landsmann's men could chase him across most of Germany. Same problem as the southern route — too much time in hostile Germany. He would face scrutiny at every train station, bridge, and road intersection. The German-French border was well-guarded, with distrust on both sides. Even if he could get to the Rhine River, crossing it would be treacherous. The French would shoot anyone sneaking in, and the Germans would stop anyone trying to flee without authorization. Very risky.

North to Denmark? That option had possibilities. Denmark was a neutral country and had maintained working relations with all the warring parties. Its territorial boundaries were intact and unchallenged. Little fighting was going on there. Communist activity in Denmark was, so far, minimal. Freikorps activity in the German territory of Schleswig-Holstein on the Danish border was relatively light, and there was less insurgent activity there than in other parts of Germany.

To get there, he would either have to pass through Hamburg over land, or book passage or stow away on a ship sailing to Denmark. Despite working around New York's dockyards, he did not know ships or their routines well, and sneaking onto a ship was dangerous. If he reached Hamburg over land — it was only 160 miles away — then what?

Andreas Sund's papers were still in his possession. Keller was about the same age as the unfortunate sailor he had shot in the butcher shop. At a glance, they resembled each other. Better, Sund was from Bremen, so no one would be suspicious that Keller would be traveling in the Hamburg area. Problems? Keller's accent was not northern German, but he figured he could bluff that. Failing that, he could pretend he had suffered some kind of head injury during the war. Men with brain trauma were frequent enough these days.

Keller's concerns about the northern escape route grew, because he had never been to the area and did not have maps. He would avoid back roads and small towns, where he would be too conspicuous. If he got lost, he would likely say something wrong and compromise himself. His inevitable pursuers would think the same way and would concentrate on the main routes. Therefore, speed was paramount. He knew nothing about Denmark's reaction to the end of the war and its subsequent policies, specifically how well it controlled its borders. On the positive side, once inside Denmark, Keller figured he could easily reach the U.S. embassy in Copenhagen and sail to France under American protection.

This option presented transportation and money problems. He would use his last *pfennigs* to buy a train ticket to Hamburg. There, he would be just another wandering soldier with no way to get home. Beg? Too much competition for too little silver. Steal? Might have to. Going north was the best of his horrible options. His biggest obstacle was how to break away from his unit.

When he dressed that morning, Keller decided to carry Sund's papers with him at all times. If he was under suspicion, his room would be searched. If Jacob or Kolbar found the papers on him, one more piece of incriminating evidence would not matter.

Keller's senses were working overtime when he walked outside to muster for roll call. Couriers were coming and going at a normal rate. Motorcycles stood ready to speed the next messengers away. A few men in civilian clothes were waiting by the front door leading to Colonel Landsmann's office, suggesting an important visitor would arrive soon. Jacob and Kolbar were not among them. A large Mercedes, escorted by an armored car, pulled up to the front door. Five well-armed men piled out, and a Freikorps major wearing an Iron Cross First Class exited the Mercedes and opened its back right door. A platoon of soldiers marched forward and formed a protective cordon from the Mercedes to the front door. Keller did not see who got out, but he had seen enough generals and ranking civilians come and go from the Eden Hotel to know few men had this kind of security.

Although Reick knew everything going on in the battalion, Keller decided he should not draw attention to himself by asking questions. The dignitary walked into the building while Keller's formation remained at attention. Once the dignitary was safe, the formation was dismissed. As he walked away, Keller heard Jawbreaker tell Dengel that the dignitary was the man who secretly financed the entire Freikorps. Keller pretended to ignore them and walked on.

"You, Sergeant Brandt, come here."

Keller froze.

"Report to Colonel Landsmann on the double," Dengel said. "Jawbreaker and I will escort you." He led the way.

Keller tried to stop his knees from wobbling. Jawbreaker stayed three paces behind. The colonel seemed relaxed. He appeared to be joking with Reick, who looked up and said with a smile, "You should be following Sergeant Brandt, Sergeant Dengel. Not the other way around. He's the hero."

Hero?

"You're to receive a medal, Sergeant Brandt. Our visitor this morning wants to present it to you himself. You saved the battalion at Alexanderplatz."

A medal? From the mysterious head of the Freikorps? How ironic.

At the back of the colonel's office, a well-dressed man was looking out the window and talking to a general Keller did not recognize. There was something familiar about the leader's voice that Keller could not place. When the man turned around, Keller recognized Matthias Weil, the German spy he had ensnared at the Speaker's Corner in New

York City more than three years ago. *My God*! How had he gotten back to Germany? Weil would surely recognize Keller as the cop who had nearly arrested him.

Keller was trapped.

Chapter 50
Run

Berlin: May 1919

Keller's trench-tested nerves held steady as he faced his old adversary, now the Freikorps's banker and one of the most powerful men in Germany. What would happen if Weil had known the real Karl Brandt during his spy days in America? A real possibility.

Engaged in conversation with a Freikorps general, Weil had not recognized Keller yet. Keller looked much different now from his disguise as the unkempt anarchist Weil had seen years ago, but he knew Weil would remember him soon enough.

Seconds mattered. Before Weil could give him a close look, Keller doubled over, grabbed his stomach, and groaned loudly — an old shadow's trick. Conversation stopped, and all eyes turned to the bent-over soldier.

"What's wrong, Brandt?" Reick asked.

"Old gut wound, Captain. Bullet's still there." Keller exaggerated the pain. "It must have moved. I'm sorry, sir."

"Get him out of here." Weil waved his hands as if he was shooing away a bug. "His bawling gives me heartburn."

"I can make it to the infirmary," Keller said, adding another groan for effect. "Permission to leave, Colonel."

"Go," Landsmann said. "And I thought you were tough."

Keller, still bent low, saluted, making sure to hide his face from Weil.

Keller clutched his stomach and crab-walked to the door. "Follow him," Reick ordered Dengel.

Keller's ruse had provided escape from Weil, but he still had to deal with Dengel. He felt as if a bullet had just missed his head by inches. But, more were on the way.

Dengel and Keller exited Landsmann's office, and one of the guards closed the door. Keller sensed the Freikorps heads continuing to talk about him. He straightened up and said, "I'm better, Sergeant Dengel, thank you. Go. You've got more important duties than me."

Dengel just grunted and continued to walk with Keller. When he and Dengel were alone in the corridor, Keller feigned another stomach attack. "Move." Dengel pushed him dismissively on the shoulder.

Keller stumbled forward. When Dengel did not react, Keller saw his chance. He bent over, pulled the knife strapped to his leg, and slashed upward in one motion. The blade sliced Dengel across the throat so deeply it severed his larynx. Dengel's eyes gaped back in anger and disbelief. Keller caught him before he fell and dragged his body into a nearby closet. No time to clean up the trail of blood. He wiped the blood off his uniform as best he could with a cleaning cloth from the closet, removed Dengel's Luger from its holster, and stuck it into his belt. He ran to the back stairway more frightened than he had ever been in his life.

~

"I apologize for that, Herr Weil," Landsmann said.

"Who was that man?"

"Karl Brandt." Reick summarized what he knew of Brant's profile.

"You say this Brandt worked as one of our agents in New York until the police broke up our operations?"

"*Ja*," Reick said.

"You knew him?" Landsmann asked.

"I knew most of our agents. Brandt's name is vaguely familiar. Our New York spy ring was decimated by 1917, but you say this man did not join us until December 1918. During our retreat from France?"

"He said he was in Mexico for the last two years. Came back at the end of the war," Landsmann said.

"Something is not right," Weil said.

"That man has been acting strangely since he joined us," Reick said. "We accepted it. Brandt is a fierce soldier. He saved — "

"A number of our agents were arrested after Beck died," Weil said. "Could it be he's an imposter? After the armistice, that would have given our enemies enough time to — "

"Bring Brandt back here this —," Landsmann shouted. Jawbreaker bolted for the door before the colonel had finished his words.

~

Keller looked around, close to panic. No one had seen him kill Dengel. *Minutes to escape. Get down the stairs, out of the hotel, and into the crowded streets.* As Keller took off, he suddenly recalled the motorcycles parked in front of the hotel. *That's it! Pretend to be a courier.* Running down the inside stairway, he confronted two soldiers walking up. He waved Sund's papers — "Orders from Herr Weil to Minister Noske. Out of my way." The two men stepped aside and let him pass. On the third-floor landing, he stopped to catch his breath, and his bad leg started to cramp. *Not now.* He hobbled through the pain.

"Halt!" Jawbreaker's voice resounded behind him. Despite protests from his throbbing leg, Keller pushed himself harder and raced down the steps as Jawbreaker bounded down behind him with his usual single-minded purpose.

Gaining ground, Jawbreaker neared Keller between the third and second floors. At the point where the stairway turned on itself in two downward 90-degree turns, Keller stopped, pulled Dengel's Luger from his belt and raised it to head level. When Jawbreaker rounded the corner, Keller fired point blank, scattering Jawbreaker's brains. He had a fleeting moment of satisfaction at eliminating the fanatical killer, but Landsmann's guards were now closing in. Keller crouched low and waited. Seconds later, the two men recklessly turned the same corner as Jawbreaker and met the same fate. Keller had to move out of the way of their tumbling bodies.

Angry voices came from the stairway from above and below. The vice was closing.

Keller hurried down to the first floor. Four soldiers were preparing to advance on the staircase. As calmly and forcefully as he could manage, Keller said, "I'm a courier. There's an assassin in the building. I have an important message for Minister Noske." By the grace of God, Keller outranked them all. "There's a wounded man up there. Help him. Out of my way. That's an order."

"Are you wounded, Sergeant?" One of the soldiers pointed to his blood-stained uniform.

"Never mind. Move."

They all sprang past him. Keller's bravado bought him a few precious seconds before their confusion cleared, giving him enough time to exit the front door.

With danger multiplying behind him, Keller sprinted to the line of motorcycles, expecting bullets to hit him any second. Two men guarded the bikes. "Man's been shot. I'm a courier for Herr Noske," Keller said. "I need one of those bikes!"

The chaos he had created worked to his advantage. The guards hesitated and looked at each other.

Keller saluted and jumped on the bike, gunned the engine, and took off on one wheel. Ducking low, he accelerated away. Bullets flew around him.

Chapter 51
Roadblocks

Berlin: May 1919

Keller pushed the motorcycle to its limit as he sped away from the Eden Hotel. Without goggles, he squinted into the wind, his vision restricted when he needed it most. Rounds of bullets zipped by him at a thickening rate. Some hit the road, sending angry bits of gravel into his face and legs that stung like dozens of wasps. One bullet nicked his left calf, and he felt the blood drip down his leg and soak into his stocking. Driven by adrenaline and fear, he ignored the pain and crouched lower on the bike.

At the end of the hotel driveway, Keller put out his foot and forced the bike into a controlled skid, balancing the risk of falling against the urgent need to get away. Frantically working the gears, he figured he had at most a one-minute lead. He sped up Hitzig Strasse to Tiergarten Strasse, where he turned south then east along the Landwehrkanal. At Potsdamerplatz, he had seconds to decide whether to ditch the bike and take a train to Hamburg. He chose the bike. It gave him flexibility and speed. In his blood-stained Freikorps uniform, he could be spotted easily on foot.

He sped past Potsdamer's Central Bahnhof and headed east on Leipziger Strasse. Three hundred yards farther, he slowed down enough to look back. No one was pursuing him. He had gained ground. He eased the bike into a higher gear, relieved it had not been damaged in his escape. The engine was running smoothly. He raced through his options. He had only three bullets left and would have to make them count.

Moving east, he was heading into an area controlled by the

Freikorps. He also had to get out of his bloody uniform. How much reward would Landsmann put on him? In these desperate times, a few marks would be enough for someone to betray him. He needed money, but his first priority was to get away from the central part of town.

Keller's mind juggled conflicting needs — the constant physical demands of operating the motorcycle as fast as possible without drawing unwanted attention, versus going slowly enough to spot potential threats. How fast could Landsmann send out the alert? What direction did they think he would take? How to counter their moves? He tried to remember the location of the permanent checkpoints. Where would they place new roadblocks? Time was moving against him.

Keller reached the wide Friedrich Strasse Boulevard and opened up the bike to full throttle. His luck ended minutes later at a checkpoint on the Victory Column circle manned by two Freikorps soldiers with the usual signs: "Do not move past this point. Violators will be shot." They saw him.

He had to decide. It was too early for gun battles, and he had too few bullets. Approach and talk his way through? He shoved the engine into second gear, causing the engine to groan and slow down to nine miles an hour. The sudden deceleration of the bike made Keller feel like someone was pressing hard on his chest, and he fought to keep his head from snapping forward. Once again stable, he planned his next move. What he would do depended on the two soldiers standing guard. To Keller's relief, he noted they were from the 5th Freikorps regiment, one of Noske's weaker units. Good. A corporal and a private. He outranked them. Better. The soldiers appeared bored and seemed unconcerned when he approached. Their rifles were slung on their back. They were not looking for him. He could fight this battle with his wits.

Although it was a chilly morning, a mix of sweat and grit ran down his neck, turning his shirt into skin-scraping sandpaper. His eyes watered and his face was so scratched anyone would think he had lost a cat fight. He shook his wrists, which were cramping from his iron-like grip on the handlebars, and slowed to a stop in front of the soldiers. "*Guten Morgen*, Corporal," he said in an upbeat and friendly tone.

The corporal grunted, "Where you going?"

"I'm on a personal mission for my colonel." Keller prayed he was right that these two soldiers had not been warned about his desertion.

"In this part of town?" the corporal said. The private casually smoked a cigarette a few yards away.

"I have a note for his niece." Keller winked. "She lives in the Schoneberg district. The colonel can't make his lunchtime rendezvous. He'll have my neck if I don't reach her."

"Your uniform, it's — "

"Landsmann Battalion,"

"Best unit in Berlin. Terrific fighting at Alexanderplatz. But the blood?" The corporal pointed to Keller's uniform blouse.

"Had to take care of two Communists before I left. They won't pose any more trouble for us." Keller smiled malevolently.

"Watch those tires, Sergeant. They're getting bald."

A field radio crackled on the desk near the checkpoint. *Was Landsmann sending out word about him?* "Corporal, I must hurry." Keller revved his engine. "Please let me pass."

"Corporal Edelman, should I get that?" the private asked through the cigarette dangling in his mouth.

Keller could almost hear Captain Reick shouting over the radio. "Lift the barrier, private." The corporal turned back to Keller and waved him through.

Keller sped off. He was a hundred yards away when he heard the shout, "*Halt*!" followed by gunfire. He accelerated beyond the view of the checkpoint guards and steered into a narrow alleyway about five minutes away. He dismounted, fighting dizziness and despair. Landsmann had reacted more quickly than Keller had anticipated. He was trapped inside the central city. The ring of roadblocks would close it off.

Soon, every person in Berlin would either be after him or willing to trade information on his whereabouts for the handsome reward the Freikorps would surely offer. In today's desperate times, money trumped everything else. He would face no sympathy. Speed was his only hope. The blood on his uniform did not matter. His bleeding leg did not matter. His growing hunger and thirst did not matter. If stopped, he was dead.

His sweat-filled, blood-stained uniform and badly scratched face transformed his appearance into a monster no unarmed man would dare approach. A welcome blessing, yet also a curse — he would not have to fight off civilians, but it singled him out. He looked like what he was: a man on the run. Such men did not last long in an unruly world of hungry people controlled by a ruthless, trigger-happy military.

Think. If he tried to hide, the pressure would only mount. More important, he had to warn the Allies about the Freikorps's intention to stop the treaty signing as soon as possible. He decided to move to the western part of the city where the Freikorps's presence was lighter and less organized. He would avoid the side streets and take the main roads, choosing speed over stealth, even though he would likely face more road blocks. They would only get stronger.

What about his leg that now throbbed? A nearly empty bottle of schnapps lay in the alley. A God-given gift. Keller drank most of the schnapps and poured the rest onto a strip of cloth he ripped from his shirt. He rolled up his trouser leg and dabbed the cloth onto his wound. It was not deep, and had mostly clotted, but the alcohol stung more than he expected.

He sifted through the garbage cans for something to wear over his uniform, but everything useful had already been snatched. The gas tank was three-quarters full, enough to get him far from Berlin, if he lived that long. He rechecked the Luger and placed it in his belt where he could reach it quickly. Acutely aware of his dim chances, he said a short prayer and took off.

He worked his way south to York Strasse and turned west. At the Bahnhof, he went south at Manstein Strasse and turned west on Goerschen. A squad of soldiers was setting up a roadblock at the Potsdamer Strasse intersection. One man was watching the street as the rest fortified the barricade and completed defensive positions. No doubt who they were after. Landsmann must have alerted the entire Freikorps in Berlin. They moved with grim-faced resolve, obviously looking for revenge for the death of two of their own. One team was completing a sandbag position in front of a machine gun.

Keller saw the observer but was not spotted in turn. He took several deep breaths. *There*! He spied a gap in the unfinished roadblock.

Chapter 52
The Wannsee

Berlin: May 1919

Keller stayed out of view, surreptitiously devising his next move. The road, full of holes and slick with automobile oil and animal waste, was his first problem. Too fast would be dangerous. Too slow and he would be shot.

He counted seven soldiers in all. They must have beaten him to this spot by minutes — Landsmann's order to arrest him was fast enough to cast out the dragnet, but too slow to complete it. Two men scrambled to set up a sand-bag and machine-gun emplacement. He would not stand a chance against that much firepower. He must get past them before they finished. Four others scrambled to close the gap he had spotted.

Other threats? The street was empty except for a prowling cat. No civilians to distract the soldiers or offer protection. By now, Berliners had learned these roadblocks meant gunfire. Only foolhardy and desperate men, like Keller, approached them.

Holding the Luger and a handlebar in one hand, Keller revved his engine with the other and blasted toward the gap. Almost immediately, he hit a slippery patch and struggled to control the skidding bike. Seconds later, a pothole almost sent him flying. His legs bounced hard into the handlebars, but he held on. He fought to steady the motorcycle, more wild bull than machine. Only his extraordinary balance and adrenaline-fed strength saved him.

Keller steadied the shaking bike and raced by the men carrying the barbed wire. They dropped it and reached for their weapons. The two other soldiers yelled a warning and hurried to ready the machine gun. They were too slow. The man on watch raised his rifle, but Keller shot him in the chest before he could work his bolt. Leaning low on the bike, he hurtled through the gap to a chorus of curses and shouting and pulled away just as they began to shoot. The jolt from another pothole knocked the Luger out of his hand. The bursts of rifle fire were too powerful to stop and retrieve it.

Keller turned away from the murderous volleys into a side street that offered safety for the moment, but he was far from safe. He had not seen any vehicles at the roadblock, and they could not catch him on foot. Would they call ahead? Where? The next roadblock? No chance they would have a direct phone link this soon. No, they would call back to Landsmann, if they had the courage to admit failure. Keller had gained precious minutes.

He had to get out of the central city—fast. Nothing else mattered. The quicker he moved west, the better his chances. The Freikorps had beaten him to the Potsdamer Strasse intersection. Keller had to beat them to the next. It would probably be in the Wilmersdorf section of the city, where the Freikorps maintained few posts. Like him, they would have to dash to get there.

Racing west on Berliner Strasse, Keller passed a Bahnhof without incident. He was gaining ground. A few people stared at his badly scratched face and bloody uniform. Going hell-bent for leather on a motorcycle, he had been right. No one dared interfere.

Nearing the Grunewald at the western edge of the Wilmsdorf section and feeling confident he had outrun the initial roadblocks, he stopped for a brief rest under an apple tree. He heard a Fokker D VII aeroplane over head. *Shit. Hadn't expected that.* He waited under the tree until it flew away. He would have to move more slowly, avoid the center of the road, stay inconspicuous.

He was desperately thirsty and mentally exhausted, but he knew he had to press on. *Calm down, remember ...* . He conjured up images of his carefree high school days and the baseball game he played for the county championship. He recalled the exhilaration when he drove in the go-ahead runs. He won the game with a dazzling backhanded grab he made at shortstop. The memory always energized him and gave him the confidence to forge ahead in tough times.

His thirst gave him an idea where he could get what he needed without violence. Why hadn't he thought of it before?

~

Watching and listening for aeroplanes overhead, Keller continued on Berliner Strasse and turned southeast on Hohenzollern until he reached the Grunewald. No aeroplane could spot him through the trees. He traveled on dirt roads and walking paths through the dense forest until he reached the Wannsee, and a popular beach area by the lake. Just a short distance from the city center, the view reminded him of the Finger Lakes in upstate New York he had visited with Shannon. Who would look for him here? Luck was with him. The sunny spring day had brought several bathers. He hid the motorcycle in a dry ditch in a heavily wooded area, covered it with undergrowth, and marked a nearby oak tree so he could locate it again. Keller stripped off his bloody shirt and buried it. Naked to the waist, he was just another Berliner enjoying the beach. He was amused that the lack of clothes provided a perfect disguise.

Germany had begun allowing public bathing a few years ago due to popular demand. He removed his pants and boots, unstrapped his knife, and tucked it in his boot. He carried them as he walked in his underclothes across the sand, which massaged his aching feet. Marvelous. Northern Goshawks were chirping, and the fresh air invigorated him. Who could have imagined that little more than an hour ago he was running for his life?

He avoided the regular bathing areas surrounded by fences and made his way to an out-of-the-way spot he had heard was popular with homosexuals. He could not have invented a more perfect place to hide. The sight of several naked men walking around told him he had reached the spot. One couple sat on a blanket in deep embrace. Although their sexual proclivities baffled him, Keller knew men like these provided an easy opportunity to obtain what he needed without a fight. He removed the rest of his clothes, dropped them on the sand, and jumped in the water. He gulped in several mouthfuls. The water was brackish but refreshing. As he washed himself off, a man approached, gesturing invitingly. Keller politely discouraged him.

Feeling refreshed, Keller walked back to his pile of clothes and let the warm sun dry him. He felt cleaner and more relaxed than he had in weeks and began to observe the men around him.

Twenty-five minutes later, two men in uniform started to walk toward him. Keller reached into his boot for his knife, but relaxed when the men began to hold hands. They walked by him without a glance and placed a blanket on the ground fifty yards away. They removed their clothes and caressed each other.

Keller sat back and closed his eyes. His body begged for rest. He woke forty-five minutes later, grateful for the sleep. He peered around but saw no threats. He studied the various men on the beach, searching for someone about his size. After an hour, a young man about six feet tall with a trim build like his sat down not too far away. The man seemed nervous, as if it were his first time in such a place. He kept looking around, sometimes staring at a good-looking man. *Here's my mark*, thought Keller. *He won't be thinking about someone stealing his shirt and trousers*. It did not take long for another man to approach. After talking a few minutes, the two men walked into the woods.

Keller sauntered over and picked up the man's clothes, acting as if they were his own. There was not much money in the billfold, but it more than doubled what Keller had. He left the man enough to get back to the city by public transport. He walked back to where he had hidden his motorcycle and stayed under cover the rest of the afternoon. He heard some commotion back on the beach, but was confident it would settle down. The man who lost his clothes would be too embarrassed to report the loss — *Where did you lose them again, Mein Herr*?

Alone, well-concealed, and no longer in uniform, Keller had time to decide what to do next. *Think like a policeman,* he reminded himself. The Freikorps were using aeroplanes, which meant he would have to move in the shadows or at night. They would never think to look for him by the Wannsee. Even if they did, he would disappear into the woods. They would never find him here unless they combed the area with the entire battalion, and maybe not even then. At this moment, Landsmann's dragnet would be at maximum effect. Let them waste their time. Each passing hour increased their frustration and improved his odds. By tomorrow, his pursuers would shift their efforts to widen the dragnet, creating holes he could sneak through.

Keller felt safe and roamed the area. The nights would be chilly but survivable. Food could be found, fish caught, and water was plentiful. He would be careful using fire, but his would not be the only one in the Wannsee, a place where homeless veterans and destitute civilians stayed. Wolves were a more serious problem, but he sharpened some branches into spears just in case one approached.

He would stay at the Wannsee for another day. He was tired and needed to gain strength for his flight to Denmark. It would be a perilous journey.

Chapter 53
Heading North

Along the Elbe River, Germany: May 1919

Three days later, Keller headed back to his motorcycle. He had stayed longer in the Grunewald than anticipated, but he was rested and certain that the dragnet for his capture would have expanded so wide as to be ineffective.

With dirty hair and stolen clothes, he looked more like a destitute workman than a Freikorps soldier. Time and the beginnings of a grubby beard had altered his look. Even his facial scratches had healed. The meager sum he had when he fled and the few marks he had stolen since were hardly enough to buy a meal. For now, his belly was full of fish he had caught, berries he had scavenged, and turnips an ex-soldier had shared.

He had a moment of concern when he could not find the tree he had marked, but he closed his eyes and retraced his steps and finally spotted the oak tree with the small "V" he had carved into its bark. More than ever, he longed to see Shannon. Could he confess all the horrors? How could he tell her about the assassination of Liebknecht? He hated himself for what he had done. Would he ever become whole again? *You're on a mission. Reveal the Freikorps plot and get back to Shannon.* That was all that mattered. There would be time enough for regrets.

The motorcycle engine purred when it started up. The weather was clear. Keller would have preferred rain. One hour outside of Berlin, he heard the distinct engine of an Albatross D.V. biplane overhead. He looked up. *Shit.* There were two of them. Before he could veer off the road for cover, they dived. Keller heard the rat-a-tat-rat of their machine guns just before the bullets showered the area. *What the hell*? They could not have recognized him from that distance. Landsmann must have ordered the search aeroplanes to shoot every motorcyclist in the area. The Freikorps wanted him badly.

The biplanes completed a pass, looped around, and returned to strafe him again, raking the area with hundreds of bullets. Keller steered his bike into the woods and hid behind a stout pine tree. Bullets passed around him in powerful bursts. The aeroplanes took a last run and flew away. Keller guessed they were out of bullets, but knew they would report the incident on their return. A patrol would be dispatched immediately.

Keller had to move fast. He turned off the main street and rode for another hour. Evening was approaching. He figured it would take Landsmann's bloodhounds that long to get to the place where he had been spotted. He found a good hiding place and settled in for the night. Hungry, thirsty, and safe. The trip north was going to take him longer than expected.

~

Before he set off the next morning, he found a small stream and drank his fill. He could survive without food. Using the Elbe River as a guide, he worked his way north and west, staying off the main roads but always vigilant. Twice he had had to ride around convoys of Freikorps soldiers and camps full of dangerous and reckless men. He continued without incident until he reached Havelberg, about one-third of the way to Hamburg. The early afternoon sun, hot like July, beat down on him. The back of his shirt was wet from sweat, anxiety, and fatigue.

He turned a sharp corner, and there it was. A roadblock manned by three Freikorps soldiers. He was on top of it before he could react. He tightened his grip on the handlebars out of disgust. Without the Luger, he would have to bluff his way through. Well-armed with carbines and hand grenades, the soldiers were alert and positioned for mutual defense. The lieutenant held up his hand. "*Halt*."

A routine stop? Keller had no choice. His heart raced as he slowly drove up to the lieutenant. "*Guten Tag*," Keller said.

The lieutenant saluted, and Keller fought off the instinct to return the gesture. The lieutenant peered at him sternly. Was it just the normal Freikorps look or something more sinister? "Papers." Keller handed over Sund's. The lieutenant scanned them and looked up at Keller. "Where you coming from, Sund?"

"Leipzig." Any place but Berlin. *Say as little as possible*. The other two soldiers had him at gun point. Run? Wouldn't have a chance.

"What were you doing there?"

"Visiting a crippled comrade. No legs."

The lieutenant shook his head knowingly. "You in the war?"

"*Nein*. Armaments industry."

"Where'd you get the boots?"

The one thing in his dress that could give him away. "Were his. He don't need them no more."

"Papers say you're from Bremen. Doesn't sound like it," the lieutenant said with a curious look. "Can't place that accent."

"Born there. Lived all over. Wherever papa could get work." This was taking too long. The other soldiers were getting anxious.

"Where did you get the motorcycle? It looks military."

"My friend were a courier. The army gave it to him after a shell took his legs. Don't know why. Maybe better than giving it to the British."

"You sure you didn't steal it? Lots of thieves around."

"From a dead man, *ja*. My friend died. We all got to live. Anything else, *Leutnant*?"

"See any deserters?"

Keller stopped himself from shaking. He shrugged and said, “I passed a camp about seven miles back. I’m sure there were some there.”

“We’ll check. Go ahead.” The lieutenant signaled him through. The two soldiers lifted the barrier.

“*Danke, Leutnant.*” Keller rode on. Only several minutes later did his heart begin to beat normally.

~

As night approached and visibility decreased, Keller stopped in a hamlet about fifteen miles outside of Wittenberg. He figured he was about halfway to Hamburg. He was famished. Dare he risk exposing himself in a beer hall? It was still early. The beer hall would not be crowded. He parked the motorcycle across the street where he could keep an eye on it.

He sat in the back corner by a window where he could see both his bike and the front door. He kept his head down and tried to remain inconspicuous. He ordered a beer, a bratwurst, and potatoes and paid with the last of his money. The frothy but slightly bitter beer rolled down his throat like a mountain waterfall. The salty bratwurst jolted his taste buds alive. The potatoes filled his belly. Half-way through the meal, a man with a scarred face and red burn marks on his arm approached from a table with two other men. “You were a soldier, weren’t you?” he asked.

Trouble. Keller could not guess his intentions. The man was obviously an ex-soldier. Keller reached for the knife strapped to his leg but hesitated. *Relax. Be friendly.* “We all were, weren’t we? You look like you fared worse than me. Sit down.” Being rude to a former comrade was provocative and could lead to anything.

“Gehrke.” They shook hands.

“Sund.” Using that name seemed strange.

"What unit you in?"

"Too many. They got wiped out as soon as they were formed."

"What sector?"

"Meuse-Argonne at the end. Americans." Keller named the area he was most familiar with, even though it was from the opposite side.

"Who was your commander?"

Too many questions. Each answer was forcing him into bigger lies. "Where did you get those?" he asked, pointing to Gehrke's burns.

Gehrke's tone turned cold. "Why don't you answer my question?"

Keller changed tactics, remembering shell-shocked men he had seen in field hospitals. "I ... I don't remember." He started to shake and twist. He pinched his eyes shut and grabbed his head. "The shelling. Make it stop."

"You all right?" Gehrke sounded concerned.

Keller opened his eyes and grimaced. "I'm sorry. I get these attacks sometimes. It will pass. Best to leave me alone."

Gehrke stood to leave. "Good luck."

His meal finished, Keller walked across the street to his bike. Gehrke and another man were waiting for him. "I don't care how many shellings you faced, no man forgets his outfit. Who are you, Sund?"

"Like I said, a soldier."

"No, you're not," Gehrke said. "I think you're a Communist. One of those *Volksmarines* who joined the Spartacists. You were in Berlin for the uprising and got routed. Now you're running." Gehrke reached toward his belt and pulled out an eighteen-inch trench sword with a spiked handguard, more than a match for Keller's knife. "That your bike?"

The other man, hulking and slow, began to circle behind Keller. "I hate traitors." He reached into his pocket and pulled out a set of brass knuckles.

Keller backed up looking for a stronger weapon. Nothing. He had to fight with what he had to save the motorcycle. He bent down and grabbed the knife strapped to his ankle and stared at both men with fire in his eyes. *Who first? Gehrke?*

Gehrke attacked when he saw Keller's knife. *Fool.* He had sacrificed the advantage he had with the more lethal weapon. The other man was slow to react. They were not acting as a team. Keller had the chance he needed. He held the knife by the blade, raised it over his shoulder, and flung it. The knife bore into Gehrke's throat. A look of confusion, then acceptance, filled his eyes. He spit up blood and collapsed. Keller picked up Gehrke's sword and pointed it at the other man. "Come on, you bastard," Keller said. "I'll cut you into sausage."

The other man ran down the street shouting for help. To whom? Keller did not want to find out. He retrieved his knife, ran to the bike, and sped away.

Chapter 54
The German Delegation Arrives

Paris: May 7, 1919

Three days after Shannon's visit, Martin left his room in the Hotel-Dieu de Paris. The pain from his wound forced him to double over. The doctor stopped him and said he needed another week to recover. "If Clémenceau can go back to work a day after an assassination attempt, so can I," Martin replied.

"Stay at a desk. Running around will reopen your wound," the doctor said, scribbling Martin's release on a pad.

Today would be the most important day in the Peace Conference so far. The German delegation was coming to receive the terms. To complicate matters, Colonel House had insisted on greeting them on arrival, at the Trianon Palace Hotel in Versailles. Martin needed to be at the scene to oversee security. What calamity would occur if a German delegate, or worse the president's top aide, were killed in the streets of France?

Dressed in civilian clothes, he went to the hotel two hours before the scheduled German arrival. There, he met three trusted allies: Sergeant Cooper, under orders not to leave Colonel House's side once he arrived; the reliable Captain Durand and three squads of his men; and Shannon Keller, who could read people and assess threats as well as anyone Martin knew on the New York police force.

The exertion of walking the streets fatigued him, and the bandage over his wound began to leak blood. He ignored it and checked his watch. Any minute. Nervous tension heightened his awareness. He forgot the pain. The streets were filling with thousands of excited and uneasy Frenchmen, anxious to view the vanquished but still loathsome Huns. Cameramen and reporters were lined three-deep along the street. French flags were everywhere. Martin walked by Durand near the reception area. They exchanged confident glances. All secure. The two men Durand had placed by the front gate looked vigilant. Out of the corner of his eye, Martin saw Shannon, dressed in war-widow black, outside the gate to the hotel. Suddenly, she turned and scurried into the crowd. What had she seen?

~

Shannon had been following the husky man for several minutes. Mid-thirties, average height, he was dressed to blend in, but he slithered through the throng like a rattlesnake. A tattered civilian coat masked his physique. *Need to get closer*. He chain-smoked. At first, Shannon thought he was suffering from shell shock, but she had worked with cops long enough to know when a man was dangerous and when he was acting. And this man was well-rehearsed.

Shannon squeezed nearer. Behaving with a soldier's calm and a criminal's purpose, he looked as if he did not care whether he lived or died. His coat pocket bulged menacingly. This man had seen war up close and knew the ways of killing.

Pondering her next move, Shannon backed away, not wanting to reveal herself. At the same time, she spotted Ana Primakova ten yards to their left, studying him too. *What's she doing here? Where was her American guard?* Shannon flashed Ana a look. They locked confused eyes.

The momentary distraction allowed the man to disappear into the crowd. Panicked, Shannon scanned the area. Too many people. She pushed her way to the curb and spotted the man heading closer to the hotel. She looked back and saw Ana arguing with a Marine corporal from the Crillon Hotel guard. Ana ran, but the Marine grabbed her arm, holding her back.

Shannon hurried to intercept the man and caught up to

him twenty yards from the main gate. She maneuvered to his side undetected until she swept her hand across his coat and felt a gun. The man made a quick look, reached into his coat, but jumped away when the sound of cars approached. He pushed through the crowd trying to reach the street just as the German delegation drove past.

The throng pressed forward to get a closer look, separating him from Shannon. People pointed and strained to see the cars stop just inside the gate. Some jeered, others shouted obscenities. Six immaculately dressed men, led by Count Ulrich von Brockdorff-Rantzau, Germany's chief foreign minister, exited their automobiles. Wearing a black morning coat and a bowler hat, Brockdorff-Rantzau looked like the self-assured Prussian aristocrat he was. He flashed a walking stick. A ceremonial guard of soldiers approached the Germans. The officer raised his sword in a military salute and said something to Brockdorff-Rantzau, who frowned. A number of French officials joined them. The soldiers lined up in two rows to usher the Germans into the hotel.

The man had reached the gate and headed toward them. He was now fifteen yards from Brockdorff-Rantzau and closing, with a clear view of the Germans. None of the ceremonial guard noticed him. Frantic, Shannon strained to signal Martin at the reception area, but the soldiers blocked his view. She shoved the man in front of her, giving her room to fight her way through.

She yelled, but the noise from the crowd was too loud. Only the officer from the escort heard her. She pointed at the approaching man and gestured warnings. The officer understood and ordered his men to close ranks around the Germans. They moved in quick step. Smartly done. It looked like a parade ground maneuver instead of a defensive ploy. None of the onlookers seemed to notice the threat.

The man stopped. He had missed his chance. His hand froze

inside his coat. His face seethed with anger.

Shannon saw the Germans enter the hotel followed by Colonel House, Martin, and the French officials, including Captain Durand. She looked around but did not see the man. She sensed danger and reached for the pistol inside her purse.

"*Putain.*" The man pressed the barrel of a Lebel service revolver hard against her ribs. "No words," he said. "Down the street. Into the trees."

The crowd was too distracted to notice her plight. Alone under the locust trees, the man raised the Lebel to her face. She ducked and tried to knock him down with her shoulder, but it felt to her like she had hit a stone wall. Up close, she recognized him from Martin's police drawing and description — it was Mal, the arsonist of the fire at Le Grand Hotel. Part of his right ear was missing.

Shannon ran and tripped. She scrambled to stand, but Mal pushed her back down with his heavy boot. Looming over her, he jammed the revolver into her forehead. The cold barrel seemed to burn like a branding iron. She heard the click of the hammer and closed her eyes.

Out of nowhere, Shannon heard a crack and a moan. The Lebel landed at her feet; she opened her eyes. Mal's forearm hung at an odd angle. She looked up and saw a studded truncheon sweep down into the assassin's head. Mal's skull opened with a sickening crack. Brain matter seeped through the wound. Blood spurted onto her clothes. Mal toppled to the ground and landed with a thud that pushed the air out of his lungs followed by a cough and suffocating gasps. He started to turn pale, and his eyes opened into sightless marbles.

"Madam Keller, are you hurt?"

Blood and hair dripped off the truncheon in Ana's right hand.

~

Ana checked to see if anyone had witnessed her attack. Her Marine guard had not caught up, undoubtedly still unconscious from the blow she had delivered when he refused to pursue Mal. She was not sure if Mal was dead or alive. And did not care. She had taken revenge on her long-time tormenter. The crowd, intent on the German delegation, had no interest in the group of trees behind them. The few who glanced her way seemed unconcerned that a man lay prostrate on the ground — drunken peace celebrations were common. When a couple leaving the area headed in her direction, Ana covered Mal's bleeding wound with her red Communist arm band. "Heat stroke," she said, bending over him so her body blocked their view.

She realized with alarm that Mal was still breathing. "Madam Keller, help me move him off the street."

~

Shannon, feeling dizzy, did not respond. She looked at Mal with dismay. She touched her face where the barrel had left an impression and tried to make sense of what had happened. In a flash, her anger exploded. She bent down, picked up Mal's revolver, and aimed it at his head.

"Stop! We need to question him." Ana grabbed the gun. "You're in shock, Shannon."

Shannon turned her head, as expressionless as a signpost, until Ana shook her out of her daze. Shannon blinked her eyes and nodded. "What can I do?"

"Find Major Martin. Bring him here. Tell Captain Durand to warn his men. Another attack is possible. Go."

Shannon stumbled off.

~

Ana tensed as the minutes slipped by. Mal's breathing weakened. She could not conceal him much longer. Ten minutes later, Captain Durand and three uniformed policemen arrived. Thirty yards behind,

Martin clutched his ribs. Durand motioned Ana aside. “Let me look at that bastard.”

Ana lifted the armband to reveal the assassin’s face. “Mal. The man we’ve been looking for.” Something about Durand’s expression caused her concern. She dismissed the feeling. Too much going on.

Durand withdrew his revolver and tapped Mal with his shoe. Still alive.

Martin caught up and cut in front of Durand. “We need to get him out of here. Where can we take him, Alain?”

Durand hesitated. “Hotel basement,” he said. Two policemen grabbed Mal by his arms and feet. Durand sent the third man to fetch a doctor. “Be discreet.”

Onlookers gawked and moved on. Obviously, a police matter. The cops carried the body to the basement of the hotel followed by Durand, Martin, and Ana. Ana brushed against Durand, either to get his attention or to distract him. “Move away,” Durand demanded.

Durand looked crossly at Ana. “What’s she doing here?” he demanded of Martin. “She’s a Communist and a potential murderer. I should arrest her.” Durand gestured to his men.

“Are you out of your mind? She’s a friend,” Martin said. “She knows this man. She can help.” Mal coughed up blood and collapsed back onto the floor. “He’s going to die soon.”

“I’ll help him.” Durand put his foot on Mal’s chest and pressed down. His body convulsed.

“Stop, we need to interrogate him,” Martin said.

“I do know this man,” Ana said. The room turned quiet, all eyes on her. “He belongs to the French Communist party. He’s their main assassin.” She glanced at Martin, hoping for his support. “This man is a soldier. He would not act without orders. Someone else planned this attack.”

“Impossible. We stopped their conspiracy when we arrested Commandant Truchon.” Durand removed his foot.

“Apparently not,” Ana said. “Someone important is still at large.”

Chapter 55
Hamburg

Along the Elbe River, Germany: May 1919

Keller neared the outskirts of Hamburg in the afternoon, unhindered by Freikorps roadblocks or reward seekers. To avoid aeroplanes, he had traveled along the back roads at an easy pace, making him appear local, not someone on the run. It also reduced problems with his vision because he did not have goggles.

The slower route from Wittenberg had proved costly as well. The trip had been harder on the motorcycle than on him. The local roads were in terrible condition. Some had been dug up for the lead pipes to make shells. All were ill-maintained, full of rocks, holes, and rough surfaces. His engine misfired, and his smooth tires made steering the bike a struggle. The morning rains had made it worse. He twice hit something that caused him to bounce off his seat. Once, he skidded on a slippery corner and lost control. He fell on his left side, bruising his arm and leaving a long strawberry gravel burn across his outer leg. Had he been going faster, the fall might have killed him.

He fought off weariness and strain. By the time he entered the harbor area of Hamburg, his tires were so flat he was practically running on the rims. His gas tank was nearly empty, and the exhaust pipe spit oily black smoke. He had not eaten in almost twenty-four hours, and the left side of his body felt as though it had been beaten by a dozen baseball bats.

Despite his best efforts, his mind wandered. Then it happened. His judgment faltered. No more than two seconds, but it was enough. He chose to plow through, not around, a puddle of water in front of him. Only two feet wide, it turned out to be eight inches deep. When his front tire rammed into the pothole, Keller felt like the bike had hit a brick wall. The motorcycle stopped instantly, but Keller flew over the handlebars. He landed on his head, knocked out.

When he regained consciousness, he could not remember where he was at first. He forced his eyes open. *How long ago did I crash*? Still groggy, he looked at the position of the sun and the shadows and figured he had been unconscious for a few minutes. If anyone had seen him, no one came to his aid. He sat on the ground with his hands around his knees and fought back a growing sense of defeat. He knew the bike was *kaputt* but had to be sure. With his remaining strength, he muscled it upright and tried to start it. It sputtered, spit sparks, and died.

The bike could be traced to the Landsmann Battalion and back to him. At nightfall, he pushed it on what little rubber was left and worried someone would hear the scraping noise. He found a secluded spot by the edge of the water. Making sure no one was watching, Keller pushed the motorcycle into the water, hoping it was deep enough. He relaxed when it disappeared without a trace. His best hope of reaching friendly territory was gone.

Now what? He was mentally spent. His body ached. He had no money, no food, no transportation, and one hundred and twenty miles to go to get to the Danish border. He slept in an abandoned warehouse and fought off nightmares, rats, and unanswered questions all night. The next morning, he headed to the Hauptbahnhof, hoping to hop a train to Flensburg, the open city on the Danish border. A desperate move, but he was out of options.

~

It was about noon when Keller reached the main train station. With his ripped and grubby clothes, dazed look, and scratched, unwashed body, he looked like a man best avoided.

It was almost a week since he had escaped from the Eden Hotel. Had Landsmann's dragnet weakened? Had the Freikorps learned he was using Sund's papers? He hid them in his boot and prayed he would not be searched.

His hopes died quickly as soon as he walked through the main entrance. Freikorps soldiers were everywhere. They were showing pieces of paper to everyone they saw. Keller switched into his cover. He started to walk unevenly, and his expression became wandering and blank. *Find the train you need and get out.*

He was looking at the departure board when he heard a voice behind him, "You, there. Come here." Was someone calling him? *Don't give yourself away.* Keller tilted his head and stared dumbly at the board. He felt a rough tap on his shoulder. A blond young man in a Freikorps corporal's uniform looked at him sternly. "You stupid or something?"

Keller turned to him in surprise, "*Wass*?" and pointed to his ear. "Deaf!" he shouted.

The soldier pushed a paper into his face. Keller nearly collapsed. It was him in his Freikorps uniform. Good likeness. "Deserter" and "Gold reward" were printed in large type. Landsmann had pulled out all the stops. Gold was rare these days. On the black market, who could say how much it was worth? Keller shrugged his shoulders and breathed heavily on the soldier.

The soldier backed away. "You stink." He held up the picture again and pointed several times, almost puncturing the paper. "Have you seen this man?"

Keller shook his head and then he saluted. "Fought for the Kaiser. Wounded at Verdun." He pretended to fall.

The young man looked sympathetic and helped him up.

"Hungry." Keller put his hands to his pockets and pulled them out, empty.

The young man flipped him some coins, enough for a meal. "Get out of here." He waved Keller away with his rifle. Although the soldier had not recognized him, someone else surely would.

He spotted the man who could identify him before the man spotted him. Half-turned toward Keller, a major in a regular German Army uniform was giving orders. The blond-haired officer was in his early forties and wore an eye patch. Keller was dumfounded. There, just twenty yards away, stood the ghost of his old nemesis, Danie Caarsens, the man who had almost blown up lower Manhattan three years ago. Caarsens was presumed dead, but his ghost was real. *How in God's name...?*

Caarsens was the fiercest and savviest opponent Keller had ever faced. One look at Keller and Keller would be doomed. *Get out fast.* He needed another plan.

~

Early that evening, Keller, still shocked at seeing Caarsens, found a hobo camp around the shit-end of the dockyards. His whole body ached, but at least his belly was full. The bread and cheese he had bought with the young soldier's money gave him the strength he needed. Keller approached three men sitting around a campfire. Their downtrodden circumstances matched his own. A large man stood when Keller neared. "We don't like strangers here, friend. Go."

Keller asked for help, guessing they, like many in such hobo camps, were fellow soldiers. When they saw how torn and bruised he was, they invited him to stay and gave him some watery cabbage stew. There was little talk. The men peeled off to find their sleeping spots, each man to his own miseries.

The next day, Keller traded his good army boots for a bicycle in decent condition and a pair of shoes with soles as thin as wafers. The men wanted Keller's knife, but when he offered it blade-end first, negotiations ceased. He picked up the bicycle and pedaled away, looking over his shoulder to make sure no one reconsidered. He would will himself to Flensburg. *Shannon, help me.*

~

Keller stopped to rest for ten minutes every hour, walking the bike off the road, where he would not be seen. Spending another night with unknown men would be too risky. The bicycle could make it. Could he? He made a goal of thinking about just the next few seconds and the seconds after that. If he thought about the distance he still needed to travel, he would become disheartened. One revolution. The next. Keep pedaling. Push left foot. Push right. Don't fall asleep. Keep straight. Push left foot. Push right ...

He had not seen any Freikorps patrols or roadblocks since Hamburg, but knew they would try to stop him at the border. Push left foot. Push right ...

The sign said Flensburg, four kilometers. Almost there. Push left foot. Push right. *No. Rest a little longer this time.* Keller got off the bike and collapsed by the roadside, too weak to walk it off the road. Something was pushing against his chest. He came out of his daze with a start. A rifle muzzle pointed at his face.

Chapter 56
Brockdorff-Rantzau Responds

Paris, France: May 7, 1919

Shannon continued to shake a half-hour after Ana had saved her life. Who was Ana Primakova? A friend? A spy? A threat? Nothing made sense. Shannon was used to danger, but she had never before experienced imminent death — not even when she had been tortured by a German spy in New York.

Shannon bumped into the door frame as she entered the conference hall. Fighting for calm, she headed to her translator's chair behind Colonel House. She sat down, folded her hands together, and breathed deeply. She pressed her legs together and suppressed the urge to scream. The velvet on the armrests felt rough. The memory of the muzzle burning into her skin haunted her. She worried that the imprint left by the gun barrel still showed, despite the powder she had used to cover it.

Compose yourself. You have a job to do. Colonel House sat at the front right corner of the large conference table. He distrusted the conference translators. He wanted Shannon near him so she could correct their mistakes and interpret the gestures and body language of the participants.

Shannon looked around the room. Like many others there, she was aware that, four years ago to the day, a German U-boat had sunk the passenger liner *Lusitania*, almost drawing the United States into the war. It was no coincidence that the Allies summoned the Germans to appear today. They wanted to remind them that Britain and America had not forgotten the atrocity. The Germans were intruders at the conference and were to be tolerated, not welcomed. But, thought

Shannon, how callous. How shortsighted.

The Allied delegation sat around a great U-shaped set of tables in order of importance. Georges Clémenceau, France's Prime Minister and head of the conference, sat at the base of the "U," flanked by four chairs on either side. President Wilson sat at his immediate right, and David Lloyd George, the British Prime Minister, sat at his left. Next to them were their three top advisors. Along the outer arms of the "U" were the chief delegates of each victorious major power. On the inner side sat representatives of the smaller Allied countries. Interpreters filled the center of the "U." A small table reserved for visitors was placed in front, almost as an afterthought. Reserved today for the German delegation, the chairs were all empty.

Ever since the proceedings had begun more than three months ago, everyone had been waiting for this day with a mix of dread and excitement. Minutes to go. The Germans, waiting in guarded isolation to appear before the conference, were about to enter. Nervous chatter spread around the room. How would they act? What would they say?

Shannon hoped Germany would be conciliatory and cooperative despite the harsh terms she had helped translate into German. She felt pessimistic about the outcome. The problems were too complex, the hatreds too ripe, the nationalistic desires too strong for this, or any conference, to resolve.

The room was so crowded that people were pressed against the windows leading to the outside garden. The air had already become stale and heavy. With the thick heels of their shoes beating against the floor, the six German diplomats entered carrying heavy briefcases, led by Count Ulrich von Brockdorff-Rantzau. If the Allied delegates wanted a remorseful and compliant German, they did not get one. He maintained a military bearing and looked every bit the Prussian he was. He had a slim physique, a narrow face dominated by a thick, wide mustache, and slick hair parted in the middle. True to his aristocratic background, he acted superior to everyone present.

Shannon leaned forward and whispered to House, "My God, he's lost the conference before he's even spoken." House scowled in apparent agreement. Shannon leaned back in her chair. *Can this get any worse?*

Clémenceau called the meeting to order in a calm but commanding tone. Distinguished, with white hair and mustache, he wore a perfectly cut gray suit and his usual gray gloves. Speaking English in deference to President Wilson, he displayed the demeanor of a high court judge, dignified and controlled. After a few introductory comments, he outlined the conditions set forth in the treaty. He concluded by addressing the Germans: "You asked for peace. We are disposed to grant it to you." When the interpreters finished, he asked if anyone wished to speak.

Brockdorff-Rantzau raised his hand. Clémenceau recognized him. Brockdorff-Rantzau lit a cigarette. Instead of standing, as protocol would suggest, he remained in his seat, shocking everyone in the room. He slipped on large horned-rimmed glasses and spoke in guttural, unapologetic German. The count reminded the conference that Germany had signed the armistice on the basis of proposals set forth by President Wilson, none of which were contained in the terms. He denied that Germany was solely responsible for the war. "Such an admission would be a lie." The audience was hushed.

He then accused the Allies of wanting to carve Germany into obscure and impotent parts. Lloyd George snapped an ivory knife in two. Clémenceau turned crimson. Shannon overheard Wilson whisper to Robert Lansing, his secretary of state, "This is the most tactless speech I have ever heard."

The count continued, unfazed by the reaction. "All countries," he said, "not just Germany, made mistakes during the war." He pressed his case. Despite the armistice, the Allies had maintained a blockade that was needlessly starving hundreds of thousands of innocent German women and children. He asked why Germany would not be invited to join the new League of Nations. The treaty was humiliating to Germany and showed no respect for justice. Despite the count's harsh and antagonistic tone, Shannon agreed with many of his points. At the end of his speech, Brockdorff-Rantzau looked at his fellow delegates and bowed his head. They followed in collective agreement, and he stated their conclusion: "We are all of the opinion here that this treaty cannot be accepted in its present form."

Clémenceau glared at the Germans. Brockdorff-Rantzau reached for another cigarette with trembling hands. Clémenceau concluded the session at 4 o'clock. The Germans had two weeks to respond formally to the treaty. Shannon despaired. With reconciliation seemingly impossible, the war had not ended — it had just changed forms.

~

As the conference reached its disastrous conclusion, Martin argued with Durand in the basement of the hotel. How to deal with Mal? Ana Primakova and Durand's men stood silent in the background. Martin had feared an attack but not Durand's reaction to it. Something was wrong. What? Mal could provide answers, but he was barely breathing. Martin had questions to ask of Ana too. But, right now, she was his only ally in the room.

Durand knelt, put his hands around Mal's head and shook him forcefully. "Wake up, you swine. How dare you try to humiliate France with these attacks?"

"Durand, stop!" cried Martin.

Ana stepped forward. "You'll kill him."

Is that what Durand is trying to do? Kill him? Martin grabbed Durand's hands and pulled him away. "We need to question him."

"We know all we need to. He's a Communist assassin and a traitor. The guillotine is too good for him."

"Wait," Ana said. "His eyes. They're opening. He's trying to speak."

Durand wavered. "He's delirious."

Mal struggled to rise on his elbows and blinked a few times. Life returned briefly to his eyes. He looked at Durand and uttered in a parched voice, "What are you doing here? It is good to see you, *Comrade Ours*." He slumped over, dead.

Chapter 57
All In

Flensburg, along the Germany-Denmark Border: May 1919
Dizzy, exhausted, and confused, Keller forced himself to his knees and raised his arms. He tried to focus and make sense of the situation. He was staring down the muzzle of a British Lee-Enfield in the hands of a man in civilian clothes. He said something Keller did not understand.

"*Wass*?" Keller said.

The man repeated it. Odd accent. Germanic but ... Then the man said in German, "Come with me." Keller tried to run, but in his weakened state, he did not have a chance. The man clamped handcuffs on him and pushed Keller forward with his arm. "Danger," he warned. "Germans everywhere."

"You're Danish, aren't you?" Keller asked, suddenly certain of the answer.

"No time to talk."

"I'm American. I'm not your enemy," Keller said, looking down at the handcuffs. "I need to get to my embassy."

The Dane looked at Keller sternly. "I don't know who you are. All I know is that the Freikorps" — he spit on the ground — "wants you. Badly. That makes you valuable to us. I'm Harald." Pointing his rifle, he looked up and down the road nervously.

Relations between Denmark and Germany had been fraught ever since Bismarck had grabbed this area of Germany, Schleswig-Holstein, from Denmark in the 1860s. Many Danes, apparently including this man, still resented the loss. Uncertain of his fate, but glad to be protected from the Freikorps, Keller knew German patrols could appear any second.

Harald whistled — twice long, one short. Two men emerged from the woods to join them. They argued. Keller did not understand, but gathered Harald was winning. When the debate was over, Harald looked at Keller and said, "Let's go."

The argumentative man prodded Keller with his rifle butt. "Move. *Mach schnell.*"

"Easy Asger," Harald said. "This man didn't kill your grandfather."

"Where are you taking me?" Keller asked. Were these men his saviors or his executioners?

Asger jabbed his rifle butt into Keller's stomach, sending him to the ground. "Keep talking and I'll feed you to the Germans. He gestured toward Harald. "Despite what he says, I don't want to risk my life for a stranger. I could use the reward."

"Enough, Asger. He won't run — will you?" Harald looked at Keller, who shook his head. "Not another word out of you, or we'll all end up dead."

Keller and the Danish men drifted back into the woods. "I grew up around here," the third man said, speaking for the first time. "Follow me and we won't be spotted."

"Go ahead, Finn." Harald gestured to advance.

"Why's he so valuable anyway?" Asger asked.

"Orders are orders." Harald turned to Keller. "One mistake and I'll give you to the Germans myself."

They walked along a winding path for about a mile. Except for Finn's confident steps, Keller might have thought they were walking in circles. They came to a clearing that looked out over water. He looked questioningly at his captor. "It leads to Kiel Bay," he replied. The border between Germany and Denmark. Keller was close to escaping. But to what fate?

"Get back!" Finn called as a German patrol boat motored by. "That was close. I've never seen so much activity along the border."

When the boat moved out of sight, Harald whispered, "We'll cross tonight."

The four men sat in silence for hours. Harald uncuffed Keller, gave him some bread, and shared his canteen. It held akvavit. Keller stared across the water at Denmark and wondered. These men may have saved him for now, but friends they were not. Did they think he was a German spy? Whatever awaited him, his life was in their hands. That bothered Keller more than anything else.

~

It was just past 21:30 when Finn left the group to scout the shoreline. The night had turned chilly, but on a windless evening the water was calm. It would be easier to cross, but easier to spot them crossing. An even trade. Keller shivered in his thin summer clothes, but suffering in silence had become natural to him. Finn returned, reporting the coast was clear. "There's the safest place to cross, Lieutenant. One hundred yards east."

The four men slowly waded into the water. "It's over there, Lieutenant." Finn pointed to a well-camouflaged rowboat. "Quiet. Noise travels far on nights like this."

When they reached the spot, Asger handed Keller an oar. "You have as much reason as we do to get over there safely," he said. "But don't think for a moment that I won't push you in if I have to. Sit." He pointed to the bow.

Finn had done his reconnaissance well. They crossed without incident. An empty truck was waiting for them on the other side. *How had Harald managed that*? These men were cleverer than he thought. Finn drove for several miles as Keller sat in the bed of the truck, guarded by Asger. A sign in passing announced, "Egernsund,

3 kilometers." Before they reached town, Finn turned into a small military compound. Harald instructed Keller and Asger to follow him to a field tent where a Danish officer sat behind a desk signing papers.

"Lieutenant Fisker reporting, Major." Harald saluted.

The major returned the salute. "Thank you, Lieutenant. Excellent work. Please stay." He gestured to Keller to sit. Asger stood over him with his hand near his pistol.

Still a prisoner.

Speaking in German and acting friendly — Keller knew this interrogation technique — the major said, "Welcome to Denmark. I am Major Frederik Rask. It's lucky for you my men found you. I've had every patrol I could spare looking for you. We know the area better than the Germans. It's our land, despite what the maps say."

"I'm grateful," Keller said. *Follow his lead. He has the advantage. Develop a rapport.*

Rask ignored him and reached for a cigarette, not offering one to Keller. He took three puffs before speaking. "You are a curious man." His eyes drilled into Keller. "I have some questions for you."

They don't trust me. This is going to be tougher than I thought.

"Who are you?" Rask asked.

Keller had often been on the other end of these interviews. He knew what to expect, but in this case his job was to make them believe him. "An American soldier. Lieutenant Paul Keller. I was captured in the Argonne."

"Then who is Karl Brandt?"

The major was good. He knew when to intimidate, when to stop talking, when to drop the anvil. "Who?" Keller tried to look confused.

"Come now. Don't play games. Do you recognize this man?" The major gave Keller the drawing the Freikorps had been handing out. "A deserter apparently."

Keller pretended to study the drawing in order to buy time.

"When the Freikorps want someone this badly, he's no ordinary deserter. Something strange is going on. I sent my men to Flensburg to look for you. Steal you from them. I ask again, who are you?" Rask pounded his desk with his fist so hard pencils fell to the floor.

Keller did not flinch. "I'm an American soldier."

The major let out a sigh. "Maybe." A pause. "Then let me ask, who is Andreas Sund?"

Keller had no idea how they had found his papers. *Don't underestimate these Danes*. "A German sailor," he fumbled.

"That's all you've got to say?"

Keller could feel Rask's frustration, but he was uncertain what game the major was playing. For all he knew, they were Freikorps agents. If so, they already knew he was a spy. Time to tell the truth. "I stole his papers. I am Lieutenant Paul Keller, AEF."

"So you've said. An American? Why should I believe you?"

"I lived near Milwaukee when I was a boy."

"Prove it. Who won the World Series last year?"

"The Red Sox, four games to two. Big star for the Red Sox was their young pitcher, Babe Ruth." He detailed the three previous World Series teams, lineups, winners, and key plays. *Time to ask them something*. "Are you Danish?"

"You are in the custody of Danish military intelligence. Here are my credentials." They looked real. "My patience is wearing thin," the major said. "Tell me the truth. We both know you're not an escaped POW. Who are you really?"

The game had reached its climax.

"If I don't start getting answers that make sense, I'll hand you back to the Germans," the major declared. "They'd owe me a big favor. That would be worth a lot."

Keller knew if he said no more, the major would end the interview. After that, who could say? *Time to go all in.* "My real name is Lieutenant Paul Keller. I am not a POW. I was on General Pershing's intelligence staff at the end of the war. Karl Brandt is the name I used when I was ordered to join the Freikorps Landsmann Battalion. I deserted."

"How did — "

Keller jumped in. He hoped the major would understand, without having to say it himself, that he was a spy. "That's not important. Here's what is — I have crucial information for Colonel House. Have your representative in Paris talk to him. He'll vouch for me." Keller paused. "He'll be grateful to get me back."

Major Rask stood up. Keller couldn't read his expression. "Watch him," he said to Harald and Asger. "I have some inquiries to make."

Chapter 58
We Need to Know

Paris: May 7, 1919

Shannon sat alone in the Crillon lounge and recalled the debacle of the Peace Conference earlier that day. Nothing had been resolved except the Allies' desire for retribution. More disasters loomed. She finished her whiskey and ordered a second. If only she could talk to Paul. Where was he right now? Was he even alive? She had never felt so lonely in her life. She longed for home like a lost and thirsty runaway child. Where was that drink?

"Mrs. Keller?"

Shannon looked up, more in reaction to hearing her name than because she cared who was calling her.

"There you are." Sergeant Cooper was out of breath.

"What is it?" Shannon asked, tilting her head like a bored cat.

Six minutes later, she found herself in the downstairs gaming room. Stripped of its billiard tables, it had once again been converted, not to a decoding room, but to a listening center. Familiar with bugging procedures from her police days, Shannon recognized the listening devices, wires, headphones, and transcribers. What surprised her most was the presence of Colonel House. "Thank you for coming, Mrs. Keller. Today has been hard on you, but we need your expertise."

Shannon fought the instinct to leave. She did not want to be party to this deceit.

"I don't need to say this," House said, "but you are pledged to secrecy about ... our little operation here." He waved his hand in a grand gesture.

"You're listening in on the Germans?" She already knew the answer.

"Of course. We planted listening devices throughout their hotel before they arrived. The French helped, of course." House handed her a set of headphones. "We are in the count's sitting room. Can you provide a running translation?"

Shannon sat down, put on the earphones, and closed her eyes so she could concentrate. The air in the room was thick with humidity. The sweat of so many people enclosed together made it smell like a locker room. Shannon's shoes were too tight, but she left them on. She asked for a glass of water, and Sergeant Cooper left to get it.

Brockdorff-Rantzau was speaking to a man whose voice she did not recognize. His voice came through despite the normal crackling sounds of the listening equipment. "We have two weeks to respond. Ridiculous." Shannon translated.

"With our *observations*. We won't be able to change a word."

"I agree, Herr Noske. President Wilson has betrayed us."

Shannon's head jolted back as a crash resounded in her ears. Everyone looked at her. "The count apparently threw a chair against the wall," she commented.

"To be expected. They're riled." House's mouth turned down in a combination of chagrin and resignation.

Shannon returned to translating. Brockdorff-Rantzau was again speaking. "We never would have signed the armistice under these conditions. Our army could have pulled back and defended Germany. We would be better off if they had."

"I just arrived yesterday, Herr Count. This is the same hotel the French commission used when they were pleading with us to end the 1871 war." Noske.

"Yes, with Paris encircled by our army. How times have changed." Brockdorff-Rantzau.

"The Allies insult us and break all diplomatic protocols. And they think *we're* barbarians. An outrage. You were right to stay seated when you spoke."

"That devil Clémenceau wanted me to stand like an accused criminal. This was not a trial, and I was not guilty. I was not going to give him the satisfaction of standing."

"What will we do now?" A voice from the background.

"We play by their rules, Captain Reick." Brockdorff-Rantzau. "We'll send translations back to Germany and leave as soon as we can. We will give them our response from Berlin. In the meantime, we must discuss alternatives." A pause. "Herr Noske, what options do we have?"

"Nothing militarily. We've already surrendered most of our heavy weapons. If the Allies choose to invade, we cannot stop them."

"No, something else."

"In the works." Another voice in the background.

~

In the basement of the hotel, Martin, too shocked to speak, looked at the dead man at his feet. *Had he heard correctly? Comrade Ours?* It was not possible.

"What did he say?" Durand asked.

Ana stepped forward. "He called you a Communist."

"And *Ours*, the bear," Martin added, using the name from the decoded message. "How would he have known that?"

Durand swallowed hard, but waved his hand as if swatting away a fly. He remained calm and glared disdainfully at Mal. "That man was hallucinating." Nodding his head toward Ana, he said, "She's Russian, not me. She's the Communist." A spray of saliva followed his words.

"He was looking at *you*, Captain," Ana said, her cheeks turning crimson.

"Liar!"

Ana reached for the Lebel she had taken from Mal and pointed it at the captain. Durand's two men closed ranks in front of him and drew their weapons. A Mexican standoff, advantage Durand.

Martin pulled his .45 and aimed it at Durand. "Stop! We need to sort this out." He stepped between Ana and Durand's men. In a sickening flash, he recognized that this same pair had been in charge of guarding the main gate that day.

Through the lens of Mal's accusation, the fragments all clicked into place as if Martin had shifted a kaleidoscope. Durand had arrived late at Le Grand Hotel well after the arsonist had set the fire and had disappeared at a crucial time. He was surprisingly slow to develop leads after Martin had described the suspect, and he acted disengaged concerning Ai Quoc. While Martin was searching the apartment for the code, Durand had tried to distract and deflect him and later provided little practical follow-up during the decoding. He had wanted to shoot Truchon before he could talk and could well have set up the ambush at Ana's. And today, had Durand not wanted to kill Mal immediately?

He had brilliantly played his role of righteous French democrat and patriot, but Durand was a guilty man.

"Your scent, Captain," Ana said. "My favorite Parisian soap. Lavender with a touch of lemon. Can't afford it myself. That scent was in the room where I met my Russian handlers. I'm sure of it. You stood in the shadows and gave those men their orders. "

Durand's mouth curled up fiendishly. "You were an excellent spy, Madam Primakova. Too emotional, though. I should have gotten rid of you sooner."

Martin considered his chances. Three guns against two. If he acted, Ana was surely dead. About himself, he did not care. *Stall.* "Alain, why? There must be a logical explanation."

"You're right about one thing, Major," Durand said. "I am a French patriot. Communism will be France's salvation. Democracy is corrupt and self-serving. Look at this war. The masses suffer. The powerful live. The wealthy get richer. *Vive le prolétariat.*" His gun remained fixed on Ana's head.

"We don't all have to die," Martin said, trying to guess Durand's next move.

"Do you expect me to surrender, Major? If so, you're a fool."

"Are you sure your gun is loaded?" Ana asked. "Didn't you notice something when I rubbed against you?"

"What? I … ," Durand hesitated and looked down at his revolver.

His split-second indecision gave Ana her chance. She yelled at Martin and jumped to his side, giving her a clear shot at the guard in front of Durand. Her bullet struck the man in the neck. At the same time, Martin fired and wounded the second guard in the shoulder. He spun around and blocked Ana's line of sight to Durand.

Martin fired twice more, killing him and Durand.

Ana stepped over the guards. She fired a shot into the motionless Durand and kicked him in the head again and again. "You put me through hell. Now you will rot there for eternity."

Martin rushed to embrace Ana.

Resting her head on his shoulder, she said, "I've suspected him since Mrs. Brooks's party. Good thing he believed my bluff about the gun."

Chapter 59
The Counter-Phrase

Egernsund, Denmark: May 1919

For ten days, Keller shared a barn with a sick cow and two goats. Major Rask had said he would make inquiries, yet here Keller sat, alone and uneasy. Diplomatic channels were always slow, but this delay hinted at problems. Had the Americans abandoned him? At least he was safe from the Freikorps, and the Danes were treating him well. They brought him bread and cheese in the morning and sausage or smoked fish with beer for dinner. Occasionally, they brought fresh berries, which Keller savored more than anything he had eaten in five months. In return for his promise not to escape, twice a day they permitted him to walk outside unescorted for half an hour.

Hating his captivity and still desperate to get word to Dulles, he tried to adjust to his situation. His straw bed was comfortable enough although the roof leaked on his head when it rained. After he moved his bed, the cow's mooing was his only disturbance. He did not mind when the Danes ordered him to clean up her liquid brown muck. It gave him something to do. Even the goats' human-like bleating did not bother him. He learned to milk them and was grateful when the Danes allowed him a share.

What bothered him was the solitude. He had too much time to think. His only companionship was an occasional visit from Lieutenant Fisker and the ghosts that regularly haunted him at night. He swore one took the unwelcome form of Karl Liebknecht. "I'm sorry. I was forced to do it. Please forgive me," he begged the apparition. Liebknecht's ghost faded away with a departing glare, leaving Keller with sleepless hours and pangs of remorse. He tried praying, but it did not help. How could the Lord forgive him when he could not forgive himself? Each passing day he felt worse. Why hadn't the Americans claimed him by now?

Keller received his answer the next day, when Fisker visited. As usual, Fisker brought two cups of coffee. Keller had not had a decent cup since he had joined the Freikorps. The brownish water the Germans drank tasted like nuts ground up with dirt, but the Danes had the real thing. It must have been expensive — why share it with a captured American? Keller guessed he was a valuable bargaining chip, and they needed to keep him content.

Today was different. Major Rask followed Fisker into the barn. From the look on their expressionless faces and hesitant walk, Keller knew something was wrong. Fisker handed him his coffee, and said, "I'm sorry to inform you, Lieutenant Keller, there are complications with your release."

Keller felt betrayed. After all he had done, the risks he had taken, the sacrifices he had made, his country left him dangling like this? "What's the problem?"

"The Americans don't want you. They say you don't exist."

The cow mooed and released its liquid bowels. "Let's get some fresh air," Rask said. "I believe your story," he continued outside, "but my superiors fear you might be a German spy who stole Keller's identity."

"I'm not."

"My superiors want proof. Our government can't release you unless we're sure who you are." Rask reached into his uniform jacket for a flask. "Akvavit?"

Keller took two big swigs. He had to admit Rask had a point. "What now?"

"We were hoping you'd have a suggestion."

Keller first had to determine why the Americans were rejecting him like some illegitimate cousin. Who had they spoken to? He grilled Rask. The U.S. ambassador to Denmark and their normal diplomatic and military connections. What was the response? Non-committal to dismissive. How hard had they pushed? The usual, meaning they had not. Had they used his undercover name, Karl Brandt? Yes. He's a low-level German spy currently locked up in a New York prison.

"Not true. I took his identity. My cover depended on it." Keller felt like a man pleading to a jury that was already convinced of his guilt.

"We have received no confirmation of that," Rask said.

"What about my name, Paul Keller? I was on Pershing's staff." Keller was becoming desperate.

"We learned that a Lieutenant Keller exists. Former New York cop. War hero. He's been decommissioned and is living somewhere in the Adirondacks."

That was all part of his cover. Now Keller knew: Dulles had kept his assignment so secret very few people knew his identity. And they were not talking — especially since Keller had lost contact when Larsen died. They believed his mission had failed. As far as the Americans were concerned, Keller was already dead. And they wanted to bury him deep. Keller had one faint hope. "Have you already contacted Thomas Tunney? Military intelligence."

Hesitation.

"Formerly, Captain Tunney of New York's Bomb Squad. He'll vouch for me. I married his niece."

"Sorry, I've already contacted him. Through my second cousin. He's a U.S. Army Colonel," Fisker said, "but didn't say why I was asking. Tunney might have guessed, but I'm not sure. Said he didn't know where Paul Keller was."

"My wife, Shannon Connolly, any word about her?" Keller was desperate for news.

"Colonel Tunney mentioned his niece is in Paris at the Peace Conference. She's a translator."

Keller felt a surge of elation. "Can you get word to her?"

"What can she say? Even you said she had no idea what you were doing."

Of course. That is what she had been instructed to say. "If I could see her, she'd confirm who I am."

"I'll try one more time." Rask shrugged his shoulders and walked away with Fisker.

The American stonewalling had shaken their confidence in his story. "Wait!" he called. "You haven't reached the right levels. You must speak to Herbert Hoover. I officially work for him. He knows me. Or General Pershing. Colonel House, if you must."

Rask stopped and turned around. "General Pershing can't, or won't, be reached."

"Oh, shit." Pershing had wanted to run Keller's undercover assignment himself. He had not liked Dulles stealing Keller away. Since Keller had abandoned the general, the general would not help Keller now.

"What about Hoover?" Keller's hope was fading.

"Hoover's traveling right now and hasn't returned our messages. We asked his assistant, but he's never heard of you. He claims the American Food Relief program doesn't employ spies."

"Have your ambassador in Paris go to Colonel House directly," Keller said. "He'll vouch for me." This was his last chance. He had never spoken to House directly, but he knew Dulles had informed the colonel about his mission.

Rask frowned. "He's a hard man to reach. Heavily guarded.

Always busy. Our diplomats are virtually ignored by the Big Four. Such is the plight of a small neutral country with no pressing demands."

Keller thought for a moment. What was the distress phrase? *Snow. Berlin.* "Tell your ambassador in Paris to give Colonel House this message: 'It's snowing in Berlin on July 4th.' He will give you a counter-phrase. When I give you the correct response, that will prove who I am." Keller had put his last chips down. He would either win and go home, or be handed to the Germans and die a spy. He prayed Dulles had given House the code.

~

Three days later, Rask appeared at the barn with a man Keller had never seen before. He was dressed formally in a dark suit and seemed nervous. Behind him were two well-armed U.S. Marine sergeants. "This is your ambassador, Lieutenant Keller."

The ambassador held out his hand to Keller and said with a confused look, "The pigeons delivered the news on Monday."

Keller replied with the right counter-date. "Not Sunday?"

"No, Saturday." Confirmed.

Keller's eyes turned moist with relief.

The ambassador smiled. "Good to meet you, Lieutenant Keller. Are you ready to go home?"

SECTION V

GERMANY SIGNS PEACE TREATY

May 1919-June 1919

Chapter 60
Have We Got Them All?

Paris: May 1919

Martin sat stiffly in Colonel House's office, shifting his weight in the hard seat, trying to get comfortable. In the chair next to him, Ana Primakova adjusted her posture more discreetly. Martin had long concluded the stiff chairs were by design. House did not want anyone to relax in front of him. Over the last few months, he had come to admire House's abilities, if not necessarily his close-to-the-vest personality.

Ana had gained House's confidence by saving Martin and helping to prevent a disaster with Brockdorff-Rantzau. A vital source of information about the French Communists, which had led to the arrest of Durand's accomplices, she had been staying at the Crillon for her own protection, and was now detested in the U.S. delegation. Shannon, still believing Ana was a threat to Martin, avoided her. Ambitious men, who coveted her access to Colonel House, schemed against her. Communist-haters, who should have thanked her, could not forget she was Russian. Military men, intimidated by her martial prowess, questioned her femininity. Only admiration for Martin and respect for diplomatic protocol prevented outward aggression toward her. Martin sensed the underlying tension and did not care.

Martin waited silently while House read the report that Martin had edited and translated, summarizing the roundup of the rest of Durand's Communist accomplices. Nine people had already been detained and arrests for another six were in progress. The report had been written by Durand's replacement, Major Victor Fauchaux, with whom Martin had much in common.

Fauchaux was methodical, efficient, and religious. Martin had once worked with him during the war, when he was assigned as the liaison for the U.S. 2nd Infantry Division to French headquarters. Fauchaux and Martin had worked together through military, cultural, and language problems to improve the combat readiness of the American troops and to ensure they performed well under French command. The 2nd Division had performed admirably in Belleau Woods.

House looked up from the report. "Have we got them all?" he asked, looking at Ana Primakova with skepticism.

"Yes," Ana said. Her strong chin and confident voice left no doubt about her certainty.

"How can you be so confident, Mrs. Primakova?"

"I know these people. I talked with them. I ate with them. I shared my bed with more than one."

What? Martin's eyes widened. A discussion for another day.

"I've been to their secret meetings and talked with their leaders. I know their contacts and their weaknesses." She paused. "We have them all," she said firmly.

The telephone rang, followed by a knock on the door. Sergeant Cooper peeked in from the entrance. House had told him he should not be disturbed. "You need to take this, Colonel," Cooper said softly.

"What is it?" House asked, in a tone that showed his annoyance.

"The call you were expecting from Denmark."

~

Keller, wrapped in his thoughts, felt someone shake him. "We're here, in France," Keller's Marine escort said. Keller felt safe, yet overwhelmed by doubts. He no longer had to worry someone would discover his true identity or cut his throat at night. He was among friends, not sadistic fellow soldiers in the Freikorps. But his mind was filled with questions. Having been part of that malignant world, could he ever regain his decency? Was he doomed by the sickness that had engulfed him? Would his colleagues trust him? What would he tell his wife? Would she still love the man he had been forced to become?

Dressed in an ill-fitting U.S. Marine lieutenant's uniform, Keller disembarked the British destroyer *Defiance* at Calais. The rough tide splashing against the hull of the warship pushed away the seaweed floating by its side. The crisp, salty air and light breeze coming off the sea revived him. They reminded him of New York, home. Had it only been five months since he had left?

Keller walked unsteadily to the gangplank on the rocking destroyer. He was escorted by the Marine sergeant who had guarded him since his release in Egernsund, Denmark, more than ten days ago. "Can't take no chances with you, Lieutenant Whoever-you-are," the sergeant said between chews of gum.

All those involved with Keller's return were under orders to keep his identity a secret. Both the Americans and the Danes wanted the Freikorps to believe he was dead. To support the ruse, Major Rask had returned Keller's "Sund" identity papers to the Germans along with the badly decomposed body of an unfortunate fisherman whose features matched Keller's. "You wanted him. Here he is," Rask told them, and asked for the reward. The next day, Rask reported that he thought the Germans had swallowed the story but refused to pay.

"You're important. That much I know," the sergeant said. He spat the wad of gum into the sea. "Let's go. I want to finish this assignment and get back to my nice job in the embassy."

Keller almost fell as he stepped off the warship and felt his boot touch land. His foot had fallen asleep, and he had to pound it into the ground several times to regain feeling. "Where to now, Sergeant?"

"The station. Next train to Paris."

"Do we have time to eat? I'd like a decent meal." Keller's ribs poked out through his once-muscled chest, and his army issue belt was three notches narrower than when he had left America.

"No, sir. We've only got a few minutes. We need to hurry."

Keller ignored the demands of his growling stomach. Duty first. He was tired of duty. "Good," he said. "I need to see the head of U.S. security in Paris as soon as possible." After this was over, he would go away somewhere with Shannon for a while. Somewhere peaceful. Someplace away from it all. Someplace where no one knew them. That is, if Shannon would have him.

"Major Martin is in charge, sir."

"Major Gil Martin? One of Pershing's staffers?"

"Don't know about that, sir. All I have is a name and an address, Hotel Crillon. I gather the U.S. delegation is staying there."

Must be Martin. Thank God.

Chapter 61
Reunion

Paris: June 1919

Keller and his escort left the train at the Gare du Nord in Paris and headed to the main entrance, where a Cadillac touring car with a U.S. flag on its hood awaited. A major, his service cap pulled low over his brow, jumped from the rear door before the driver could open it. He had a familiar build, but not until the officer looked up did Keller recognize his old friend. Gil Martin opened his arms and smiled broadly. "Paul, my God, it's good to see you!"

Keller stood speechless for a moment, shaking his head in disbelief. Suddenly overwhelmed with joy, he hugged his old partner and did not want to let go.

Martin broke the embrace. "We have a lot to do. Colonel House wants to see you right away." He thanked the Marine, handed him orders and travel documents, and dismissed him. The sergeant saluted and trotted back into the station like a dog freed from his leash.

As the Cadillac sped along, Keller was taken aback by the striking contrast between the peaceful streets of Paris and insurrectionist-torn Berlin. Stability versus chaos. Bounty versus deprivation. Paris's street markets had fresh food. The French people were weary but savored victory. The German people were hungry, angry, and feared the future. Fatigue and grief were common elements. Tree stumps marred both cities, wartime casualties of the need for heat.

After a few minutes of silence, Keller found the courage to ask Martin, "How's Shannon? I understand she's in Paris."

Martin placed his hand on Keller's shoulder. "Shannon knows you're here. She's waiting for you at our hotel. She can't wait to see you. She was worried sick."

Calm came over Keller. After his ordeal in Germany, happiness was a strange and welcome emotion. Content, he closed his eyes and reveled in his thoughts. *Have I really made it back*?

~

Ten minutes later, Keller felt Martin's nudge. "We're here, Paul." He would have preferred to rest a while longer in the car. A Marine guarding the front of the Crillon Hotel walked to the Cadillac, opened the door, and saluted. Martin exited and returned the salute as Keller stumbled out. The Place de la Concorde was lined with rows of captured artillery pieces collecting bird droppings. "The war is not over, despite this plunder," Keller said.

Sergeant Cooper was waiting at the entrance to lead them to Colonel House's office. House stood up and waved them in. Dulles was already there. After a few formalities, House offered wine. Keller preferred water. *Need to keep sharp. Much to say. Much not to.* Before House could start the interview, Keller said, "Colonel, I want to thank you for getting me out of Denmark."

"Glad it worked out. I know you're anxious to see your wife. She's done a wonderful job here." House smiled. "Before we begin, let me say that everyone in this room is authorized to hear what you've been up to."

Dulles nodded in agreement. "Yours was a dangerous mission, Paul. You have performed a great service for America."

"Thank you, Captain Keller," House said, extending his hand. "You'll get your new bars tomorrow."

"Here, here," Martin said, lifting his wine glass in a toast.

"I'm back in the army?" Keller felt invigorated by the news. A promotion too. A stiff brandy could not have done more to revive him. He had done enough spying for a lifetime.

"Now, tell us everything you've learned."

Keller detailed every major event since he had joined the Freikorps except his involvement in Liebknecht's murder. That was between him and God. He highlighted Larsen's death and meeting Weil. Everyone wondered how Weil had managed to escape America after the Bomb Squad had learned he was a German spy three years ago.

"Houdini couldn't have managed a better disappearing act," Martin said. "We had every law enforcement agency in the country looking for him."

Keller ended by describing the conversation he had overheard between Weil and Colonel Landsmann about stopping the signing of the Peace Agreement. "I believe they mean to do it."

"Why do you think so?" asked Dulles.

"The Germans are desperate. The nation is splitting apart. The Freikorps is fighting to preserve it. They can't live with the terms of the treaty."

"Why do you say that?" House inquired.

"I saw the treaty."

His statement met with astonished silence. "How?" asked House. "That must have been weeks ago. We hadn't even presented Germany with a copy yet."

"It's possible," Martin said. "Remember the day I was shot? We reported a copy was missing. Somehow a German agent must have stolen it from under our noses."

"Or bought one," House added. "We have to assume they've either infiltrated our inner circle or have a very capable agent in Paris."

"There's another problem," Keller said.

"What else?" House sighed.

"Danie Caarsens is with them."

Martin looked stunned. "So those rumors from those soldiers

we captured in the Argonne were true. I didn't want to believe them. We probably faced each other across no-man's-land. Are you sure, Paul?"

"I saw him in the Hamburg station. Same build, deep tan. He wore an eye patch and the side of his face was partially burned, but yes, it was him. You never forget the face of a man who almost shot you dead. We must assume he'll be part of the attack."

"I thought he was killed when the Germans tried to destroy New York," House interjected. "That's what the report said."

"We tricked you and everyone else," Martin said. "We never found the body."

"So, he's still working for the Germans," House said. "What can one man do?"

"With Danie Caarsens, anything is possible," Martin said, brandishing a white-knuckled fist. "Despite everything we did to catch him in New York, he was always one step ahead of us. He came within the length of a short fuse of blowing lower Manhattan off the map. He's a genius at disguise, an explosives expert, and a master at commando tactics."

"He's the most dangerous man in Europe," Keller said.

Chapter 62
The Most Dangerous Man

Garches, Outside of Paris: June 1919

The one-eyed man in a priest's robe walked down to the dank wine cellar of the burned-out chateau, the warped stairs creaking under his weight. The wine racks were empty, and the remains of broken bottles covering the floor crunched under his heavy boot. Scurrying noises along the walls indicated he was not the only intruder.

Danie Caarsens flipped back the hood of his white robe with one hand and brushed away the cobwebs with the torch in his other. The abandoned chateau in Garches, located seven miles west of Paris, suited his operational needs. Three men followed him to a large table in the center of the basement. No one spoke. Caarsens put down the torch, lit four candles, and spread out a large contour map he had stolen from the French general staff. It detailed the area, roads, and military bases around Versailles.

Caarsens's tanned and furrowed face was weathered from years of farming under the African sun and hardened with a desire for revenge. He cracked his knuckles. He liked the sound. "Let's begin." The other three men, all in civilian clothes, leaned in and listened intently: Freikorps Captain Reick, who had arrived in France through Austria and Italy; Wolf, recently recovered from his bout with influenza; and the renowned pilot, former Lieutenant Colonel Hermann Goering. Reick remained stationary, but studied the map intently. Wolf, his thumbs hooked inside the waistband of his trousers, shifted his weight from one foot to the other with the pent-up energy of a rat released from its cage. Goering, his hand resting on his chin, outlined military options.

Caarsens, the former Boer commando and German agent, was

the commander of the strike on the signing of the Peace Agreement. He had returned to Germany after his failed attack on lower Manhattan in September 1916. Wounded and burned, he had escaped capture by swimming a seemingly impossible distance against a strong current. He had dodged a powerful manhunt, using various disguises and identities to flee into Mexico and parts south, where he shipped out as a work hand on a cargo freighter bound from Panama for the Netherlands. Back in Germany, he had employed his extraordinary military skills to help the German Army refine its infantry tactics.

At the end of the war, Caarsens had commanded a battalion of elite German storm-troopers. His unit achieved a successful breakout, but once again, victory was denied him when insufficient reinforcements and lack of ammunition forced him back. During the retreat, a shell landed near him, knocking him unconscious. He woke up in an army hospital minus an eye and a kidney. Shrapnel fragments remained near his spine, the possibility of paralysis his greatest fear. Since his release in late 1918, he had shuttled through Switzerland to France and Germany, working as a German agent in Paris and advising the Freikorps in Berlin.

Halfway through his briefing, Caarsens paused. “Comments?” he asked, looking intently at the three men surrounding the table.

“Thorough, but risky,” Reick replied. “You know your business, but we need more troops.”

“And heavy weapons. I’ll get them,” Caarsens assured him.

“Kill ’em. Kill ’em all.” Wolf spit out the words like a venomous snake, his hand clutched to his well-notched trench sword.

“I need more time to work with my pilots,” Goering said. “Continue, Herr Caarsens.”

“We are Germany’s last chance for an honorable peace,” Caarsens said, knowing this attack was his last chance to strike a fatal blow at Britain, the hated enemy who had murdered his family in 1901, and Britain's paramour, America. He knew the chances were limited. It did not matter. This time, he swore he would succeed or die.

"What do you know about this Major Martin with the U.S. delegation?" Reick asked. "All my reports say he's a competent man."

Bile rose in Caarsens's throat. "They are correct, but he is just one man. Let me deal with him." Silently, he cursed Martin for thwarting his attempt to destroy New York in 1916. Caarsens had been shocked to see his old foe in Paris, when he first encountered him in January at Le Grand Hotel, the night it almost burned down. Using the same priest's disguise he had donned tonight, he talked his way past security to mingle with the dignitaries at the hotel. His fluency in English, French, and German had allowed Caarsens to listen in on conversations of boastful men who spoke too loudly. He had noticed Martin and left the ball before Martin spotted him. Standing across the street as the fire blazed, he once again admired, however grudgingly, Martin's courage and coolness amid the chaos as he carried an injured woman to safety. After Martin had left the scene, Caarsens visited the triage center, giving blessings and performing last rites in a French-Canadian accent.

Caarsens saw Martin a second time at Mrs. Brooks's party in the spring, but quickly left when he noticed Mrs. Keller talking to Martin about him. The third time was at the Crillon Hotel, the morning Martin was brought in wounded. Martin's injury had provided a welcome distraction that made it simple for Caarsens to accomplish his purpose, and he easily stole a copy of the treaty off the front desk. He now looked forward to confronting Martin again. This time he would kill him.

Nearly finished with the briefing, Caarsens rolled up the sleeves of his robe, exposing circular cigar burn marks, courtesy of the British officer who had tortured him during the Boer War. He reached into his robe and pulled out his razor-sharp Demag bayonet. To him, the Demag was an extension of his hand. He scraped it across his two-day-old stubble. The feel of its cold blade so close to his jugular exhilarated him. Facing death made him feel alive.

The Demag had been with him through countless fights and had saved his life many times. The most potentially fatal encounter was in a Manhattan brawl-to-the-death with a renegade German agent, whom he had been sent to kill. The memory caused Caarsens to nick himself at the ridge where his neck met his chin. He ignored the droplets of blood falling on his map. The others ignored it too — blood bothered none of them.

“How many men do you have for this mission, Captain Reick?” Caarsens asked.

“Two hundred. They’re spread out in farms near Versailles.”

Caarsens raised an eyebrow.

“We’re trying to sneak more men into France this week,” Reick said.

“I’ve overcome worse odds before. We will make up for lack of numbers with diversions and firepower. Fast, Boer style. The Allies will think five times that number are attacking. They won’t have time to react before the aeroplanes swoop in.” A taunting smile took over Caarsens’s face. “And pilots, Herr Goering. How many?”

“Enough.” The German ace visibly resented reporting to Caarsens.

Caarsens ignored the rebuke. “What is your plan?”

“My men will be ready,” Goering said. “The maintenance crews have been practicing. We’ll truck in our own bombs and equipment. We can be armed and airborne in twenty-five minutes.”

“Good. Flying French aeroplanes will not be a problem?”

The ace laughed. “A plane is a plane. Besides, we’ve inspected

SPAD XIIIs and Nieuport 28s like those at the airport. Once we're in the air, no one will be able to tell if we're friend or foe."

Caarsens nodded and turned to Reick. "I'm concerned about that deserter of yours, Captain. I recognize the picture of your Karl Brandt. I know this man. He was a New York cop, Paul Keller." Caarsens was as gifted at recognizing others as he was at disguising himself. "I shot him during my time in New York. Too bad, it was only a wound."

"Brandt is dead," Reick said.

"You sure?" Caarsens wiped blood from his chin with his sleeve. "I understand he overheard some of your conversation with Herr Goering. He knows our intentions."

"The Danes returned his body and his papers," Reick said, backing away a bit as if intimidated by a man who feared death even less than he did. "The body was decomposed. Hard to identify. The papers were real."

"Then we must assume he's alive and with the Allies. A complication." The chance to kill Keller provided an additional reward. Caarsens pointed the Demag at Reick. Light from the candles glinted on the blade. "Your men will have the toughest fight, Captain. Can they do it?"

"Or die for the glory of Germany."

"I'll sing when I machine gun those dignitaries," Goering said. "Good fun. And you?"

"This is not a game," Caarsens retorted.

"Where is our staging area?" Reick asked.

Caarsens closed his eyes, then exploded. "*Fokking* Allies!" He drove the bayonet into the map and nearly cleaved the table in two. "Our fate will be decided here. Nine miles south of Paris. The AEF's Air Acceptance base at Orly."

Chapter 63
Confession

Paris: June 1919

The most dangerous man in Europe? Martin and the others in House's office considered the implications of Caarsens's involvement in the plot. The office was crypt-like quiet except for the comings and goings from the street below. Martin pressed his heels into the rug to check his emotions.

House tapped his fingers on his desk. "How will Caarsens attack?"

"A hundred different ways," Martin said.

House frowned, stood up, and began to pace, his hands clasped behind his back. "What does he hope to accomplish? He can't possibly succeed." Martin had never seen him so agitated.

Keller struck the arm of his chair with his right fist. "These are determined and ruthless men."

"If I were them," Martin said, "I would blame the attack on the Bolsheviks. Demands for war would follow. Germany could renegotiate the peace terms by pledging to join the Allies in an all-out assault against Russia."

"That won't happen," House quickly replied. "We've already considered it. But we never suspected the Germans would preface their negotiations with a sneak attack."

"They'll come at us from all directions. I saw Hermann Goering at Freikorps headquarters," Keller said.

"An attack from the air. Another possibility," Martin said.

"I'll go to Brockdorff-Rantzau," House said, "and threaten Armageddon if anything happens at the signings."

"Be careful," Martin warned. "We can't let Caarsens know we're on to him. That knowledge is our main advantage. Besides, Caarsens is leading a renegade group — military, not diplomatic. Brockdorff-Rantzau is not involved."

"Captain Keller, you know these Freikorps people. Any thoughts?" House scratched his cheek, a rare sign of uncertainty.

Keller was glancing at the door, anxious to leave. "What? Sorry. The Freikorps? Yes, they are fanatics. The only way to stop them is to kill them."

"Can we change the venue of the signing, Colonel?" Martin asked politely.

"Impossible. Our Allies want to make it a big event. Versailles it will be." House stood up and reached for his coat. "I think we've discussed everything for today. This meeting is adjourned, Major." He paused and looked at Martin. "If you are to maintain our advantage, keep your suspicions quiet. If anything goes wrong, you'll end up in Leavenworth, either as a guard or an inmate."

~

Keller left the meeting and headed straight to Shannon's room. He did not know what to expect, and his trepidation mounted with each step. With his strained face and serious loss of weight, he had changed since she had last seen him. His boot caught the underside of a loose rug, and he tumbled to the floor. He picked himself up, swept himself off, and reflexively tried to straighten his hair. Before the war, Shannon had loved to run her fingers through his long, unkempt hair, now so short, so German. What would she think?

Keller reached the 3rd floor stairwell; his mouth was dry as he struggled between anxiety and excitement. How would it be to see her again? Part of him could not wait to talk to her, hold her, and feel her alluring mix of strength and femininity. Yet how could he face her, knowing what he had done? How much could he tell her? Tell her all, he decided. Damn his orders not to talk about his mission in Germany. All except — no, he had to tell her that too. But would she still love him once she knew what he'd done? There was no turning back. There it was, down the hallway, room #315. *What should I do? Knock? Call out?*

Before he could decide, the door opened. Shannon. Her eyes beamed with joy. She smelled like paradise. "Here you are." She wrapped her arms tightly around his bruised ribs, but they did not hurt. They moved inside and kissed a kiss Keller would remember for the rest of his life. He became overwhelmed and loosened their embrace.

"What's wrong?" she asked.

Keller backed away hesitantly. He did not deserve such love. He felt unnerved, not knowing what to say or how to say it. He — she — it wasn't supposed to be like this. He loved her, needed her, but he had to tell her. "I — I'm not the man you married, Shannon. I'm sorry. I ..."

Fear filled Shannon's eyes. "What do you mean, Paul?"

"I can't tell you. I can't even admit to myself what I've done. I ..."

"For God's sake, say it."

The words burst out. "I've committed an unforgivable sin."

"Whatever you did in Germany, you did your duty. You have nothing to atone for."

They sat on a couch. It took Keller a few minutes to find the words. "Germany was a horror." He fought back tears. Shannon stayed quiet. He began his story at the point he crossed the Rhine with the Freikorps, and stopped when he got to the night of Liebknecht's death. A breeze swept in from an open window; Keller felt a piercing freeze run through him and he bowed his head. "I feel a hundred years old."

"I can't image what you've been through, my love." What is it that you can't tell me?"

~

Keller's words came slowly. "I'll never forget that night. The night I killed Karl Liebknecht."

"My God! I read about his death in the Communist papers, but didn't believe them. That was you?" Shannon swallowed hard and steeled herself for worse to come. "Go on."

Keller bowed his head and folded his hands as if in prayer as tears welled up in his eyes. "I had no choice."

"You're not a killer, Paul." Shannon's stomach knotted. "You're not telling me everything." She paused. Her marriage depended on what she would say next. *Say what's in your heart.* "I'll love you whatever you tell me."

~

Keller felt a dam break inside his head. Could he believe her? Just maybe? "You mean that?"

"Of course." She held his hand and kissed it. "You're a good man. I'll always love you, just like we promised."

Keller half-smiled. Shannon responded with a reassuring look. His resistance melted. "I'm haunted by ghosts."

~

A breakthrough! "I'm not your judge or jury," Shannon reassured him, "but I can help redeem you from yourself. What happened?"

~

Minutes passed before Keller spoke. "It was one of those nights — spooky, calm, new moon," Paul recounted. "The kind of night when scavengers stay hidden, as if they knew more than people do. Noises traveled funny distances that night. We were worried someone might hear a gunshot. The owls stayed alert. Their hoots echoed around me. Light winds whistled through the trees. Were they warning me? The air was still. A fog cloaked the ground. My boots sunk into the soft earth. It felt like it was trying to pull me down.

"After we dragged Liebknecht out of the car, Reick hands me his pistol. 'You do it. Kill him,' he says. 'If you don't, I will. The second bullet goes into your head, Brandt.' I push Liebknecht a few yards away so Reick and Jawbreaker can't hear me. I stare right into Liebknecht's swollen face with its purple welts, broken teeth, and half-closed eyes. 'I'm not a butcher like them,' I tell him.

"He fights to say something. 'I know.' I was shocked and reel back. Did I hear that right? Jawbreaker is making cat-calls. 'Get on with it,' Reick says. Liebknecht looks faint and collapses to the ground. The other two hoot. Jawbreaker must have thought I hit him. 'That's better,' he says. Liebknecht struggles to his knees.

"I kneel down and talk to him real quiet.

"I don't want to do this, but you know you have to die. He nods. My friends over there want a good show, but I don't know what to do.

"Reick says, 'Stop waltzing about, Brandt. Shoot him, will you? I want to go get a beer.'

"Liebknecht stands. He fights to remain dignified. He wipes the blood off his face and brushes his clothes with his swollen hand. It must have been painful. I chamber a round in the Mauser and point it at his head. 'Close your eyes,' I say.

"'No,' he says. 'Let me.' He takes the Mauser — he was so steady, like he was reaching for a loaf of bread — and points it up, under his chin. Doesn't flinch. 'For the Fatherland. May God have pity on what it will become,' he says, and pulls the trigger. His brains splatter across my face.

"Jawbreaker cheers and claps. 'Excellent! You even made him do it himself.' Reick laughs. 'I'm impressed. You're one of us again.'

"The three of us roll the body in a blanket and dump it into the trunk. I force myself not to get sick. We drive through the Tiergarten and unload the body in front of the morgue. There was lots of celebrating that night. I pretended to go along." Keller raised his hands, palms up, like a man before a priest.

"So you didn't actually kill him," Shannon said.

"Yes, I did. All but pulled the trigger. Liebknecht humbled me. I'll never forget that."

"What else could you have done?"

"I could have tried to kill Reick and Jawbreaker and escape, then and there."

"If you had, they would have caught and executed you. Liebknecht was a revolutionary. He gambled and lost. Men like that die. It's an old story. Don't blame yourself. If you had done anything else, you would have failed your mission. That mission has given us priceless information. You did the right thing."

"You think so? I didn't think you'd understand. I committed cold-blooded murder."

"Liebknecht killed himself before you and the Freikorps broke into his flat. Once he failed, he had to die. By his hand or yours, it doesn't matter. I would have done the same thing as you. My uncle would have done the same thing too. I'm not so innocent, either. War is war. It forces you to make hard calls. I let a guilty man escape. I couldn't kill him. It was the right thing to do. Now let's get those bastards who forced you to do this."

Chapter 64
Only the Devil

Paris: June 1919

For ten days, French police, military intelligence, and gendarmes scoured the city and outskirts looking for Caarsens and the German assault force. The searches, done discreetly under orders from Clémenceau, caused no panic in the civilian community. The investigations had uncovered nothing. Martin pleaded with House to urge the French to call out their army. "Not happening. Clémenceau will not be intimidated," House said. "Warnings have been given. The Germans will not be stupid enough to attack during the signings."

Martin disagreed. Since Keller had returned with the news about Caarsens, a wave of bombings and strange incidents had occurred around Paris and Versailles: a warehouse fire, an ammunitions explosion at a military depot, and a train derailment that paralyzed Parisian railroads for several hours. The authorities blamed events, those that were reported, on poor maintenance and neglect during the war. Martin suspected something more sinister. The disappearance of a French Renault 17 tank and a disciplined bank robbery by men with military haircuts and weapons expertise worried him the most. The bank robbers were reported to speak French with an Alsatian-Rhineland accent.

Martin was certain these events were meant to distract, frustrate, and weaken local defenses as a prelude to an attack. If he had been planning the operation, he would be doing the same things. No question, Caarsens had announced his presence. But where was he?

~

Caarsens studied the stockpile of rifles, heavy weapons, grenades, and explosives stored in the basement of an abandoned warehouse north of Paris. Captain Reick and former Lieutenant Colonel Goering looked on. The munitions cache had been bought or stolen in the last two weeks. Seven trucks were hidden nearby and ready, but Caarsens wondered if it would be enough. His plan was bold — coordinated diversions followed by a pinpoint strike on the American airbase at Orly. Reick's storm troopers and Goering's air assault on Versailles would determine success or failure.

Caarsens turned to Reick. "The pilots can fly away, Captain, but I'm afraid we'll need to fight our way out."

"My men are prepared to die. When will we receive final orders?"

"I'm waiting for instructions," Caarsens replied.

~

Colonel Landsmann reported to Matthias Weil's office near Unter den Linden in the heart of Berlin. He was escorted to a back room with thick walls and no windows, where Weil sat in front of a large mahogany desk that looked uneven. The colonel saluted. "The campaign to disrupt the signing is proceeding," he reported. "Our man in Paris awaits final orders."

"It's not sure when we will get them," Weil said. "There's been a development. Count von Brockdorff-Rantzau has offered to sign the treaty conditionally. He has asked that the clause stating Germany is responsible for starting the war be removed. The Allies rejected his request. The signing must be unconditional. He has resigned as foreign secretary. I applaud him." Weil reached for his usual afternoon delicacy: chocolate cake, a scarce commodity.

"Will President Ebert find someone to replace him?" Landsmann asked.

"He's looking. If he can't find anyone willing to sign, his

government may fall," Weil said, washing down the rare remaining cake crumbs with coffee. "I can't imagine who he'll find. Whoever signs that treaty will be considered a traitor. Or a fool."

"If it does fall," Landsmann said, "Defense Minister Noske is the only man who can lead the country. Then we will fight."

"General Groener disagrees," Weil said, referring to the army chief of staff. "The army has no will to renew the struggle. Even with your Freikorps, we cannot hold back a full-scale Allied invasion."

"Not now, but we could maintain defensive positions," Landsmann countered. "Then we rebuild the army with a compulsory draft. I'm sure the German people will respond to save the Fatherland."

"Groener says no. The German people are tired. If the blockade continues much longer, hundreds of thousands will die. The people will not fight. Noblemen like us must carry the banner. Will your man's plan succeed? I'm not comfortable giving such responsibility to a Boer."

"He's the best man for the job," Landsmann retorted in a sure voice. "Trust me when I say he's as committed to its success as any German. Our strike will paralyze the Allies and give Germany time to recover — to rearm, rebuild our army, and fight back."

"If not, Germany could be broken into small regions and destroyed. Quite a gambit, Colonel. The devil's dealing a strong hand."

~

That same morning, Martin met Keller for breakfast. Keller had been on leave with an order to rest since his return. Today was his first day back on full assignment. He felt full of energy and anxious to get to work.

After the meal, they went to House's office to discuss the progress to thwart Caarsens's plans. "There's some news," House said when everyone was seated. "Count von Brockdorff-Rantzau has resigned as foreign secretary."

"What does that mean, Colonel?" Martin asked.

"Hard to predict," House replied. "I believe President Ebert wants to sign, but he is facing opposition. It's his only reasonable option, but common sense might not triumph. If Germany does not sign, I've been informed that the Big Three have ordered General Foch to prepare to invade the Rhine with more than a hundred thousand men."

"It can't come to that — another war." A cold chill ran up Martin's spine. "Surely there are other options."

"Only two." House's brow deepened into a frown. "Either the signings proceed as planned and we risk a German attack to stop it, or we invade if they refuse to sign. Either way, the world will be watching us."

Martin placed his hands over his bent head. "Only the devil will win," he moaned.

Chapter 65
Orly

Orly, France: June 1919

The one-eyed French-Canadian major stopped his black Renault touring car in front of the entrance to the American Air Service Acceptance Park in Orly, nine miles south of Paris. A French corporal approached and gestured for him to shut off his engine. *A Frenchman. Not Americans? What has changed since I was here two weeks ago?* Caarsens wondered. He turned to his two passengers and said in German, "A complication. Let me handle this. Say nothing." The two civilians, dressed in well-cut business suits, folded their arms and grumbled. Caarsens rolled down the window, saluted the corporal, and said in a friendly tone, "Major Trottier, 22nd Regiment. *Bonjour*. I'm here to see your commanding officer."

"*Papiers*?"

Caarsens reached inside his uniform blouse and handed over the documents. His military identification was a perfect forgery, copied from that of a French-Canadian officer captured at the end of the war. "Fire inspection. There's been a report of an incident. We're here to investigate." The orders were "signed" by the commander of the Canadian Corps, General Arthur Currie. His companions' papers indicated they worked for the French aeroplane manufacturer Nieuport.

The corporal gave the documents a cursory look. He returned them with a smile and saluted. "Captain Leblanc's office is one hundred yards across the field, in the main building, to the right." He pointed and ordered the private at the gate to lift the barrier and let them pass.

The commander — only a captain? Strange. Caarsens drove

onto the base. An open area larger than two football fields side-by-side formed the inner compound. Cheap one-story wooden buildings rimmed the field to form a solid wooden rectangle open at the main gate. A dirt road crisscrossed the main field, and patches of overgrown grass bordered brown splotches of neglect. A flagpole with the French tricolor stood as the lone sentry to the building marked "headquarters." Two weeks ago, sandbag emplacements three feet high had been positioned at each corner of the compound. Machine guns had pointed out from each position, forming interlocking fields of fire across the compound. At the time, these had worried Caarsens, but they were gone. *I hope the aeroplanes are in better shape than this base.* He spotted possible targets and made a mental note of distances so his mortar teams could calculate the range on the day of the attack.

Except for a few soldiers milling around talking or raking dirt, the compound was empty. Had the Allies learned of his plan? *Too late to drive away.* Caarsens feared a trap, but had to continue the bluff, hoping he was mistaken. He turned to his civilian-dressed passengers and told them to pull out their weapons. They already had.

Caarsens studied the roofs, windows, and potential ambush positions looking for snipers or other threats. All remained quiet. He breathed deeply, relieved but baffled. Had the gods of war finally chosen to reward him with good fortune?

Caarsens stopped the Renault in front of the headquarters. A soldier sitting on the front step eating bread and drinking wine ignored him. Caarsens told Reick and Goering to stay in the car and say nothing. They were to wave away anyone who approached. One mispronounced French word could compromise the entire operation. "I know what to do," Goering huffed, Luger in hand.

Reick spoke enough French to get by, maybe, but Caarsens did not know about Goering. He had not wanted to bring Goering on this reconnaissance mission, but the ace had argued he was the only one who had the knowledge to inspect the aeroplanes. Caarsens exited the automobile and addressed the soldier sitting on the steps. "*Capitaine Leblanc*?" he inquired.

The soldier looked up, saw the officer's insignia, and jumped to attention. "Inside, Major."

The poorly lit room reeked of stale cigarette smoke. As Caarsens entered, Leblanc was signing something at a desk overflowing with papers. The captain looked up with tired eyes as Caarsens approached. Caarsens saluted and handed his papers to Leblanc, maintaining an attitude commensurate with his rank. "Headquarters has concerns about the fire security here," he explained. "I understand there was a fire a few days ago."

"You're aware of that? How ... ? We didn't ..." Obviously surprised by Major Trottier's inside knowledge of the fire, Leblanc stopped talking. He did not challenge the questionable jurisdiction of a superior officer's orders.

Caarsens himself had set the fire. During his last visit, he had hidden a cigar bomb with a twelve-day delay mechanism in the warehouse. "The two men with me are from the Nieuport aeroplane factory. They need to inspect their aeroplanes to make sure they are in good condition. They will arrange to take them back next week." Caarsens hesitated for effect, folded his hands behind his back, and leaned forward. He towered over the sitting captain. "We need to look over the entire compound."

Leblanc leaned back to keep his distance. If he detected anything not quite right about Caarsens's French-Canadian accent, he did not say anything. "Please do what you must. Is there anything I can do to assist you?"

"No. We prefer to work alone," Caarsens said. "Frankly, Captain, I'm surprised by the deplorable condition of this base."

"I am as well," Leblanc said. "I apologize. We took over the base about ten days ago when the Americans left. *Vacated* is a better term. They took everything that was theirs and left everything else about the way you see it. The aeroplanes were still ours. I have few men and, since the end of the war, discipline is not what it used to be. I am doing the best I can."

By leaving the base to such poor soldiers, the Americans had virtually handed it over to Reick's troopers. They could occupy this base with little effort and hold it for longer than expected. Caarsens hid his delight and adopted a gracious tone. "I understand your position, Captain Leblanc. I see the same thing at my headquarters. Let me investigate and make my report. I'm sure I will not find anything worth noting."

Leblanc visibly relaxed. "The fire you mentioned was easily contained. Nothing alarming."

"I just need to check," Caarsens said. *Of course it was not alarming. I planned it that way. Just big enough to get attention, but too small to report.* "I'm sure you are doing your best. My colleagues and I will do a routine check and file our report. We will not bother you again." Caarsens started to leave and stopped. "Oh, the fuel? It could be a fire hazard."

"The base is full of it, all properly stored. It's the first thing I did."

"Good. Thank you." Caarsens was pleased. Another important element in his plan was secure.

"At your service, Major."

"One last thing," Caarsens said. *The most important. Make it sound trivial by mentioning it as an afterthought.* "The aeroplanes. Are they in good order?"

"Fine shape, Major. Hardly flown. They were well maintained.

I'll give the *Sammies* credit for that. We have thirty of them, mostly SPADs, a few Nieuports. Top of the line, ready to fly right now. They are in the hangars."

"Excellent." Caarsens's battle plan was coming together perfectly. "We will give those a look too. Thank you again for all your help, Captain." Caarsens left the building and went back to the Renault where Reick and Goering were waiting.

"What took you so long?" Goering asked petulantly.

Caarsens was tired of the fighter pilot's contempt. He ignored Goering's attitude for the moment and instructed him and Reick to go to the hangars to inspect the fighter aeroplanes and available ordnance, while he himself pretended to complete his investigation.

~

In the hangar, Goering climbed into the seat of a light-blue SPAD XIII with its red-blue-and-white roundel American markings. The cockpit seemed more cramped than his white Fokker D VII, but now, several months after the war, his waist was expanding. Assuming all went well, which it usually did for him, Goering would not be airborne for long. Versailles was a short distance by aeroplane. He closed his eyes and imagined an American on his tail. Goering barrel-rolled out of danger and maneuvered into a kill, his machine guns, an extension of his deadly will, barking death. Reick's words interrupted his imaginary victory, number twenty-three. "*Wass*?" Goering looked up, his face ready for combat. "Repeat that."

In front of the plane, Reick had lifted the cowl and was inspecting the engine. "I said it looks fine. No leaking oil," he repeated in German. "How are the machine guns?"

Goering leaned forward and inspected the twin Marlin machine guns, synchronized to fire through the whirling propeller. "They look fine too. Not much different than ours. Start it up." Reick placed his hand on the top of the propeller and spun it down with all his strength. The SPAD engine coughed and grumbled to life. Goering revved the engine and had it running well in a few seconds. "The fuel gauge is full. This will do nicely," Goering said, pretending to work the machine guns.

~

"What are you doing here?" The voice came from the front of the hangar, twenty yards away. A French private. "Did I hear German?"

Reick pointed to his ears, pretending not to hear. He gestured the private over, glancing about for a weapon. His pistol would make too much noise. *There, a wrench.* Goering jumped out of the SPAD and murmured something. His meaning was clear to Reick.

It was clear to the Frenchman as well. Reick motioned for him to relax, but the private backed away, then turned and ran. Goering tackled him before he could reach safety. "*Aidez moi!*" he shouted. "*Au secours!*" His last words. Goering punched him in the throat, silencing him. Reick picked up the wrench and smashed it into the private's head. It opened like a watermelon. Had anyone seen? Reick looked up, but the area was empty. Goering pulled the body deep into the hangar, and Reick found a greasy rag to clean up the mess.

Reick and Goering ripped the insignias from the private's uniform and removed his identity papers to make it look like he had abandoned his post. Reick spit on the papers and placed them on the desk in the hangar — no deserter would keep them. "We have to bury this man. Find a shovel," Reick said. They wrapped the body in a tarp, dug a shallow pit in a secluded rubbish area, and covered the grave with dirt and debris. Reick was satisfied it was sufficiently camouflaged and that no one had seen them.

"Only three days left," Goering said. "No one will find him before then."

"What do we tell Caarsens?" Reick asked.

"Nothing. He doesn't have to know."

Chapter 66
The Day Before

Paris: June 27, 1919

It was late afternoon, and Martin was fighting back his fears as he walked to Major Fauchaux's office. There was little time left. The signing was scheduled for the next day. President Ebert had appointed Dr. Johannes Bell and Hermann Mueller, obscure government officials, to represent Germany in place of Count von Brockdorff-Rantzau. Martin sensed the same tension at the headquarters of French military intelligence that he had felt in the corridors of AEF headquarters before a big push. Men looked panicked. Orders in various degrees of loudness echoed across the hallways. One man waving papers about, urging people to move out of his way, nearly barreled Martin over. Men in cramped offices pounded away at typewriters.

Martin felt impotent. Tomorrow, the heads of every major Allied nation would all be gathered in one place. And it was Martin's job to keep them safe. He did not know if he could. "How are the Germans going to hit us?" he asked himself again and again. His keen mind had devised so many ways Caarsens could attack that Martin feared the countermeasures he had recommended to the French would be ineffective. *Too many. Too weak. Too spread out.* A determined and concentrated force could overwhelm any of them.

Martin needed a clue. His police instincts told him that some incident, a German mistake perhaps, would lead him to Caarsens. Stop the attack before it starts — this was the mission Martin had set himself. But the last week had been quiet, too quiet. Nothing unusual had been reported, but there had to be something. Caarsens was out there — a hurricane waiting to crash onto land — but Martin did not know where.

Martin entered Major Fauchaux's office hoping for a break. Fauchaux stood waving his phone with one hand, pointing to a map on his desk with the other, and shouting orders as two aides scribbled notes. He looked over and saw Martin. "Good," he said. "You're here."

"Anything new?" Martin asked, dispensing with formalities. Fauchaux abruptly hung up the phone and gestured *no*. Martin fought back his frustration. The aides prepared to leave, but Fauchaux said, "Stay. You need to hear this. Major Martin, sit. There," he pointed. Martin had sat in that chair often in the last two weeks.

Major Fauchaux, his aides, and Martin began their discussion of potential threats. A *one-man suicide mission to shoot "the Big Three" at close range*? No. All heads of state would be heavily guarded. No one could get within thirty yards of them.

A sniper? Impossible. No sniper could get close enough. Versailles was a huge complex surrounded by wide-open spaces. All potential sniper posts would be watched. Ten of France's best marksmen would be positioned discreetly around the area as countersnipers.

A direct assault on Versailles by a large force? Inconceivable. A regiment of French "dress parade" guards would ring the area. Caarsens would need more than a thousand men. Just in case, three brigades of crack French troops equipped with tanks and heavy weapons had been sent to guard the outskirts of Versailles. A cavalry unit was positioned in the stables for fast deployment.

A poison gas attack? Out of the question. There was no way to deliver the gas. The Germans did not have the necessary artillery. Could mortars be employed? No. Soldiers would patrol the perimeter within a mortar's range. Even if a German was able to get a mortar close enough to use it, he would not have time to deploy it.

An attack before the dignitaries reach Versailles? Possible. But every precaution would be taken. All roads and railway tracks would be swept clean for possible mines. Every dignitary would ride in an armored car and take a different route. They would leave Paris at different times. Military escorts would guard each man. The cavalry would lead the way once they neared Versailles.

An attack on the German signatories? Unlikely. They were in a hidden location near the palace under heavy protection. How they would be taken to the signings was a secret.

An air attack? Hard to conceive. The Germans would need to get many aeroplanes in the air. Where would they get them? Active Allied airbases were secure.

This last point gave Martin serious pause for thought. *Active bases?* "All of them?" he asked. "You sure?"

"Yes," Fauchaux replied firmly. "Squadrons of French biplanes will be on alert, ready to take off at a moment's notice. They can reach Versailles in minutes."

"They won't be airborne until a threat appears?"

"No. Clémenceau does not want them to interfere with the proceedings. Four observation balloons will circle Versailles. They will give us sufficient warning in case of danger. In addition, the army has placed several batteries and machine guns around the palace to guard against an air attack."

Martin was reassured. Caarsens had no way to get the aeroplanes, but … . A thought lingered. No matter — just one more possibility. They had done what they could for now, but Martin continued to ponder other potential threats.

~

At the same time Martin was leaving Fauchaux's office, Caarsens stood in the loading area of his warehouse. He was feeling confident. How could the Allies stop him? There were too many possibilities to defend against. Even if they had a broad idea of his plan, it would not be much use. It would be like looking at a sign one thousand yards away without binoculars — the sign would be there, but impossible to read. Only three other men knew the full scope of the operation: Colonel Landsmann, back in Berlin, who had helped craft it; Captain Reick, the troop commander; and Goering.

Caarsens watched Reick and Goering supervise the loading of four military trucks he had acquired over the last two weeks. Two were filled with bombs and belts of machine-gun bullets to be fitted to the aeroplanes they would commandeer at the Orly base. The third sat low on its tires, full of weapons and battlefield necessities — machine guns, mortars, mines, hand grenades, bullets — that Reick's men would need to storm and defend the airbase. The fourth truck contained everything the maintenance men needed to service the SPADs and Nieuports and get them in the air: extra petrol, oil, struts, engine parts, tools. The money from the bank robbery had gone a long way. When the men were done loading the trucks, Goering complimented their work and dismissed them.

Caarsens was pleased. Every contingency had been addressed. He had never had an operation so thoroughly supplied. He walked with Reick and Goering to the basement where the individual mission leaders were waiting. Caarsens and Colonel Landsmann had handpicked each man for boldness, battlefield excellence, and independent thought. They were the cream of the Freikorps — motivated, dedicated killers, all willing to die. Goering's twenty-seven pilots were there, since success or failure ultimately rested with them. They all applauded when the three leaders entered.

Wolf stood by a keg, filling steins with frothy beer. When everyone had been served, Caarsens raised his glass. "To our success!" He drank to cheers and shouts. Soon getting down to business, Caarsens then sought out each mission leader to review final plans and discuss last-minute concerns.

The Orly attack team? Reick was confident. Each man in his company of one hundred and fifty soldiers knew every detail about his assignment. They were eager to go.

The maintenance crews? All seventy-five men practiced and ready.

The diversionary explosives squads? The squads should not face many obstacles. The sappers were safely in Paris. Starting at 07:20, they would place their satchel bombs at key locations across the city. Planned to go off at different times, the bombs would spread panic and confusion.

Blocking teams 1, 2, 3, and 4? Prepared. The men were staying in barns or abandoned buildings near their targets. Railroad tracks would be destroyed so no train could leave Versailles. All roads out would be closed off with mines, machine guns, and grenades. Each team had a portable armor-piercing weapon. "Remember," Caarsens told Mission Leader One, "We want them to get in, not out. No one should escape the killing zone alive."

Caarsens greeted his old friend Sergeant Albrecht, an Iron-Cross recipient who had been wounded three times and had fought in Caarsens's battalion during the war. His platoon would block the main road, a key assignment. They talked for a long time. "I can't wait to get into action again," Albrecht said. "I guess the good Lord has kept me alive for this last mission. I won't let you down."

Goering's pilots? Caarsens approached Goering's second-in-command, twenty-two-year-old Captain Reinhardt Voss, credited with fourteen kills in seven weeks. Had the war continued, Voss could have become one of Germany's greatest aces, greater even than his renowned cousin. German newspapers bragged he could not be shot down. Once, after out-flying and downing three British SE-5's in one engagement, he returned to base with his Fokker D VII's cloth wings so shredded no one could believe it still flew. "What do you think of your chances, Captain Voss?" Caarsens asked.

"Excellent, sir."

"How many aeroplanes do you expect to get through?"

"We'll have losses, but I would guess at least ten will reach the target. That many can do a lot of damage. We'll drop our bombs, then strafe the area with machine guns. It's a perfect killing zone — an open area, one building that's easy to spot, crowded. No escape."

"There shouldn't be. What about French aeroplanes patrolling the sky? Are they a threat?"

"Herr Goering and I considered that. Our aeroplanes will have American markings. It won't be obvious we're the enemy. We know U.S. tactics. No one can tell we aren't Americans. Is there any chance the French will ground American aeroplanes that day?"

"I can't imagine why," Caarsens said. "Anyone looking at your aeroplanes will see you're carrying bombs. I can't imagine this would be the case for any Allied aeroplanes in the air that day. Won't they make your aeroplanes look suspicious?"

"There's a chance, but we will be flying high to avoid detection. The maintenance men have already painted the bombs to look like the underside of the Yank aeroplanes."

"What happens if you are intercepted before reaching the target?" Caarsens asked.

"In case they are watching us, we are going to be flying in two waves, one led by Herr Goering, the second by me. Each wave will have two sections. The first section will act like the aggressors and the second section will pretend to pursue them. It will look like the second wave has intercepted the aggressors and are trying to shoot them down. Anyone looking on will think the first group is being chased and will back off. This should give us enough time to drop our bombs."

"Good." Caarsens had liked the plan when Goering proposed it, and Voss had further improved it. "Good luck, Captain." Caarsens liked Voss.

"Thank you for selecting me for this mission, Herr Caarsens. It's what I live for. My wife and infant daughter starved to death back home during the war. Most of my comrades are dead. My only friends are the men flying with me tomorrow. All I have left is Germany."

Life had been a similar hell for Caarsens, since his wife and child died in British hands in the Second Boer War. The desire for revenge had sustained him ever since — a desire so far unfulfilled. Tomorrow would change that, one way or another. He returned to his room, slumped down on his bed, and opened his Bible to the Book of Revelation 9:13. "And the sixth angel sounded, and I heard a voice ..."

Chapter 67
What's Happening?

Paris: June 28, 1919

08:32: Martin had been up all night; his mind was racing. He finished his third cup of coffee and hurried out of the Crillon dining room. The signing was scheduled for three o'clock that afternoon, and he had cause to worry. A series of bombings across Paris had just been reported behind Sacré Cœur, in the Jardin du Luxembourg, and along the tracks outside the Gare St. Lazare. What the hell was happening?

Martin had assigned his normal bodyguard duties to Cooper. The main German threat was sure to come, and he needed to remain available. He first had to ensure that House left safely for the pre-signing meeting with President Wilson. A small explosion crackled across the street just at the moment House and Cooper drove off. *Surely, it couldn't be the Germans — no, not here.* Martin reached for his .45 and scanned for danger. It was only a dumb kid with fireworks, having his own little pre-signing celebration. *Calm down. It will be a long day.*

House's car turned safely out of sight, and Martin returned to the telephone center that House had established in his office. First task, call Fauchaux. He dialed, identified himself, and asked the operator to connect him. He tapped his feet while he waited. When Fauchaux finally picked up, Martin jumped in as soon as the major said his name. "What's going on?"

"There's trouble," Fauchaux said.

"What do you make of it?"

"Seems random. No reported injuries. It's no coincidence, I'm sure."

"This is part of Caarsens's plan," Martin said. "A diversion to make us move resources away from Versailles."

"If so, it's one I cannot ignore. I must pull men from other duties to investigate," Fauchaux replied. "Everyone's on edge."

"What about the major signatories on their way to the signing?"

"We've doubled the guard around them. Altered their routes. We're rechecking all the roads to Versailles, looking for ambushes and mines. Railroad lines too. Men are on standby. Do not worry, *mon ami*. The Boches will not succeed."

That's easy enough for you to say, thought Martin. *You don't know Caarsens like I do.* "Let me know further developments."

Caarsens had already seized the initiative. Martin's worry mounted. He stayed by the telephone for the next hour, chewing his fingernails. He tried pacing to relieve the stress. Nothing helped. He watched from the window as Keller escorted Shannon and Ana to a Ford with U.S. military markings. Shannon and Keller were arguing so hard that Shannon's hands quivered in apparent frustration. She took a heavy-looking haversack from her husband and jumped into the car without looking up. Keller closed the door and waved goodbye. He kicked the street with the heel of his boot as the Ford drove out of sight.

I don't want them to go either, my friend, but try stopping those two.

Martin returned to his chair in front of House's desk and clenched his fists. Every few minutes he checked his watch. Why wasn't it moving? His fingers cramped. He ignored them and plotted possible moves. When the telephone finally rang, it startled him. He picked it up on the first ring. "Martin."

"There's been a development," said Fauchaux. His colleague had just begun to explain, when Martin realized he had the clue to unravel Caarsens's plan.

~

On the Road to Orly

The Alsatian truck driver slowly approached a group of French troops along the road, the third one he had seen that day. Caarsens sat at his side dressed in farmworker's clothes, and the Freikorps men in the back wore French uniforms. Their truck was loaded with weapons. Behind them were two cars with more soldiers. The troops along the road waved as they passed. Good sign. They did not look like a threat. Around the bend, they came upon other soldiers inspecting the road as if looking for mines. Bad sign. These men suspected something.

Similarly disguised, the other three trucks they had loaded the night before traveled by different routes. They could not afford to give the impression of a military convoy. Most of the men assigned to attack the airbase were already in position, making final preparations.

A road sign at the bottom of a small incline read, "Orly 4 km." Nearly there. When the truck reached the crest, Caarsens looked down and discovered a French sergeant and five soldiers setting up a roadblock below them. A precaution? Someone looking for them? It was too late to turn around. If the French soldiers saw his men, there would be a fight. Caarsens reached for his Mauser trench-sweeper automatic. He liked the 10-bullet clip. "Follow their instructions," he told his driver. "Remember, we're just farmers making deliveries." He knocked three times on the metal plate separating the cab from the loading bay, his signal for danger. He heard the men in the back ready their weapons. The driver obeyed the sergeant's signal and stopped at the wooden barrier. "What's going on?" he asked.

"What's in the truck?" the sergeant demanded in a firm manner.

"Farm equipment."

The sergeant frowned. "This road is barred to all non-essential vehicles. Mind if I look?"

The driver shrugged and looked to Caarsens for instructions. "Go ahead," Caarsens said. He looked for targets — the sergeant, two men by the barrier with rifles slung on their shoulders, three more looking on. No machine guns. Foolish soldiers. Caarsens pointed the automatic across his driver's face and shot the sergeant in the cheek. He jumped out of the truck before the other guards could react and shot the two men at the barrier. Reick leaped out the back and killed the others.

Caarsens searched the sergeant's body for a clue to the reason for the roadblock, but found nothing but cigarettes, a few coins, and some condoms. He instructed his men to hide the bodies and remove all traces of the roadblock. "We'll have to move fast. Something's gone wrong," he privately informed Reick as they searched the area together for a phone. Finally satisfied that the roadblock was not equipped for communications, Caarsens gave the order to move on. "Take the back roads, and move fast," he told his driver.

~

Paris

11:46: Martin found Keller in the hotel lobby. "We've had a breakthrough," he said excitedly. "Fauchaux has just issued orders to set up roadblocks into Versailles. They've found the body of a French soldier at Orly. It was set up to look as though he had deserted, and at first they bought the story. But when the body was discovered, there were clear signs of murder."

"I thought that was a U.S. base," Keller said. "What was he doing there?"

"We abandoned that base while you were in Germany," Martin said. "The French took it back." Martin related the news from Fauchaux that a Canadian major and advisors from the Nieuport factory had visited the Air Acceptance Base a few days previously. "And the Canadian wore an eye patch," he concluded.

"Caarsens!" Keller pounded his hand. "Damn him! He pretended to be a Canuck when we investigated him in New York too."

"Caarsens plans to take over the airbase, and — "

"Goering!" Keller exclaimed. "That's the plan. He'll lead an air assault on the signings at Versailles."

"Now we know what base he'll use. I have to call headquarters."

"I need to warn Shannon."

Martin waited five tormenting minutes to reach someone at AEF headquarters. He demanded to speak to General Pershing directly. "He's not here," the operator informed him. "I'll connect you to Lieutenant Colonel Hartwood. He's the highest-ranking officer present." Martin did not know Hartwood. When the colonel took the phone, Martin explained the urgent situation and demanded all American aeroplanes be grounded. "I don't have the authority," Hartwood kept repeating.

"I do," Martin said. "I speak for Colonel House."

"He's a civilian. I don't take orders from him. Who are you again?"

Martin struck the phone against the desk. It was lucky he didn't break it. "Listen, Hartwood. If any American plane flies today, I'll make sure you'll be broken to private and assigned to Panama. You can sweat your life away with the mosquitoes. Goodbye." When he looked up, Keller was standing there staring at him.

"I can't reach Shannon. I'm worried," Keller said.

"She can take care of herself."

"You're right." Keller calmed down. "You should call Fauchaux. Maybe he can do something."

Martin dialed Fauchaux immediately and fidgeted through

another long wait before he was able to recount the problem at AEF headquarters. "We must get through to Generalissimo Foch. As overall Allied commander, he can order the grounding of all U.S. aeroplanes. That will stop any U.S. aeroplanes the Germans might take at Orly from mixing with French aeroplanes defending Versailles."

"It'll take some time."

Martin hung up, defeated. "Fauchaux's going to try to get through to Foch."

"We'll stop Caarsens. We've stopped him before. We'll stop him again," Keller said.

"We'll have to stop him on the ground. If Goering gets his aeroplanes in the air ..." Martin was unwilling to finish the thought. "How much time do we have?"

~

On the Road to Versailles

Albrecht's sapper dashed to the cover of the woods on the main road to Versailles, five miles away. "All done, Sergeant. Last mine planted." Wide, unpaved paths for foot traffic or slow-moving carts stretched along either side of the two-lane road. It now contained a mine field fifty yards deep.

"Good job."

"No one gets through without triggering an explosion."

"Go to your post. It won't be long now." Albrecht's fifty-man platoon was dressed in French uniforms and expertly placed. While Reick and the main German units attacked the airbase, Albrecht would ensure no one escaped Versailles once Goering's pilots started to bomb the palace. This was critical to Caarsens's plan. They formed a defensive perimeter in the shape of a ninety-degree angle along the top of a sharp dog-legged curve in the road. Behind the tree line, the men had dug shallow pits, fronted with rocks, dirt, and fallen timber. Machine gun emplacements at the center of each line in the angle permitted the gunners to hit anything coming from either direction with interlocking fire. A mortar team positioned in a clearing a hundred yards back had already marked off the distance to every section of the road and tested the range. Whatever survived the minefield would succumb to their deadly accuracy.

The sound of an automobile neared, coming from the direction of Paris. *That's running late.* "Ready, men. Wait for a mine to explode," Albrecht ordered. He eased the stock of an inferior French Lebel rifle into the crook of his arm. He preferred the smooth bolt action of a German Mauser.

~

Shannon bounced up and down on the seat of her Ford so hard she twice hit her head on the roof. Next to her, Ana remained silent as if she sensed trouble. The haversack Keller had given her rested at Shannon's feet. It contained a .45 and extra clips. "I won't need this, Paul," she had insisted, but took it anyway. It wasn't worth the fight. She leaned forward and said to the driver, "Can't you go any faster? I have translations to do before the signing." She was angry that the argument with her husband and unexplained stops along the way had caused delay.

"Tell that to *him*," her driver said, pointing to the automobile in front of them. "The road is bad, and the roadblocks were not my fault."

"We'll be fine," Ana consoled her, sitting to Shannon's right. "It's not much farther."

"I can't miss the signing. Not after everything — "

The automobile in front of them exploded into a fiery ball. "Get down!" the driver shouted, braking hard. Shannon and Ana ducked as heat from the blast radiated toward them. Gunfire opened up from their right side, shattering the windshield and peppering the driver with glass shards. Shannon heard his last desperate breath as debris and lead flew over her crouching body. The automobile behind them slammed into their rear. Bullets pierced the car doors like small hammer blows in rapid succession. Shannon heard voices in the automobile behind them shriek out in pain.

"Grab your weapon," Ana ordered. She raised her eyes to the window and peeked outside. "Get out. Your side." Ana clutched an infantryman's pouch full of grenades, a French Lebel revolver, and a handful of extra bullets. She followed Shannon out the left door, opposite the gunfire.

The two women crawled on all fours to the safety of the adjacent woods, bullets cracking over their heads, and stopped behind the base of a stout tree. Bullets pounded into it and zipped past them. Behind the cover of the tree, Ana returned fire. "Save your ammunition," Shannon said, slamming a clip into her .45. She peered around the tree and viewed the carnage. A noise from the woods. Breaking twigs.

"Germans." Ana touched Shannon's shoulder. "They're circling around."

"What do we do?" Shannon asked.

"Fight. Take some grenades."

~

Outside U.S. Air Acceptance Base

12:44: Caarsens's truck drove into the starting point for the attack, a farmyard close to the airbase. Its owners were newly dead. Caarsens had not encountered further problems on his way. The other trucks had already arrived, and the men were unloading Caarsens's truck as Goering and his pilots put on their flying gear. The maintenance men reviewed their checklists. Ten teams of four men each were responsible for readying the aeroplanes. Their leader assured Caarsens they would get the full assault fleet airborne as planned.

Caarsens changed into his French-Canadian major's uniform. He took out his binoculars and studied the base about one-and-a-half miles away. It looked the same as it had on his last visit. Excellent. The wide open fields surrounding the base presented the biggest tactical challenge. Anyone approaching could be seen for more than a mile. His men would have to advance in open territory, a disaster if the defenders were expecting an attack. To counter this, the first part of the plan called for Caarsens, again impersonating the Canadian major, to drive up to the base accompanied by three Germans. If the ruse worked, they would gain entry without a fight and could start the attack from within. Two mortar crews would then move into range and shell the base. They knew their targets.

The rest of the men would advance double-time. Separate units would move to one of three different weak points that Caarsens and Reick had identified. The tank would follow, ramming through the front gate and eliminating any remaining opposition. Wolf would man the tank gun. He wanted to start immediately and became angry when ordered to wait. He pouted and set to sharpening his trench sword with a stone.

Caarsens reviewed his plan one last time. Half an hour to take control of the base. 13:15. Another forty-five minutes to get the aeroplanes ready. They would need to defend the base until 14:00. He added fifteen minutes, just in case. The aeroplanes would attack by 14:30 or a bit later, when all the signatories and officials would be crowding into the Versailles Palace. Timing was tight, but adequate. Caarsens felt confident as he gave his men their final instructions. "Be careful," he ordered. "We can't shoot up the aeroplanes. Take as many prisoners as you can. We'll use them as shields. If the French attack, they'll be reluctant to shell us and kill their own men." This would be an infantryman's fight, and Caarsens's Freikorps was the better infantry.

He looked at Reick.

“Ready,” Reick said.

“Attack.”

Chapter 68
The Attack

Paris:
Martin checked the clock over the fireplace. Time was short. He was glad to be moving. His senses sharpened into pre-battle awareness. Everything he had done since arriving in France mattered little if he failed today.

Keller jumped to his feet. “Can we get there in time?”

“Orly is about nine miles away,” Martin said. “About twenty to thirty minutes. Maybe longer today. Depends on traffic. We have to arm ourselves. To the armory,” Martin said. “We’ll meet Fauchaux at Chevilly. French units are assembling there.”

Dressed in battle fatigues and weighted down with guns, extra ammunition, and grenades, Martin and Keller ran to their staff car. Martin hopped into the driver’s seat. “I know all the shortcuts.”

Keller looked around. “Just us? What about the other men?”

“I need the rest of them to guard our people in Paris. The French have enough troops.”

“What about Shannon?”

“She’s on her own. If you need to go after her, I’ll understand, but I have to move fast.”

“I’m with you, but what are we going to do at Orly?”

“Kill Caarsens.”

~

On the Road to Versailles
The man in a French uniform raised his rifle and snuck through the trees. Shannon caught a glimpse of him from the corner of her eye, swiveled from the waist, and killed him with one shot. Coldness grabbed her heart — her first kill. *Think about it later*. She crouched low next to

Ana, taking cover behind the tree. Back-to-back, the women surveyed the ground, Shannon pointing forward to the road, Ana covering their rear. Except for the crackle of flames coming from the first automobile, the entire area had gone quiet. "They're closing in," Ana whispered. "See anything?"

Shannon had never faced a combat situation like this before. She was going on instinct, her reflexes heightened, her skin turned to gooseflesh.

"I'll shoot the first thing that moves," she said to Ana. Pungent smoke from the burning car began to fill the woods. "How many are out there?"

"I can't tell," Ana whispered. "We need to move. They know our position."

"But the others. We — "

"They're dead. Come, or we'll be joining them."

Shannon heard a twig snap about ten yards to her right. Ana pointed toward the sound and squeezed off two rounds. A soldier fell face first from the bushes and moved no more. "Rainer's down," someone called in German. A new volley of bullets swept toward them. Shannon and Ana clung so close to the ground they tasted dirt.

Ana, flat on her stomach, fired every round in her revolver as more men approached from the woods. Two more screams. The voices retreated back into the trees, and Ana rose slightly, scrambling to reload as Shannon drove others off with well-placed shots. To her surprise, Ana lobbed a grenade at the attackers. "Cover your head!" she yelled at Shannon as she dropped down.

Shannon was stunned by the force of the explosion. A wounded man cried out. Grisly body parts landed in front of them. Shannon heard orders, and two soldiers dragged a body away. Concentrated rifle fire bored into their position. Broken tree branches and chunks of burning bark landed on her head.

"Must be a good twenty men out there," Ana said. "Not sure how long we can last." She tossed another grenade. "That'll keep them at bay for a moment."

This was not how Shannon had expected to die. The thought of Paul that morning as he begged her not to get in the car flashed through her mind. Her regrets vanished when she heard the clanking whine of an approaching tank.

~

Orly

13:18: The Renault touring car with Canadian military markings drove slowly up the road to the U.S. Air Acceptance Base. The surrounding fields were deserted. Caarsens persistently scanned his surroundings for the perfect chance to spring his attack. Five hundred yards — so far, so good. The engine of his car began to overheat, but he drove on, keeping to a steady twenty miles an hour. At one hundred yards from the entrance, he moved into a zone of peril, the point at which the French would start shooting if they intended to fight.

Two muscular Freikorps soldiers, each armed with carbines and four stick grenades, sat in the back of Caarsens's car. He could hear them breathing fast and deep like sprinters about to take their marks. The man in the front passenger seat carried a portable British Lewis machine gun. "Just tell us when, Major," the Lewis gunner said, his finger tapping the stock.

"Not yet." Sensing no threat, Caarsens drove on. The closer he got, the more lethal his punch. At fifteen yards, he waved to the French private manning the gate. "Get down," Caarsens said to his men. He pressed the accelerator hard. His Renault rammed through the wooden barrier, splintering it into kindling and crushing the guard behind it. He stopped ten yards into the base, and he and his men scrambled out. Caarsens shot the two remaining guards. The grenade men destroyed a sandbag emplacement, wiped out six men running at them, and blasted the nearby buildings. The Lewis gunner sprayed the windows across the compound. Caarsens and his men took up defensive positions behind the car. Begin phase two.

With perfect timing, the mortar team began shelling the compound. The first shell veered toward a warehouse Caarsens had previously identified as the armory. On target, the shell triggered secondary explosions that shook the base. Fire erupted among the remains. Caarsens began to sweat. The second round hit the main barracks, followed by one to the canteen. The measurements he had taken on his last visit were as precise as his mortar team was accurate. The next round landed in front of a group of ten French soldiers preparing for a counterattack. The shell felled half, and two of Caarsens's riflemen downed the rest. Caarsens glanced behind him. Thirty Freikorps soldiers were hustling along the road he had just traveled, followed by the Renault tank with its deadly 37mm gun. Hidden behind his splatter mask, Wolf's head stuck out above the turret. He fired a round at a Frenchman about to toss a grenade, nearly cutting him in two. He removed the mask and cheered his comrades on with youthful glee. They entered the compound with overwhelming force.

The explosion to Caarsens's left was right on time. Another Freikorps platoon was blasting its way into the compound through a flimsy wooden building. Screams of dying men reverberated from inside. Three French soldiers charged from across the enclosed field. The Lewis gunner stopped them with a sustained burst. The inside compound was Caarsens's.

Gunshots coming from the hangar area announced the presence of Reick's main force. The firing lessened for a few moments, then all went quiet. “All secure,” Reick called.

Caarsens cuffed his hands around his mouth and shouted in French, “Captain Leblanc? I urge the rest of your men to surrender. There’s no need for more to die.”

“Cease fire! We’re coming out!” Leblanc and four men emerged from headquarters, hands raised. Leblanc was bleeding from a head wound. One soldier clutched his arm, another limped badly, and the fourth looked dazed. Leblanc ordered the rest of his men to drop their weapons. Across the compound, rifles were thrown from open windows or dropped from the roof. Caarsens estimated they had eliminated three-quarters of the garrison with a coordinated aggressive attack and deadly mortar support.

Caarsens shot a green flair into the air — the signal for Goering, his pilots, and the maintenance crew to approach. Four trucks sped onto the base, drove across the landing strips, and headed to the hangar area. It was all over in fourteen minutes, at the cost of three slightly wounded men.

Caarsens ordered Reick to set up the defensive perimeter. He walked up to Leblanc and said, “Time to talk.”

“You killed my men, you swine.” Leblanc charged at Caarsens. The Freikorps private next to Caarsens punched Leblanc in the stomach, buckling him over. Leblanc looked up. “Who are you?”

“Inside.” Caarsens waved his Mauser toward the headquarters building. They entered Leblanc’s office to the sound of a ringing telephone.

“Pick it up,” Caarsens barked. “I’ll be listening. Everything is calm. There’s nothing to report. Got it?” Caarsens jammed his automatic into Leblanc’s lower jaw. “Or you die.”

A shaken Leblanc picked up the phone. He listened, responding in muted tones, and hung up the receiver. “They’re coming,” he said.

"That was a warning from Paris."

"How soon?" Caarsens had been expecting this.

"Fifteen minutes. Maybe twenty."

~

Chevilly, Staging Point for the French Counterattack

Martin and Keller arrived in Chevilly in twenty-two minutes. Martin drove like a madman, relying on his horn as much as his gearshift. On the way, they passed five military trucks pulling heavy artillery pieces and two platoons of tanks heading in the same direction. Squadrons of Nieuport 28s flew overhead. Keller prayed they were French, not American, and was relieved when he identified their red-white-and-blue roundel markings. The French air force was moving in on Orly.

Martin slowed down when he saw a regiment marching forward. He saw Fauchaux by the roadway, talking to a French colonel. An angry-looking sergeant signaled the Americans to stop. Martin identified himself, and Fauchaux waved them over and introduced him to Colonel Favre. "He's in charge of the attack."

Martin saluted. "Do you know what you're up against, *mon Colonel*?"

"No. We assume the Germans are in control of the base. My men heard gunfire and explosions originating there. We'll have to take the base or destroy it."

"How many aeroplanes are at the base?" Martin asked.

"Around thirty. My airmen have orders to shoot down any plane that takes off." Favre gestured to the sky. "No one will get near the palace."

Hubris has caused many defeats. All it would take is just one plane.

"Every one of the German pilots is an ace," Keller said.

"Care to join my attack?" Favre asked.

"Just give us time to grab our weapons," Martin responded.

"I have some debts to settle with these Germans," Keller said, his face flushed with anger.

"I intend to chop through them like a cleaver through a chicken's neck," Favre said through gritted teeth.

Keller nodded in agreement. "Make them suffer."

Martin grabbed his favorite weapons from the trunk of the car, a Winchester Model-12 pump-action shotgun, and a .45. He stuffed bullets into his pockets. Keller snatched a Browning Automatic Rifle (BAR), extra magazines, and several grenades. His knife was already lashed to his ankle.

A lieutenant on a motorcycle rode up to Favre, jumped off, and saluted. "My advance scouts say the Germans have taken prisoners, *mon Colonel.* They are using them as shields. The main building is on fire. The Germans are setting up barbed wire and mines."

Explosions sounded in the distance. "The Germans are blowing up buildings to create better defensive positions," Martin said.

"Let me investigate," Keller interjected.

"Go, but be careful, Paul."

"This may be more difficult than I'd expected," Favre said.

~

On the Road to Versailles

"Listen. A tank," Albrecht said from his position behind the middle car. He ordered all but one man back to their original positions. He told the remaining man to get behind the women and keep them pinned down. "They've already killed six of our men." He turned to his second-in-command. "Tell the mortar crew to get ready. Runner!" The youngest man in the unit sprinted toward Albrecht. Albrecht pointed toward the curve in the road that led to Versailles. "Rudi, find out what's coming at us."

Minutes later, Rudi returned. "Battalion strength at least. Two tanks in the lead. Armored car follows. They have a field gun."

"How're they deployed?"

"They're coming for a fight. Standard French attack formation. Disciplined. Be here in five minutes."

"*Scheisse.* Those damned women have taken away our surprise. Get Bruer here on the double."

A private with a flamethrower on his back reported within seconds. "Get as close as possible and remain hidden," Albrecht commanded. "Wait as long as you can, then spray the lead vehicle with fire. Block the road. Stop their advance."

Albrecht ordered his men to move their defensive line up the road. He instructed his second-in-command to pass the word. Open up when Bruer shoots. The mortar crew should follow and fire two hundred yards behind the disabled tank. Walk their rounds ten yards closer with each shell. Each rifleman was free to choose his target.

French skirmishers led the way, advancing along the side of the road. Two tanks rolled thirty yards behind them. Albrecht's men remained hidden, waiting to spring their ambush. When the point man rounded the bend, he saw the burning automobile. Positioned on the farthest part of the German line, Bruer unleashed a spray of flaming death. The lead tank erupted into a fireball, and the Germans opened up. The mortar team lobbed shell after shell. The third one disabled the second tank. Albrecht's soldiers worked their rifles feverishly, but all knew it was only a question of time before the French numbers would overwhelm them.

The French lost fifty men in the first minute, yet managed to seize the advantage. They backed away their armored car, set up a 37mm infantry-support artillery piece, and fired on the outgunned Germans. The lead French unit, a company of one-hundred-and-sixty men, raked the German positions with a powerful fusillade. Twelve Germans fell instantly. The French moved forward, throwing grenades and killing six more Boches.

Simultaneously with this action, two companies of French troops moved into the woods and eliminated the mortar team. Albrecht heard their dying pleas — the French were not taking prisoners. The enemy was closing in on two sides, and Albrecht realized his few remaining men would be flanked. "Fall back," he ordered. Seven men, including Rudi, followed him along the roadside toward the burning auto. The last machine gun team stayed and continued to fight. An artillery shell silenced them. Three retreating Germans fell next to Albrecht.

Lead the French into the mine field. Kill as many as possible, Albrecht thought. *We've done our duty.* He told the four remaining soldiers they were free to leave. They laughed and reloaded their weapons. "I'll be in Valhalla soon," Rudi said with a smile, and tossed another grenade.

~

Pinned down by a German rifleman, Shannon peered cautiously around the tree as the Germans retreated back to the burning car. Kneeling next to her, Ana kept the German soldier behind them at bay with well-placed shots. The young, brown-haired soldier in front of Shannon threw a grenade. It was his last act. An artillery shell passed harmlessly over the remaining Germans and exploded near the women. A fragment of shrapnel skirted the tree protecting them and grazed Ana in the side of her head. She appeared dazed but remained upright. The next shell landed near the Germans, knocking down all but the leader.

Distracted by Ana's plight, Shannon momentarily forgot the rifleman behind them. He saw his advantage and dashed into an open space for a clean shot. "Shannon, watch out!" Ana yelled. She pulled herself upright, trying to aim her revolver.

The German hurried his shot and missed. Shannon turned and fired. Her bullet hit him in the chest, nearly spinning him around. She stood up and looked back at the road. One last German remained. Her bullet passed through his heart. Administering death was becoming easier.

Six French soldiers emerged from the bend and raised their rifles, thinking the shots from the woods were intended for them. "*Ne tirez pas!*" cried Shannon. "Don't shoot! We're friends!" Too late. They unleashed a volley right at her. One bullet nicked Shannon in the leg, another grazed her face. Ana slumped over beside her. She looked surprised and placed her hand to the spot where blood was spurting from her chest.

"Stop shooting! I'm a woman." Shannon called out and tossed her .45 onto the road. This time the French soldiers listened. "My God," she uttered, as she examined Ana's wound.

Ana gestured for Shannon to come closer.

Shannon bent over to hear her. "What?"

Ana smiled. Spitting out a mouthful of blood, she muttered, "Tell Gil ..." Her words faded.

"Ana! Stay with me!" Shannon cried. "Tell me again!" She looked into Ana's face, but Ana's lips did not move.

Chapter 69
I've Found a Way

U.S. Air Acceptance Base, Orly

14:03: *What was taking the French so long to strike?* Martin wondered, staring through his binoculars. *Would Keller spot weaknesses in the German defense on his scouting mission?* The Germans were fortifying their positions. A few fighter aeroplanes appeared on the runway, their propellers whirling. Behind him, the French were setting up their 75mm artillery pieces, but their tanks had not yet arrived. A battalion had moved into attack formation. The men were quiet. They had done this before.

Martin turned to Colonel Favre. "Why haven't your men moved forward?"

"I have two companies of men circling around to attack from the rear. I must wait until I can apply maximum force with my tanks."

"You can shell them, at least. Stop those aeroplanes from taking off."

"The situation is delicate, Major Martin. The Germans are using their captives as shields. A soldier is roped behind every plane on the runway. I'll kill a Frenchman for every German. I won't do that."

Martin did not hide his disapproval. "You must."

"The situation is under control. I remind you, you are just an observer."

Keller returned and reported back to Martin. "I've found a way." He pointed to the farm behind the base. I've recruited ten volunteers to join me. They want to liberate their countrymen."

Martin nodded his head in agreement. "Colonel Favre?"

Favre checked his watch. "The tanks will be here in twenty

minutes. You have that much time, Captain Keller. We'll then attack with everything we have. Save as many Frenchmen as you can."

When Martin and Keller were alone, Martin said, "Your plan is reckless, Paul. You don't have to do this."

"Yes, I do. I saw my old Freikorps commander in there. He's leading the defense of that base. I owe a debt to Sund and Liebknecht. I must kill him." Keller extended his hand to Martin. "We've been through a lot together, old friend. I'll attack the base. The hangars are your responsibility. When this is over, let's go back to New York and forget this cursed war." Keller hesitated as if to add something, then turned away. He signaled his volunteers to get ready. He carried his BAR, a pouch full of hand grenades, and a .45. His knife, strapped to his ankle, provided insurance.

~

Caarsens looked skyward from the front of the main hangar. The odds were mounting against him. Fifteen French aeroplanes appeared over the base. "How did they get here so fast?" he asked Goering. "Someone has betrayed us."

"We have to accelerate our plan." Caarsens looked around. The hangar was full of bombs and belts of machine gun bullets yet to be fitted onto the remaining aeroplanes.

Caarsens called to Voss, who was discussing something with one of the maintenance men. "If we can get the aeroplanes in the air, some of my men will get through. It'll be three or four against one, but we can do this," Voss said.

Goering agreed. "The men are repainting the roundels to the French colors. It's delayed us, but eight aeroplanes are ready to take off."

"I'll lead. Let me go," Voss said.

"Good luck," Caarsens said. *Brave man.*

Voss saluted and ran to the white SPAD waiting for him on the landing strip.

"Can you direct your guns against those French aeroplanes?" Goering asked.

Caarsens was calm. "I'll have to. Back soon."

~

Positioned in the farmhouse near the back of the base, Keller studied his target: the far corner of the buildings that formed the outer circle of the compound. The Germans had improved their defenses with barbed wire, sandbags, and riflemen pits. A tank blocked the entrance. Keller's team hustled to an irrigation ditch that extended to within thirty yards of the building — a blind spot except for the sniper on the adjacent roof. French aeroplanes overhead improved his chances.

Keller led the way, crawling on his knees, belly, and elbows through the muddy ditch. It smelled of rotting carcasses, fertilizer, and stagnant water. No man spoke. Several grunted from the exertion. It took seven minutes to reach a position nearest the buildings. He looked for an opportunity to attack.

~

Caarsens returned to the main hangar in five minutes with two machine gun teams. They immediately prepared their guns to shoot at the French. "I've stripped my defense so you can take off," Caarsens said to a worried Goering. "Every man I've got has orders to keep the French away from your pilots."

From the cockpit of his SPAD, Voss signaled the other pilots to follow him. The maintenance crews untied their prisoners. Voss gunned his engine and started down the runway. Five French Nieuport 28s swooped down on him, but he managed to get airborne.

The German infantrymen unleashed a wall of bullets at the attackers. Elevated to shoot skyward, the 37mm tank gun provided the deadliest fire. Two Nieuports crashed to the ground. The other three climbed to avoid the same fate. In addition to Voss, five other aeroplanes made it off the ground. Two French pilots, new to the fight, banked down and sprayed the runway with machine gun fire, ignoring German bullets.

The lead German aeroplane waiting to take off began to burn. The pilot in the second slot was dead. Maintenance men ran to help, but the two diving Nieuports gunned them down. The last two German SPADs on the runway scrambled to get around the disabled aeroplanes in front of them. The French aeroplanes circled back and fired, crippling the scrambling SPADs. Gunfire brought one of the diving Frenchmen crashing down in a fireball to the outside field. The second Frenchman flew away, his engine spewing smoke.

Voss circled around and pursued a diving Nieuport, closing in for the kill. His machine guns chattered. The French pilot slumped down, dead. Voss climbed to join his other five men in the dogfight. Although the German aeroplanes were outnumbered, their odds improved every minute. Four French aeroplanes, their engines burning, had to flee. The cost? Two German aeroplanes.

Caarsens watched the aerial acrobatics above him. The scene resembled a mesmerizing dance: graceful, beautiful, deadly. Explosions behind the east side of the compound seized his attention. What was happening?

~

With the Germans focused on the battle in the air, Keller saw his chance. He borrowed the rifle of his English-speaking sergeant and aimed at the German on the roof. The bullet struck his heart. “Good shot, *mon ami.*” Keller signaled Fauchaux to unleash the mortars. The first round arced toward the compound and blew away the back of the building. The second exploded inside, clearing a path to the inner compound.

"Advance!" yelled Keller. He grabbed his BAR and led his men through the gap.

The Germans reacted quickly. In the inner compound near the front entrance, the tank shifted position to confront the new threat with its 37mm gun. The first round killed two of Keller's men. Splotches of blood mixed with mud and sweat on Keller's uniform. The smell of cordite was everywhere. Smoke thickened, making it hard to see. Another burst. The severed arm of one man smacked Keller on the leg. Unfazed, he unloaded a full twenty-round clip of his BAR, stopping three advancing Germans. Both sides exchanged grenades. Deadly fragments scattered in all directions. Wounded men from both sides screamed. The tank fired, decapitating Keller's English-speaking sergeant.

Keller and his remaining two men retreated into the ruins of the adjacent building, surprising a German guarding three captives. His BAR empty, Keller pulled out his .45 and shot the guard before he could react. With poor French and sheer adrenalin, Keller made the captives understand they were to go back to their lines and order the artillery to fire. Another 37mm round exploded over his head. *How to stop that tank?*

Plowing through the debris, the rumbling menace neared. Sixteen yards. Fourteen. Keller would soon be flattened. The German gunner paused to reload, and Keller took his chance, tossing a grenade in the tank's path. The explosion blew off the tread, stopping its advance. The gun turret turned toward him, unleashing another shell that passed inches from his ear and exploded behind him. The air turned gray with debris, making it hard to take in air. *Where was his artillery?*

Keller and his last man scrambled to the back of the building. A 37mm shell landed in the position they had just vacated. Pinned down by rifle fire, Keller had only one thing to do: Stop the tank. He slammed another clip into his BAR and handed it to the Frenchman, who unleashed a spray of covering fire, driving back the German attackers. Keller zigged and zagged, denying the tank gunner a clear shot. Increasing smoke hid Keller's moves. He ignored bullets from the German riflemen and tried to jump on top of the tank, but his bad leg betrayed him and he fell. Luckily so — a bullet flew directly in the path of his jump. He summoned his inner strength, ignored the cramps, tried again, and made it. He moved so the tank's turret protected him from German bullets, which now were bouncing off the tank's steel skin. Ping. Ping. Ping. He signaled his man to stop firing, shot a bullet into the air, and faked a loud dying moan. A few seconds later, he tapped on the top of the tank hatch. In German, he called to the gunner, "They're dead. Come out."

To Keller's surprise, a familiar face emerged. Wolf. Mutual recognition turned to mutual hate. Wolf ducked and tried to close the hatch. Too late. Keller lowered his .45 into the tank and fired off a full clip. He heard Wolf's body slump down. More from hate than necessity, Keller dropped a grenade into the tank and jumped off. The explosion blew off the tank turret and scattered fragments of Wolf's trench sword into the air. *I hope you rot in hell.*

Keller looked up and saw four Germans charge. At the same moment, the French started shelling the inner compound. *Finally.* The first shell landed among the charging Germans, killing all but one. As the French bombardment intensified, Keller and the remaining German ran to the relative safety of the nearest building, reaching it just in time before the next round exploded in the area they had just abandoned.

Keller dived and covered his head. He rubbed his eyes. The German next to him did the same. Reick.

~

14:28: Amid the explosions and gunfire, Caarsens knew he could not help the men in the compound. He had to get Goering's second squadron in the air. They would soon be overrun or shelled into oblivion. The hangar next door was already burning. Overhead, the dogfight was slackening. The two German SPADs left in the air were fighting four French aeroplanes. The two German aeroplanes split off. One barrel-rolled and made a frontal attack, downing one Nieuport and smashing head-on into another. The other aeroplane, Voss's white SPAD, downed one French aeroplane and damaged the other. He accelerated toward Versailles, free of pursuers.

Caarsens ran into the hangar and confronted Goering. "What now?" The inner compound was being overrun. The French artillery bombardment intensified as French troops advanced on the hangars. The German aeroplanes on the runway had been destroyed or were riddled with bullets. Few French aeroplanes remained overhead. They had either been shot down, disabled, or had left the fight to chase Voss. Caarsens ordered the French prisoners released and sent back to their lines.

Goering ran up to him in a rage. "You can't do that."

"These are honorable men, Herr Goering. They don't deserve to die."

"And *we* do?"

"It was our choice." Caarsens raised his Mauser and pointed at Goering's two maintenance men. They protested. One raised his rifle, but Caarsens was faster and shot him in the arm. He pointed his gun at the other man's face. "You next? Untie them," he ordered. When the soldier protested, Caarsens fired, clipping a quarter-inch off the top of his head. He quickly untied the remaining five prisoners. "You are on your own," Caarsens said in French. "My men will not shoot you."

Goering's face turned crimson as they ran.

"Your plane is armed and ready, *Oberstleutnant,*" said the head maintenance man, pointing to a sky-blue SPAD XIII, its engine growling. He held his hand to his bleeding ear.

"Excellent," Goering said, checking his flight gear.

"Join Voss. Maybe one of you can get through," Caarsens said. "My men can hold off the French until you get in the sky. We haven't lost yet." An artillery shell landed near the hangar, shaking it to its foundations with a deafening explosion.

Goering looked at Caarsens skeptically. "Are you crazy? The French know our plans. You can bet more aeroplanes are on their way. At least a squadron is protecting Versailles right now. Voss doesn't have a chance." Another explosion blasted the back of the hangar, sending shrapnel toward them. "I need to get out of here," Goering said.

"You running?" Caarsens shook Goering by the lapels of his leather jacket. "Coward!"

Goering pushed Caarsens away. "Back off!" he commanded, Luger raised.

"If you're as good as they say, you can get through."

"Hah! If you were as good as you claimed, I'd be flying over Versailles right now!" Goering exclaimed.

Caarsens raised his Mauser and aimed at Goering's head. He saw Goering look over Caarsens's left shoulder, his blind side. At the same moment, the head maintenance man swung a crowbar into Caarsens's back. Caarsens managed to hold onto his pistol and shoot him in the lung. Another gunshot. Caarsens felt a burning agony in his side. Goering holstered his Luger and dashed to his SPAD.

Caarsens dropped to his knees and placed his hand over the wound, the side that had already lost a kidney. *Not dead yet.* Fighting pain and dizziness, he fired three shots blindly at Goering, now taxiing away.

Caarsens crawled after him leaving behind a trail of blood and losing distance by the second. By the time he reached the front of the hangar, Goering was in the air, his blue SPAD streaking southward, away from Versailles. "Damn you, you *fokking* bastard!" Another artillery round landed in front of the hangar, lacing Caarsens with shell fragments. He rolled over and closed his eyes.

Chapter 70
Your Man Is in Trouble

U.S. Air Acceptance Base

14:32: "Reick!" Despite his watery eyes, Keller was certain the German lying next to him was his old Freikorps captain. Recognition turned to fear. Where was his .45? *Must have dropped it.*

Reick raised himself on his elbows and glared at Keller. "Brandt? How in God's name ..."

A shell landed just outside their building, covering the two prone men with debris. Flames crackled next door. Gunfire outside made it difficult to hear, but no words were needed to convey their loathing. Reick reacted first and reached for his holster. Empty. He spotted his Luger yards away, amid the wreckage of the door though which they had just escaped.

Reick scrambled for his pistol on hands and knees, as Keller reached out to grab him. Reick pulled away, but Keller seized a foot-long piece of lumber and slammed it into Reick's right calf. Reick howled and kicked back like a horse, cracking Keller square in the nose. One more step and Reick would reach his gun. Keller lunged, tackling him at mid-thigh. Reick spun around and threw an elbow that Keller blocked with his forearms. It felt like a blow from a nightstick. While Keller tried to recover, Reick pulled him into a wrestler's grip.

As the two tangled together, punching, cursing, and biting, Reick managed to get on top. Keller felt his rival's thumbs inching up toward his eye sockets. He tried to yank Reick's arms away, but the Freikorps captain was too strong. Keller reversed his motion and pulled Reick toward him, simultaneously lifting his chest and head-butting Reick, stunning him long enough for Keller to roll Reick onto his side. Head throbbing, Keller tried to knee Reick in the groin, but only hit his utility belt. His next blow caught Reick in the kidney with no effect. Reick forced himself upright and began to pummel Keller with punches.

The German seemed indestructible, except ..., Keller raised his leg and pounded his heel into the spot where Reick's left toes had been amputated. Reick shrieked and backed away, giving Keller a chance to force him onto his back. Keller jumped up and placed his right forearm on the German's neck as his left hand pressed down on his right, doubling the force. Reick fought wildly and refused to yield, but Keller used all his weight to suffocate him. Something suddenly slammed into Keller's spine. He rose in pain, releasing his grip, and saw a broken chair leg in Reick's hand. Keller barely managed to dodge the next blow.

Desperate, Keller broke away and reached for the knife at his ankle just as Reick jumped for his Luger. Keller lunged and jabbed Reick before he could aim. The knife drove into the soft area of the chest just below the collarbone. Stunned, Reick dropped the gun and pulled out the knife. Keller jammed the lumber he had used earlier into Reick's belly, doubling him over. Shifting his grip so both hands held either end of the wood, Keller raised it upward as if he were forcing open a window. He caught Reick in the chin, standing him upright.

Keller swung the wood down on the back of Reick's head, cracking open his skull. Reick grunted and dropped to the floor. Keller swung again, smashing the wood at the knife wound. Never had he struck a more satisfying blow. The German sprawled at his feet, smiled oddly, and gestured Keller to come closer as he fought to speak his last words. "You were always a good soldier, Brandt."

"And you don't die easily." Keller picked up the Luger and fired two rounds into Reick's face. "That's for Liebknecht and Sund," he said. Emotionally spent and too exhausted to move, Keller sat down so covered in blood he could not tell Reick's from his own.

His retribution complete, Keller felt his humanity begin to return. He looked up to realize the walls around him were starting to blaze.

~

Martin, shotgun in hand, stood with the main body of French troops waiting to attack the airbase across open farmland. He ignored the dogfight above him and calculated how best to advance in the face of stubborn German resistance. French mortar shells exploded inside the main compound, the signal to start the attack. Colonel Favre waved his men forward.

French artillery began to shell the German defenses. The advancing soldiers spread out, ten paces between each man, to avoid being mowed down en masse, as they had been decimated in 1915. Two German machine guns opened up when they reached four hundred yards. The French ducked to the ground and waited. Their artillery barrage intensified, and three French tanks plodded forward. The lead tank, a twenty-three-ton Saint Chamond, armed with a 75mm cannon and four machine guns, could not be stopped by infantrymen alone. The Germans understood the mounting crisis and concentrated all their firepower on it. Mortar shells ranged in on the slow-moving monster. One shell disabled its engine, rendering it immobile but still deadly. Two more finished it off. The other two tanks, light Renault FTs, circled around the steel wreck and advanced.

German fire around the airfield continued despite the bombardment as German riflemen quickly erected effective defenses, allowing them to pick off French soldiers. Freikorps troops were falling just as fast.

Martin heard an aeroplane engine. A light-blue SPAD XIII approached from the main hangar and accelerated down the runway.

"Stop him!" French soldiers redirected their guns to the plane, but to no avail. It reached the sky. No French aeroplanes remained to intercept it — the Nieuports still airborne had sped after the white plane. To Martin's amazement, the light-blue SPAD banked south, away from Versailles.

Martin stood and signaled forward with his right hand. "Follow me." Three hundred French soldiers stood up as one and charged headlong into German machine gun and rifle fire. One out of four fell immediately, but the rest kept coming. One of the two remaining tanks hit a mine and toppled onto its side. A French shell exploded near one of the German machine guns, silencing its crew. The last tank moved forward, spraying the German lines with devastating 37mm gunfire. French soldiers followed close behind.

Twenty yards from the German front, Martin pulled the pin of his Mills grenade and heaved it into a foxhole, where a German with a telescopic sight continued shooting until the end. Martin felt German resistance slackening. French soldiers threw F1 grenades, and the remaining tank broke across the primary German trench, crushing a man. French troops followed and spread out across the runway. The airfield was theirs.

Martin counted twenty-five Germans still fighting from the ruins of aeroplanes on the runway, sandbag emplacements, and the hangar. Fauchaux had moved all his troops forward and was calling for German surrender. The major was shot in the face three times. No quarter either side. The French troops shot the remaining Germans at point blank range.

The gunfire ceased. *Where was Caarsens?* Martin wondered.

"Watch out!" someone called.

Martin turned as two Germans ran at him. The lead man carried a rifle with a fixed bayonet. Martin raised his shotgun and blew a fist-sized hole through his abdomen. The second man angled to Martin's left to avoid the shotgun. Martin followed his movement and pulled the trigger. His last cartridge, a miss. The German sensed his advantage and raised his rifle. Jammed. "Damned French rifle!" he shouted, and ran at Martin with a trench knife. Martin reached for his .45 and fired. The first bullet grazed the German. He kept coming. Martin's second bullet stopped him as if he had hit a wall. The third knocked him flat, unmoving.

Stillness. Favre's second-in-command blew a whistle, the battle over. Martin searched the dead bodies looking for Caarsens. "Major Martin, come," a lieutenant requested. "You're needed at the main hangar."

Unsure of what he might confront, Martin reloaded his shotgun and ran to the hangar. A Canadian officer lay prostrate in the rear corner, near a stack of bombs and munitions. Martin recognized Caarsens immediately. Caarsens's hands were covered in blood, and he was staring into the distance. *Still scheming, no doubt.* Martin pointed his shotgun and said, "I should kill you right now, Danie Caarsens." He pulled the trigger. The spray of lead passed eight inches over Caarsens's head. "Next one, your head'll be gone."

Caarsens did not flinch. He looked up, his face turning whiter by the second. "I'd do it myself if I could. Hand me my pistol."

Martin kicked the Mauser farther away from Caarsens's reach. "Not a chance. I may regret this, but I'm going to bring you to trial. Let American justice take care of you."

Caarsens started to laugh. "Stand in line. I'm wanted across the British Empire. Now France, I'll wager."

"A trial and a firing squad. I don't care who does it." Martin suppressed the urge to pull the trigger.

"Did that white SPAD get through?"

"No," Martin lied. He did not know and was not going to give Caarsens any satisfaction that it might have.

"Always the odds. What went wrong?"

Martin told him about the dead French "deserter" found at the base.

"That bastard Goering. He's a coward. You want him? He's flying the light-blue SPAD that took off a few minutes ago."

"That won't help your case," Martin said.

"Just get him. *He* deserves a firing squad. I know where he's headed." Caarsens struggled, but managed to reveal Goering's escape plan. He coughed and spat out blood. His right hand moved to his head. Martin leveled his shotgun. "Easy," Caarsens said. "You've won, Major Martin. You are a worthy and honorable opponent. You fought well and bravely." He struggled to catch his breath. "You're a religious man, I believe." His eyes showed no more fight.

Martin looked at Caarsens curiously. How could he know? "What's it to you?"

"I know you. We're alike, you and I. Different sides of the same coin. Given different circumstances, we might have been friends. At least allies."

Martin had thought the same thing after the battle they had fought in lower Manhattan almost three years ago. He lowered his gun. "We were on opposing sides. Friends? Never. Justice calls. I'll get a doctor."

"I'm dying. Can you find a Bible? There's a quotation. Corinthians ..."

"I know the one." Martin ordered a French corporal to watch Caarsens. "He's dangerous." Outside, he heard a scream. A man being knifed. Martin cursed himself and ran back toward Caarsens. Before he could reach the hangar, a blast knocked him down and blew the roof off. Martin picked himself up. “You wanted to die your way, didn’t you, Danie?” he said with grudging respect. Even near death, Caarsens had outwitted him.

A French soldier looked at the remains of the hangar. “Nothing survived that, Major,” he said.

Martin shook his head. He had expected Caarsens’s death would give him more satisfaction. Another soldier approached amid shouts from the main compound. “Your man Captain Keller is in trouble.”

~

Over Versailles

14:46: High in the clouds, Voss had two worries. He was alone, and his engine was coughing oil. Could he get through? He figured he was four minutes from the Versailles Palace. He had enough fuel, but what could one plane do? His machine guns were armed. The two twenty-five-pound fragmentation bombs under his wings could kill a number of people if he dropped them in the right spot. He might not stop the signings, but he could strike a blow for Germany. After that, he did not care.

Where were the French aeroplanes? Voss flew at an altitude of 12,800 feet. The air was thin, and he was cold despite his goggles, thick leather jacket and helmet. He liked that; it focused his mind. He put the aeroplane into a dive, coming down fast under the cover of clouds. He used all his strength to stabilize the SPAD as his engine protested with misfires, and the fuselage shook. His wings groaned at the stress. Breaking through the clouds, he spotted several observation balloons, their machine guns cranking out streams of lead. Voss flew through them as bullets pinged his engine and shredded the fabric on his wings. If one took out a strut … . *Ignore what you can’t control.*

He crossed himself and accelerated further into his dive, pushing the SPAD to its limits. He saw the palace. Forty seconds until he dropped his bombs. To his horror, four French Nieuport 28s circled below, waiting for him. Another maneuvered behind him, guns blazing.

Voss banked hard to avoid being hit. His damaged SPAD protested, vibrating uncontrollably, about to break apart. Flames burst from the engine, threatening to spread to his upper wing as the Nieuport 28 on his tail continued to rake him with bullets. He felt a sharp pain in his right shoulder. His arm went numb. The plane inverted and began to spin. He fought unconsciousness, trying to right the plane with his good arm as the ground below loomed larger and larger.

~

U.S. Air Acceptance Base

Martin ran to the burning building. "Your man is in there, Major Martin," a sergeant informed him. "We think he's alive, but ..."

"Keller!" Martin yelled at the top of his lungs. No response. Three men with a fire hose ran up to the building and started to douse the flames. "That man saved my life," one declared. "I've got to save his." Rivulets of sweat poured from Martin's face in the heat. "Keller!" he called. "Keller!"

"Here!" came the faint response. "I'm trapped!"

"Soak me," Martin said to a fireman. "I'm going in." He wrapped a wet cloth around his nose and mouth and donned a French helmet and heavy gloves from one of the tank men. Someone handed him an axe.

"Hurry! The building's going to collapse any minute."

Martin rushed in, bent low. Fallen debris and burning objects made for treacherous footing. He tripped over a broken chair and stepped on upturned nails, saved only by the solid soles of his army boots. Smoke blocked his vision and choked his lungs. He used the axe as a blind man would use a cane, tapping into the furnace-like heat. "Paul, where are you?" he called, as flaming chunks of plaster fell from the ceiling.

"Here! In the corner!" Martin heard two rounds fired in quick succession. He found Keller on the floor near the far wall, a dead body next to him, surrounded by a circle of burning furniture and debris.

"I can't move," Keller yelled above the roar of the flames. "I'm pinned!"

Martin cleared a path with his axe, his energy sapped, and his breathing labored. "Thank God you're alive!" he declared, reaching his friend. Behind him, the fire had strengthened. Martin pulled the debris off of his friend.

"We're doomed," said Keller, coughing hard as the fire crept toward them.

Martin had one option — to hack at the outside wall with his axe. Keller followed as best he could, jabbing at the lower boards with his piece of lumber. Grudgingly, the wall gave way. Daylight appeared and oxygen poured in, both helping their breathing and stoking the fire. Martin's wet clothes protected him, but Keller's pants ignited. He snuffed out the flames with his hands and yelled desperately for help.

Martin hacked twice more with the axe, but realized he was out of time. He braced himself and charged like a fullback at the goal line. He broke through and somersaulted onto the ground, twisting his ankle. Unable to stand, he crawled back to the wall, reached in, and grabbed Keller, pulling with all his might. Lifting his good knee to a forty-five degree angle and bracing his foot, Keller levered himself away with Martin's help.

The building collapsed just as Martin pulled Keller to safety. Four French soldiers ran to them and carried them away from danger.

~

While medics tended to Keller, Martin reported to Colonel Favre. The base was secure. The treaty had been signed, and no German plane had gotten through. Martin relayed what he had learned about Goering's escape plan, though he admitted the need to save Keller had caused a delay. They might be too late to catch Goering. Favre telephoned orders to local units to head to Goering's location with urgent haste. He reported on return that Goering had escaped.

"We'll have to deal with him later, I'm sure," replied Martin.

"He's sympathetic to the Freikorps," Keller interjected. "I'm afraid of what he'll turn out to be."

"Something dirty, I'm sure," Favre said. "I fear the Freikorps will metastasize into something worse. Oh, before I forget, I have something for you, Major Martin." Favre handed Martin a German Demag bayonet.

"What's this?" Martin asked, although he was certain it belonged to Caarsens — it had been his close-in weapon of choice in New York. "So this is what Caarsens used to stab the guard. How could I have neglected to search him before I left?"

"This is all we found of the German. He — "

"Caarsens. He was the field commander."

"His body disintegrated in the blast."

"You mean there's no confirmation of his death?" Martin's face fell.

"The bayonet. Here." Favre handed it to Martin. "A gift."

"Not enough." Martin wanted proof. Caarsens had been declared dead once before without physical confirmation. Martin did not want to make the same mistake again.

"All you'll get. Feel free to search the wreckage. Maybe you can find a fingernail." Favre paused, pulled out a paper from his uniform blouse, and opened it. He gave Martin a stern look. "Orders from my president's office. The official word is that the incident at this base never happened. The explosions were caused by leaking aeroplane fuel. They triggered a series of fires that destroyed the base. The tanks and my regiment were on maneuvers."

"What about the dogfight?"

"An aerial display. A show in celebration of the signing. The crash was an unfortunate incident caused by an overzealous pilot."

"Do you really think the public will believe that shit?" Martin asked. As he well knew, a compliant press and disciplined military control could deceive the masses. New York City had achieved the same thing after Caarsens's nearly successful attack there. The French would do the same. Manipulations by the powerful would win again. Martin shook his head.

"You and your captain will receive decorations. *Merci.*" Favre saluted and extended his hand.

Martin shook it. There was nothing else he could do.

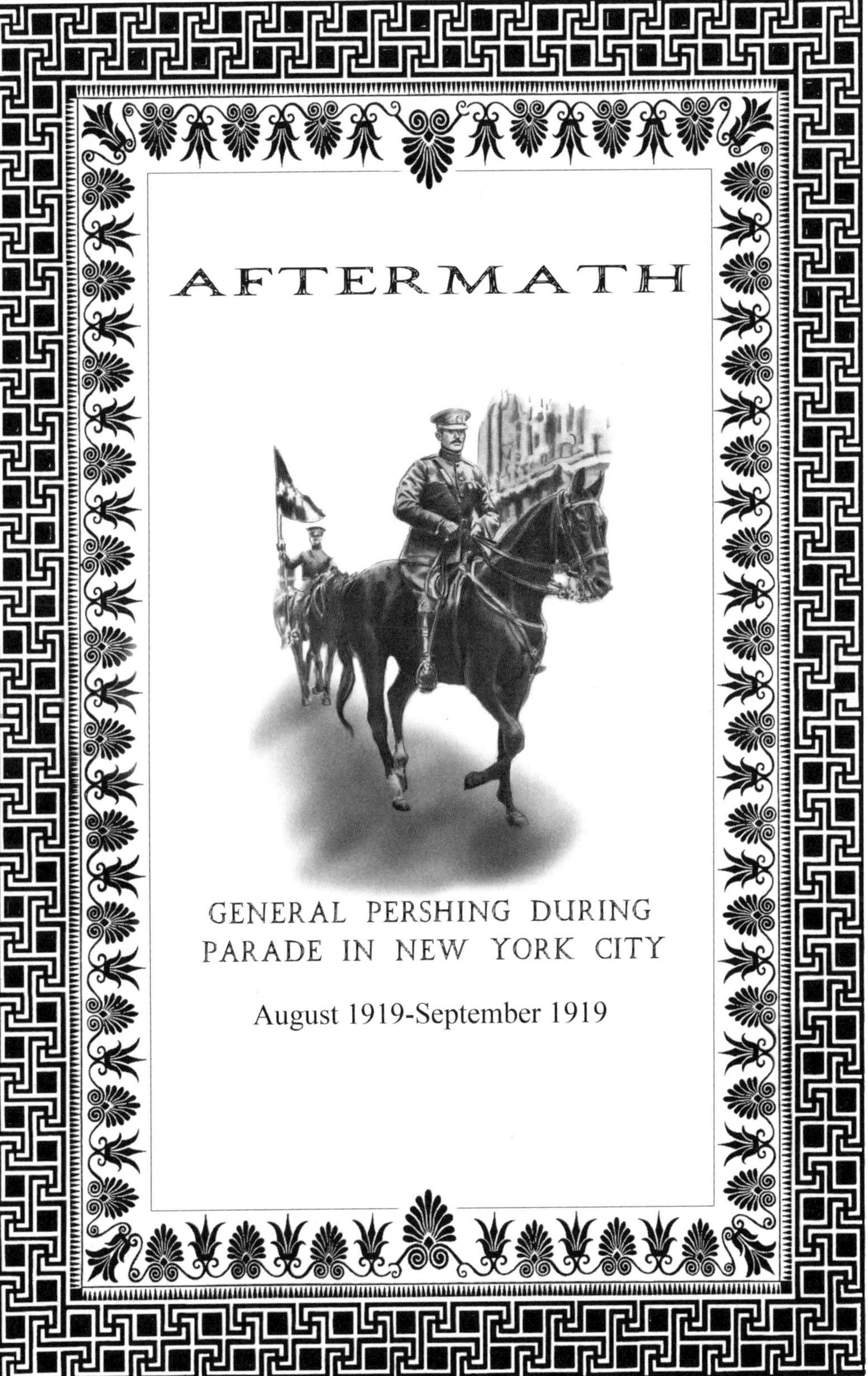

AFTERMATH

GENERAL PERSHING DURING PARADE IN NEW YORK CITY

August 1919-September 1919

Aftermath

Atlantic Ocean: August 1919

Martin, Keller, and Shannon departed France on the *S.S. Leviathan* with little fanfare. Like the liner that had brought them to Europe, the *Leviathan* was a former German ship sheltered in New York Harbor, commandeered when the United States declared war. The joy the Kellers felt at Shannon's pregnancy was tempered by Martin's grief at Ana's loss. "Let me remain in the past a while longer," Martin told them the first night at sea. "I hope I never go back to Europe."

During the voyage, Martin rested in his cabin and joined the Kellers for meals, which he merely picked at. He remained polite during the journey, mentioned all the right things about the baby, but said little else. News bored him. He attended Mass daily, often arriving at the chapel half an hour before services.

Keller understood and left Martin alone. Two loves lost in just over three years was an ordeal for any man. Add to that the horrors of combat and his burdens during the Peace Conference, and Martin had every reason to be despondent.

"I'm worried about Gil," Shannon said over afternoon tea on the second day. "He's losing weight. He looks as if he's not sleeping."

"He'll be back again," Keller said. "Give him time." He did not want to trouble Shannon, but wondered what could pull Martin out of his quagmire. To Keller's knowledge, all Martin had left were memories, his friendship with Shannon and him, and his love of New York City.

After Martin returned to his room, Keller and Shannon sat quietly, deep in their own thoughts. Shannon broke the silence. "What are you going to do when we return home?"

Keller perked up. “I wanted to surprise you. I’ve already spoken to Dulles. I’m going to work for him.”

Shannon nearly exploded. “You can’t go back to being a spy! Not with our baby on the way.”

Keller stayed calm. “I agree, but I can teach others how to be one. If Larsen had had better ...” He let the thought drop. “I’ll work directly for Dulles. I can stay in Washington. Would you like to live there?” Keller held his breath. “I’d be one of his top men. Paid well too. I’d start next month.”

Shannon looked at Keller with an intensity that matched her determination. “You mean it? No danger?”

“I’ll hold Dulles to his word. If that doesn’t work, you can shoot him yourself.”

She smiled. “Good. Let’s have another drink.”

“One more thing. I fulfilled my promise to Sund.” Before he had departed from France, Keller had been able to have someone from Hoover’s Food Relief group deliver $1,500 to Regina Sund in Bremen. She was grateful but wanted to know about her benefactor. She was told it was a gift from a sympathetic friend who had been with her husband when he died in the Berlin revolt; he owed Sund his life.

As they entered New York Harbor, Keller persuaded Martin to join them on deck while they sailed past the Statue of Liberty. Keller and Shannon cheered with the rest of the passengers, but Martin stood impassive. Keller noticed Martin wipe a tear away and heard him say, “I wanted to show it to her. She was so excited about coming here. Got that wrong too.” He returned to his cabin.

~

They stayed that night at the Waldorf Astoria, courtesy of the city’s Mayor John Hylan and a grateful nation. The next day dawned cold and dreary. Keller and Shannon followed Martin, his every step an effort, as he walked toward the water line in Battery Park. Martin's head was bent and his shoes shuffled along the pavement. He carried a seventeenth-century silver urn, a gift from the Versailles Palace with thanks for helping prevent a catastrophe.

When they neared the water, Martin blinked away the wetness in his eyes and turned to his companions. "Give me a minute. I need to do this myself."

"I owe her my life," Shannon said as tears rolled down her face.

"God bless her," Keller added. "If we have a girl, she'll be named, Ana."

Keller took Shannon's hand, and they moved back solemnly.

Martin walked the final steps alone. The Statue of Liberty looked down on him in silent majesty. He looked up at her as if to seek her approval. Behind her rotted the scarred remnants of Black Tom Island. So much had happened in three years.

Martin said a few words and held the urn over the water. He opened it. Ana's ashes fell into New York Harbor and mixed with the murky water, sinking into oblivion. Martin weakened and almost dropped the empty urn. He turned and slumped, resting on his heels, his elbows on his knees. His head fell into his hands. How many times must a man lose a love? He closed his eyes and lost track of time, thinking of Corinne and Ana.

Martin felt a hand on his shoulder. He looked up. Darkness was overtaking day. "Come, my friend. It's time to go home," Keller said

"Where is that?"

~

New York City: September 1919

A few weeks later, the *S.S. Leviathan* once again returned from France with General Pershing and his staff. New York City was electrified. A victory parade to honor Pershing and the U.S. Army was scheduled for the next day.

Martin and Keller joined the entire 25,000-man 1st Division in upper Manhattan as it formed for the march down Fifth Avenue. A *Croix de Guerre*, awarded by the French government for bravery, adorned each of their uniforms, along with numerous ribbons. Keller estimated the parade would take three hours. Every soldier was dressed in full combat gear, including rifle and fixed bayonet. New York City was going to see the full might of a U.S. division, complete with artillery, combat wagons, field kitchens, and ambulances. Marching bands were excluded. This was a display of power.

At 10:30, General Pershing, astride a grand horse, headed the procession. His general staff, including Martin and Keller, followed on foot. Keller kept pace, his injuries from the fight nearly healed. Overhead, aeroplanes soared. Martin, his memory fresh from the battle at Orly, ducked at the sound. Keller put his hand on Martin's arm. "Calm down, Gil. They're ours."

Ten-deep on the sidewalks, the crowd cheered and waved American flags. People everywhere called out Pershing's name. Women handed out flowers. Along the way, church bells rang; sidewalk bands struck up tunes; and drums beat to the cadence of the marching soldiers. Paper streamers and confetti rained down, so thick at times that it blocked Keller's vision. He felt the crowd's deep joy, profound gratitude, and unrestrained excitement. He looked at Martin but could not read his thoughts.

The parade stopped when a young woman broke through the crowd and tried to kiss General Pershing. Keller knew his friend was beginning to enjoy himself when Martin whispered, "If she only knew what he is really like." Keller saw the outlines of a smile on Martin, who began to march with more vigor.

The parade stopped on 51st Street at St. Patrick's Cathedral.

Pershing dismounted to receive a bouquet of American Beauty roses from a Knights of Columbus war worker. Pershing shook hands with Cardinal Mercier of Belgium and other church dignitaries. Meanwhile, Keller noticed, Martin's hands were folded in prayer.

At Madison Square on 24th Street and Fifth Avenue, they passed an arch that Keller did not recognize. The colonel next to him explained it was a Victory Arch, a huge, temporary wooden and plaster monument.

Martin shook his head and chuckled. "Typical New York. Of course they'd build something like this. Success measured in size." As they approached Washington Square, the end of the parade route, he turned to Keller and said, "I love this city. I want to be a cop again."

Author's Note

Once again, as with my first book, *Over Here,* it is time to set the record straight and to separate reality from fantasy. Although *So Beware* is a work of fiction, it is grounded in fact. As I have done in *Over Here,* I strove to stay true to the passions and controversies of the times. I worked hard to portray the actual places and events fairly and accurately. By transporting the reader back to 1919 Paris and Berlin, I hope I have provided insights into the complexities that arose after World War One. Much of today's world is the way it is because of what happened, and what did not happen, after the November 11, 1918 armistice. One hundred years later, little has changed.

My main characters Gil Martin, Paul and Shannon Keller, and Ana Primakova are fictional. Danie Caarsens and Matthias Weil are my creations, as are the Freikorps soldiers from Landsmann and Reick down to the enlisted men, the Marine guards and personnel at the U.S. embassy (with the exception of James Brown Scott), and the various French and Danish soldiers. Commandant Emile Truchon and Captain Alain Durand were fabricated. Any resemblance to real people is a coincidence.

Aside from the main characters, the Paris peace talks play a central role in this novel. Almost unique in history, most of the leaders of the world gathered together in Paris for almost six months during 1919. At the same time, Paris became a magnet for other dignitaries and figures to plead their cases. Others wanted to be near the history-making events.

Among the actual Americans who appear in this book, Colonel Edward House takes the same essential role in the story as he had in Paris. He was President Wilson's principal advisor until their split during the Peace Conference, as suggested in the book. AEF Commanding General Black Jack Pershing, a known womanizer, appears briefly. Herbert Hoover did manage the U.S. Food Relief effort to Europe after the war, and Allen Dulles was partly responsible for starting America's early spy efforts. Their connection to this book's events is fictional. In all cases, their actions and words in *So Beware* are mine, and I regret any mischaracterization of them I may have made.

John Maynard Keynes is also a central character in the story. He was a highly respected economist, a key member of the British delegation to Paris, and was highly critical of the peace terms. I do not know to what extent he played chess, but he certainly had a mind for it. I apologize if my book depicts him falsely in any way. By the way, I created the code that he and Shannon break. It is based on the actual chess match cited.

I have folded into the story some of the more colorful characters who were present in Paris at the time. My readers might be surprised to learn that Nguyen Ai Quoc was the man later known as Ho Chi Minh. He actually wrote the *Eight Claims of the Annamite People* as mentioned in the book. Lawrence of Arabia did "bomb" Paris with toilet paper. Mrs. Brooks really lived at 71 rue de Lille (it exists today), and her parties were popular among members of the U.S. delegation. She became General MacArthur's first wife, but the marriage did not last. Queen Marie of Romania was as colorful and provocative as I have portrayed her. She dressed in much the way I illustrate and was able to secure an excellent deal for Romania in the talks. The roles of these colorful characters in the story are purely my creation.

Several real-life Germans are critical to the book. Hermann Goering is a well-known World War Two figure. Few people know he was a German ace in World War One and won the coveted Blue Max. Although he had imperialistic leanings and was sympathetic to the Freikorps cause (as proved by his later actions), his participation in this book is my creation. It was my choice at the end of the book to have him flee rather than attack Versailles on a suicide mission; I have no doubt Goering was a brave pilot. German Foreign Minister Count von Brockdorff-Rantzau's arrival to receive the terms of the armistice, and his speech to the conference, happened largely as I have recounted, with the exception of Mal's invented attack and the related participation of Shannon and Ana. Defense Minister Gustav Noske's role in the German government and his relation to the Freikorps as depicted in the book are accurate. Their personality traits and dialogue of these Germans as contained herein are mine.

A few historical notes. The reader will be, as I was, shocked by the casualties suffered on the last day of the war. American casualties alone were approximately 3,500. Sadly, they are part of the historical record. Chapter 1 is fiction, but it characterizes actual events. Allied generals indeed ordered attacks before the 11:00 armistice took effect. Their motivations included a need for glory and a spiteful desire to bloody the Germans one last time. In a few cases, orders to cease attacks were never received.

By early 1919, the Allies perceived Bolshevism and the rise of international Communism as a central threat. They feared its spread. Russia was shunned and deliberately not invited to the Paris Peace Conference. France thought Russia, by suing for peace in 1918, had abandoned her in her time of need. It is true that Allied troops were stationed in Russia to support the White Russians, who were fighting Lenin's Red Army. Uprisings and workers' revolutions took place in Hungary, Bavaria, and elsewhere after November 11, 1918. Communism had to be stopped.

The Freikorps was formed to supplement the shattered German Army in the winter of 1918-1919. Some Freikorps elements did metastasize into Hitler's Brownshirts and contributed to the Nazi rise. The Freikorps suppressed the Spartacist and March revolutions in Berlin as dramatized in this book. The climactic attack on the signing of the treaty is pure fiction. I know of no actual threat to Versailles. But

I have no doubt that somewhere in Germany, someone was thinking about a way to stop the signing by violent means. The sentiments displayed by my Freikorps members were common among the soldiers. The German people's reaction to the peace terms, included in these pages, is largely accurate.

Many important scenes in *So Beware*, though dramatized, actually occurred. Others did not. Which is which?

In France, Wilson's triumphant arrival in France happened as portrayed in the book. The assassination attempt on Clémenceau occurred in much the way I describe. Emile Cottin was an anarchist who always insisted he acted alone. The suggestion that there was a conspiracy to murder Clémenceau is purely my own. There is much controversy about Wilson's illness during the conference. Understandably, the severity of his condition was minimized at the time. However, he did suffer from the symptoms I describe. Combined with his later medical history, I have come to the conclusion, shared by others, that he had a stroke in Paris.

German Foreign Minister Brockdorff-Rantzau did refuse to sign the treaty and resigned his post. President Ebert had to recruit the unfortunate Johannes Bell and Herman Mueller to take Brockdorff-Rantzau's place at the signing. The signing doomed the new Weimar government, which was blamed for the perceived injustices imposed by the treaty. The Allies in fact bugged the German delegation's hotel in Versailles but not as I have described it.

In Germany, the withdrawal of the German Army from France and the start of the "stab-in-the-back" theory are factual. The German people were largely unaware that the German Army had virtually collapsed in late 1918. The arrests and murders of Karl Liebknecht and Rosa Luxemburg are true. Obviously, Keller's participation and the specific related details in the book are fictional but reflect these crimes. The fate of their bodies is real. The start of the Weimar government as presented in the book is accurate. The battle at Alexanderplatz during the March 1919 Berlin revolt occurred, although I have created the details of the fight from my imagination.

In Russia, the William Bullitt mission happened, even if Gil Martin's involvement did not. The specifics concerning whom Bullitt met, the terms he agreed to with Lenin, and the reaction by the Allied leaders are accurate.

The November 11 celebration in New York City and Pershing's victory parade down Fifth Avenue at the end of the book are faithful portrayals of the events.

A few final comments. The United States did impound German ships harboring in its ports when it declared war in 1917. The British and American delegations actually stayed in the Majestic and Crillon hotels, respectively. The passageway from Maxim's to the Crillon existed even if the shoot-out between Martin and Mal did not. The fire at Le Grand Hotel happened only in these pages. The propaganda pamphlets from Moscow Magda are my creations. The Café Josty in Berlin was a popular restaurant in 1919 and has been rebuilt in the new reunified city. The Freikorps really used the Hotel Eden (no longer in existence) in Berlin as one of its headquarters. The U.S. Air Acceptance Base at Orly existed, but its role in the book is fictional.

I have done as much as I can to make this book accurate. Any errors are mine, and I deeply regret them. I have conveyed to you the times as I have come to understand them. I look forward to doing the same with the planned third book in my "World War One Intrigue Series," *Send the Word.*

- James Hockenberry